TALES OF IAIRIA
TRIAL OF A MAVEN

by

Tyler Tullis

authorHOUSE®

AuthorHouse™
1663 Liberty Drive, Suite 200
Bloomington, IN 47403
www.authorhouse.com
Phone: 1-800-839-8640

© 2008 Tyler Tullis. All rights reserved.

No part of this book may be reproduced, stored in a retrieval system, or transmitted by any means without the written permission of the author.

First published by AuthorHouse 5/29/2008

ISBN: 978-1-4343-7417-2 (sc)

Library of Congress Control Number: 2008902041

Printed in the United States of America
Bloomington, Indiana

This book is printed on acid-free paper.

for
Mom and Dad

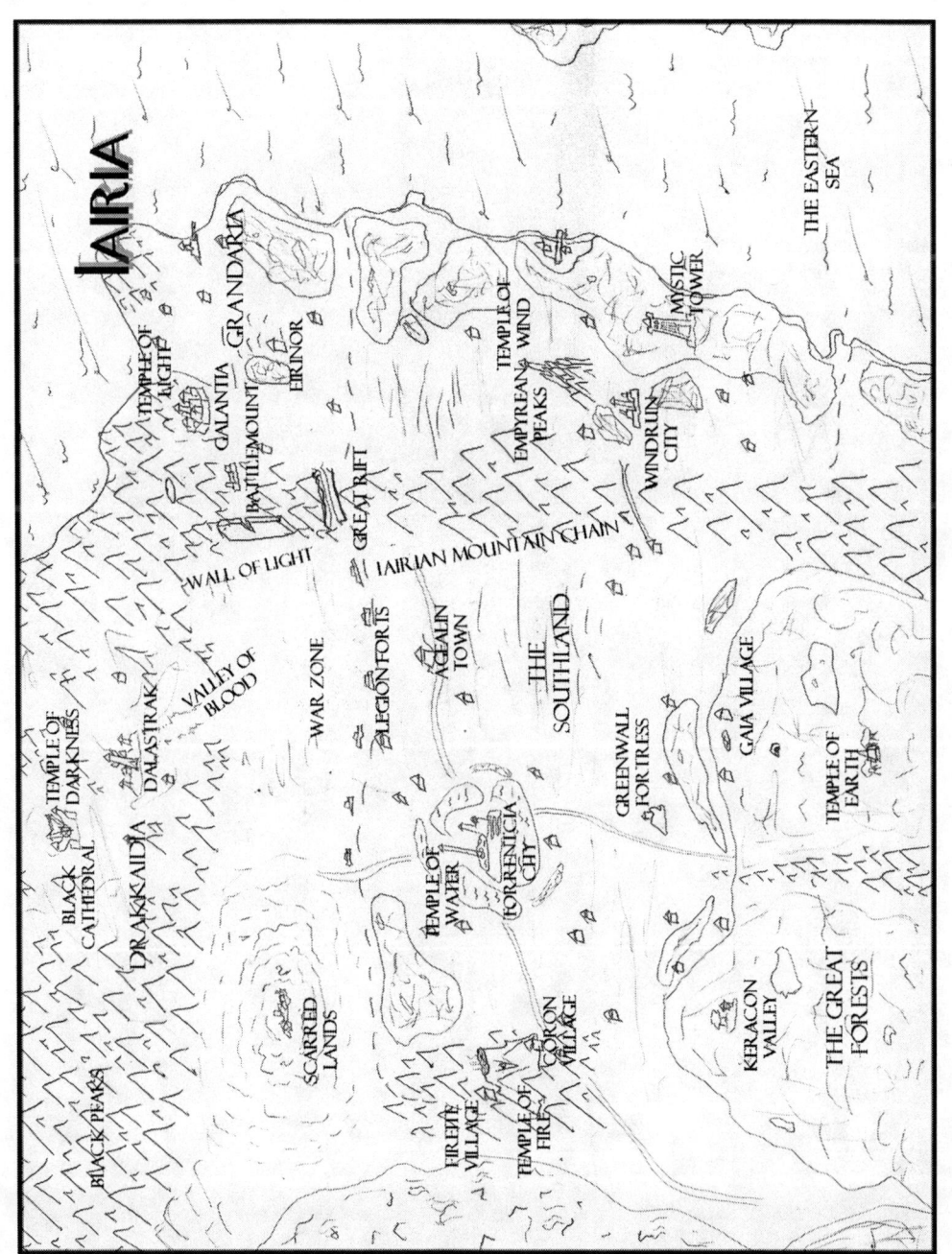

Prologue

The Fission of Drakkaidia

Almost twenty years after his coming, incredible tales of the rebirth of the Warrior of Light continued to spread throughout the golden land of Grandaria and all of Iairia. They told of how a mere boy stood up with a band of diverse allies to defeat the greatest evil the world had ever known. Few Grandarians knew however, that in the wake of their salvation a revitalized surge of chaos and hatred was sweeping through the hearts of their enemies to the west. After Valif Montrox's abrupt death, the people of Drakkaidia were left torn and ravaged by the hordes of unholy demons he had loosed upon them. Desperately hungry for answers and justification to the senseless destruction and loss of life, the people turned to the oldest establishment of power in Drakkaidia—the Black Church of Drakkan. Its authority usurped by the throne and the House of Montrox centuries ago, the Church saw the sudden absence of Montrox as its long awaited opportunity to reclaim ruling power.

Quickly selecting a new High Priest to take control, the Dark Mage Zalnaught was anointed. With traditionalistic views of hatred for Grandaria, Zalnaught rallied the populace to him and the Church, boasting fabrications that Valif Montrox had been assassinated by ancient Grandarian magic which had purposefully released the demonic horde upon them. Outraged at this false revelation, thousands vowed to follow the High Priest in fulfilling their fallen king's ambition to reignite the Holy Wars and annihilate Grandaria once and for all.

Arriving home from his travels, Verix, the son of Valif Montrox, was shocked and appalled at the sudden shift of power in his home. He knew better than any the contempt the Black Church held for his family and that without an active king on the throne it could not be controlled. Though Verix voiced to his people that Grandaria had actually battled to save their lands and now was not the time for war, his seemed to be the minority view. Thus came the fission of Drakkaidia. The smaller portion of the populace that recognized Verix Montrox as the next in line for the title of king gathered around the ruins of Dalastrak and took on the name of the Loyalists to the Throne. The rest of the nation departed their homes on a veritable pilgrimage to the Cathedral of Dalorosk further north, calling themselves the New Fellowship of Drakkan. As political tension rose between the two factions, a besieged Verix began to sense the High Priest concealing motives beyond what he preached.

Part One
Legacies

Chapter 1

Incursion

There were more of them than he thought there would be. But then, that was always the way it was with the marauders of the Purging Flame. Despite their near destruction at the hands of the Southland Legion twenty years ago during the Days of Destiny, their number was always cropping back like a weed—choking the life from the Southland. Edge let out an inaudible sigh of vexation as he reaffirmed his grip on the thick rope he held, keeping him stealthily suspended on the steep cliff wall overlooking a compact encampment of the marauders. The world was consumed by the dark of a moonless night, masking the Purging Flame just returning from their raid on an unsuspecting village along the northern border of the Southland. Edge turned his intense eyes to one of the makeshift tents below him as a man cloaked in deep purple robes appeared from under the long flaps of the doorway, carefully securing it with rope and ordering two sentries to stand guard as he left. Edge narrowed his eyes. His objective had to there. It would be well guarded, naturally, but it would be no problem for him. He was a Maven after all.

Edge sighed again and shifted his attention to the various gear strapped to his body, most of it midnight black to conceal his position in the darkness. He wore his standard black vest and pants that tucked his faded and frayed blue tunic underneath, with thick black gloves and boots covering the ends of his limbs. His short dark hair aided to camouflage his body into the night, slightly swaying back and forth in the subtle breeze nipping at his lean, controlled face. Despite his obvious youth, he harbored an expression of maturity and self-discipline about his visage that portrayed the professionalism and control with which he operated. Black leather straps with worn silver buckles were strewn across his hard body, tightly securing the various supplies, weapons and other accessories littered over him. A thick belt ran along his waist with satchels containing hooks, knives and bolts for the compact crossbow that hung behind his back alongside his trusty broadsword. Though the assortment of heavy steel worked against him when he needed his speed and agility, Edge had learned to compensate for its presence from the years of experience he had accumulated in his profession.

Mavens had a somewhat dubious reputation across the lands of Iairia. Adept mercenaries that rented themselves out for any job an employer could offer, they were known for their tactlessness and indifference to the laws or codes of ethics that governments established and common decency upheld. The worst of them were the Red Mavens that specialized in assassinations and other jobs of such vile nature. While Edge certainly did not consider himself a Red, he did find himself about to stealthily enter a marauder encampment and do whatever he had to in order to complete his mission—a morally ambiguous assignment for a Blue Maven such as he. Edge quietly lifted his right hand to take hold of the ends of his faded blue scarf gently massaging his face in the breeze and threw it back behind his right shoulder. One could always tell a Maven by the scarves they loosely wore around their necks. It was the last remnant of the guild once in place to manage the Maven's of the world, long since disbanded.

As Edge began to plot out the position where he would enter the camp, a faint noise from below him in the bushes some twenty feet down caught his acute attention. He brought his pale gray eyes down to find a small humanoid creature steadily ascending toward him. It was no more than a foot high, not including the pair of small wings mounted on its back and the tail feathers protruding from just below. As it softly beat its wings harder to rise to Edge's level, the Maven's seemingly impenetrable aura of seriousness softened and a faint smile spread across his lips. When the winged creature rose to within a few inches of his face, Edge locked onto its deep purple eyes.

"Did the bush give you some trouble, Zeph?" he whispered with a coy grin. The miniature winged creature hovered before him silently beating its wings and raising its arms to pluck out the foliage that had lodged itself in between his feathers.

"Very funny," the creature quietly retorted from behind its wide yellow beak, brushing off its white feathered torso.

"If you want a partner that can maneuver through leaves in the black of night, you should go find a Cronom. Maybe you haven't picked up on this yet but I'm a *Sky Sprite*. You know, that soars through the sky? Hence the name?" Edge silently chuckled and shook his head.

"Oh come on, partner," he started playfully, "don't get all sour on me. You know you're the only sprite for me." The other merely scowled at him and continued to purge the undergrowth he had picked up in his feathers from his reconnoiter into the Purging Flame's camp. Sky Sprites were the mystical race of fairy creatures that inhabited the Empyrean Peaks in the eastern Southland. Though humanoid in appearance, they stood only a foot tall and were finely feathered from head to toe in diverse assortments of colors. Their defining attributes were the pair of wings located high on their backs, the miniature beaks spread across their faces, the lengthy tail feathers below their wings and their talon like feet.

Some years ago Edge had been traveling north past the Empyrean Peaks in the Southland when he found a Sky Spite lying on the forest floor in a broken heap. Barely alive, Edge knew he would not last more than a few hours alone and defenseless in the woods so he picked him up, set his broken wings in a splint and gently nursed him back to health while he traveled. When the sprite finally regained consciousness he revealed his name was Zephyr and he had been banished from his people and their colony in the high peaks. His wings were broken as further punishment and he was thrown from the peaks. Ever grateful for saving his life, Zephyr pledged to remain with Edge until he could repay the debt. Being an outcast as the sprite viewed himself, the reclusive Maven reluctantly accepted Zephyr's offer and ever since they had become each others' only true friends.

Edge exhaled softly and rotated his darkly clad body to allow Zephyr a position to land on his shoulder. The sprite gently secured his talons onto the boy and pulled in his outstretched wings.

"Which tent is it in?" the Maven whispered with his stern resolve restored. Plucking the last obtrusive shred of foliage from his wings, Zephyr outstretched his arm and pointed to the single tent at the opposite end of the encampment erected perpendicular to the rest.

"I don't think the old man was kidding about that medallion's value," he began in a low hush, "because the Purging Flame locked it up in a chest apart from the rest of their pillaged loot. It's inside the leader's tent at the end of the site."

"Recall that the old man is the noble of his village," Edge reminded. "If any of the junk these idiots plundered has any real value, it would belong to our employer. Now what about guards?" The Sky Sprite shook his miniature head and shifted his extended arm toward another much larger tent in the center of the others.

"The leader of this lot is still on his way here from another village they raided, so most of the marauders are in there looking over the spoils of their efforts. Say about thirty. That's probably where they'll stay until the boss gets here. There were only two half drunken sentries playing cards in front of our target tent. The bad news is they've got a Bulloct behind it." Edge shifted his focused gaze from the encampment to his gear, opening the satchels containing assortments of pointed steel to make sure the tools of his trade were in order. Sealing them tightly in approval, he angled his worn but ever steady sword above his right shoulder to easily pull it free should he need it.

"Move into the branches of those trees along the treasure tent and keep watch for the leader or anything else that gets too close," Edge ordered. "I'll cut through the shrubs you popped out of and move around the tree line behind the tent. I won't be able to see any movement through the camp so give me a whistle per man for anybody coming my way." Zephyr raised his feathered brow.

"Behind the tent? And just how do you intend to get past the Bulloct lying back there? Because I can tell you right now there is no way I'm playing bait with one of those things again." Edge did not respond but turned his body to face the cliff and prepare to descend down the rope.

"I'll take care of it," he whispered at last. "Now get into position. You know how much I hate this kind of job but we're stuck with it so I want this quick and clean. No blood—understand?" Zephyr just shrugged.

"Why don't you tell that to the bloodthirsty marauders we're about to steal from?" the little sprite quietly returned, lifting off the boy's shoulder back into the air. Edge's expression remained hard.

"I'm not kidding, Zeph. If one spots us they all will and I don't want to get backed into the corner. It's been almost a year since I've..." The boy's already hushed voice failed him for a moment and a slight cringe rippled through his suddenly vulnerable body. Zephyr's feathered frame loosened knowingly, aware of where his friend's mind had drifted.

"We'll be fine, partner," the sprite assured him, then hovered closer to pat Edge on the back twice. "They don't call you Lightning's Edge for nothing." The melancholy glaze over Edge's face lingered a moment longer before he abruptly tightened his frame, silently kicked off from the cliff wall and covertly slid down the rope for the earth beneath them with his blue scarf flailing behind. As the boy disappeared into the darkness of the foliage below, Zephyr hovered above a moment longer before empathetically shaking his head and gliding back down into the tree line to find his position.

At the base of the cliff wall, Edge relinquished his rope and unbuckled it from his belt keeping him safely harnessed. Spinning his crouched form around, he could make out the faintly lit camp of the Purging Flame through the dense shrubbery. The largest tent full of the loud and obnoxious marauders was in the center of the site, nearly thirty feet away. As he began to quietly push through the bushes around him, the Maven swiftly came to the end of his immediate cover. The tree line was fifteen feet away and all that rested between it and the bushes was a massive boulder sunken into the earth. Taking a quick look at the tents and up to the branches of the trees to listen for any warning from Zephyr, Edge silently leapt from his position and rolled along the earth to plant his back against the boulder.

Preparing to jump once more for the tree line, Edge froze when the soft but strident call of a crisp whistle sounded through the night air. Calmly checking his surroundings, he turned his head back behind the boulder to find a figure cloaked in deep purple robes exiting the primary tent and making his way toward him.

"Where the hell are you going, Janns?" a drunken voice from inside the treasure tent called.

"I emptied half of that keg, fool," the man outside shouted back, still on his way toward Edge. "I've got to piss or I'm going to explode!" Turning back to hide his face, Edge listened as the footsteps grew closer. Reaching down to his belt for a knife, his hand hesitated and he shook his head, unable to draw one. As the man was nearly on top of him, Edge quickly unfastened the scarf around his neck and pulled it taut in his hands, waiting. At last the footsteps stopped on the opposite side of the boulder and the marauder began to unfasten the button on his pants. Leaning over to conduct his business, his eyes suddenly burst open to find the black clad figure crouched behind the boulder. Before he could so much as open his mouth to call for help, Edge threw his scarf up behind the man's angled head and jerked down, forcing his face into the boulder with nearly lethal strength.

Quickly rising to seize the man before he collapsed, Edge took hold of his frame and silently brought him around the boulder to tuck him behind it. Though he would have the worst headache of his life and a massive lump on his forehead when he woke, the marauder would still have his life. Checking to be sure he was clear again, Edge leapt from the boulder to the tree line and stealthily crept behind the rows of tents to the last one situated at the end of the camp. Like Zephyr had reported, there were two drunken guards at the front and a massive Bulloct chewing on a bone behind. Bullocts were known across Iairia as the largest dogs with the most ferocious tempers that could be found. They could easily break a human bone in half with one clamp of their powerful jaws. Taming one was no easy task.

Aware he was running out of time, Edge pushed aside the hesitation of what he knew he had to do and slowly appeared out of the trees before the creature. The Bulloct saw him at once, its colossal skull and short but pointed ears alertly shooting up. Like most predators, it matched its prey's stillness—waiting for it to make the first move. Edge was still in a crouch on the earth, his gray eyes locked onto the other before him. As the moments ticked by, the air around Edge began to softly stir while a palpable blue mist of glowing energy formed and boiled off of the boy's frame, only to dissipate once it rose an inch above him. As the alluring blue light shone off Edge's figure, his eyes began to softly glow deeper and bluer than an ocean depth, mirroring an infinite sea of tranquility and peace. The very grass and leaves around him seemed to grow greener and larger in response. Struggling to maintain some emotion deep inside, a single tear dropped form his cheek onto the swaying grass below.

The Bulloct before the tent gradually responded as well, its once biting eyes full of enmity now calm and serene.

Trial of a Maven

As its rigid head lowered, it slowly rose toward the Maven to drop the bone in its enormous jaws and sit next to him with its muscles loose and relaxed. Watching the Bulloct sit, Edge relaxed as well and the blue mist around his body gradually dissipated. The boy casually lifted his hand and placed it over the Bulloct's head, gently scratching the now docile beast behind its ears. Patting it on its broad chest and wiping the tear from his face, Edge rose and silently crept into the exposed tent.

It was dark inside, illuminated only by the dim torchlight from outside the camp. Taking a look around, Edge quickly found his target. A large chest at the end of the tent next to a round chair lay guarded by an oversized padlock. Creeping toward it, Edge unfastened one of the pouches along his belt and pulled free a thin knife with two rounded blades protruding from the miniature hilt. Inserting it into the keyhole, he slowly turned it in circles, pinching the two blades together in sequential patterns. After a few moments, the lock clicked open and Edge set it on the floor and shoved his tool back into the pouch in his belt. Slowly opening the lid, he gazed in to find a cylindrical object wrapped in cloth. Picking it up and freeing it of the concealing fabric the Maven found what he was looking for. The medallion the Purging Flame had stolen from the noble of Bolsek Village rested safely in his hands. Mission accomplished.

No sooner had he completed this thought, Edge heard a sudden series of whistles from outside in the trees. Not one or two but dozens. They came so fast Edge could tell his partner was frantic. The Maven quickly turned his keen attention outside into the camp where he began to detect the sound of hoof beats fast approaching. Tucking the medallion into his tunic pocket he turned, heading for the back exit to avoid whatever hindrance to his plans was approaching. The sentries out front abruptly came to attention and two more of the marauders came scrambling into position out back. Stopping short, Edge cursed under his breath, realizing he had let himself become surrounded.

Forcing himself to sit tight and listen intently in the darkness, he heard several horses ride into the camp from the back side where he had entered along the cliff wall. Judging from the sudden scrambling of feet amongst the Purging Flame, Edge could only guess their leader had finally arrived—his cue to leave. When he was about to rise and incapacitate the two guards behind him then make a run for Zephyr, he overheard something that froze him.

"But sir, this is Janns!" a familiar voice called. Nervous, Edge peered out a slit in the tent lining and found the marauders and their leader swarming around the boulder where he had left the unconscious man. They had him picked up and were examining his motionless form. "He wasn't drunk enough to pass out, sir." The hulking form of the leader threw his hands into the air.

"Then how do you explain..." the man stopped there, looking down peculiarly behind the boulder. As he came back up, Edge was horrified to find him holding a long blue cloth in his hands. Throwing his hands up to his neck, Edge realized he had forgotten to tie his scarf back around his neck after he had used it against the marauder. Writhing the scarf in his hands, a look of boiling hatred swept into the leader's eyes. "There's a Maven in the camp! Search the tents, you fools!" As the chief marauder's booming words echoed into his ears, Edge grit his teeth in rage, infuriated at his stupidity and the situation he now faced because of it. Before he could so much as reach down to his belt, the sentries on both sides of him opened the tent flaps pouring light down onto the lone black figure.

The next thing that happened was the one thing Edge did not want—his instinct took over. There were two guards no more than a foot in front of him staring in disbelief, two more in the back ten feet away and another marauder rushing toward them from the front. Striking like lighting, the boy's hands flew to his legs to pluck free two of the four throwing knives strapped to his thighs. In one fluid motion before any of his foes could let out a scream he rose to his feet and slammed his steel into the two men before him, wrenched the blades free and flung them over his shoulders with such force and precision the guards behind him dropped to their knees as the steel came soaring squarely into their chests. With his hands already behind him, Edge took hold of his sword hilt to heave the blade out and slash it through the air to come sailing down into the final marauder charging him.

Watching the sentries fall from where they stood and the charging man suddenly fly back in the opposite direction with his chest torn down the middle, the rest of the Purging Flame turned in astonishment to the other end of the camp to find Edge standing at the entrance of the leader's tent with sword in hand and complete focus encompassing his visage. Incredulously pushing his way through the front line of his men, the chief marauder's face tightened with rage.

"*Kill the Maven!*" he bellowed, wrenching free the rusty cutlass under his dark purple robes. With that, the entire encampment of over thirty of the Purging Flame drew their weapons and came charging for Edge. While the Maven could easily have leapt into the forest and all but disappeared from the band of raving brigands, there was a vertical cliff wall on either side of the camp that boxed him in. They would find him eventually. He also could have outrun the marauders in the open field ahead of him if he dropped his equipment but never the horses many of them had. Three of his four walls were not an option.

He had been backed into a corner.

Edge grit his teeth with throbbing rage tearing through him. The only way out of this was straight through them. No, he thought. He would rather die than let it happen again. He vowed it would never happen again. He would kill himself first. Unfortunately, the Maven was left with little time to make any choice at all. The marauders were on him in moments, thrusting their stained blades out for him. Edge spun to his right and slammed his broadsword through the closest post holding the tent sheet aloft. As the fabric began to fall without its support, he thrust the tip of his sword up to catch its ends and slashed forward to cast the entire sheet over the first row of charging marauders, confusing and slowing them down.

As the Purging Flame continued madly advancing on his position, Edge could feel it beginning to take hold on him—the hopeless inevitability of what he knew would happen if he couldn't stop it. There was no other way. He had to try and take down as many as he could before it took control. He couldn't let it happen again; even to men as wicked as these. With fierce determination, Edge leapt forward into the charging mass, jumping onto and over the men covered in the tent sheet and into the rest of the crowd. Maybe he could pierce through the marauders and get to the leader to barter for his life, he thought. As he slashed down through the robes of three oncoming foes and spun around to parry away a cutlass sailing toward him from another with one hand, his other was reaching into a pouch at his waist to pull free a handful of barbed spheres that he cast into enemies to his left. Dropping three at once, another five came swarming over them.

    Edge quickly realized getting to the chief of the group was all but impossible. He was now completely surrounded and even for him, thirty against one were not good odds on open ground. He fought them back continuing to savagely slash his sword while twirling over the earth and downed corpses around him, all the while emptying his satchels of steel into their number. It was another ten downed marauders later when one of them at last penetrated the Maven's ferocious defense and cracked him on the back of the head with the swinging end of his hilt. Edge grunted and stumbled forward, catching the blade of a cutlass down his left arm. Wheeling to block an incoming attack, one of the Purging Flame rushed forward and violently slashed downward straight into Edge's middle. He screamed out and fell to the earth, the blood of both he and his enemies slowly soaking through his clothes and hair to his skin. As he fell, his senses seemed to blur and fade in and out, yet he could still hear the cries of one man shouting to the others to leave him be.

    No, Edge thought. Kill me. Kill me now. Kill me before it happens. But no killing stroke came. Only the monstrous frame of the purple cloaked leader suddenly standing over him. The man smiled and shook his head, still holding Edge's blue scarf in his hands.

    "Nothing but a child," he scoffed, dropping the blue cloth down over Edge's bloodstained chest. The man slowly picked him up by the shirt and pushed a knife to his throat. Edge winced. Not at the steel but at the sensation threatening to rip through him. It was going to happen. "But you'll die like a man." As the chief marauder prepared to thrust his blade down into the boy's throat, he stopped. Edge could see a suddenly confused, even frightened, look in his eyes. A fervent red mist of brilliant energy was beginning to appear around Edge's body and his eyes were morphing from pale gray to heated crimson. As the seconds ticked by the grass beneath the boy slowly lost its color and withered while the Bulloct still behind the leader's tent began to moan and ran off into the trees.

    It was happening.

    Edge felt overwhelming anguish encompassing his mind as realization that he had broken his vow sunk in. It was too late to stop it now. By now the throbbing around his wounds was all but gone and the man holding him down had released him and taken several steps back. As the mesmerized marauders grew nervous, one resolved to finish it himself and plunged his blade downward with such force it stabbed through the boy's chest down into the earth. Edge took the blow but did not move, save for his eyes, now changed. They were consumed by some uncontrolled presence within him, piercing red along with the shining scarlet mist growing brighter and larger as the seconds passed by. A heated layer of semitransparent energy was building beneath the mist, quaking to be unleashed. Edge's body tightened and the near invisible force around him abruptly exploded out, detonating the very air. All at once, everything around him, living and not, was blown away—crushed by the force erupting from Edge's body. A field of exploding energy ripped through time and space crushing bones, shattering tree trunks and splitting the earth.

Then, as soon as it started, it was over. The explosion of invisible force was gone and all that was left was a clearing full of fragmented earth and corpses. The trees had all been uprooted and blasted into the now bowed cliff walls along with the lifeless members of the Purging Flame. Their bodies were broken and gnarled, as if a beast had torn them apart. The clearing was absolutely quiet but for the menacing hum of the crimson energy now once again hovering around Edge's motionless form. Everything was still for several lingering moments until the Maven at last moved. His eyes, still burning red, opened once again and he pushed himself up with his right arm. Slowly standing at full length, he noticed the rusty cutlass still lodged inside his chest. Reaching up, he casually took hold of the hilt and heaved it out to cast it aside onto the cracked and bowled earth where he had just lain closer to death than ever before.

As the faint red mist faded, Edge at last found his conscience mind again. His eyes shut then opened slowly like coming out of a deep sleep but were instantly confronted by the malicious image of the devastation around him. It had happened. He had let it happen again. He had dispersed death a way in which it was never meant to be dealt; so violently it looked as if the Netherworld itself had erupted from below. The young Maven's heart fell to mesh with his guts. He wanted to die. This was never supposed to happen again. As he stood there suppressing his tears, Edge felt the sudden presence of a miniature hand on his shoulder.

"You couldn't have avoided it, partner," Zephyr's voice quietly told him. "You would have died if you hadn't used it." Edge sealed his eyes tightly shut as he ran his bloody sleeve along his face to wipe away the salty water.

"I should have died, Zeph," the boy responded almost silently. The blood stains on his body remained but the wounds that made them were completely gone. It was as if he had never been touched. Another tear formed in the corner of his eye prompting the boy to look down and avoid Zephyr's gaze. Spying his blue scarf lying on the ground under his boot, the boy leaned down to pick it up and gradually fastened it back around his neck, still damp with blood. "But here I am, still alive..." The Maven dryly chuckled in spite of himself, obvious ire in his words. "You okay?" Zephyr tried a faint smile as he moved in front of Edge's face, smoothing out his tail feathers protruding behind his body.

"I knew it was coming and got up into the sky," he returned.

"Hence the name, right?" the Maven stated emotionlessly. Zephyr merely nodded, searching for the something to say. Edge beat him to the punch. "How do I live with myself, Zeph?" Knowing the boy was beyond the reach of trying to justify why it happened, the Sky Sprite just sighed.

"Let's start by walking out of here, Edge," he offered calmly. "We can talk later." After a long silence, Edge at last breathed deeply and started slowly walking forward with his partner quietly flying behind.

Chapter 2

A Lucrative Offer

It was almost noon the next day when Edge rose from the stump where he had been sitting on a hillside overlooking Bolsek Village, one of the border towns the Purging Flame had plundered the previous day. He crossed his arms and motioned with an upward nod of his head for Zephyr to move from his shoulder to the branches of the small, dying tree next to them. As the feathered Sky Sprite spread his rich purple wings and lifted off toward the leafless branches, he looked down to the gates of the charred village to observe a single horse drawn cart exiting and making its way up the dirt pathway for the hillside where they waited. Edge's precise vision spied their employer at the reins the moment it appeared.

By the time Edge and Zephyr had made their way back to the village, the sun had risen on a new day only to be blotted out by an overcast sky that painted the world in melancholy shades of gray. Though they had hiked through the entire night not taking any breaks along the way, the usually swift and invisible Maven moved sluggish and carelessly, once again weighed down by the only true terror he had ever known. He and Zephyr had patched his attire as they traveled through the hilly borderlands but every one of his lethal wounds from the battle with the Purging Flame the night before had vanished along with the indiscriminate power that had erupted from the boy's body.

A silent cringe tore through the Maven once more. Though he felt more like dying than living after what he had allowed to happen the previous night, he stood firm over the rocky road with his arms crossed and his bloodstained scarf gently dancing behind him with the faint breeze blowing past his face. At last the cart carrying the town noble and another figure beside him rose to the top of the hill and halted before him, the aged brown horse setting down its front foot to loudly clap against the stones underneath. Edge's employer this time was a tall but portly man with a balding head but a full grey beard. His visage had yet to be pleasant in the Maven's presence but Edge received this reaction from most people he encountered for being what he was.

The portly man slowly rose and released the reins, stepping out of the cart to extend his hand up to it again and help an adolescent girl down alongside him. Edge raised an eyebrow, not having expected the other. The girl had shoulder length chestnut hair and a vibrant green dress, nicer than any a plebian village girl would have. From her appearance and from the unabashed way she stared at him, running her eyes up and down his battle weary figure, Edge guessed she was the noble's daughter. They both walked around the cart to within five steps of the darkly clad Maven, neither saying anything. When the girl at last tried an uncertain smile at him, Edge remained cold and detached, still unmoving with his arms crossed. At last the noble spoke.

"It would seem you've run into *some* kind of trouble since we last spoke," he started dryly, observing the blood stains on his apparel. "Was it the Purging Flame?" Edge remained silent but reached into his tunic pocket behind his dilapidated black vest and pulled forth the medallion he had recovered.

"That group won't ever be causing you trouble again," he affirmed in an emotionless tone, still holding the medallion. The noble eyed him and the object in his hand peculiarly.

"I thought you said you were a Blue Maven," he stated inquisitively. "That you didn't like killing." Edge's eyes sharply met with the man's.

"I don't," he returned not missing a beat. "All the same, they won't be back." The noble shot an uncertain glance at the girl beside him, and then turned to the cart to pull free a medium satchel of Seir.

"I didn't think you'd need much of this," he said haughtily, turning back. "I told you that you were free to any of the treasure you pleased in their camp. It doesn't look like you seized on the opportunity." Edge extended his arm and opened his hand for the satchel, raising an eyebrow at him.

"Was all that treasure yours?" he inquired. The noble's brow furrowed, moving forward to toss the satchel at him.

"A great portion of it was but of course not all—"

"Then how can you offer me what is not yours?" Edge cut him off. "I'm a Maven, not a thief. All that they plundered is still up there. Tell the other villagers they are free to collect it by the twin cliffs at the edge of the Borlien Hills but I wouldn't send any women or the weak of heart it if I were you." Before Edge was about to hand back the medallion to the noble, he paused. "Out of all that they took, why was this all that you wanted me to recover? There were plenty of more valuable trinkets up there."

"It's my mother's," the chestnut haired girl at last spoke in a slightly offended tone of voice, taking a small step forward. When Edge's cold eyes shifted to meet hers, she lost her confidence again. The boy maintained his grip on the pendant, waiting for the words he could tell she still wanted to say to him though they were much softer this time. "Please. It's all that I have left of her." Studying the girl for another moment, Edge decided he had misjudged her and slowly stepped forward to offer her the medallion. The girl's eyes softened with gratitude as she smiled and raised her hand to take it but her father reached in and plucked it from Edge's palm first. He quickly pulled the girl back and leaned down to whisper in her ear.

"You know Maven's are not to be trusted," he admonished quietly. "We're lucky I could find one that didn't just steal the medallion and leave. Now get back in the cart." The girl quickly pulled back, obvious disapproval and frustration in her eyes. She turned to Edge, aware he had heard her father's words and politely bowed.

"Thank you," she said sincerely. Rising, her eyes spitefully passed back to her father's and she disappeared around the cart, stepping back in. The noble turned back to the boy before him and frowned.

"Thank you for your services, now take your Seir and go," he advised strongly. On any other day Edge would have loved to unpleasantly respond that he was nothing more than an oversized blob of greed that should aspire to be more like his daughter, but today the Maven merely narrowed his eyes and slowly turned his back for the hills, his Sky Sprite partner and blood crusted scarf following close behind. When he disappeared from view, the noble entered his cart and turned it back for the ravaged village with the loud clapping of the horse hooves on the flat rocks on the road.

~

His fatigue finally catching up with him, Edge decided to spend the night on the outskirts of Bolsek Village to rest before traveling to another township closer to the Southland capital to refresh their supplies. He and Zephyr set up camp near a dusty forest road beside a small thicket of thick oaks and a short rock wall dropping off from a higher ridge like many littered over the hills of the region. The moon had just appeared from behind the Iairian Mountain Chain to the east, bordering the massive Southland from its eastern side and the golden land of Grandaria—two places Edge had no desire to go. As the final rays of light began to retreat across the skies to the advancing night, the boy built a small fire while his partner warmed some of their last rations. Edge had removed his heavy sword and belt and laid his back against the short rock wall behind him, eager to just sit and remain still after all the moving around the two had done over the past few weeks.

Business had been slow lately. With all the negative attention those in his profession were getting from the Red Mavens descending ever further into their crevice of ethical ambiguity, it was difficult to secure even the usual jobs with the mounting fear of getting entangled with a Maven. They were struggling to make ends meet. Edge's hair was a tangled mess of black, along with most of his frayed clothing. His face, illuminated orange by the small fire, was placid and devoid of energy as it had been since the prior night. Zephyr glanced at him as his miniature hands took hold of a little grass salad he had made himself, a standard snack for any healthy Sky Sprite. The two hadn't spoken much since it happened and Zephyr could tell his friend wasn't coping well. The little sprite tried his best to smile and speak normally as he dropped out of the air to take a seat on a small rock beside the fire and begin shoveling his salad through his wide yellow beak.

"I don't know if my taste in humans is anything like it should be," he started, chomping away at his dinner, "but that noble's daughter was cute, wasn't she?" Edge's distant eyes remained fixed into space before him. "I mean, I'm not saying we should give it all up and run back there so you can have her forever or anything, but I bet it makes you think about where you'll eventually settle down someday, huh? A quaint little village like—" The boy slowly turned his glazed eyes to the sprite and interrupted him mid-sentence.

Trial of a Maven

"You'd bring that up, after last night?" he murmured in icy disbelief. Zephyr stopped chewing and slowly let down the rock he was using as a plate, letting a long silence hang as they stared each other down.

"Edge, how long are you going to keep thinking that way?" he asked eventually. "Look, we both know it only happens when something triggers it—when you're in danger so grave it threatens your life. What reason would it ever have to happen in a harmless village like that?" Edge stared at the sprite for a long moment before reaching down for his flask of water. He gulped the rest down then threw the empty flask to the rocky basin where he sat.

"You saw one last night," he declared bluntly. "Suppose we *were* living in a village. What happens when it's attacked by marauders; or it catches fire; or some of our Maven buddies come looking for us wanting to settle old scores; or the Draks come down from the war zones like the rumors say? Or what about the dream, Zeph? Did you forget what happens then?" He shook his head incredulously at the sprite, his voice and temper escalating with every word. A faint red mist of swirling energy began to sweat off of the boy's skin. "Anything can set it off, Zeph. That's why we stay on the move—to keep me away from people. That's why I do this. That's why I can't ever 'settle down.' That's why I always win this argument and that's why I keep telling you not to bring it up! You knew this was the way it was when you joined up and this is the way it has to stay! Now *shut the hell up*!" As he finished his tirade, the crimson power radiating over his skin faintly burst to life and they were both surprised to hear the massive stone wall behind them cleave and split in response.

Wheeling around in surprise, Edge saw the gaping fissure in the rock and realized what had just happened. Not able to believe he lost control and acted this way toward his friend, the boy tore his gaze away and rose to his feet to step away from the fire. He slowed before the dirt road beside them, letting his hands limply drop to his sides. All the bottled emotion he had suppressed from the previous night rising out, he fell to his knees on the ground trying to fight tears. The red mist around his skin slowly softened into a hazy blue, and quickly after a soft drizzle of rain coming down over the small camp. Zephyr remained calmly on the rock he had been seated on, somewhat taken aback but not surprised at his friend's outburst. After giving him a moment to cool, he spread his wings and hovered over to the boy through the mist of rain to put his small hand over his shoulder. Edge was the first to speak, shaking his head.

"I'm sorry, Zeph," he managed, his voice taut with tension. "I didn't mean it, I just..."

"I know, buddy," the sprite offered with a smile. Edge shook his head and sealed his salty eyes shut.

"You're right, Zeph. I don't want to do this forever. But... I have to. You know that. I can't risk letting it loose on innocent people. I've killed too many of them. Doing this... being a Maven... it's all I can be. I don't have a choice."

"There is always a choice, young Maven," a deep voice from behind them on the road suddenly spoke. Though besieged by all his emotion, Edge's trained instincts immediately seized control of him and he wheeled around with a blade in his hand. What was left of the pale blue mist over him evaporated instantly as did the quiet rain. Zephyr was still just realizing the voice had spoken by the time Edge was on his feet facing the darkness from where it had come.

"If you want to keep your life you'll show yourself right now," the Maven commanded, stern resolve emanating from his words. No reply came but a sudden wisp of wind blew down the dirt road, picking up leaves and other foliage along its path.

"Your reputation is indeed well deserved, Lightning's Edge," the voice sounded once more, still concealed behind the cover of darkness.

"Though it never precedes me—only my blade does that," Edge informed him brusquely. "Now come out before you find that out first hand." After another long silence, the voice spoke once more, this time directly behind him.

"Save your threats, Maven; they will have little effect on me," it articulated still calm and controlled. Stunned to hear the voice suddenly behind him, Edge wheeled once more and flung his knife at what turned out to be a tall man, hooded and cloaked behind thick dark robes. While it penetrated the figure's person, however, it went completely through as if he was not even there. Edge could even hear the blade thud into a tree trunk behind the figure at full strength. He took a slow step back and thought about rushing for his sword but as he stared into the darkness of the unmoving other's hood he remained frozen in place.

"What is this?" Edge breathed slowly, his eyes uncertain for the first time in years.

"As I said," the figure responded in its low, easy tone, "you have a choice. I am here to offer it too you." Edge remained still, his eyes searching.

"Choice?"

"That's right and should you make this choice, it will yield to you the path you are looking for, Edge." The Maven shot a quick glance at Zephyr, hovering next to him with eyes wide, his beak open in disbelief.

"Who are you and how do you know who I am?" the boy grilled. The figure shifted slightly, his face still concealed under the hood.

"Who I am is not significant or relevant to my presence before you tonight, so you would do well not to dwell on it while I am here," the figure stated informatively, aware it was not the answer the boy was looking for. "As for how I know you, let us just say your reputation does in fact precede you farther that you know. I am here to make you an offer—a very lucrative one. I am in need of a Maven; one who can provide protection to one who cannot protect herself. You are capable of providing that protection." Edge sneered.

"If you're talking about a blood run you should be talking to a Red. It's not my line of work," he retorted heatedly.

"I know you are no Red Maven and I would not be here if I thought you were," the figure responded quickly. "I merely have a friend who is in need of a bodyguard while she makes a journey. She has no enemies but she needs protection nonetheless." Edge loosened some at this, taking another look at the Sky Sprite to his right, already staring at him with hopeful eyes.

"Who is this friend? And where is she going?" Edge pressed, folding his arms.

"She is a Grandarian and must make her way across that nation," he replied. Edge was already shaking his head no.

"Not interested," he decreed quickly. "I can get plenty of work here in the Southland without having to trek all the way to Grandaria and then march around for Granis knows how long playing babysitter for a little girl on some pilgrimage to Galantia or whatever she's doing. Find somebody else."

Tales of Iairia

"As I said," the figure picked up quickly, ignoring his answer, "this will be a very well paid job. You're deluding yourself if you believe you can get work in the Southland with the fear over Mavens of late. You will not find a better way of income anywhere in Iairia." When Edge was about to decline more passionately, he felt Zephyr tapping his shoulder.

"Partner, this sounds like it might be right up our alley," he whispered. "He's right about the Reds. We're having a tough time digging up good jobs anymore. But this is long, easy work for what sounds like good money and no risk of *it* happening." Edge paused for a minute, letting the last comment sink in. Slowly turning back to the figure, he narrowed his eyes.

"How do I know this is for real?" he asked flatly. "You won't even tell me your name." The figure was still for a moment then spoke once more.

"My name will be revealed in due time." Edge stared skeptically, still unconvinced.

"Well then what assurance can you give me to trust you? Why should I believe a word you say?"

"Because the chance for you to discover the truth about your past and why *it* keeps happening to you is too rare and valuable an opportunity to pass up," the figure spoke slowly. Edge's eyes grew wide, both awe and anger mirrored there.

"...What are you talking about? How do you know anything about me?"

"I know more about you than you know yourself, young Maven. And if you wish to learn more, you will arrive in Eirinor Village of Grandaria in exactly one week's time to meet with me again and begin your task." With that, the figure took a swift step back and rapidly began to blend in with the darkness of the night. His muscles tightening, Edge burst forward after the figure. By the time the Maven had ran past where he was standing however, the gray robed figure was gone into the night as if he had never been. Another wisp of wind blew down the road into the air carrying the stranger's voice upon it. "You have a choice, Edge. Choose wisely."

After the voice faded and the wind dissipated into the night once more, Edge slowly turned to face his partner, staring back at him incredulously.

Chapter 3

<u>Child of Light and Dark</u>

Kaylan Tieloc gazed at the transparent glass she picked up with the wet cloth in her hand and shook her head with a smile, observing the thin layer of filth still present from the last person to have drank from it. She turned her head toward the large elderly man to her right behind the bar, drying off a plate he had just submerged in a tub on the floor.

"Could it be that the great innkeeper Carfon Doyrl has at last begun to lose his touch?" she asked in a dramatic tone of voice, pointing to the soiled glass with her opposite hand. The aged man slowly turned his bulky frame toward her, eyeing the object in her hand. At last he coyly smiled back and shook his head.

"Young lady, I have been running this inn since before even your father was born," he began slowly. "When you are my age, see if you fair any better. I may be getting on in years, but that's why I have my favorite employee to assist me in keeping this place up." Kaylan grinned and walked to the tub of soapy water to immerse the glass beneath its surface and start scrubbing again.

"I'm flattered, Carfon," she replied quickly, "but it might mean more if I wasn't your only employee." The innkeeper chuckled and nodded, reaching down into the water to take the glass from her.

"Even if I had an army of help around here, I have no doubt you'd still be my favorite, Kaylan," he complemented earnestly. "You've been working all morning and we've barely had a customer. Why don't you step outside and keep an eye on your little brother and the Garrinal boys for a while?" The girl put her hands on her hips and furrowed her brow at him.

"I just got back from my break, Carfon," she reminded him kindly.

"Oh it would hardly be a break knowing those boys," Carfon chuckled shaking his head. "Judging from the pintsized battle cries out the back door I'd guess our three man wrecking crew is still raising mischief in the big oak behind the inn. With your parents away and your uncle out on his hunting trip, somebody's got to keep an eye on them *all the time.*" Kaylan rolled her eyes and began to unstrap the soiled white apron wrapped around her light blue tunic and short brown pants.

"Don't I know it," she knowingly sighed with a smile. "I'll go watch the boys for a while then. Call me if you need anything, all right?" Carfon quickly nodded and told her yes, to which she set her folded apron on the back shelf and exited the bar for the rear of the inn. The closer she walked to the back door through a long pantry, the louder the already shrill screaming of her little brother and his best friends became. Kaylan couldn't help but grin. As she walked out the door for the green back yard behind the inn, the girl unfastened the ponytail she kept her hair in while she worked and let her golden tresses down to gently caress her shoulders as they fell. Her shimmering light hair was the only trait she had not inherited from her parents.

Everyone always told Kaylan that she was the embodiment of both her parents, Tavinious and Arilia Tieloc. They were two of the most renowned people in the whole of Iairia after their adventure almost twenty years ago that they always told her about. Fate had ordained Tavin as the fabled Elemental Warrior of Light when not much older than Kaylan was now, granting him the power to wield the legendary Sword of Granis on a mission to save Grandaria and the entire world from the evil of the Drakkaidian tyrant Valif Montrox and his demonic minions. Tavin and his best friend Jaren Garrinal, the last of the Mystic Sages named Zeroan, two warriors from the Southland and the Elemental Warrior of Fire that would eventually become Tavin's wife, Arilia Embrin, set off on a quest to find the missing shards of the Holy Emerald—the most powerful talisman of magic in existence—before sinister forces in Drakkaidia could do the same.

Over the course of their adventure together, the Drakkaidian prince Verix Montrox defected to their cause,

Tavin spoke with Granis, the God of Light himself, an army of demons was mobilized and defeated, and Drakkan the God of Darkness was sealed forever into a void world apart from Iairia. Though tales of this adventure still spread through the lands like wildfire, most Grandarians had come to call these events the Days of Destiny, when the ancient prophesy of the Three Fates was fulfilled and the world left to be molded by the hand of mankind alone.

After their adventure Tavin and Ril had met with Zeroan's spirit one last time in the mystical village of the forest creatures called Cronoms in the Southland and then traveled back to Ril's home village in the west to rebuild after the attack there by Valif Montrox. After nearly a year, they returned to Grandaria to be married and so Tavin could resume his new responsibilities as the Warrior of Light. Though they lived in Galantia for two years, when Ril became pregnant with Kaylan they decided to move to Tavin's home village of Eirinor in the south to raise her and their son Darien, who was born ten years later. Kaylan was now eighteen while her little brother Darien, named after Tavin's father, was eight. When Kaylan was born, Tavin and Ril could sense both light and dark power dormant in her veins from theirs. Though they feared what having both Grandarian and Drakkaidia power in their children's blood might someday mean for them, they knew it would remain dormant unless activated like all magical power in the world and resolved to keep it that way for their own good.

Though it was sometimes daunting to live in her parents' massive shadow, Kaylan had inherited their strength and resilience. Like her father, Kaylan's bravery and kindness extended to all she met but her blood heated at the sight of injustice being done unto others. Tavin often observed her mother's fire and independence in her as well when she became passionate about something, just as stubborn to have her way. Aside from her golden hair she was physically a mirror image of Ril, if not somehow even more beautiful. Kaylan had long been the object of desire for many boys of the village and beyond, constantly receiving gifts and devotions of their feelings for her. As her mother had been before meeting Tavin she was unimpressed by the constant barrage of most of her would-be suitors, realizing such frivolous relationships led to nothing in the end and her time was better spent working toward more meaningful endeavors.

Also like Ril she often opted to participate in activities thought inappropriate for a girl her age, such as learning the way of the sword from Tavin when he had time to teach her. Kaylan was always quick to stand up for herself and what she believed right when anyone dared to put it down. Like both of her parents, her determination and will to act were unparalleled by her peers. Once when she was helping her father and "Uncle" Jaren paint a shed for Carfon as a child, she refused to come in for dinner until it and she were dripping in paint, having promised him they would finish. When Tavin turned to Ril for help, she would just shrug and sarcastically remind him that a Tieloc never gave up.

Now that she was coming of age, Kaylan's parents entrusted her to watch after her little brother while they were away in Galantia and elsewhere on business. As the Warrior of Light, Tavin had a place on both the Galantian Council and the Senior Council of the sovereign of Grandaria, the Supreme Granisian. In these troubling times with the debate over the divided Drakkaidia raging in the hearts and minds of Grandarians nationwide, they were more and more frequently called away to advise the Supreme Granisian on how to respond.

Kaylan let her mind ease into more uncomplicated matters as her brother and the Garrinal boys came into view. They were in the branches of the massive oak tree behind the inn with paper armor strapped to their body and blunt wooden daggers Tavin had made them in their hands. They were all screaming out at each other that the fort was under attack and Drakkaidian troops were trying to invade.

"Pardon me, brave soldiers," Kaylan called once more placing her hands on her hips, "but maybe you could lower the sounds of battle just a little bit. Some of us are trying to work, you know." Hearing the girl's call, the younger of Jaren's two boys looked over and pointed his wooden blade in her direction.

"Watch out! It's a Drak spy!" he bellowed in a high pitched call. Kaylan's eyes narrowed at him. Uncle Jaren's two boys Roan and Jak were eight and ten years old. From what she knew of her Uncle's behavior when he was their age, they were mirror images of him in that they were magnets for trouble. While Darien was thankfully a little more cautious of the world around him, sitting safely in the lower branches of the tree while the others were on the end of a thin branch, playing with such hazardous friends was making him prone to trouble himself. Darien had pitch black hair, though currently concealed by the lightweight paper helm sunken over his cranium. Ril had guessed that their children's hair was a reflection of the power inherited from each parent; Kaylan portraying the light from her father and Darien the darkness from his mother.

"No, it's just my sister," the younger Tieloc replied informatively. Jak slapped his forehead and shook it back and forth, shaking the tree branch he and his brother sat on.

"I told you that you have to use your imagination, Darien!" he reminded impatiently, adjusting the armor over his little chest. Kaylan frowned at how much they were causing the undersized branch to quake, remembering the large pit where Carfon was digging a well was adjacent to the tree and right beneath them.

"Jak, Roan, please stop shaking the branch. You need to come in closer to the trunk or you could fall," she advised quickly. The boys just laughed and made dim-witted faces at her.

"Don't be such a scardy-cat, Kay," Roan giggled, standing up to start hopping on the branch like it was a trampoline. Kaylan took a heated step forward and extended a pointed finger up to them with a glare.

"I'm not joking, Roan!" she barked at full volume. "Come down from that branch before it—" Her words were precluded by the sudden snapping of wood high up in the tree. The already thin and rotted limb of the oak they were straining abruptly gave way from the force of the jumping, sending it and the two boys plummeting down for the earth below. While it would have been a painful enough landing on the grass almost ten feet down, both boys managed to fall right into the gap where the well was being dug, dropping them another fifteen feet down. Kaylan's eyes bursting open with worry, she blasted forward and slid to the opening of the hole to stare down into the darkness. With the sun-filled summer sky to aid her, she managed to locate the boys lying in a heap on top of one another, both crying.

"Jak! Roan! Are you alright?" she frantically cried down to them. Though they tried to respond, their words were too muddled by their tears for the girl to make any sense of them. From the way Roan was grasping at his leg, she guessed he had broken it. Realizing she had to get them out without delay, the girl instructed them to hold on while she found help. As she rose and turned for the village, however, she remembered most of the men were out on their hunting trip and Carfon was too old to be of any assistance. Rapidly scanning her mind for an idea, she burst into the small shed next to the back of the inn and reemerged with a thick rope slung over her shoulder.

Calling for Darien to get out of the tree to run for help, Kaylan mounted determination to her face and heaved what rope she could over the closest strong branch on the oak. Racing to pull the rope down the opposite side of the branch, she paused. She listened to the little boys crying out in pain and knew there was no way they would be able to hold onto the rope if she tried to pull them up. She would have to go in and get them out herself. Throwing the rope into the hole and heaving down on the branch to be sure it would not budge, she exclaimed to the boys she was coming for them and lowered herself into the damp earth.

She descended quickly, the oozing mud on the walls smearing against her slender frame as she went. When she reached the bottom and turned to examine the boys, both crawled and latched onto her, sobbing.

"Kay, my leg hurts!" Roan cried, tightly squeezing her arm.

"It's all right, you two, you're going to be fine," she assured them, just glad they were both still alive. When she quickly looked them over in the weak light shining in from the surface, she observed Roan's leg was indeed broken and it looked like Jak had a deep slash down his midsection. "All right guys, I need you to hold onto me tight. I'll pull us out of here but you need to hold me really tight, okay?" They both agreed and nodded through their tears, firmly wrapping their arms around her waist. Though Kaylan was no frail little girl with her well built frame, packing two of the boys out at the same time was going to be a challenge. She didn't want to have to leave one behind, though; even for a moment.

Taking solid hold of the thick rope, Kaylan grit her teeth and started to pull herself upward. Instantly she realized this would be harder than she thought. The slippery mud-spattered walls were difficult to work her feet into and the boys were squeezing her so tight she could barely move. Just as she had managed to work them about a quarter of the way up the hole with every ounce of strength she could muster, she heard another snapping sound from above. Looking up apprehensively, the girl quickly realized it was not the branch but the rope thrown above it. She could see a tear in the very threads holding it together that she must have missed before.

Before she could so much as warn the boys to hold on, the rope snapped altogether and the three Grandarians were sent plummeting back down to the bottom of the hole with the rope falling in after them. Picking herself up from out of the mire, Kaylan felt her heart sink with the desperation of her circumstances weighing her down. Their only way out had just fallen in with them and the boys were crying louder than ever. Even when Darien alerted someone of the situation, most of the men were gone and there would be little help to get them out. They could be in here for a very long time. The girl wiped the mud streaked on her face away. She couldn't give up. It wasn't in a Tieloc's character.

Just as she was about to try shouting out for anyone to hear her, she looked up to find more rope falling in down the side of the hole. This time however, one end remained secured at the top.

"Grab on and I'll hoist you up," a voice called out from the surface.

"All right!" Kaylan yelled out, not sure who the voice belonged to. It sounded a bit like one of her father's friends but younger. Not caring who her savior was at the moment as long as he could pull her and the boys free, she once again firmly took hold of the rope and instructed the Garrinals to do the same to her. The next thing she knew they were steadily rising through the hole. It was still hard to hold onto the rope for the three of them but they ascended so quickly that before she knew it her muddied head was exposed to fresh air once more.

Straining to lift the boys out as she clung to the grassy earth, Kaylan barely had time to observe the lower half of their rescuer. What she could see of him was all clad in black garb, not reminding her of anyone she knew. Looking to the boys first, however, she turned back to be sure they were both completely out of the hole and safely pulled away from it. Assuring them that they were fine now and everything was going to be all right, she at last turned only to find her mysterious rescuer disappearing behind the inn wall.

Instructing Jak and Roan to remain exactly where they were for a moment, the girl rose and swiftly trailed after him.

Rapidly turning the corner of the inn, Kaylan failed to notice the small creature hovering in the path just before her. Letting out a yelp of surprise, she fell to the ground on her bottom, staring up in disbelief. There was a small purple bird of some kind struggling to regain its altitude after she had run into it. Though she was shocked enough at its appearance, her mind was blown away when she heard it speak.

"Yank my tail feathers, where did that come from?" it spoke from behind its widespread yellow beak. Regaining its composure, the little creature's eyes fell down to her, suddenly nervous. "Oh... this is probably awkward. Um..." As the little creature let the silence hang, Kaylan shook her head in pleasant bewilderment.

"What... are you?" she inquired slowly, a quirky smile spreading across her lips. The creature's hand rose to the long feathers bunched over its skull, running its fingers through them like a human would with its hair.

"Well..."

"Zeph!" a familiar voice called from beyond the next wall of the inn. Spinning around, the winged creature and the girl on the ground watched as a figure in black stepped out from behind the wall. While it looked as though he was about to grab the purple figure hovering before him and continue on his way, his pale gray eyes fell onto the muddied girl on the earth staring back up at him in bewilderment. The boy let out an inaudible huff, shooting a glare at the bird creature to his side.

"Are you the person that just rescued us?" Kaylan managed after an uncomfortable silence. The boy stared at her for another moment, then gave a single nod.

"Rescue's a big word," he stated preparing to turn. "I was just passing by and heard the rope snap so I pulled you out. That's all." As he motioned with his eyes for the creature to get in front of him and move, Kaylan quickly picked herself up and continued.

"Wait!" she pleaded. "Who are you? I've never even seen you before."

"That's because I've never been here before. I'm no one you want to know and you'd do well to let me be about my business." Kaylan gave the boy a peculiar gaze, taken aback at his curtness.

"Well let us repay you for your help before you go," she insisted. "I can arrange a free meal for you at the inn or—"

"I just want to be on my way, girl," he interrupted intolerantly, reestablishing eye contact to impart his impatience. She stared at him for a moment, studying his appearance. His entire form was dark—from his attire littered with satchels and buckles, his black, wavy hair and the hostile look in his eyes. It was not until she spied the blue cloth tied around his neck and trailing down over his back that the girl's eyes widened with realization.

"You're a Maven?" she asked softly. The boy rolled his head from her once more, beginning to walk away.

"Don't worry, I'll be leaving as soon as I can," he informed her quickly. Kaylan shook her head and raised her hands defensively.

"No I didn't mean it like that," she corrected, following after him, "it's just I've never heard of a Maven being so... young." Hearing her voice still trailing him, he spun around swiftly to confront her a final time.

"Look, what's your problem? I'm just trying to get on my way, now would you let me shove off?" Kaylan halted where she stood, a confused and offended look encompassing her face.

"My problem?" she repeated with wide eyes full of insult. "I'm just trying to thank you for saving—"

"What you're doing is wasting my time," the Maven cut her short again. "Leave me alone. Don't you have some children to be watching after? You do such a magnificent job of it." Kaylan stood frozen in place, amazed at how rude she was being treated when all she was trying to do was express her gratefulness. She stood there petrified watching the coarse boy disappear around another building corner. Her incredulous eyes drifted to the purple Sky Sprite once again uncomfortably hovering before her.

"Sorry," it tried uncertainly. "His bark is worse than his bite." With that, it thrust its wings and jetted off after the Maven, leaving the mud-covered girl standing behind confused and embarrassed.

Chapter 4

<u>Strangers in the Night</u>

It was late evening by the time Uncle Jaren and the rest of the men out on the hunting trip returned to Eirinor Village to find both his sons ailing in bed with broken bones and an assortment of painful cuts littered over their miniature frames. Kaylan had since sought out the village's favorite healer and conveniently, Jaren's wife, to attend to the injured boys. While Mrs. Garrinal had been horrified to find her boys once again mangled by their own recklessness, she threw her arms around Kaylan with a mother's gratitude after hearing of her daring rescue. Though Kaylan maintained she should have been watching them closer to have precluded it from happening in the first place, Mrs. Garrinal merely gripped her tighter and told her she grew more like her parents by the day. After she released Kaylan, she and a few other women rushed the Garrinal boys into their house to begin patching them up. Realizing Kaylan would want to clean herself up as well, she insisted she use the warm bath she had prepared upstairs while she attended to the boys.

All too happy to accept, Kaylan instructed Darien to keep watch for their Uncle Jaren and not to disturb Mrs. Garrinal while she worked on Jak and Roan. She then retired to the washroom, discarded her mud soiled clothing into the wash basket and set to working the crusted mud away from her trim form under the surface of the steaming water. She let herself lay in the in the confines of the soapy tub until the torrid temperature completely seeped through her submerged form, saturating her with its comforting warmth. At last she emerged to quickly dry and drape herself in the casual white tunic and skirt Mrs. Garrinal had left out for her. As the girl unwrapped the towel she had secured around her damp golden hair and loosely pulled on some light summer shoes, she heard the sarcastic groans of a familiar voice from downstairs in the boys' room. A smile adorning her soft face, Kaylan rose from the chair, shoving her heels into her shoes, and made for the door.

Descending the staircase for the surface level of the house, Kaylan turned down a hallway with an open door at the end. She couldn't help but giggle at the banter coming from the two adults inside.

"...and if it wasn't for Kaylan, both of them could still be in there crying or worse," the woman's voice finished. "Why I couldn't have civil, well behaved children like the Tielocs' I'll never know." Kaylan moved down the hall and leaned against the frame of the door, her shimmering blond locks gracing her soft beaming face as they rolled over her shoulders. She found her Uncle Jaren with a grin seated on one of the two beds that held his incapacitated sons. His green attire and small sets of daggers were still dirtied from his hunting trip, from which he had obviously just returned. After all the years since his adventure with her father, both of Kaylan's parents told her he was still the flippant, impulsive but bighearted kid he had always been.

"It's because they're mine," he stated proudly, looking down at Jak and scratching his short rugged beard. "You *are* both mine, right?" Both of the boys giggled despite their pain and nodded voraciously, to which Jaren ruffled their hair with his dirty palms and rose. Kaylan's smile widened, observing his natural talent to make people laugh no matter how bad things seemed. Mrs. Garrinal merely scowled and slapped her husband out of the way, commenting that he ought to be taking the Tielocs home to get their things for the night. Kaylan and Darien always spent the nights with the Garrinals when their parents were away.

"Glad to see everyone smiling again," Kaylan at last spoke, taking a step into the room toward her uncle. Jaren turned with a smirk and rolled his eyes toward his wife.

"Well, almost everyone," he said, to which his wife merely slapped his arm again and cheerily greeted Kaylan. Jaren quickly followed in suit, lifting her off the ground with a hug. "So your mom was right after all this time," he laughed setting her back down. "I guess the hero thing really does run in the Tieloc family." Kaylan giggled again and leaned in to peck him on the cheek.

"If I was a better babysitter I wouldn't have to be a hero," she commented quickly, "but thanks."

"Oh give yourself some credit, Kay," he quickly retorted, "*I* can't even control these two hellions."

"You can say that again," Mrs. Garrinal caustically commented, applying a warm cloth over Roan's forehead. "So why don't you leave our children to me and take Kay and Darien back to their house to gather their things?" With that, Darien popped into the room from the hallway beaming and nodding, challenged his uncle to a race there, then disappeared as quickly as he had arrived. Kaylan rolled her eyes as Jaren laughed heartily and pulled her along after him.

As the two exited the house after the younger Tieloc, Jaren inhaled a deep breath of the humid evening air into his lungs and looked into the starry sky. The last remaining rays of light from the looming mountains to the west had now vanished into the warm night air, illuminated now only by sporadic torches throughout the main village roads and the large moon above. Beginning their walk down the road for the Tieloc residence, Kaylan imparted to her uncle how she had saved Jak and Roan with the help of the mysterious boy clad in black. After she was finished, Jaren came to the same conclusion about his being a Maven and reminded her they were not the friendliest group of people in Iairia, accounting for his churlish behavior. He followed up with giving her another hug and repeated what his wife had told her about growing more like her parents with each passing day, something she could be proud of.

Approaching the Tieloc house, Kaylan eyed her brother standing peculiarly still before their old fence, staring. Squinting in confusion to Jaren, he cocked his head as well and shrugged.

"What are you doing, kiddo?" he questioned with a laugh, walking up to him. "You know you've got to touch the door to win the race." While Kaylan expected her little brother to concoct a new rule of the race neither of them had ever heard before, he merely pointed toward the kitchen window of the house with a straight face.

"The light's on," he spoke plainly. Curious, Kaylan and Jaren shifted their views to survey what he was talking about. Peering into the house, they both saw a candle had indeed been lit and placed on the kitchen table. Her confusion suddenly turning to unease, she looked over to her uncle.

"I didn't leave a candle lit, Jaren," she stated nervously. "I haven't even been in there all day." Jaren's face quickly lost its playful appearance, replaced by one of troubled concern. Taking a more careful look inside the window for anything else out of the ordinary, he motioned for Darien to stand behind Kaylan.

"Both of you wait here. I'll check it out," he told them reaching down to the hilt of his larger hunting dagger and looking to Kaylan. "If anything happens, you know what to do."

"I do?" she asked uncertainly. When her uncle frowned, she shrugged it off and nodded. With a firm grip on his hilt, Jaren quietly began creeping around the Tieloc's old fence toward the back entrance of the house that opened into the kitchen. As he disappeared around the corner, Kaylan breathed deeply, nervous for him and curious why anyone would intrude into their home and put a light on in the process. Standing in wait amidst the silence of the night with Darien behind her doing the same, her keen eyes locked back onto the window with alarm. There was a sudden movement from inside the house; one that did not belong to her uncle. Her heart leaping up into her chest with apprehension, she knew she had to act. Turning and instructing Darien to remain where he stood and to run for help if she didn't come back in a moment, she wheeled around and began sprinting after Jaren to alert him of the other inside the house before he stumbled in to meet whoever was in there.

Wildly careening around the corner of her home, she observed her uncle silently stepping through the back door to the kitchen. Screaming out to him in warning, she sped through the fence and leapt into the doorway after him. Inside she found only her surprised uncle turned around with anxious uncertainty tearing through his face and the lone candlelit table amidst the darkness.

"Kaylan, what is it?" he grilled rapidly.

"There's someone else in here," she managed to quietly mutter, out of breath. No sooner had she completed her last word, a soft sound from the darkness of the opposite side of the room caused them both to jump. Unsheathing his dagger and spinning around to face whatever lurked in the shadows, Jaren found the silhouette of a lone figure leaning against the wall.

"What are you doing in here?" the Grandarian archer asked harshly. "Who are you?" Though the figure remained bolstered up with its back against the wall, it slowly raised its empty gloved hands in a defensive gesture. Though no reply came, the figure then thrust itself off the wall and took a few slow steps forward into the light, its hands still open and at rest. The intruder's body now illuminated by the slowly burning flame, Kaylan's blue eyes opened wide. Taken aback, she recognized the figure as the dark boy that had saved her earlier in the day. Her mouth open but too stunned to speak, she watched as the boy's brow furrowed upon seeing her as well. His hands dropped limply to his sides and he exhaled sharply.

"If you're Kaylan Tieloc, I quit here and now," he spoke suddenly, his voice agitated. Jaren's frame tightened as he identified the boy as a Maven from his long blue scarf.

"What are you talking about?" he questioned callously. "What the hell are you doing here?" The boy's expression was no friendlier than that of Jaren's but his tone was controlled.

"I was invited here," was his factual reply. Though Kaylan and her uncle shot tentative glances at each other, Jaren scoffed.

"*Invited?*" he repeated incredulously. "Invited by who?" Though they could see the boy was about to respond, he paused, shifting his gaze to the side of the room by the window. A moment later, a faint breeze rustling around the outside of the house came blowing through the dark kitchen, gently twirling Kaylan's bright golden tresses about her shoulders and sending a strange sensation tingling down her spine. After the gust had subsided, the Maven's expression eased.

"By him," he spoke again, motioning with his eyes for the two to turn around. Confused but taking the hint, they both rotated their heads to find another figure suddenly standing in the doorway. Though Kaylan jumped in shock at the ominously large and cloaked frame, as the moments ticked by she was again surprised to find her Uncle Jaren still as stone as he looked upon the figure, his jaw slightly dropping and his eyes widening. He slowly let his previously taut frame loosen and his short blade fall to his side, an incredulous expression encompassing his face. As Kaylan silently stared in frightened bewilderment wondering who this man could be to provoke this kind of reaction from her boisterous uncle, she saw Jaren's lip was actually quivering. At last, he finally managed to utter sound.

"It can't be... no..." he mouthed almost inaudibly. The figure shifted underneath his flowing robes and gave a faint nod from behind his concealing hood, to which Jaren merely shook his head in further disbelief. "Z... Zeroan?" A long silence hung about the air then, Kaylan's eyes slowly expanding at the mention of this name.

"Hello again, Jaren Garrinal," was the deep but affable voice from behind the figure's hood. Kaylan could see her uncle sweating at his words, though skepticism was still mirrored in his eyes.

"...It can't be..." he repeated. "You ... Zeroan died."

"This is true," the figure spoke softly. "Yet death is merely the next step in the journey of life, and for a Mystic Sage, not one that separates me from this world all at once. I am the spirit of Zeroan; his will, temporarily returned to the mortal realm until my last affair is done." Jaren softened then, the doubt and disillusion in his eyes fading as a wave of remembrance at his old friend's speech flushed through his mind.

"...Zeroan," he spoke quietly. "It really is you, isn't it?" Though the figure's face remained shadowed behind his hood, everyone could tell his was faintly smiling as he took a step into the house.

"It is, my friend," he affirmed softly. "But my time here is very short; restrained now by forces beyond my control and I must be brief." Zeroan looked up then toward the darkly clad other standing with arms crossed beyond the two Grandarians. "I am glad to see you again as well, Edge." Kaylan rotated her head around in surprise, having almost forgotten the Maven was still there. He silently nodded in response.

"Why have you come back, Zeroan?" Jaren inquired curiously. "What is this last affair of yours? I thought everything was done the day Tavin gave up the Holy Emerald." The sage shifted in his robes once more, pausing before he began.

"The prophesies of old have been fulfilled, my Grandarian friend. I have returned to this world and to this village in response to a... disturbance I sensed from beyond. As I asked you so many years ago, please trust that which you hear for all that I offer tonight to all of you is the truth." Seeing them all nod in hesitant understanding, the sage paused once more, collected his thoughts, then began again slowly. "Since I last spoke to Tavinious and Arilia in the Southland after the God of Darkness Drakkan was defeated and his evil sealed, my spirit has been adrift in the winds of Iairia, waiting for my final task to be completed. While I was waiting, I sensed a disturbing occurrence to the north. One that if left unchecked, threatens to reverse all that we fought for and accomplished in our quest." Zeroan's spirit waited once more, noting the apprehension on the faces of those before him. "To put it simply, there is something wrong with the seal to the portal that holds Drakkan at bay. It is weakening by the day." While shocked dread overcame Kaylan's face at this revelation, Jaren staggered where he stood as if someone had punched him in the gut so hard he couldn't draw a breath.

"*What?*" he practically shouted. "How is that possible, Zeroan?" The sage exhaled deeply before continuing, as if remembering Jaren's volatile impatience from so long ago.

"It is difficult to hear, I know, but it is nearly as difficult to explain, so please listen well. Since I am no longer a part of the world of the living, my senses have weakened significantly from what they once were. I did not detect this disturbance until recently but I now estimate it has been going on for some time. A dark shroud of power is seeping forth from around the portal. It is still too faint for Tavinious to notice but he would have in the near future were it not for my intervention. I cannot directly tell why this is happening because my sight, though far and widespread in the afterlife, is blurred by the presence of other magics and powers. All I can tell you with any certainty is that the seal is deteriorating as we speak and if it is not restored, it will fail altogether in the not too distant future. If that happens, no Warrior of Light or any other power in this world would be able to stop Drakkan's wanton evil from escaping and destroying everything." Pausing once more to let the sage's words digest, Jaren shook his head in disbelief, voicing the question abound in all their minds.

"But how could this happen?" he asked horrified. "I thought Tavin sealed Drakkan into the void forever."

"He did, Jaren," the sage responded, "but something has happened since that has impaired the strength of that seal. That is the reason I am here." He turned his hooded face to Kaylan then, unmoving. "The portal itself is constant; constructed at the hand of a god to hold another for eternity. The only possible explanation for the seal's failing would rest with the Sword of Granis that now locks it in place." Jaren raised an eyebrow at this.

"You're saying something's wrong with the sword?" he asked bemused. Zeroan nodded.

"It is the only feasible way for a breach in power," he affirmed. "I'm not sure how or why but something must have happened to the Sword of Granis that is loosening its grip over the portal and in turn the seal. Someone must venture to the portal to ascertain what is happening there to cause this dangerous phenomenon, and it must be someone who can handle the sword. By right, that someone is you, Kaylan Tieloc." There was a long silence then. The color in Kaylan's face flushed away, the sage's heavy words pounding through her. It was her uncle who at last broke the silence.

"Excuse me?" he spoke incredulously.

"You heard right, Jaren. A new threat is upon the lands of Iairia and they are in need of Kaylan." Jaren was shaking his head as he at last sheathed his weapon at his side.

"What do you mean they need Kaylan?" he repeated baffled. "And how do you even know about her? You were gone long before she was even born."

"As I said," the sage picked up, "I have wide vision of a nature you cannot yet comprehend, Jaren. I have seen much of what has transpired in the world since my death and this daughter of the House of Tieloc is the only one who can fulfill this charge."

"Oh no, Zeroan," Jaren interrupted, waving a hand before him defensively. "I've heard this before. The last time you came looking for help you nearly got Tavin and me killed 'fulfilling our charge.' I'm not about to let you take Kaylan when her parents aren't even here to hear this. She's just a girl. And if you need help with the Sword of Granis, why didn't you appear before Tavin? He's the Warrior of Light. Why can't he see to the sword for you?" Zeroan shook his head.

"To start with, the last time I came looking for your help despite the fact it nearly led to your deaths it was to save the world. It is the same this time. I need someone with the ability to manipulate the Sword of Granis should the need arise, but it cannot be Tavin. I would have come to him because he has wielded the sword before but as he is the current Warrior of Light this advantage would work against us. Should he so much as lay a finger on the hilt of that sword with his awakened power he would inadvertently release it from the portal, breaking the seal and freeing Drakkan. Tavin cannot go. The only ones besides him with the blood right to touch the sword are his two children. His son is far too young, so it must be his daughter. Kaylan is the only one who can properly inspect the Sword of Granis and see to its safety if anything is indeed wrong."

"Then where exactly do I fit into all this?" a voice from behind Jaren and Kaylan finally sounded. Turning, they both found the darkly clad Maven taking a step forward with an impatiently confused expression over his tense face. "I knew whatever you really had in store for me was going to be more than what you said but this story is pretty far out there. I still don't believe half of what I'm hearing." Eyeing the forthright boy peculiarly, Jaren wheeled back to face Zeroan.

"And just who is this, anyway?" he grilled frustrated. "How do you know a Maven?"

"This Maven has a part to play in this as well, should he choose to accept it," Zeroan answered with assurance. "His name is Edge. He is a skilled and dependable warrior and will serve as Kaylan's bodyguard as she travels to the void portal." Jaren began vigorously shaking his head once more at this.

"Now just stop right there, Zeroan," he decreed avidly. "First off, I wouldn't trust this girl I love like a daughter to any Maven ever, but second, I won't have to worry because she's not going." Kaylan looked to her uncle, then back to Zeroan, nervous of what his reply would be. It was slow to come but after a long moment he took an unhurried step forward. Though all of them expected him to state otherwise, he merely spoke two words.

"She must," he said stoutly. Seeing the antagonism building in her uncle's face, Kaylan at last broke her silence and spoke to the sage to prevent an outburst.

"Zeroan, what would happen if I don't go?" she asked quietly. The sage turned his head toward her comparatively small frame.

"We are racing against time once again," he answered. "If nothing is done to stop it, the seal will eventually fail in the weeks to come and Drakkan will be unleashed." The girl forced herself to swallow, countless questions and thoughts of doubt clouding her mind.

"But... I don't think I could help you even if I wanted to," she confessed hopelessly. "I don't know the way, I wouldn't know what to look for if I got to the sword, and I wouldn't know what to do even if I did find out what was wrong."

"You forget your heritage, young Tieloc," Zeroan informed her. "There is power in your veins, dormant just as it once was with your father. You are connected to the Sword of Granis as is everyone in your bloodline. You will be able to feel what is wrong with the sword as you would feel discomfort in your own body once you reach it, which you will be able to do with Edge's help. You must trust that." Jaren was still beside himself with skepticism.

"This is ridiculous, Zeroan," he scathed. "You're asking her to travel to one of the most inaccessible place in the world with a total stranger to do something she has no idea how to do. How can you expect her to even consider this?" Zeroan remained still and responded.

"Was it any different when I came looking for Tavin before your quest began?" he asked calmly. "You had nothing to trust me by then either, yet you still believed in the end. I was right then, and I am right now. You must trust your faith. You must go, Kaylan." Seeing the sage's words work on her as they once did with him, Jaren grit his teeth and moved to take her by the shoulders. He stared her straight in the eyes.

"Kaylan, you have to listen to me," he told her avidly. "You know all about Zeroan from all the stories your dad and me have told you. You know he's a great person but remember everything else we told you. There's always a secret behind Zeroan; something else he hides from you that you don't find out until it's too late. You can't do this. Your parents wouldn't approve if they were here either. He'll just have to find another way."

"Just as it was with her father last time," Zeroan interjected, "it is the same with her now. She is the only one who can do this. There is no other way." Jaren wheeled on him in anger.

"And what are you holding back from us this time, Zeroan?" he grilled so heatedly it surprised them all. "This has got to be more dangerous than just going on a journey to the portal. If I've learned anything about magic, it's that when something's amiss there's a Drak behind it. What's out there that she would need a Maven bodyguard to protect her from?" Zeroan took another step forward to tower over Jaren. His words came with greater urgency and power.

"The only antagonist we battle now is time, Jaren," Zeroan stated. "There will be no dark force after Kaylan as there was with Tavin and you. She merely needs protection from the unknown. What you need to remember here, my stubborn Grandarian, is that this is Kaylan's decision. She is practically as old as you were when you embarked on your journey and if she inherited anything from either of her parents she has more fortitude than most to successfully complete this task. Be mindful your words do not carry the stain of hypocrisy." He then turned to Kaylan and locked his view onto hers, still frightened and unsure of his words. "I know you have little reason to trust me, Kaylan, but this must be done. There is some risk for I do not know what you will find when you arrive at the portal, but should you remain here as Jaren would have you do, you place yourself and the entire world in far greater danger than you assume by embarking on this quest. Jaren is right that it is not fair for me to ask this of you, but it was not fair of me to ask your father either. Fate is never fair. For the sake of us all, you must do this."

As the sage's words soaked through her, Kaylan suddenly felt all three pairs of eyes in the room locked upon her, waiting. Still unable to believe any of this was happening and with a thousand thoughts racing through her mind, the girl shrunk back and shook her head.

"I need... time," she softly stated. "Can I sleep on this, Zeroan?" Both Jaren and Zeroan's faces frowned at this but the sage at last gave her a single nod as he shifted in his signature gray robes.

"As I said, time is short and *my* time is even shorter," he reminded carefully, "but you may have the night to reflect on this. Think well, Kaylan Tieloc. Everything rests on your answer." With that, the sprit of the Mystic Sage Zeroan turned, the ends of this robes flying up behind him and he walked out the door. As if anticipating a frustrated barrage from the young Maven still silent in the room, he spoke as a faint wind rustled down from the trees into the kitchen. "You have the night as well, Edge. You will get your answers tomorrow once Kaylan provides me with hers." The moment

Trial of a Maven

his final word was finished, the sage disappeared into the darkness and the wisps of wind, gone into the night.

As the last remnant of the breeze faded into the sky, Jaren and Kaylan shifted their uncomfortable gazes back to the Maven they had found upon entering the Tieloc house. Before Jaren had a chance to ask him how he got sucked into this, the boy started for the door himself with the small winged creature Kaylan had encountered earlier lifting off from the shelf behind him and following him out.

"Tomorrow then," he spoke plainly, stepping through the doorway. Finding himself once more alone with the young Tieloc, Jaren turned back to look on her uneasy form with frustration.

"All right, miss," he began putting his hands on his sides, "let's go back to my place so we can talk—"

"No Jaren," she cut him off in a distressed voice, her full blue eyes falling to the floor. Her uncle became quiet, surprised at her reply. "You take Darien back to your house. I want to sleep in my own bed tonight…" As she trailed off, Jaren brought his hand up to massage his forehead.

"Kay, I don't think you understand how serious this is. You can't—"

"Jaren," she interrupted again, swinging her eyes to his. She breathed heavily then, walked toward him to take his hand in hers. "Thank you for caring like you were my dad but remember what he said—it's my choice to make just like it was yours. I'm… overwhelmed, and I just need to rest. We can talk tomorrow. Please do what I ask." She leaned in and gently kissed his rugged forehead. Jaren sighed, obvious aggravation but sensitive understanding in his eyes. He nodded and told her he was just a few houses away if she needed him. With that, he tightly secured the back door behind him and left Kaylan and her thoughts to themselves in the empty Tieloc house.

Chapter 5

Decisions

The next morning arrived with an overcast sky blotting out the sun from the green Grandarian countryside. Edge stood stationary with his back propped up by the rear wall of the Tieloc house in the center of Eirinor Village, his arms crossed and his pale gray eyes closed. The Maven had trained himself to sleep half awake and standing up to lessen the chance of having the dream. Zephyr always marveled at how his partner ever had any focus during the day getting the little sleep he did. Edge had rested particularly poorly the previous evening in the trees on the outskirts of the village. All night his mind had been burning with new uncertainties and doubts after his second meeting with his employer now revealed as the spirit of the legendary sorcerer Zeroan. He knew the tales of the Days of Destiny and the Mystic Sage Zeroan's involvement in them. He was the one who practically organized the entire effort to stop Drakkaidia from destroying the world. The question of what such a renowned and powerful figure would need with a Blue Maven, after his death, was raging about his head. To think that the Mystic Sage Zeroan somehow knew of his past and the answers to his horrible power boiled his blood with anticipation all the more.

Edge's pale eyes opened swiftly, his eagerness to meet with the sage's spirit once more tearing through him. It was brighter than when he had reentered the village almost an hour ago waiting for Zeroan to reappear, but the sun's warming rays remained obstructed by the barrier of inert billows above. Edge repositioned his back on the reverse side of the Tieloc house and exhaled sharply, his impatience getting the better of him. At last as a faint breeze began to caress the tail of his long blue scarf against his cold face, he heard the miniature flapping of wings from above and looked skyward to find Zephyr descending from the roof of the house to his level. Hovering before the boy's face, the purple sprite yawned.

"All this mystery and suspense makes me hungry," he stated rubbing his white feathered belly. "Do you think we could eat after this?"

"She's coming, then?" Edge asked quickly.

"She's been awake in her room for half an hour," the sprite reported with a nod. "She's coming down now so she ought to be out in a minute." Edge breathed heavy and nodded, rotating his head to the left. Figuring Zeroan would appear again when Kaylan Tieloc was ready for him, Edge had posted Zephyr on top of the Tieloc house when they returned that morning to watch for her. Thrusting off the house to make his way for the front door, Zephyr cut in front of him to cast an accusing look in his direction. "And maybe this time you could try smiling; or at least not biting her head off." Edge frowned and raised his black gloved hand to swat the purple sprite away, shaking his head. When he and Zephyr arrived yesterday, Zeroan had appeared in the shadows and told them to find the house of Kaylan Tieloc and wait for her there. Edge couldn't believe that this girl would turn out to be the same one he had abrasively encountered just moments later. She seemed pleasant enough when she spoke to him but as he told Zephyr time and time again, he didn't have the luxury of friends and brushed her off accordingly. Edge brought a hand down his face and grit his teeth at his bad luck. His strict policy of burning bridges would come back to haunt him if he was stuck with her now.

As the Maven broadened his shoulder to allow Zephyr a place to perch, he rapidly scanned his mind for some way to avoid the awkward meeting in store for him. Quickly rounding the corner of the house with his concentration elsewhere, Edge was surprised to find another person appear in his path, running into him. Falling to the grassy earth in shock, he looked ahead with mortification to find it was the blond haired girl again. She fell uncomfortably on her backside landing with a thud, her surprised face cringing upon impact. Kaylan Tieloc blushed bright red to find it was the Maven she had collided with, in disbelief that her every meeting with this boy was so sudden and surprising. She was dressed in brown hiking pants and a long sleeved blue collared tunic, both tightly fit against her curving frame. Though the light was dim outside, the girl's blue eyes were vivid and bright along with her shimmering golden hair that messily draped over her shoulders from her fall.

When both remained silent only staring at each other, it was the little Sky Sprite struggling for altitude that managed to smile and break the silence for his partner.

"We just can't seem to stop running into each other, can we?" he tried with a forced laugh, quickly fading as he realized no one else was laughing. At last Kaylan shook off her discomfiture and bolstered herself up to offer the Maven a hand.

"Good morning," she spoke softly, a hint of ambiguity in her voice. Though Edge had expected her to visit his curtness and impatience from the day before back on him, it appeared he was getting a second chance. Coming back to his senses, he nodded but avoided her hand by rolling on his back onto his feet. Kaylan withdrew her arm and let it drop to her side with a small discontented huff. Realizing Edge was not making strides in acquainting himself with the girl, Zephyr put a smile over his beak again and swept down to her to outstretch one of his hands.

"Hello," he smiled. "Sorry to have kept our identities in the dark for so long. My name is Zephyr. I'm a Sky Sprite." Kaylan gazed at the little creature for a short moment before raising one hand to wipe a silky lock of her hair behind her ear and another to take his tiny limb in between her fingers and shake it, all the more amazed at his appearance.

"I'm Kaylan," she said with an estranged smile appearing. Zephyr beamed.

"We're glad to meet you, Kaylan. This is my partner, Edge. As I think you've gathered by now, he's a Maven. A *Blue* Maven." Kaylan released the sprite's hand and uncertainly shifted her gaze toward the boy standing behind him, giving her a silent bow of his head. She uncomfortably tipped hers in response.

"So how did you two end up in this?" she inquired slowly. "Do you... did you know Zeroan when he was alive?" Edge raised an eyebrow.

"Hasn't he been dead nearly twenty years?" was his rhetorical question. "Even if I was that old, I would have been a baby in his final days. We didn't even know this guy *was* Zeroan until last night." Kaylan's face was both unconvinced and cynical.

"Then why are you involved in his business?" she pressed, returning his brusqueness.

"Because of who he is," answered a familiar deep voice from all around them riding the wind down from the clouds. As a sudden gust blew through the alley between Kaylan's home and the adjacent one, the three figures turned to the back of the house to find the wisps solidifying into a bundle of gray robes, lengthening to drape down and form the towering frame of the spirit of Zeroan. Though his massive outline was still an ominous sight, both Kaylan and Edge noticed he was somewhat hunched over and what little of his face was visible had grown haggard since the previous evening.

"Are you alright?" Kaylan asked after a long silence. The sage gave a single nod from behind his hood.

"As I told you before," the deep voice began quietly, "my time here must be short, for what power is left in this world that allows me to be here draws low." He shifted in his robes and tried to straighten himself. "Have you made your decision, Kaylan?" Edge and Zephyr turned back to face the Grandarian girl, her usually confident face tense with unease.

"I think I should wait for Jaren..." she trailed off, to which Zeroan shook his head.

"He is on his way, young one, but you cannot allow his feelings for you to influence your judgment. It must be your own." Kaylan inhaled a large breath of the crisp morning air and nodded, looking down into the trim grass beneath her booted feet.

"My father has always told me we all have to make a choice in our life that will decide our destinies. Maybe this one is mine..." At last she raised her resolved blue eyes to Zeroan's, clenching her fists. "I don't know of what help I will be, but if something is threatening all that my parents battled for in the Days of Destiny I have no choice but to do what I can to stop it. I will go to the portal of the void to find out what is wrong with the Sword of Granis." Edge was curiously taken aback at her sudden determined and self-assured words in the face of such a massive charge, forcing him to question his judgment of what he had assumed to be another helpless village girl.

"Very well," Zeroan said slowly. "You have chosen wisely, Kaylan Tieloc. I can see your parents' courage is alive in you." The sage paused then as the swift footsteps over the grassy road stretching through the village sounded in the distance. Kaylan turned to find her Uncle Jaren quickly striding toward them, an upset look harbored on his face when he saw the other figures with Kaylan.

"And here I thought you wouldn't even be up yet," he stated sarcastically entering the alley beside the young Tieloc, turning to face him. As their eyes met, Jaren's taut frame loosened with defeat as he observed the look of familiar fortitude that he had seen in her father's so many times. "You've decided to go then." Kaylan was still for a moment but at last gave him a single nod looking for the approval she so desperately wanted from him. Jaren exhaled deeply and turned to Zeroan. "If she's going to do this I'm not letting her do it alone. I'm going with her." Zeroan's spirit was calm and controlled as he opened his mouth to respond.

"It is true that she will not be alone," he started, "but it is not that you will be joining her. Kaylan will have the protection of Edge and his Sky Sprite companion. There is need for you here, Grandarian. As I informed you last night, there is no specific danger that worries me over this matter but the unknown can be a dangerous and unpredictable beast. You must watch over the younger of the Tieloc children in his parents' absence. All members of this bloodline must remain safe and accounted for in this moment of uncertainty." Jaren scowled at the sage and put his hands on his hips.

"The more I hear about this the more I think there's something you're not telling us, Zeroan," he commented coldly. "I know your ways too well. I don't want Kaylan doing this without me."

"They are young and will travel faster without you, Jaren," Zeroan answered. "And again I assure you everything is on the table with regard to the Tieloc family. It is the other young man before you who now requires answers to questions." The sage paused then and stared along with the Grandarians at the Maven clad in black.

"I still don't know how you could know anything about me but since you are who you are and you seem to, I'm ready to hear it if you're finally ready to tell me," Edge spoke, masking his eagerness with impatience. Zeroan's spirit shifted in his flowing robes and nodded, preparing to begin again.

"As I once told you, I know more about you than you know yourself, Edge," he stated with assurance. "Whether you are ready to accept this truth or not will soon be revealed but all that I offer is that. By telling you all this I am breaking the code of the Order of Alberic that has been in place to protect our secrecy for centuries, yet now that we are no more I am compelled to break tradition for this case." The sage paused again and tilted his head up to reveal his spacious eyes to the boy. "There is a question you have asked yourself and Granis on high since you were a child. I know the answer. I know why it happens. I know why you can't control it. I know what purpose it serves and I know what your purpose is because of it.

Zeroan stopped once more to give Edge a moment to brace himself, observing the anxiousness in his eyes threatening to drive him mad.

"The answer to all your questions, Edge, is in who you really are. Not who you have trained and masked yourself to be but who you were born as. You have a gift, Edge, not a curse as you believe it to be. A gift I too possessed but unlike you I was not born with it; I learned it through years of study and practice over the course of an entire generation of sages. Yet every generation of sages begins and ends with one who is born with this gift. You are the beginning of a new generation, Edge. The eighth one, in fact. You are the next Scion of the Order of Alberic." The sage's spirit stopped there. While Edge and Zephyr stared at him nervously, baffled at what this title meant, Jaren squinted at Zeroan with a look of hesitant remembrance in his eyes.

"I thought that was the true name of the Mystic Sages," he recalled to which Zeroan nodded.

"After the first sage that lived thousands of years ago—Alberic," Zeroan confirmed. "He was the first Master Sage with power far broader and more potent than that of a normal member of the order. It is this power that this young man is in possession of, in its raw, untamed and undisciplined form." Edge took a slow step forward, painful bewilderment encompassing his face.

"Zeroan," he started skeptically, "I'm... a Maven. Before I was just a baby born in an impoverished Southland village. How could I possibly be connected to the Mystic Sages? I've never even been to your tower in the east." As Zeroan was about to respond a strange and sporadic ripple of transparent energy spread down his form, causing him to hunch over further and the bottoms of his flowing robes to disappear.

"What's happening?" Kaylan worriedly asked. "Are you alright?" Zeroan attempted to lift his frame once more, the ends of his from dissipating into the air.

"My power in this world is nearly gone, young one," he answered. "If I am to meet you again after your journey, I must fade now." He turned back to face Edge again, his eyes still racing with questions. "You may not believe it, young Maven, but the same power that once flowed through my veins flows through yours, and far greater than mine ever was. With time and training you can learn to control it and use it at will for good. I am sorry I cannot reveal more to you now but I must go. I will divulge to you the rest after your journey to the portal. Kaylan," he said staring back to the blond Tieloc girl as his form began to unwind like threads in the wind, "I know you are besieged by doubt at your task but you must trust your instincts and follow your heart. They will lead you to the portal and the Sword of Granis. Remember that it is a part of you. You will know what is wrong. I will come to you once more when you do. You are the only one who can protect Iairia now. I know you will not let us down..." With that, Zeroan's now transparent form unwound into the faint wind blowing through the trees and carried his tired spirit away once again.

Kaylan Tieloc was left both empowered and daunted by the Mystic Sage Zeroan's parting words to her. Though she knew she had to accept this charge and trusted his revelation that her dormant power would lead her to the portal, the weight of the world was something she had never expected to be on her shoulders despite the fact that her parents constantly told her it could be one day. After the sage's spirit had disappeared for the time being, she and Jaren set to packing her things together for her trip. Though he offered once again to come with her if she wanted, she told him that no matter how much she wanted him to he had to stay with Darien to keep him safe until their parents returned.

Strapping on her stoutest hiking boots and wrapping her golden hair in a ponytail behind her back, she slung on her backpack and marched outside to meet the boy named Edge. Though she was nearly overcome with nervousness at what she was about to set off doing, perhaps the most frightening aspect of the journey was traveling with the abrasive Maven. He was now all the more unstable in trying to cope with the revelation that magical power of the Mystic Sages was instilled in his body. Though she still had no idea what any of it meant or what he was all about, she had no choice now but to trust him. At least she would have the personable Sky Sprite named Zephyr along with them to lighten the mood as he had in the past.

Making her way toward the boy leaning against her neighbor's home with his arms crossed as was his custom, his pale gray eyes came open and he thrust himself off with Zephyr taking to the sky from his shoulder. Jaren also exited the house and made his way to them to outstretch his arm with another pack identical to Kaylan's in his hand.

"Rations for nearly a month as well as some extra clothes for the cold weather," the Grandarian archer informed Edge. "Kaylan can get you a Lavlas Rock along the way to keep you warm up the mountain but it's a constant blizzard up there so keep yourself wrapped tight." Edge eyed the brown pack for a lingering moment but at last gradually accepted it, mounting it on his back behind his worn broadsword sheath. Jaren had suggested that they stop at the Battlemount before they venture into the Border Mountains where the portal to void lay. There they could pick up a Lavlas Rock—a fragment from the rocky skin of the Lavlas Boars that once lived under the Border Mountains before the Grandarian presence there. The small stones gave off a tremendous amount of heat but somehow never burned anything. General Ronus was stationed at the Battlemount and knew Tavin well from years of serving on the Galantian Council under the Supreme Granisian. He had met Kaylan before and would certainly grant her a Lavlas Rock they kept for troop excursions into the mountains.

With all their things packed and ready, Jaren walked the two to the outskirts of the village where the Hills of Eirinor commenced. He took Kaylan in his arms and hugged her tightly, telling her he didn't feel good about this but that he was proud of her for having the courage to do it. Reminding her to be careful in everything she did and to watch out for whatever might be out there that Zeroan had chosen to leave out in their earlier discussions, he let her go with a teary smile and a promise to keep watch over Darien. Kaylan could feel a tear roll down her own soft cheek as she smiled back and nodded, promising to be back soon. Turning to the north, Kaylan, Edge and Zephyr flying above set out into the hills for the white mountains on the horizon.

Chapter 6

Politics

Tavinious Tieloc stood motionless in the grand hallway connecting the Supreme Granisian's throne room to the conference chamber where the sovereign met with the numerous advisors and generals under her command. It was the latter room that the veteran Warrior of Light had once attended a council in the Days of Destiny led by the Mystic Sage Zeroan to decide how they would go about stopping Valif Montrox from destroying the world. A dry huff echoed out from behind the Grandarian warrior's closed mouth as he blankly stared out one of the gaping windows that looked down on the rest of the Golden Castle in the center of Galantia. Though he had discussed the impending doom of all Iairia in that chamber before, he dreaded his next conference inside its illustrious walls far more than he ever had as an adolescent.

The Fission of Drakkaidia in recent years had torn a rift down the heart of Grandaria as well. Though tales of the Days of Destiny and rumors of the true heritage of the Drakkaidian people had been spreading and enlightening the minds of Grandarians for nearly twenty years, the majority of the populace remained the way Tavin had been brought up: to hate Drakkaidians and stay on the offensive when it came to safeguarding their golden land. This traditionalistic enmity for the people of darkness had been proven false when Granis revealed to Tavin that Drakkaidians were merely Grandarians that had been taken and twisted by the taint of Drakkan's evil power, but two decades had proven not long enough to purge a millennium of hatred and most of the populace remained hell-bent on maintaining the old policies of aggression toward the dark nation.

It was these policies and deep routed biases that Tavin now found himself desperately struggling to overcome. Since he had been officially anointed the Warrior of Light by Supreme Granisian Corinicus Kolior at the end of the Days of Destiny, he had been imparting to the Grandarian people the truth of Drakkaidia's lineage and that Lord Granis had no desire for further Holy War against them. Though this had always been a difficult tale to swallow for any proud Grandarian, the new situation with the unstable Drakkaidia made Tavin's task all the more difficult. With the aggressive New Fellowship of Drakkan in control of virtually all of Drakkaidia's armies mobilized under the late Valif Montrox, battalions of rogue soldiers were filling the war zones west of the Wall of Light by the month in response to the new High Priest's sermons calling for the destruction of Grandaria.

While the majority of Grandaria saw this as a clear throwing down of the gauntlet from their age old enemies and that they must move to counter any mounting attack, Tavin remembered Verix Montrox's pledge for peace and was desperately trying to avoid conflict. He and those who credited his story about what Granis had told him knew that this reforming of the Drakkaidian people was the first chance for peace in history and was too valuable to pass up without fighting for. As a valued and respected advisor to the Supreme Granisian, it had been up to Tavin to persuade her to give Verix and his Loyalists a chance to contain the fission and not to spark conflict by mobilizing Grandarian troops in the war zones. Though she wanted to believe him and wait for the situation to stabilize, the rest of the military staff on her council had been demanding action to keep the New Fellowship in check. Every meeting with them ended in heated debate without any compromise on either side.

"I thought you'd be here," a pleasant voice sounded from the opposite side of the hall, rousing Tavin from the depths of his thoughts. Turning his clean shaven face toward the source, he found a beautiful figure wearing a light auburn tunic with a simple red dress underneath strolling toward him with a soft smile. Drawing near, she swept a flowing lock of her crimson hair away from her eyes and sighed, pulling in to gently peck him on the lips. "Are you alright?" Tavin stared into her deep red eyes for a moment, a trait she had inherited from the Drakkaidian side of her family, and pulled her in by her slender waist to quickly kiss her again.

"Considering I'm about to get into a war to prevent one," he began knowingly, "I'm fine. What about you? How did the greetings at the Gate Yard go?" The woman let out a long huff of breath and looked Tavin straight in the eyes, attempting to brace him for what she knew was coming.

"Considering I just avoided a war with your favorite general," she repeated sarcastically, "I'm fine." Tavin released her and grit his teeth, turning toward the window once more.

"If anyone can make it all the way from the Wall of Light to Galantia in under a week just to be here to tell me off, it's Sodric," he grilled to himself. Tavin looked down into the city as he exhaled once more. "This is a big one, Ril. I think Miless has convinced Mary to act today. I wish you could be in there with me." Tavin's wife shook her head then pulled in to lean it against his shoulder.

"You know it's just the Senior Council this time," Ril reminded him softly. "You'll have to manage without me today." When there was no response after a long moment, Ril shifted her gaze up to her husband, who was once more staring blankly into space. Observing the aloof glaze over the face of the man she knew better than anyone, she spoke curiously. "Are you sure nothing's wrong, Tav?" The Warrior of Light once again stirred out of his thoughts but this time looked upward into the clouded sky.

"Something doesn't feel right, Ril..." he trailed off uncertainly.

"You're just nervous for the council, is all," she said rubbing underneath his lightly armored shoulder. Tavin shook his head, setting his blue eyes on her.

"No, it's something else. Something... out there. Like something is out of place..." Ril held his gaze for a long moment before shaking her head and raising her hands to straighten Tavin's blue and gold cape around his neck.

"You just keep your mind on this council and Sodric," she admonished gingerly, smoothing out the wrinkles in her husbands bright blue tunic that stretched down to his embroidered white pants. "If he and the other generals convince Mary that she has to send troops past the Wall of Light we could be looking at another Holy War." Tavin focused his mind back on the task at hand and nodded, pulling in to kiss her one last time.

"Thanks, dear," he said taking her hand. "Sometimes I think you'd do better at this job than me."

"Sometimes?" she smiled, pushing him off down the hall for the massive arching doorway in front of him. Grinning as he turned leaving her behind in the golden hallway, Tavin passed through the doorway and into the small room adjacent to the conference chamber with another two doors in front of him and to his right. Stopping before the much larger one plated in gold, Tavin rest his hands over his belt waiting for the smaller door on the opposite wall to open. As he stood letting his smile fade in the faintly lit windowless room, the Warrior of Light overheard muffled voices entering the conference chamber beyond. A louder more obnoxious one sounded above the rest and Tavin caught himself writhing the ends of his blue tunic with apprehension, having matched the voice with General Sodric.

At last, the smaller door in the room opened wide and two royal guards adorned in shining silver armor stepped out with an undersized lance in one hand and an oval like shield bearing the crest of Grandaria in the other. As they rhythmically parted and moved to flank the doorway, Tavin watched as the regal form of Supreme Granisian Maréttiny Kolior walked in behind them. The beautiful woman was draped in the finest blue dress Tavin had ever seen. Brilliant yellow lining ran up from the hemming at its waving ends to thin straps over her delicate shoulders adorned with smooth overlapping gold plates engraved with Grandarian emblems from the Temple of Light itself. Her shimmering crown majestically rose from her chestnut hair neatly draped behind her back in light curls. Apart from Ril, Tavin had to admit she was the most gorgeous woman he had ever met.

Maréttiny Kolior, whom Tavin still called Mary when in private with her, had only been anointed Supreme Granisian a year ago when her father at last passed away in his sleep. She had still not married and with no male heir in the Kolior family Mary was the only living successor for the throne of the golden nation. Along with her father's title she had inherited the political mess over the Fission of Drakkaidia and now found herself caught between her military staff and Tavin advising her how to respond to it.

She beamed at Tavin as she entered the room along with her Chief Advisor directly behind her, a wise and well spoken old man named Miless Cerbru. Though Miless had been the Chief Advisor to the Supreme Granisians for over a decade now and Mary had come to trust him with anything,

Tavin had in essence become just as influential and vital to her. She spent nearly as much time with him as any of her other advisors when he was in the capital and valued his opinions greatly. She had even increased the authority of his position when she took control of the nation by granting him additional emergency power over both the armies and government should anything ever happen to her in a crisis.

The Warrior of Light bowed with a smile as he always did when meeting her before a Senior Council meeting.

"Good afternoon, Your Eminence," he spoke softly. "You look ever ravishing today."

"Why thank you, Tavin," she replied with a bow of her own. Miless, scratching his thick white beard with one hand, outstretched the other for Tavin as Mary's private guards opened the doors for them. After a warm greeting, the Warrior of Light and the Chief Advisor entered the conference chamber flanking the Supreme Granisian on either side. The occupants of the ornately decorated room seated around the long oak table in its middle rose at their coming. The table was long enough to seat over twenty, usually filled with the full Galantian Council. Moving to his seat on the right of the Supreme Granisian, Tavin scanned the faces of the few present. There were only eight members on the Supreme Granisian's Senior Council including herself. The others were her Chief Advisor, the Warrior of Light, the High Granisian of the Temple of Light, the Minister of the People, the Envoy of Foreign Affairs, the First General of the armies and the Commanding General at the Wall of Light—a recent addition to the council because of the current situation.

After two more of Mary's elite guard waiting at the table tucked her chair in behind her she smiled and greeted the group with a slight bow which they returned in unison. As everyone took a seat and her guards exited through the ornate doorway at the front of the room, Mary softly cleared her throat and began.

"Very well then, gentlemen," she addressed proficiently, "this session of the Senior Council is in order. Thank you for all being here today. I know our meetings have been frustratingly frequent of late, but you all know as I do the need for decisive action over current affairs is growing more apparent by the day. Miless?" The white robed figure to the Supreme Granisian's left leaned forward in his seat and folded his hands over the table.

"The focus of this council is to analyze the most recent reports from the Wall of Light and come to a decision on how to respond to this newest Drakkaidian troop movement. General Sodric, please." Tavin turned his gaze down to Sodric, already staring at him in his chair with intolerant eyes. Sodric was a large muscular man wrapped in rough skin adorned with a collection of scars from the minor skirmishes against bandits and marauders that had been foolish enough to foul Grandaria's lands with their presence. The troops under his command joked that his shortly cut hair matched his short temper. He leaned forward with a collection of thick papers in his hand and shifted his edgy gaze to the Supreme Granisian.

"Your Eminence, the latest reports from the war zone by our scouts indicate there is a new swell of enemy movement from the Valley of Blood. Battalions of Drakkaidian forces are mustering there and are gradually drifting south into the war zone. Our best estimates place the number of Drakkaidian soldiers at twenty thousand and building."

"This report should be a wakeup call to us all, Your Eminence," General Tycond took over. "This marks over a year since our scouts have first seen Drakkaidian troop mobilization in the war zone. They haven't set foot past the Valley of Blood for a century but now they're trampling around the war zone like they own it. They are completely unchecked. Now is the time for action, Your Eminence."

"And what action are you proposing, general?" the Warrior of Light spoke from the opposite side of the table, folding his hands on its surface with his cape rustling behind him as he leaned in. "The Drakkaidians haven't so much as hinted aggression of any kind in the year they've been there."

"Haven't hinted aggression?" General Sodric repeated aghast from beside Tycond. "What do you think the Draks are doing if not preparing for aggression? They've been building their numbers and weapons in the neutral lands for months. You don't string an arrow in a bow if you don't plan on firing it, much less mobilize for battle without intentions to start one."

"And how many battles have we fought with these Drakkaidians so far, general?" Tavin pressed.

"The Valley of Blood War, near constant conflict for over a thousand years in the disputed land, and two holy wars,

Warrior of Light," Sodric answered, his voice challenging. "Would you have us wait for the third to start without us?"

"That's enough, gentlemen," Mary cut in with a cold but controlled tone of voice. "Tycond, have we confirmed the affiliation of these newest Drakkaidians yet?" Tycond breathed deeply with obvious irritation before giving a single nod.

"Our intelligence reports that these troops are marked with the emblem of the New Fellowship, but enemy forces are enemy forces, Your Eminence. If anything, these troops are more of a threat now than in the past because there is no direct leadership behind them. They are acting on the innuendo High Priest Zalnaught has been spewing in his cathedral to the north. They are rogue troops and could attack all on their own."

"The truth of the matter is that they haven't attacked because they *are* under control, general," Tavin stated confidently. "You forget that the troops in the war zone are essentially the army that Valif Montrox built when he was alive. They are professionally trained and will not act without a clear order from Zalnaught. And while Drakkaidia may be split into two factions, this new High Priest will not give an order for an attack with Verix Montrox there to stop him." Sodric almost laughed in spite of himself.

"Montrox and the Loyalists are less than half the number of the New Fellowship, Warrior of Light," he reminded curtly. "They are powerless to stop Zalnaught."

"You don't know Verix Montrox, General Sodric," Tavin stated powerfully. "As I've said before, Verix promised us peace under his rule after the Days of Destiny. Verix doesn't want civil war but he'll move to stop Zalnaught if it means avoiding war with us. Zalnaught must know Verix would kill him and take control of the New Fellowship by force if he tries to make open war with Grandaria directly. The High Priest won't risk it."

"And neither will I," Sodric stated plainly. "I don't have the luxury of going off my gut instinct like you when it comes to defending a nation, Tieloc. All I know is that there are twenty thousand Drakkaidians massing in the war zone just beyond sight of the Wall of Light and they aren't there for a picnic. Would you have us sit on our hands while they march on the wall? It is our responsibility as Grandarians to counter—or at least defend against—aggression from our mortal enemies. Their mere presence there is an insult to Lord Granis—that should be all the reason we need to send in troops."

"Have you forgotten what Lord Granis revealed to us in the Days of Destiny, Sodric?" the High Granisian of the Temple of Light returned, sitting forward with frustration in his eyes. "Drakkaidians are not the evil people we always thought they were—they are the ancestors of our brothers corrupted by the taint of Drakkan. Our responsibility is to work for peace, not war."

"Our responsibility is to defend our people from those who would kill them, no matter who they *once* were. If we don't fortify our defenses at the wall and match our enemy's strength in the war zone we leave ourselves open to invasion."

"Putting troops in the war zone would be casting a torch in a lake of oil," Tavin continued. "It's the excuse Zalnaught is looking for to go to war without ordering it directly and having to go through Verix. We have to give the Loyalists their chance to calm the New Fellowship and for Verix to assume control of the Black Church. Once he does he'll pull the troops back."

"And what if the New Fellowship doesn't wait that long? What happens when they attack on their own like I said in the first place? We don't have time to wait for the Loyalists to gain control, which there is no reason for us to assume they ever will. This entire Drakkaidian fission may be an elaborate ruse. What if these two factions are just meant to give us false hopes of peace to lower our defenses? I don't trust this Montrox of yours any more than I trust Zalnaught. He may have aided you in the Days of Destiny but at the end of the day he's still a Drak. I won't pin our survival on what you think that lying piece of garbage *might* get the *chance* to do." That was the comment that broke Tavin's back. In one fluid motion, the Warrior of Light shot up and wrenched free the sheathed sword at his side, directing its point in Sodric's direction. The entire table jumped back in surprise, uncertain dismay of his intensions mirrored in their eyes.

"You will never, under any circumstance, speak of Verix Montrox that way," Tavin breathed with ice hanging from his every word. "That 'Drak' is more of a hero and has done more for this nation than you will ever begin to fathom, Sodric."

"Tavin, lower that weapon," Mary ordered in a commanding voice, rising to her feet. The Warrior of Light kept his deep blue eyes focused on the uneasy general before him for a long moment before at last flipping his hilt around his hand and dexterously throwing the blade back into his sheath. As he unhurriedly took his seat, Mary remained standing.

"I will not have my Senior Council, or my nation, divided to the point of violence, *ever*," she spoke sternly to them all. "This behavior is unacceptable and I will not tolerate it. Either control yourself or be dismissed from your service. Sir Tieloc, your point is made so you will remain quiet for the duration of this meeting, and Sodric, while the Warrior of Light was out of line, he is right. You will not ever refer to Verix Montrox in a disrespectful manner." As she stood above them all with her petite gloved fists clenched, the silence hung about the golden chamber. When she sat, she turned to the Minister of the People next to the silenced Warrior of Light. "What are your thoughts, minister?" The white and golden robed figure tilted his head trying to properly impart his opinion.

"The populace as a whole is concerned that Drakkaidia has free roam of the war zone unchecked but most of them do not know the extent of this volatile situation. As before, I advise increased caution and readiness at the Wall of Light but no direct military action against the Drakkaidians until it is warranted by direct aggression on their part."

"I agree," the aged Granisian of the Temple of Light voiced from beside him. "Lord Granis does not desire a Third Holy War. We would surely spark one more violent and long lasting than ever before if we provoke these leaderless soldiers in the war zones." Mary nodded and turned to the Envoy of Foreign Affairs for his thoughts.

"While I do not wish for war, Your Majesty," he began, "I am first and always concerned for the safety of our people. We must at least prepare for aggression. The Drakkaidians in the war zone may be professional soldiers as Sir Tieloc reminds us but they are in fact acting on their own recognizance at the moment. This dangerous blaze may spark into a wildfire on its own. We must be ready for that." Mary turned to Miless, already staring at her.

"You know my mind, Highness," he stated quietly. "I believe in Tavin but too much of his argument rests on chance. If there was one thing I learned from your father, it is

Tales of Iairia

that one cannot trust chance when ruling a nation. I advise no direct action but some precaution must be taken." Mary held his gaze for a lingering moment then broke off to stare down the center of the long oak table, her soft eyes placid but intense all at once. At last, she lifted her head with assurance and swept the room with her gaze.

"I am deeply troubled by this situation," she began. "As the Warrior of Light and the Granisian of the Temple of Light remind me, another Holy War is not what Lord Granis desires for us. The revelation that the Drakkaidians are not born from the black hand of Drakkan weighs my decision greatly, but the safety of our land and people weigh it the greatest. While I believe that Verix Montrox has some power over the High Priest Zalnaught and I wish to give him time to gain direct control of this divided Drakkaidia, the simple truth is that he is not in control of it at present and there are no assurances he will gain it before something happens to spark conflict, which would inexorably lead us to war anyway. Therefore, I will compromise the best I can. By my order, no Grandarian soldier will set foot in the war zone under any circumstance, but so long as Drakkaidians remain there we will strengthen our own ground. The Battlemount and Wall of Light are to be sent reinforcements at once and are to maintain an increased state of readiness. Hopefully this will allow us to defend ourselves but at the same time maintain this fragile peace hanging between the nations."

With that, the Supreme Granisian rose from her seat, the rest of the Senior Council doing the same immediately after. "We will meet again in the full Galantian Council next week. If your duty allows your presence, General Tycond, I will expect new reports on the situation in the war zones. General Sodric will return to the Wall of Light to oversee the strengthening of our forces. The rest of you may return to your duties. That will be all." With that, she turned for the massive doorway at the end of the room lurching open as the guards pushed it forward. Turning with Miless following, Tavin strode out of the room after her.

Once they were back in the small room adjacent to the conference chamber with the doors closed, Mary turned to face Tavin.

"I hope you realize that if you were anyone else and had drawn that sword in my presence my elite guard would probably have killed you on the spot," she stated letting her regal tone dissipate to her natural voice while Tavin met her gaze. "I know it wasn't the decision you were hoping for Tavin, but it's the best I can do." The Warrior of Light shrugged but civilly held her gaze.

"It's your decision to make, Your Eminence, and I respect it," he responded quietly. "I'm sorry for my behavior."

"We both know Sodric is an impulsive traditionalist," Mary acknowledged. "He was trying to set you off. He resents you because of the power you potentially have over him if there was ever an emergency."

"Let's hope I never have to use that power," Tavin stated gloomily. "All it takes is one mishap anywhere with any soldier on either side. One spark will turn into an inferno. If this spirals out of control we won't be able to stop it. Valif Montrox's old armies have been reassembled under Zalnaught bigger than ever. Verix has him in check for now but it won't hold if we give Zalnaught an excuse for war. The Drakkaidians will side with him if they think we struck first." Mary gently shook her head as she bowed goodbye.

"That's why we won't give him the excuse," she answered softly. "I'll see you soon, Tavin." Bowing back to her, Tavin bid farewell to Miless and found himself alone in the small room. While his thoughts remained fixed on the tense council, Tavin could still sense something else tingling in the back of his mind. Something dark. Though he couldn't identify what it was, he could feel something apart from all this was wrong.

Chapter 7

Resurgence

Since their departure from the Hills of Eirinor almost two weeks prior, Kaylan Tieloc and her Maven protector Edge had made it to the frozen base of the Border Mountains north of Grandaria. They had traveled light and quick across the green Grandarian countryside, a near constant air of silence around and between them. Both of the usually confident youths had set out from Eirinor constricted by doubts and uncertainties of the journey they faced, unnamed fears of danger beyond stirring within. While Kaylan was still in a state of shock from finding herself in circumstances similar to those of her parents as they embarked on their quest nearly twenty years ago, Edge remained besieged by the revelation that he and his dangerous power were somehow connected to the Mystic Sages. Everything he had ever known or trusted felt shaken and his partner Zephyr could see it by his continued sullenness. The only thing that granted any of them focus was to concentrate on the mission at hand.

All three had remained sharp on their expedient quest across Grandaria. While Edge had expected his beautiful Grandarian charge to move sluggish and fatigue quickly, she had led the way for the trio with speed and fortitude that matched his own. Never slowing or complaining once, he quickly found she did not need his help getting from camp to camp on the journey. Kaylan kept a wary vigil as she hiked through the plains and into the rugged terrain of the Border Mountains, a watchful eye and a wondering thought alert for whatever dark force might be lying in wait for her of which the spirit of Zeroan had not seen fit to inform them. All the while, even the amiable Sky Sprite Zephyr felt exceedingly uncomfortable as the awkward silence between his two human companions lingered.

Trial of a Maven

After trudging through the opening gap in the Border Mountains to the north, the party had arrived at the Battlemount—Grandaria's military base that reinforced the Wall of Light from behind. Four to five garrisons of troops were usually stationed here but with the recent concern over the rogue Drakkaidians in the war zone, an additional three were amassed around its perimeter. Mindful of their dwindling time, Kaylan had speedily entered and requested to see General Ronus to acquire a Lavlas Rock, the enchanted stones from the backs of Lavlas Bores that lived underneath the Border Mountains. Though Kaylan had difficulty assuring the validity of her identity to the guards and captains under Ronus, when Tavin Tieloc's old friend finally recognized her he was quick to let her through to his quarters. After hearing the abridged story of what she was doing and what she needed from him, he was confused and unsure of releasing her so she could trek up the inhospitable ice capped mountains for reasons she would not disclose. Nevertheless, he hesitantly bestowed her with a Lavlas Rock and his blessing.

With the means to keep them dry and warm, Kaylan and her protectors embarked onto the steep roads of the northern Borders Mountains into the endless white before them. As the infrequent snow flurries transformed into fierce blizzards, Kaylan found herself increasingly worried she had no idea where she was going. Yet whenever she was confronted by doubt of her path, she forced herself to halt and calm down to find a tingling sensation slowly pulling her in the right direction once more. It was as Zeroan had said; she could feel the presence of something connected to her off in the distance as though it was a part of her. Though Edge and Zephyr both frequently thought to themselves they would surely be engulfed by the infinite winter never to escape, Kaylan always pressed on after her brief stops with confidence that assured them both they were indeed on the right path.

After days of trudging through thick snow banks, steep glaciers and unyielding snowfall from the tempestuous sky with only their trust in Kaylan and the magical warmth of the Lavlas Rock to sustain their energy, the group at last arrived at the same road another trio of heroes had once trekked up twenty years ago. Standing at its base, Kaylan could feel the friendly radiance of a somehow familiar feeling directly before her. Sensing what she guessed to be the Sword of Granis close enough to be calling to her, she pressed up the sharp incline with newfound purpose and honest excitement. The ends of his long blue scarf whipping behind him in the frigid wind, Edge looked up in amazement at the girl. How she had not knelt over in aching fatigue by now was beyond him. He had never met a simple village girl with such stamina. Zephyr's eyes peered out of the Maven's largest pouch strapped over his back, desperately trying to keep as warm as possible in the freezing air. Even with the radiating warmth of the Lavlas Rock enveloping his purple feathered frame, the Sky Sprite's teeth were chattering behind his wide beak.

Trailing behind her along the top of the glacier for another hour, the Maven at last looked up to find Kaylan at rest. She stood with her arms almost limp at her sides, staring ahead at whatever lay before her. Guessing they had finally arrived at the portal to the void, Edge quickly pushed his way up the gap between them. Though nearly out of breath when he took a stance beside the Grandarian girl, his jaw slowly dropped and what little breath his lungs retained escaped him. In all his travels over Iairia he had never seen something like what lay before him now. Nearly thirty yards away was a gargantuan stone platform that stretched for hundreds of yards in a massive circle. It was so huge Edge could not see its end—only a faint golden light at its center. Amazingly detailed engravings graced the stone surface in shapes of flowing angelic wings similar to those in the Temple of Light, converging around the circular pedestal in the center. The Maven shot a quick glace to the girl standing in awe next to him. Her soft face was captivated and her deep blue eyes glazed over with wonder. As the now faint breeze gently caressed her golden locks behind her shoulders, Kaylan began slowly walking toward the massive portal. Edge silently followed in her footsteps, unsure of what was going to happen now that they had arrived.

As the two figures made their way to the edge of the sprawling portal, Kaylan locked her eyes onto the shimmering light at its center. Staring for several long moments, it seemed to shine brighter in response to her presence. She could feel it reaching out as if asking to be made whole with her. After a long moment to confirm her thoughts she slowly opened her mouth to speak.

"I have to go out there," she said plainly. Edge broke his curious gaze off from the portal and set it on her.

"That's the Sword of Granis out there?" he asked, to which the girl nodded. The Maven exhaled deeply before unfolding his arms and repositioning the broadsword slung over his back. "I'll go first." Kaylan turned her head back to face him and blinked.

"No," she stated softly. "I have to do this alone. You need to stay here." Edge raised an eyebrow, his pale eyes searching.

"Why?" he pressed. The girl held his gaze but shook her head.

"I'm not sure," she admitted, wrapping herself tighter in the confines of her thick brown traveling coat. "I just... need to do this alone." Edge frowned and crossed his arms.

"I'm not being paid to stand around while you do something that could be dangerous," he reminded her grimly. Kaylan's blue eyes remained on his, resolute as ever.

"I know, but you have to trust me," she said. "Please." The Maven took another deep breath of the chilled mountain air and blew it out between his closed lips. Staring into the girl's unyielding but genuine eyes, he somehow knew in his heart that though this couldn't be safe he had to let her do it alone. There was a touch of destiny exuding from the portal that felt beyond him. Giving her a single nod, he took a step back and told her to be extremely careful. Replying she wouldn't be far off if anything did happen, Kaylan turned and placed her right boot onto the portal. As soon as her entire body stood over the indented border, her unsure face loosened and lit up with wonder. Just like her father had told her of his visits to the portal, the moment she stepped onto it a wave of warmth rushed through her that made her forget she was in the cold at all. Staring down in curious amazement, she began to gradually walk out to the platform's center while Edge and Zephyr nervously waited behind at the border.

As the Grandarian girl closed the gap between the perimeter and the center, she couldn't help but smile at what she was seeing. The portal looked exactly as it had been described to her by her parents. Intricate Grandarian emblems similar to those she had seen so many times in Galantia were strewn across its exterior, beautifully curving and arching with flowing detail. Kaylan soon forgot about the stunning appearance of the portal, however, drawing nearer to the glowing object protruding from its center. The Sword of Granis. Slowing to a crawl she spoke its name out loud to convince herself what she was seeing was real. Stepping within a few feet of the powerful Grandarian talisman, its every detail sparked a memory of its depiction from her father. It looked exactly like she had always imagined. From the rich blue leather handle over the sterling silver hilt with gilded engravings to the razor sharp golden blade stretching down into the stone portal beneath it, its regal appearance almost brought tears to the girl's eyes.

Though Kaylan could feel the golden energy radiating off of the sword almost familiar, a strange qualm was present in the bowels of her being as well—a presence of something foreign to the righteous power that contradicted its very existence. Peering around the base of the blade, Kaylan narrowed her eyes to notice the faint mist of dark light hovering around it. Lowering herself to her knees to investigate closer like Zeroan had instructed her, she could see a murky haze weakly seeping out of the cracks around the pedestal. Worry flooding her mind, Kaylan brought her gaze back up the illustrious hilt of the weapon. Turning her attention to the Granic Crystal Tavin had told her about, she caught another troublesome blight on the sword. Staring at it for a long moment, the color in her face washed away with shocked horror.

There was another crystal mounted on the blade right below the Granic Crystal.

A black one.

Kaylan shook her head with alarm. Her father had told her of the time when a dark imposter crystal attached to the Sword of Granis had almost killed him with its sinister power. This crystal before her was in the exact place he said the imposter had been. Though Kaylan wasn't sure how this dark addition to the sword had come to be there, she didn't have to think twice to guess it was the reason for the breach in the sword's power. She had to get it off. Unsure of how to purge it from the blade, however, she curiously raised her hand to examine it. Pulling the thick brown glove off her right hand and spreading her delicate fingers, she reached out to run them down the hilt of the sword.

It hit her the moment the tip of her outstretched finger contacted the dark crystal's sharp exterior. An incapacitating sensation of emptiness sweeping through every cell in her being, Kaylan suddenly felt as if she was trapped suffocating where she sat. As the girl remained locked in place with horror, the once faint black mist hovering around the base of the sword violently blasted upward, growing and thickening by the second into a swirling wind of sharp, dark particles. Beginning to churn around the Sword of Granis and the incapacitated girl fixed to it by some mysterious force, Kaylan could see it spewing out of the elaborate engravings in the portal where the radiant light had once shone. As the darkness spread around her and her vision began to dim, the cold of the endless blizzard set in again, invading her vulnerable form. Desperate to be free of this assault on her body from the shadowy mist around her, the girl mustered all her strength to try and pull away from the sword. Yet no matter how hard she heaved, she could not remove her finger from the surface of the dark crystal; she could not sever its grip on her.

  When her senses had all but blurred over and all light abandoned her to the violent foray of darkness, she could feel the crystal behind her finger suddenly shatter. The next instant the entire surface of the massive portal exploded with the dark spray, ferociously tearing out from its exterior and racing like hurricane wind for the defenseless girl at its center. As it painfully rushed around her body, Kaylan could not help but scream out in terror. The dark waves of haze immediately seized on the breach in her defenses and rushed into her open mouth with rays of black light shining out as it came. The penetrating emptiness Kaylan had felt a moment before was suddenly replaced with a wanton presence filtering into her every cell, consuming her like a ravenous predator. With each passing second of the dark mist flowing into her, she could feel herself falling into a world of shadow beyond the one she had been in moments before.

  After the longest and most horrifying moments of Kaylan's life, the final surge of the black spray rushed into her screaming mouth and was gone from the now blank atmosphere around her. All at once the maelstrom of dark power was gone, absorbed into her immobile form. Besieged and violated like she had never thought possible, the terrified girl's beautiful frame went limp and her conscience mind went blank. She fell to the once more normal platform with a soft thud, numb to everything around her. The moment her motionless hand fell into the mess of golden locks around her head and all was completely still once more, a final movement broke the silence of the quiet mountain air. The

Tales of Iairia

Granic Crystal, its usually beaming golden light now all but dead, lurched free of its mounted position on the hilt of the Sword of Granis and dropped to the portal beneath it with a tiny tingling of crystal on stone. Resting seemingly lifeless, its final rays of dim light faded as a gloved hand of a lone figure scooped it up and hoisted it beside the equally inert girl already in his arms.

Chapter 8

Dark Usurper

Dalastrak had always been an inhospitable city with regard to anything one could imagine, but after the death of its late ruler Valif Montrox, it had become a veritable graveyard. Not one of its occupants had survived the demon horde that had been mobilized there, and the explosion of evil power from the depths of the Netherworld at the coming of Drakkan had left it in ruin. Upon Verix Montrox's return shortly after, he and his Loyalists to the Throne had rebuilt and repopulated the barren cityscape as best they could but the once towering capital had been unofficially moved to the Cathedral of Dalorosk further north once High Priest Zalnaught took control.

It was this dark edifice the veteran Drakkaidian prince Verix Montrox now found himself riding toward, flanked by rows of elite royal horsemen that had set out with him from Dalastrak three days ago. His coming to the home of the New Fellowship was a rare and momentous occurrence as he had not set foot there in almost ten years on the day he last officially confronted Zalnaught about his abuse of power not rightfully his. Though that volatile meeting nearly ended in the outbreak of civil war, Verix had not been ready to plunge his all but broken nation into another conflict that could have left it destroyed after they had suffered such a blow during the Days of Destiny. Recent events, however, had forced Verix back to the heart of his enemy's territory once more for another confrontation with the High Priest Zalnaught.

No one in the Cathedral of Dalorosk or the surrounding city was aware Verix was coming until he arrived that morning amid the rolling storm clouds and crackling lightning always present over Drakkaidian skies. Though Verix implored his Loyalists to exercise control when Zalnaught and New Fellowship forces visited Dalastrak, the High Priest gave contrasting encouragement to his own people with regard to the Loyalists. Verix's party of horsemen received a cold welcome as they made their way through the towering walls and tightly built city to the sprawling Cathedral of Dalorosk at its center. The cathedral was similar to Galantia in that it was more of a fortress that surrounded the Temple of Darkness at its core as the Golden Castle did with the Temple of Light. It was the most elaborate and sophisticated structure in all of Drakkaidia and one of the largest in Iairia.

Since his adolescent travels with Tavin Tieloc, Verix Montrox had matured into a fierce, battle hardened warrior that towered over most. His physique was composed of bulking muscle, littered with scars from the Days of Destiny and after. While trying to unite his divided country he had also been contending with frequent barbarian raids and the occasional Ogren Siege from the north to protect both his Loyalists and the New Fellowship. As he and his elite riders dismounted before the massive staircase leading up to the doors of the Cathedral of Dalorosk, he noted the unfriendly faces of the citizens and soldiers staring them down and quietly lashing out threats. Touching down to the earth once more, Verix's piercing red eyes swept into the mob of antagonists closing in on him, freezing and silencing them instantly. Even the most obnoxious and foolish of them knew better than to challenge a man as formidable and infamous as the Drakkaidian prince. Watching the crowd slowly push back as his icy gaze swept through their number, he pushed a hand through his long crimson hair and turned for the steep stairs of the cathedral with the ends of his frayed gray cape flying up behind him. His elite crimson guards closely followed behind him in pairs of two as they began rapidly ascending it, adorned in light riding armor bearing the newly created Loyalist emblem resembling the old Drakkaidian flag. Though Verix's composure was cold and controlled as always, the men trailing him were far more anxious, aware their unannounced presence here could easily spark conflict.

At last arriving at the top of the stairs, Verix threw his arms forward to slowly heave the twin crimson doors open with a lurching echo. A faintly lit foyer lay beyond, branching off into the east and west wings of the cathedral and to the Temple of Darkness above. Another pair of elaborately engraved double doors before them led to the dark sanctuary at its center. All eyes in the chamber nervously spun to the Drakkaidian prince and his guards as they hurriedly entered and made their way for the closed black doors. Four Dark Mages, the magically endowed sentries of the cathedral always hidden beneath black robes and hoods, stood guard before them. As Verix came within a few feet of them they quickly lowered the spiked lances in their grasp into a cross, blocking the way. The prince slowed to a halt but before he could utter a word the elite guard at his right side wrenched free the blade at his side and extended it to one of the mage's faces.

"You dare block the Prince of Drakkaidia?" he barked fiercely. The Dark Mages did not flinch.

"We do not answer to you, brute," one of them spoke behind his hooded face. "The High Priest is performing a ritual and is not to be disturbed." Before the Loyalist guard could take a step forward to viciously remind him of his place, a hand on his shoulder forcefully pulled him back. The guard turned to find Verix glaring at him with hard eyes.

"I have not spent every ounce of my stamina maintaining peace in this nation for twenty years to have you waste my efforts now," he whispered with ice hanging from his words. Feeling Verix's eyes burning through him with each passing second the guard humbly bowed and sheathed his sword, stepping back into formation. Verix's penetrating gaze shot back to the Dark Mages.

"I must see the High Priest," he told them quickly. "Step aside." A long moment passed but none of the mages moved a muscle. His expression still as controlled and focused as ever, the prince took a large step forward until his was within an inch of the first mage's face. "You may not answer to my guards, but as long as I am the Prince of Drakkaidia and you a Dark Mage, you *will* answer to me. Now raise your lance before I raise the four of you off the ground." Though fearful of the consequences later if he allowed the prince in, the mage was far more fearful of what would happen to him if he ignored a Montrox now. With a hesitant jerk, the mages pulled up their lances and took a step back.

His path clear, Verix pushed the doors open and entered the massive sanctuary beyond. It was an arching chamber boasting a ceiling rising over fifty feet from the floor with diamond shaped windows of black glass embedded near the center. Streams of ominously slow burning fire flowed along the center aisle and symmetrically on the ceiling, forming ancient Drakkaidian glyphs that were taken from the Netherworld Portal Verix had seen so many times in his own citadel. At the end of the sanctuary was an ornate altar with a massive dais at its center that rose through a carved hole in the ceiling into the upper level of the cathedral: the Temple of Darkness.

Verix remained unaffected by the forebodingly majestic architecture around him, his unyielding eyes fixed on the lone figure at the front of the altar. He was draped in a collection of black and crimson robes, the top layers stretching to his shoulders while the lower ones extended to the floor. His bald head was concealed by a towering black cloth helm with a Drakkaidian Rune embroidered over its front. As Verix neared the figure he turned back to his guards.

"Go back and wait at the doors," he commanded quietly. Though they shot uncertain glances at each other, they immediately turned when the prince narrowed his heated eyes. With his Loyalists gone, the prince wheeled around for the figure. A black flame was nestled in between the other's hands which he lowered onto the wick of a candle. As Verix stopped behind him the figure at last turned to reveal his smirking face. There was a long silence as their eyes met but at last he spoke in a soft yet dangerous tone.

"It's been too long, Your Highness," he began with his twisted smile growing. "Why, since you last booted me out of Dalastrak I thought I wouldn't be seeing you for a quite a while longer than this." Zalnaught was a medium seized man, seasoned by almost twice the number of years Verix had seen. He had been a Dark Mage when Verix's father was alive—before the Black Church robbed the ruling power of the nation from Dalastrak. Zalnaught quietly chuckled at the prince's presence and slowly stepped down from the altar to pick up a simple wooden staff at its base, an odd item for a High Priest to keep in his possession. Verix crossed his arms below the chain on his chest that kept his cape secure, opening his mouth to speak.

"I'll come straight to the point," were his first words, containing the impatience behind them. "The disturbance in the Border Mountains three days ago—what do you know of it?" The smile over Zalnaught's face quickly faded, a dramatic look of confusion encompassing his visage.

"Disturbance?" he repeated.

Trial of a Maven

"You think my senses are so obtuse they could miss it?" Verix spoke belittlingly. "Something happened at the portal to the void. Did you have a part in it?" A look of realization swept across the High Priest's face, obviously toying with Verix.

"Ah yes, the portal," he conveniently remembered. "I sensed this disturbance as well but I obviously could not have had anything to do with it as it is a Grandarian edifice—"

"The power there was dark, Zalnaught," Verix interrupted. "A sudden swelling of it then it completely disappeared. Do not attempt to allot blame for this on Grandaria." The toying expressions on Zalnaught's face dispersed, replaced by a serious gaze that matched Verix's.

"I think you forget, young prince," he began taking a step toward him, "that the portal and the dark power sealed within are now locked in place by a Grandarian talisman that only one from a chosen bloodline can manipulate. If you search for the perpetrator of this occurrence, you should be looking in the direction of Galantia."

"What possible reason would the Warrior of Light have to remove the Sword of Granis from the portal?" Verix pressed intolerantly. "He was the one that put it there in the first place." Zalnaught shrugged and placed both hands atop the wooden staff propping him up.

"I have warned you for years, young prince; your precious Warrior of Light along with the rest of his nation will eventually seek to destroy us. You may have last parted as allies but you know he now serves on a Grandarian council that is urging their Supreme Granisian for war against us. Their people plead for it two to one. Do you really think Tavinious Tieloc and his council will sit idle with this kind of outcry?"

"The Grandarians still don't know the extent of the situation," Verix argued. "Tavin and the Supreme Granisian do; they know they have nothing to gain from further Holy War as you would cast us in."

"I merely seek to defend our nation against these provocations for battle like you sensed three days ago," Zalnaught responded. "The Warrior of Light is the only one who could incite such a display of power at the portal by tampering with the Sword of Granis. He is trying to provoke us by threatening to remove the sword and gain its power once more."

"You would do well to stay your tongue if it is incapable of uttering logical thought, High Priest," Verix bit at him. "I am not the idiot you must believe me to be. Tavin would not unleash Drakkan just to gain the sword's power again."

"Wouldn't he?" Zalnaught said, beginning to slowly walk around Verix. "What if I told you that our scouts have reported Grandarian troops building at the Wall of Light over the past weeks? It seems obvious they are preparing for something. Grandaria is ready for war and when it comes to that, the Warrior of Light knows he will need the power of the Sword of Granis to defeat you when you meet on the battlefield. If he unleashes Lord Drakkan as a result he must assume he will be able to beat him back with the power of the sword. Whether you and your Loyalists believe it or not, young prince, the path we are on now inexorably leads us to war." Zalnaught unhurriedly shifted his gaze down to his hands, slowly churning over the top of the staff in his hands. "Yet, there may still be a way to avert this fate." His eyes rose back to Verix's and he began to slowly saunter toward the prince. "The troops in the war zone belong to the New Fellowship of Drakkan. As its head these troops... credit my advice. If I were to call for their return to the Valley of Blood it may lower tensions in Galantia and lessen the Warrior of Light's resolve to threaten us with the Sword of Granis."

Zalnaught leaned in to whisper into Verix's ear, a faint smile appearing over his face.

"I could be easily persuaded to issue said advice to these rogue troops," he spoke, pulling back. Verix's eyes trailed him as he turned and tread back to the front of the altar. "All I would require is to see a certain chamber of your ruined citadel at Dalastrak for a brief moment. Just for a moment—and this entire situation could be calmed. War could be avoided. All I would need is a moment. I could be easily persuaded, young prince." Watching the High Priest's sinister head rotate back to return his gaze, the prince's face tightened. Unfolding his muscular arms, he vigorously marched forward to take hold of the priest's robes, lift him off his feet and push him into the face of the towering altar with an audible thud. The suddenly nervous priest dropped his wooden staff to the floor in shock.

"I'm not young anymore, Zalnaught," Verix quietly snarled, his temper unleashed. "I'm not the politically powerless boy you stole rule from after the Days of Destiny.

You've been spewing your lies about how Grandarian magic killed my father and unleashed the demon horde upon us for years despite knowing it was Tavin and Grandaria that saved us. I know there are motives behind your war mongering, Zalnaught, and whatever you want with the Netherworld Portal you *will not have it*. Not while I draw breath." Letting the heated silence hang for a long moment Zalnaught's frightened expression gradually hardened into one of knowing hate.

"You would like nothing more than to kill me, wouldn't you?" he asked. "To remove the man who threatens all that you strive to accomplish and defend. There is nothing you wish for more." Zalnaught leaned his face closer to Verix still hoisting him against the altar, his eyes locked onto him. "But you won't. Because the only thing you fear more than another war with Grandaria is civil war here. You know how fragile the peace is between the Fellowship and your Loyalists. You know that if you kill me my armies will march on Dalastrak and raze what's left of that hellhole to the ground. Your beloved nation will tear itself to shreds until nothing is left, and you won't be able to stop it because another like me—like your father—will just keep coming to take my place. You may be able to snap me in two with your physical strength but you lack the real power to lay a finger on me, and you know it or I would have stopped breathing years ago." Zalnaught could see the hate boiling behind Verix's crimson eyes, ready to explode with dark power. "Now lower me down before I order my mages inside to see the assassination attempt on my life."

Though all the instincts in his body told him to tear the manipulative autocrat in half, Verix knew his every word was right. He slowly set the High Priest back onto his feet and released his robes. Zalnaught unhurriedly smoothed out the creases on his dark attire and repositioned the large hat covering his round dome. Leaning down to pick up the wooden staff once more, his eyes drifted back to Verix as if surprised he was still there.

"You may leave now," he informed him factually. The prince remained still as stone, the loathsome passion in his blood burning his veins. After a long moment of staring each other down, Verix took a step forward once more.

"There has been an unspoken truth between us since you robbed my birthright as king from me all those years ago," Verix announced, "but today I say it aloud for you to hear. I know you have direct control over the troops in the war zone and I know you have the power to do what you say you can do, but heed this well. If one New Fellowship soldier so much as unsheathes his sword toward the Wall of Light, I'll come back here again—and it won't be to talk. If you start another Holy War with Grandaria you won't live to see the end of it. *I'll* make sure of that. If civil war is the cost of preventing war abroad so be it, but the days of blind hatred and tyranny here are over, Zalnaught. That is my word, and you would do well to heed it."

With that the prince wheeled around and began marching down the long aisle of the sanctuary for the double doors at the end. As they lurched open and Verix disappeared, Zalnaught exhaled deeply, eying the simple wooden staff in his grasp once more.

"That went as expected, I suppose," he stated plainly. A black robed figure from behind the altar stepped out of the shadows then, making his way beside Zalnaught.

"You must know the Netherworld Portal is not an option anymore," it spoke from behind its hood. Zalnaught nodded.

"I've known that for years," he responded turning to face the Dark Mage. "We'll have to continue with the current plan. What did you find at the portal?"

"It was as you suspected, Your Excellency. The sword still remains but both of the crystals are gone. Things are moving faster than we expected." Zalnaught nodded to himself, turning back to meander down from the altar.

"Then it wasn't the Warrior of Light at all," he spoke quietly. "It must have been another from his bloodline—one with dark power in his veins as well. This complicates things." Zalnaught spun around and locked his eyes on the mage. "You are to assemble a taskforce from the mages to find this human vessel. We need that power to activate the staff. Use all available resources at your disposal. Do it quickly." The Dark Mage bowed and turned for the back of the sanctuary, disappearing into the shadows once more. Alone in the massive chamber, High Priest Zalnaught slowly ran his fingers along the length of the wooden staff in his hands. "Montrox may hinder my plans now, but after I collect the vessel and harness its power both the Loyalists and Grandaria will crumble beneath my feet." A slow chuckle echoed from his throat into the rafters of the sanctuary.

Chapter 9

Demolition

Edge let out an impatient and admittedly worried huff of breath as his gray eyes drifted back to the unmoving door of the Medic Quarters that contained the Grandarian girl he had been charged to protect, the one who now rested unconscious, possibly dying, because of his failure to protect her. The Maven ran the word through his head a second time. Failure. It was not something he was accustomed to experiencing. Yet here he stood, helplessly waiting to hear if the girl would be alright.

After the explosion of dark power at the portal to the void three days ago, Edge had collected Kaylan's unconscious form and rushed her back down the Border Mountains as fast as his body could move. Though he didn't feel good letting Kaylan step onto that portal by herself in the first place he could never have predicted what would happen as a result. The worst part was he still had no idea what had happened. All he knew was that she was still alive but needed help as quickly as she could get it. Aware that the Grandarian controlled Battlemount miles behind the Wall of Light was the closest friendly outpost they would find, Edge made good time down the mountains and back to its gates to find the man who had given Kaylan the Lavlas Rock, General Ronus. He had been busy coordinating new troops from Galantia that had been arriving in droves to reinforce the Wall of Light, but when he discovered Kaylan Tieloc had returned in critical condition he immediately allowed her into the Medic Quarters for help. She had been in there for half a day now and none of the healers had any clue as to what was wrong with her.

Edge clenched his fists tighter, battling to keep his emotion suppressed as always. He shouldn't have let her just stroll up to the sword without checking it out first. Stupid—

Tales of Iairia

why wasn't he thinking when it mattered? Now, more could be at stake than just the girl's wellbeing. He was listening when Zeroan told them about the weakening of the seal holding the God of Darkness in place and the repercussions of this mission's failure. Had he allowed Drakkan to be free of his prison as well? No, if the God of Darkness was free he would know it, he thought. Something else must have happened at the portal.

As the perturbed Maven stood running the past days through his bewildered mind, a familiar sound drew his attention out past the Medic Quarters into the courtyard beyond. The constant snowfall from the mountain had turned to rain when he arrived at its base and continued softly drizzling all the way back to the Battlemount. Looking out through the falling showers he found Zephyr descending through the rows of trees adjacent to the Medic Quarters with frantic immediacy in his movements. He whistled again and motioned with a swooping gesture of his arm for Edge to come. Thrusting his back off the wall, the Maven exhaled softly and quickly strode over to the edge of the covered porch he stood on to eye his partner.

"He's back again," Zephyr rushed, answering Edge's question before he asked. "At the end of these trees around back. He said to hurry." Edge nodded with a surge of relief pouring through him and stepped off the porch area into the mud of the courtyard.

"It's about time," he mouthed to himself irritably but admittedly grateful. "Stay here and keep watch on the door. The second something happens I want to know about it." Turning and striding down the wet path toward the trees before Zephyr could respond, Edge began formulating his first questions for the tense conversation surely in store for him. As the boy strode into the rows of trees behind the Medic Quarters, the gentle rain began to fall harder and Edge could almost feel a familiar presence around him. Slowly halting and checking to make sure he was alone, he shouted out into the downpour. "Where are you?" Sweeping his eyes around, Edge at last found a unique column of rain drifting together behind him. Watching as the column of liquid collected and structured itself into a loosely based figure hooded and cloaked, Edge clenched his gloved fists again. All at once the towering form of the Mystic Sage Zeroan was before him.

Trial of a Maven

"Hello again, Edge," the apparition spoke more distant than before.

"It took you long enough to say that," the boy spoke curtly. "Where have you been Zeroan? She's been out for days and *this* is first I see you again?" A look of sudden puzzled dread encompassed the sage's face then and his liquid form took a step forward.

"What do you mean 'she's been out?'" he responded quickly. "What happened at the portal?" Edge raised an eyebrow incredulously.

"You mean to tell me you don't know what happened to her?" he replied in disbelief. Zeroan frowned and shook his head.

"As I told you before, my sight is blurred by the presence of other magics," he reiterated. "If I could see around the portal to the void I would not have needed Kaylan in the first place. I have no idea what transpired in the mountains—you must tell me everything." Stumbling over himself in aggravated confusion, Edge threw his arms up and exhaled deeply. He swiftly but thoroughly related to the Mystic Sage all that transpired from their arrival at the massive portal to their return to Battlemount that morning. Throughout, Zeroan frequently interrupted him to ask for clarification, needing to know exact details to help him believe the bizarre and disturbing tale. At the conclusion the sage could barely keep his eyes on Edge, as if processing the parts of the story to try and make sense of what had really happened for himself.

"And she's been in there since this morning, still out cold," Edge finished blankly. "I know I should have taken some precaution before I let her go onto that damn thing but I've never dealt with anything like this and it seemed as though she knew exactly what she was doing when she left. I tried to get out to her when it was happening, but the force from that hurricane of light wouldn't even let me on the portal until it was dying down. By that time it was too late so I took her and got the hell out of there." Trailing off, Edge let the silence hang between them with only the rain pouring into the muddy earth around them echoing through the atmosphere. Still staring into the ground with glazed eyes, Zeroan shook his head again and mumbled something to himself. Edge crossed his soaked arms as the sage turned his back and paced backward in the rain. "So what happened, Zeroan? Is the seal still in place? Is she going to be alright?"

Zeroan said nothing at first but at last turned back with obviously painful confusion on his face.

"This makes no sense," he stated more to himself than to Edge. "Kaylan's potential power over the Sword of Granis is still dormant—she could not have affected it enough to free its seal over the portal. Something else must be at work here... I need more detail." Edge shrugged and narrowed his discouraged gray eyes.

"Well that's all I could see from back there. I'd tell you to ask her but she's been unconscious ever since," he stated sardonically. "Can you help her or not?" Zeroan did not appreciate the impatience in the boy's voice and he spun around to face him.

"Any aid I could provide would first require greater knowledge of what happened than you can offer, Maven. Surely there is some other detail you have neglected to mention. Even the smallest thing you might have noticed could provide me with greater insight. Think back to how you found Kaylan. Was there anything peculiar about her when you found her? Or the Sword of Granis—had she manipulated it at all?" Edge raised an eyebrow again.

"Not that I'd know what that thing is supposed to look like normally but it looked to be in perfect condition. Sitting perfectly erect in all its Grandarian glory. And the girl was just unconscious. There wasn't anything else. After I picked her up with the crystal and started down the mountain it started snowing heavier but other than that—"

"Wait," Zeroan interjected quickly, almost throwing himself forward toward the boy. "Crystal? What crystal?" Surprised at the sage's apparent outburst, Edge struggled to remember back again.

"...This little golden crystal was lying between Kaylan and the sword so I grabbed it as I was scooping her up. I thought it was hers..."

"And you still have this crystal?" Zeroan continued to cut him off. "Where is it now?" Confused but complying, Edge reached into one of his satchels along his waist and took hold of a pale diamond shaped golden crystal and presented it in his open palm to the sage. Zeroan's eyes widened and his mouth slipped opened.

"I don't get it," Edge stated looking down to the gem in his grasp. "Why is this important?"

Trial of a Maven

"You're sure you found this on the ground, Edge?" Zeroan asked hurriedly, to which he again replied yes. "And was it this color when you first saw it? Has it lost any vibrancy since you picked it up?"

"I don't think so..." he replied vaguely, to which the sage frowned.

"Now is not the time for uncertainty, young Maven," he grilled. "This is critical." Edge placed his confused gaze back on the crystal and thought back to finding it on the portal surface.

"No, it was like this when I picked it up. Dull and pale. There were little shards of broken glass all around it but obviously not from this because it's completely intact." Zeroan's expression intensified further at this.

"Shards? You're sure of what you saw, Edge?" he pressed. The Maven answered yes again. "Then this is beginning to piece together after all..." The sage nodded to himself and placed the palm of his hand on his forehead to massage it gently, obviously lost in thought.

"I don't understand what this crystal has to do with anything," Edge at last spoke aloud, water dripping from his chin as he spoke. "Why is this significant?" Zeroan slowly looked up into the cloudy sky, the drops of rain falling down to mix into the surface of his watery face.

"The Granic Crystal's life extends far longer than this. It can't be natural. The Sword of Granis has been sabotaged before..." he trailed off, as if trying to convince himself of something. "And if this is indeed the case, this entire chain of events was set in motion by intent..." Letting the sage mull over his thoughts, Edge impatiently but tolerantly waited for Zeroan to address him directly again. At last the sage's spirit turned to face him. "Edge, I know you are still waiting for answers of your own right now but I must ask you to be patient for a while longer. There may be more going on here than I originally thought and it is imperative that we—" All of the sudden Zeroan stopped, the perfect fluidity of his liquid figure suddenly sloshing unevenly back and forth. Though he could tell the sage was trying to speak once more, Edge could not decipher what he was trying to say and before he could do anything Zeroan's entire figure lost its form and fell to the muddy earth along with the rest of the pouring rain between them.

Edge stared down into the mud with an uncertain look about his face, unfolding his arms and calling out the sage's name. There was no response but the continued falling of rain. Baffled at why Zeroan would just leave him when he was so enveloped in Edge's story, the Maven grit his teeth and kicked the muddy ground beneath him in aggravation. Looking around the courtyard clueless at what had just happened, the soaked boy prepared to walk back to the Medic Quarters to check on Kaylan. As soon as he took his first step the sudden shock waves of a huge explosion rocked through the Battlemount and the boy tripped back into the trunk of a tree in surprise. Regaining his balance, his terrified eyes shot over the roof of the Medic Quarters where billows of smoke were rising. Observing an ominously similar aura of massive dark energy hovering around the thick smoke like the one he had seen at the portal to the void, Edge remembered what Zeroan had said about how he could not exist around the presence of other powerful magics. Dread of what might be free upon them now coursing through him, Edge grit his teeth and shot forward for the central courtyard.

As the Maven came careening around the corner of the smoking Medic Quarters his jaw dropped at the extent of the damage. The entire front of the building had been blown apart from what looked to be the inside out. Fiery debris was still falling down along with the rain, landing all over the massive central courtyard beyond where groups of soldiers were mobilizing in panic. Trying to stare into the building past the billows of rising smoke and the residue of the dark aura of energy dissipating into the air, Edge realized the room where Kaylan was laid to rest had been incinerated. There would be nothing left of her. His face twisting with furious confusion, he heard a familiarly quiet cough from behind him. Wheeling around he found Zephyr lying in the mud of the road struggling to rise. Quickly rushing down into the courtyard and kneeling to his partner's side, he gently scooped him out of the mud and laid him in his lap.

"Zephyr, are you alright?" Edge asked quickly. "What happened?" The little Sky Sprite coughed violently again and struggled to prop himself up with his miniature arms.

"I'm not sure," he managed, obviously still dazed from the explosion. "I was perched on the roof of the porch when I saw this deep purple light shine through the cracks of the building and the next second the whole thing just blew up.

Something flew past me when I was falling to the ground but I think the girl—" Before the shell-shocked sprite could finish another detonation of the dark purple light and fire rocked the Battlemount, once more catching Edge off guard. Jerking his head back toward the opposite end of the central courtyard in the heart of the Grandarian base, he saw more smoke rising into the sky and ranks of soldiers running from the barracks toward it.

"Hold on, Zeph," Edge commanded, his instinct taking over. "I need to see this for myself." Tucking his partner into the largest pouch where he frequently rested behind his back, Edge shot up with rage threatening to tear his body and sprinted into the mob of Grandarian soldiers rushing into the central courtyard. As they ran Edge tried to shout out and ask what was happening but none of them could hear him over the chaos of the moment. Tearing into the muddy courtyard Edge gazed around them in disbelief. The Battlemount was a sprawling collection of barracks, training yards and armories all fortified by thick walls and towers along the perimeter. Aside from the Wall of Light itself it was the pride of Grandarian Army, yet now columns of smoke rose on either side and chaos ran rampant throughout. Looking past the rows of confused soldiers scurrying back and forth across the sparring grounds before him Edge could see another row of barracks lying decimated in flames.

Slowing to a halt, Edge forced himself to stop and focus. Running aimlessly was doing him no good—he had to find the source of this devastation. Anything so destructive and obviously powerful couldn't hide for long. Sweeping his eyes around all corners of the courtyard another flash of strange light caught his attention from above. Locking his gaze onto the furthest tower on the opposite side of the courtyard nearly fifty feet in the air, Edge was amazed to find a figure standing on its lofty shingled spire with a dark purple light menacingly whirling around its hands. Squinting uncertainly, he could make out the slender figure of a girl faintly illuminated by the sporadic lightning now crashing behind her. Taking a nervous step forward in bewilderment, he watched as the girl threw her head back with giddy laughter and spread her previously clenched fists into open hands. Instantly the soft glow emanating from them intensified into a massive surge of dark energy and a rolling wave of exploding power came blasting from around her open palms down into the tower.

Edge defensively brought an arm up to protect his face as the entire structure exploded with dark purple energy and twisting flames blasting outwards. Losing the figure of the laughing girl in the detonation of foreboding light Edge watched as the soldiers turned toward the explosion in fear and raised their shields to avoid the onslaught of rubble falling around them.

His target marked and his final shred of patience gone, the darkly clad Maven tightened his expression and darted into the concealing dust filtering through the soldiers. As he disappeared in the veil of dirt and smoke, the Grandarian soldiers lowered their shields and looked back into the sky where the tower had once stood to find the silhouette of a winged figure superimposed in front of the dark clouds slowly descending toward them. Though frightened out of their minds, not a single man budged in the coming moments. As the dust and smoke cleared over their heads, a girl with a pair of jagged glowing wings mounted high on her back abruptly dropped out of the sky with a spiteful giggle. She hit the ground with a powerful wave of deep purple energy electrifying the earth around her, fragmenting the rock beneath her feet. The soldiers all took several steps back, creating an uneven perimeter around her radiating form.

"Fun, fun, fun!" she spoke to herself in a threateningly gleeful tone, running a hand through her midnight-black hair that stretched down to her waist. It was tangled somewhat from soaring through the rain but she remained comparatively dry. The girl swept another lock of silky hair behind her ear and shifted her attention onto the faces of the men surrounding her, their weapons tightly gripped. She raised an eyebrow at one of them, a playful smirk spreading across her lips. "But you didn't like it?" It was more of a question than a statement and she made an overly dramatic expression of regret. "Well maybe I'll have to do it again until we start having some real fun." The Grandarians said nothing but remained fixated on her as the large pair of bat like wings bleeding dark purple light on her back suddenly dispersed in a flowing mist. The girl ran her hands down her sides as if to smooth out the short purple skirt she was wearing. Her top was covered in a skintight black and white tunic with elaborate but jagged violet emblems stitched throughout, forming what appeared to be designs of a Drakkaidian origin. There were large shining rings adorning her hands and thick high heel boots housing her feet. Her arms and midriff were bare but for a thin semi-transparent layer of abnormal black material stretched over.

There was a supernatural quality radiating from the girl's every movement that kept the frightened soldiers intoxicated with wonder. Though every man present knew how dangerous this girl was from what she had done and had the capacity to do, not one could bring themselves to lunge out at her. She was young and beautiful with a slender body and striking face that toyed with them as it passed through their ranks, her bright purple eyes capturing their attention but instilling a chilling sensation of trepidation. Her appearance exuded an innocence that contradicted what they all knew she really was. At last the girl tilted her head with a loud chuckle and placed her hands on her hips.

"Oh come on, boys," she stated teasingly, "what's everyone staring at? Haven't you ever seen a girl before?" She locked her gaze onto one of the trembling soldiers directly before her and narrowed her eyes. "Then maybe you want a closer look." The girl raised her hand and pointed at the man, then swept her fingers back toward her. The same instant the man was gripped by a field of constricting purple energy and abruptly flew toward her only to stop an inch away from her face. The rest of the soldiers finally shocked back to their senses at last reacted, pointing their weapons in her direction and assuming battle positions. The girl's smile widened. "Boys and their toys. So cute."

"Don't be fooled men!" one of the higher ranked soldiers shouted. "It's some kind of demon from the north—destroy it!" The smirk on the girl's face quickly dissipated as the soldiers nervously started toward her, raising their sword points. She dropped the man in her supernatural grasp and spun her head toward a broadsword sailing down toward her body.

"Excuse you!" she bellowed annoyed. Throwing her hand up a blast of dark energy flew from her palm and flared out to strike her incoming assailant in a flash of sinister light and send him careening back through the air to land far behind the rest of the men. Her brow angled downward in a state of disgust and she clenched her glowing fists. "If you don't want to play nice we won't play at all." With that an aura of purple energy rapidly flamed to life around her and detonated out to throw the falling rain and all remaining soldiers back through the air to land in the muddy earth.

She scowled and turned her head to the man who had last spoken, calling for her death. Striding over to him with a burst of lightning flashing through the sky as she came, she leaned down over his cowering figure and outstretched a pointed finger at his head. A ball of dark light formed at its tip. "That wasn't very nice, now was it? How would you like it if somebody killed you?" As she was about to fire the energy at the tip of her finger straight through the man, she stopped, a curious sensation on her neck. Looking down, she observed a blade was pressed against it leading up to her left. Rotating her head she found a boy clad in black standing above her with an intolerant look on his visage. The girl narrowed her eyes. "Well aren't you sneaky."

"Step back," Edge spoke icily, water dripping from his chin. The girl raised an eyebrow and sneered.

"You first," she replied disgusted, raising a hand to touch his blade. The moment she laid a finger on it a wave of purple electricity shot down its length to spread onto Edge himself. Overcome with constricting pain holding him in place, Edge was forced to drop his sword. With the sharp steel away from her neck, the dark girl stood full length once more and fixed her gaze onto Edge, studying him. When she was about to ask him something she remembered what she had been doing before being interrupted. She spun her dismayed head down to the cowering man below her and used her free hand to summon a blast of the dark purple energy forth to slam into his body with an explosion of light, pounding a crater into the earth and incinerating all that lay above it. Helplessly witnessing the execution, Edge furiously struggled to be free but still couldn't move.

"What the hell are you?" he questioned with what strength he could muster. The girl put her attention back on the boy squirming in her grasp.

"I hope you can tell what I am," she stated dryly. She smiled then and ran her fingers through her hair once more. "I'm a beautiful girl. But you can call me Kaotica. And you are... cute." She took a step closer and ran the boy up and down with her deep violet eyes. "Yes you are. Does the cute boy have a name?" Edge remained fierce, desperately struggling to be free. He could feel his rage building and the horrible feeling of inevitability of what was going to happen soon after unless he was freed.

Trial of a Maven

"You just murdered dozens of men," he managed heatedly. The girl raised her brow at him once more, her smile fading.

"You say it like they matter," she said dismissing his rage with a belittling tone. "So some random idiots got blown away. Big deal. There are greater tragedies, you know." She paused for a moment, looking into his eyes. They had been pale gray before but they were slowly turning heated red.

"And a helpless girl," he added caustically, a fervent red mist beginning to palpitate off his skin. Now the girl's expression turned sour.

"Oh, don't spoil the moment with her," she said dismayed. "It's Kaotica time, not blondie's." Edge's burning emotion continued to build at this. He knew it was coming now and nothing was going to stop it. Kaotica paused sensing something happening inside the boy as well and curiously released him from her grasp, a genuinely intrigued expression overtaking her face. Edge fell to his knees in the mud covered ground, struggling for breath. Though his power had been ready to explode once more, the faint red mist subsided around him as his freedom was restored and he looked up to face the girl once more. She was staring at him with interested eyes. "You have a nifty little something inside you too, don't you?" She studied his face for another moment before folding her arms with a frown. "Well if you want to see your precious little blondie again so bad, fine. I'm tired of all this mud and you sticks in it spoiling my fun. It's too wet out here." Kaotica leaned in toward the panting boy then within an inch of his face. "But I like you so we'll see each other again. Till then, stay cute."

With that, the girl straightened herself and winked at him as an aura of dark purple energy expanded out from her skin to cover her entire form under its dark glow. The force of its emergence blew the falling rain back into Edge's face as he watched surges of black and red electricity slowly morph into softer waves of brightening golden light radiating upward. Confusion of what was happening bombarding his mind, Edge remained still as the once midnight black energy covering Kaotica's dark form morphed into a brilliant golden glow that softly faded into a gentle aura of light wrapped around her body now lying on the earth. As the shimmering light began to fade, however, Edge's gray eyes opened wide to find it was not Kaotica lying before him asleep in the mud. It was Kaylan.

Chapter 10

Renewed Charge

    Kaylan Tieloc's eyes opened slowly the following morning, confronted by the fervent rays of light pouring in from the window to her right where she lay tucked beneath the covers of her bed. Squinting in puzzlement, she tried to focus all the slurred colors before her into coherent images. Though attempting to lift her head nestled into a pillow, it immediately started throbbing and she let it fall once again with a cringing ache expressed on her face. As the room she lay in at last started to come into focus a movement to her right caught her attention. She tilted her head and squinted once more to find a figure clad in black standing beside her with a steaming cup outstretched to her. Staring at him uncertainly for a lingering moment, Kaylan remembered the face of her Maven protector Edge and memories of the portal to the void came flushing through her mind in a blended fury.

    "Take this," the boy spoke emotionlessly after seeing her come back to her senses. "You've been unconscious for over four days—your head has to be hurting. This will help." Kaylan's gaze shifted from the boy's pale eyes back to the mug he held and she sluggishly summoned her hands from beneath the sheets to gingerly accept it with a single nod of thanks. Lifting up to lean her back against the wooden wall behind her she brought the steaming liquid to her soft lips and sipped it's warmth down her throat. Her brow furrowed uncertainly at the taste—raw and unsweetened but warm and comforting all the same. As her bright blue eyes drifted back up to the boy standing patiently before her, a look of awkward confusion composed her expression.

    "Where am I?" she asked softly at last. Inwardly relieved to hear her speak, the Maven kept his eyes on her and folded his arms.

"The Battlemount," he replied coolly. "You've been here a day." Kaylan took another sip from her mug before tilting her head in confusion.

"I thought you said I was out for four," she stated curious. "Where was I before?" Edge broke his gaze from hers and put it on the floor, exhaling at length.

"What do you remember of the last time you were awake?" he asked slowly. Kaylan eyed him peculiarly before thinking back to the portal on the mountains and shuddered.

"The last thing I remember was making it to the portal to the void and... something bad happening," she spoke, not wanting to share her horrific experience with the coarse boy. She watched as he exhaled deeply again, making her feel as though he knew something she didn't.

"She's all yours," he stated bluntly looking to his left, to which the girl curiously followed his eyes to find something that completely shocked her awake. Over a thick candle resting on the table next to her bed was the figure of the Mystic Sage Zeroan with his flowing robes comprised of the orange flame. The glowing fire making up his frame stood a foot tall over the candle with miniature embers twisting off him every time he shifted the weight between his feet.

"Good morning, Kaylan Tieloc," his distant and ghostly voice sounded through the small room. Kaylan instantly sat up in her bed and threw the sheets over her legs in preparation to stand, her bright blond hair cascading over her shoulders in tangled but ever beautiful curls. The small sage extended one of his flaming arms and motioned for her to be still. "Please stay still, Kaylan. Whether you know it or not you are not well and you should take advantage of this moment to rest." The girl nodded slowly but squinted in confusion.

"What do you mean, 'I'm not well?'" she repeated with a hint of fear in her voice, thinking back to her experience at the portal. Zeroan's small form shifted once more before cautiously beginning again.

"Kaylan, Edge informed me about what happened at the portal but I need to hear it from you as well," he told her slowly. He could see the confusion and fear in her eyes. "Please hurry, Kaylan. We may not have much time. I need to know exactly what happened at the portal." Afraid of remembering and even more to tell him about it, Kaylan could feel herself trembling but at last nodded and began to relate to the sage her entire experience on the surface of the portal to the void from her first seeing the Sword of Granis to her falling unconscious. She could see the anxiety in Zeroan's movements as she told him of the dark crystal on the blade of the Sword of Granis. As he did when hearing the story the first time from Edge, the sage let his gaze drift down to the ground, lifting his hand out of his enflamed robes to massage his forehead.

"You are sure beyond any doubt that there is nothing you have left out?" he at last asked, addressing them both. When Kaylan replied she had told him everything and Edge merely nodded, he breathed deeply and shifted in his robes, preparing to speak. "Kaylan, I am very sorry for what happened to you at the portal—I did not have the clairvoyance to see all that was really at work here until now when it is too late." Kaylan could feel a tremor of fear shoot down her spine at Zeroan's words.

"Too late for what, Zeroan?" she asked almost quivering. "What's really going on here? What happened to me?" The sage's eyes peered into hers from behind his hood and he shook his head.

"Until now I wasn't sure," he admitted slowly. "Edge, you should take a seat as well as this is going to be long." The young Maven standing beside him peered down to the fiery figure then made his way to the single chair in the room next to the bed where Kaylan sat. When he threw his blue scarf behind his neck and was seated, Zeroan started again. "There are many pieces to this puzzle that I have not been able to put together with my limited vision in the mortal realm until today. Unfortunately for us, today I was too late to stop things from unraveling. The weakening of the seal to the portal that holds Drakkan at bay was not of natural causes as I had supposed, but by intent—the intent of one who would seek the dark power locked inside released once more. I must start, then, by telling you something that once again violates the code of my order. Something never revealed to anyone outside of it in the history of the Mystic Sages.

"This story begins shortly after my last meeting with your parents, Kaylan. As you both know, my spirit and will have remained intact throughout the winds of Iairia after the fulfillment of the prophesy of the Three Fates, waiting for something to happen. In my time waiting, my otherwise dormant spirit was awakened by a disturbance. But this disturbance was not the weakening of the seal as I told you before. It was a violation of the Mystic Tower to the east—intruders of a dark nature that arrived shortly after the Days of Destiny. I did not know it at first but they were the last of the Dark Mages of the Black Church in Drakkaidia. Without the Mystic Sages to guard our vaults, the mages penetrated into the lowest level of the tower and found the most sacred and powerful of all the talismans we protected there—an object known as the Staff of the Ancients. This staff is the last known surviving artifact that the Ancients of the old world possessed. The Mystic Sages found it during the first generation of the order by Alberic himself and in his studies of the staff he discovered it was the mighty talisman they created to build the Elemental Temples across the six lands. Next to the Holy Emerald, this staff was the most powerful talisman of magic in existence—most likely forged out of the remaining power from the shrine of the emerald. It was from this staff that Alberic based our power—it was what granted him the power of the Master Sage and gave him the ability to create the Sage's Draught which provided the regular sages their power over the years.

"Like all active talismans of magic, however, over the years the staff became dormant and lost its power. We kept it locked up in secret, never speaking of it outside the order for fear knowledge of its existence would fall into the wrong hands." Zeroan at last paused then and exhaled deeply. "Now, it has. The Dark Mages have found and stolen the Staff of the Ancients in our order's absence, which means it is now in the possession of their new master—the High Priest Zalnaught." Kaylan and Edge both shot unsure glances at each other, unsure of what any of this story had to do with the portal to the void or the situation at hand.

"So where do the Drakkaidians and this staff of yours fit into all this? What does this have to do with the portal being weak or what happened when I was there?" Kaylan finally asked, a questioning look in her eyes. Zeroan slowly turned his gaze and locked it onto the girl's, hard.

"The two of these occurrences are linked, young Tieloc," Zeroan answered. "I did not see it before but now I realize one is happening because of the other. The weakening of the seal to the void world was by intent—the intent of this Zalnaught you have both undoubtedly heard a great deal about. After the Days of Destiny and the reawakening of my spirit because of the theft of the Staff of the Ancients, I witnessed the Fission of Drakkaidia that you have both had to live through. This former Dark Mage Zalnaught usurped control of Drakkaidia after Valif Montrox's death and is trying to incite a third Holy War between Drakkaidia and Grandaria. Zalnaught and his mages must have learned the importance and potential power of the talisman they stole and are trying to activate it to further their cause. The Staff of the Ancients is no ordinary talisman, however, and cannot be so simply activated as others are. It was created to absorb elemental energy and reflect specific power when in use, but it has been dormant for so many thousands of years without its original masters that to activate it enormous amounts of energy would be required. Far greater amounts of energy than Zalnaught has access to. Even all the power of the Dark Mages combined with that of the Source of Darkness in the heart of the Temple of Darkness would not be enough to restore its former strength. Zalnaught would need either the power of *all* the Sources or of something beyond anything he could find in this world. He would need that of a god." Kaylan and Edge's eyes widened in fear at this, finally making the connection toward which Zeroan had been driving.

"Wait," Edge interrupted skeptically, "are you saying that the New Fellowship of Drakkan in Drakkaidia is purposefully trying to release the seal holding Drakkan to absorb him into this staff? How could a manmade talisman absorb a god?"

"You forget, young Maven, that the void absorbed both Granis and Drakkan at one point or another," Zeroan stated. "I know it is difficult to grasp but the Staff of the Ancients functions much in the same way. It was crafted from ancient magics straight from the Sources that have the ability to soak in any and all power around it. It could absorb the Holy Emerald itself if it was still present in the world. If the seal was somehow lifted and Drakkan freed, Zalnaught would be able to absorb the power of the God of Darkness and reactivate the staff with power beyond even what the Ancients themselves wielded."

"So Zalnaught was using the black imposter crystal I found to weaken the Sword of Granis and release the seal?" Kaylan questioned, trying her best to keep up. Zeroan shook his head.

"Not exactly, no. Our enemy in Drakkaidia has done his research and knows the role of the Sword of Granis. Remember, Kaylan, the nature of the imposter Granic Crystal. It sabotages the link between the Sword of Granis and its master—your father. Zalnaught was counting on Tavin to eventually sense this disturbance for himself and come to investigate. When he did Zalnaught would spring his trap and force Tavin to pull free the sword, releasing Drakkan. Fortunately, I managed to sense this disturbance before Tavin so Zalnaught's original plan could not come to fruition. Unfortunately, something happened as a result of our actions that is just as great a threat. The sabotaged Sword of Granis' power was so depleted from the imposter crystal that the power of Drakkan was already slowly seeping forth. That was the dark mist you saw at the base of sword, Kaylan. It saw the darkness in your blood and when you touched it this latent darkness in you provided a vessel for the power of Drakkan to escape its imprisonment in the void." Kaylan stared at the sage with painful confusion mirrored in her eyes. She looked at the boy beside her already staring in her direction. He knew what was coming and quickly looked away, unable to hold her gaze.

"...You both know something that you're not telling me," the girl said with a quivering voice, throwing her eyes back onto Zeroan. "What are you trying to say, Zeroan?" The sage shifted in his robes, the embers from his fiery figure lofting into the air. While they both expected Zeroan to give an elaborate explanation, he merely pointed up to the sunlit window.

"Look out the window, Kaylan," he said quietly. Confused and afraid but curious, Kaylan rose and started over toward the single window of the room above the table where Zeroan's fiery sprit stood. Peering out, her face tightened in bewilderment and dismay. Half of the mighty Battlemount was covered in rubble and smoldering ruin. Entire buildings were obliterated and maimed soldiers still lay dead across some of the courtyard being collected by others. Kaylan brought a hand to cover her mouth before wheeling back to face the others in the room.

"What happened here?" she asked in panic. "Did Zalnaught do this?" Zeroan slowly shook his head.

"No, Kaylan," he replied softly. "You did." The girl stared at him for a long moment, letting his words sink in.

She shook her head softly and let her hand drop back to her side. She shot an uncertain glance at Edge, uncomfortably doing the same to her.

"...What?" she replied dumbfounded. "What do you mean I did? I've been unconscious for the past four days." Zeroan nodded but shifted in his robes once again.

"Kaylan Tieloc was unconscious for the past four days but your entire person was not," he replied cryptically. "I have never encountered a situation like this before, Kaylan. What I should have realized before I sent you to the portal was that the darkness in your blood could be a factor in what played out there. The loosened power of Drakkan took advantage of the dormant darkness in you, young Grandarian. Zalnaught's plan was for Tavin to inadvertently release this power but instead it was absorbed into his daughter's blood. It was this dark side now awake and coexisting in you that took control for the first time yesterday and destroyed half the Battlemount." Kaylan took a step back, shaking her head once more.

"...You're saying Drakkan is inside of me?" she asked in horror, tears welling in her eyes. Zeroan shook his head.

"It is very complicated, Kaylan," he said, trying to keep her calm with his soothing tone. "Drakkan has not taken possession of you as he did Valif Montrox in the Days of Destiny; his power has been absorbed into the dark side of your being that you inherited from your mother. He cannot appear as himself, only through you, or, this girl that Edge encountered calling herself Kaotica. She is your opposite—you in a negative reality. She is her own person inside you, using Drakkan's power to live through your flesh. You are sharing your body with her so only one can appear at a time." Both Zeroan and Edge could see Kaylan becoming panicked.

"I don't believe this..." she said more to herself than either of the other two. "I don't have control of myself anymore? The God of Darkness is free and could appear in me anytime he wants?"

"Kaylan, you are emotional and still not grasping what I'm telling you," the sage answered. "Drakkan himself is not active inside you—his will and spirit are dormant in the spirit of this girl sharing your body. Therefore he is not yet free. He is trapped behind the will of your dark side—this Kaotica. His spirit is the blood that runs through her veins and gives her strength. But you are still in control of you—of

Kaylan Tieloc—there is just another person inside you who exists all on her own apart from your mind. As far as Kaotica having the ability to appear anytime she wants, that is going to change over time."

"What does that mean?" Kaylan pressed.

"There is yet another element factoring into all this that we have neglected to account for," Zeroan transitioned. "Edge?" Looking back to the Maven, Edge nodded and slowly pulled forth the small crystal he had been keeping in his pocked for the past four days. Opening his hand to reveal it, Kaylan immediately knew what it was.

"The Granic Crystal," she said quietly. "Why is it not on the Sword of Granis?"

"It was weakened by the imposter crystal over the months or years it has been attached to the sword and now the Granic Crystal is failing," Zeroan reminded her. "So much in fact that it fell off the sword after you were seized by the power of Drakkan. Without the crystal, the Sword of Granis is inactive once again. Therefore the Granic Crystal is the key to reversing what happened to you at the portal. After its empowerment from Granis himself in the Days of Destiny, the Sword of Granis now has the potential strength to vanquish the darkness of Drakkan. If it is activated again it can purge Kaotica and in effect Drakkan from you, pulling him back into the void. But without a power source the sword is useless."

"So do we have to go put this crystal back on the sword?" Edge asked from the bed, outstretching his open palm to reveal the pale gem in it. Zeroan shook his head no.

"No, that crystal is almost dead from its exposure to the imposter crystal for so long. The only way to reactivate the Sword of Granis now is to augment it with a *new* Granic Crystal." A renewed gleam of hope shone through Kaylan's eyes.

"You mean if a new Granic Crystal is attached to the Sword of Granis we can put all this right again?" she asked expectantly. Zeroan nodded but his face remained stoic and hard.

"That would dispel this darkness from you, but as I said earlier, things are going to change over time. What I haven't had a chance to tell you yet is that we are in a race against time once again on more fronts than one. The more your dark opposite reveals herself and is allowed to expand her power, which she will try to do more and more as time passes, the stronger she will become. As her strength increases so will Drakkan's. If she grows too powerful Drakkan's true self will eventually emerge through her and take possession of both you and Kaotica. If this happens, you will be lost, Kaylan." The Grandarian girl swallowed hard at this, struggling to suppress fresh tears welling in her blue eyes. "In the meantime, Zalnaught and his minions will be looking for you. They will have sensed Kaotica's first appearance yesterday and are surely on their way here even now. If you are caught by Zalnaught he will use the Staff of the Ancients to absorb the power of Drakkan from you. None will survive if this happens. And beyond Zalnaught, these explosions of power are being sensed by Tavin, Ril, Verix and others with the ability to feel them. These disturbances are sure to inflame the volatile political situation between the two nations. If Verix is persuaded to take his Loyalists to war he may allow Zalnaught use of the Netherworld Portal where there might be enough dark elemental energy for him to bypass the Drakkan's power altogether and make his war. If any of these things are allowed to happen all is lost."

Kaylan Tieloc stared at the flaming figure of the Mystic Sage Zeroan, his words of the coming doom pounding through her. She couldn't believe any of this was happening. The God of Darkness was inside her along with an evil version of herself festering to be free, a Drakkaidian tyrant was after her, her father could be forced into a third Holy War because of her actions, and the one thing that could fix all this was broken itself. The Sword of Granis was powerless in its current state and if it wasn't restored soon the world would face the same doom that once hung over it during her parents' battle in the Days of Destiny. She shifted her gaze toward the pale little dying crystal resting in Edge's gloved hand. It was the key to their future—their only hope now. Kaylan raised her arm to wipe the tears away from her eyes and set her now resolute gaze onto Zeroan.

"Then I have to get a new Granic Crystal before any of this can happen," she stated powerfully. Edge raised his head to look at the determined girl, amazed at her sudden fortitude and focus in the face of such besieging circumstances. Zeroan nodded.

"Yes you do, Kaylan Tieloc," he answered with a soft smile. "Your parents' courage is indeed alight in your heart.

Trial of a Maven

And you will need it all for the trial that lies ahead of you now." The spirit of the sage shifted in his robes, the flames shooting up from the wick of the candle dimming and weakening suddenly. Zeroan quietly groaned to himself. "Listen well, young ones, for my time with you is almost completely gone. Kaylan is right. This world's only chance now rests with the hope that you can find a new Granic Crystal for the Sword of Granis. Its light is the only way of dispelling this darkness before it consumes all of Iairia. I wish I could be of more help to you, young Tieloc, as I was to your father during his quest, but I have cheated death for far too long as it is. The last bit of power that allows my final presence in the world is all but gone and I will not be able to return to you until my final task is done." The sage's dimming form turned to face Edge. "My final affair that I first spoke of in Eirinor was not to wait for this impeding doom but for the new Scion of the Order of Alberic. That scion is you, Edge. You are the reincarnation of our power—the eighth one of your kind. Because you possess this incredible power you are connected to the Staff of the Ancients just as all the Mystics Sages before you have been. If it is somehow activated only the power of a true Master Sage could ever hope to control it. Whether you acknowledge this or not, young Maven, is up to you, but I tell you now that this is your destiny. Remember this well—the key to controlling your power is by first accepting it, Edge. It will surely awaken before this quest is over and you will have to accept it or it will destroy you. I would tell you more but my spirit wanes and you will have to find the answers for yourself at the Mystic Tower, where you must first go."

Zeroan turned back to Kaylan, the flames making up his body drifting into the air and his already distant voice fading into oblivion.

"There is a place where the first Grandarians found the means to forge the Granic Crystals but I do not know where it is. It will be recorded somewhere in the libraries of the Mystic Tower, so you must first go there and gather what information you can. Take the old crystal and guard it well, for whatever remnant of its former power that remains will be of invaluable defense to you should you encounter the forces of darkness before the end of this journey. From there it is up to you..." With that the final flame of the candle extinguished and the wick fizzled out, along with the Mystic Sage's physical form. As the smoke rose into the air it formed into his hooded face and spoke one last time. "...Fate is never fair, but it has chosen you both as it chose those who came before you... ...You are bound to each other in this quest... ...Go with Granis and restore the light..." As the faint smoke faded from view, Kaylan Tieloc and Edge's eyes met as if for the first time.

Part Two
A New Quest

Chapter 11

Tension

    There was always a massive swell of activity outside the golden gates of the shining capital of Galantia that made it difficult for caravans of merchants or travelers to get in and out of the city. Though Tavin Tieloc had experienced this himself time and time again after his hundreds of visits to the gleaming municipality, never before had his need to get past them and into the city with all speed been so great. He rode as fast as his horse could carry him with his sword drawn commanding passing merchants doing business with the city's citizens to clear the path leading to the towering city gates. Noting his dignified appearance and commanding voice, the jostling masses quickly parted for him as he blasted his way through their ranks onto the enormous downed draw bridge leading into the city's military stronghold known as the Gate Yard. Upon his dramatic entrance several units of passing soldiers recognized the caped figure as the Warrior of Light and took several steps back as he blasted his steed passed them and into the first tier of the city with urgency and determination mounted to his face. Many of the armored soldiers shot uncertain glances at each other as they watched him disappear into the city, silently worrying if something could be wrong.

    After the latest meeting of the Galantian Council, the Supreme Granisian had ordered Ril to go the Southland capital of Torrentcia City. Having the strongest ties to the Southland of anyone on the council, Ril had become Grandaria's emissary to the Sarton to inform him of important events and news regarding Drakkaidia. Tavin had gone with her, ordered by the Supreme Granisian herself to take a well deserved break from the capital after all the tense meetings of which he had been a part. As they were traveling through the Great Rift that connected the two nations through the massive Iairian

Mountain Chain that stretched from the Border Mountains in the north all the way to the bottom of the Southland, they had both sensed the explosion of dark power in the Border Mountains and knew something was terribly wrong.

Terrified of what had triggered the sinister display more powerful than anything they had sensed since the Days of Destiny and what it would do to inflame the tension between Grandaria and Drakkaidia, Tavin told Ril to keep going without him to meet with the Sarton while he returned to Galantia. Aware the Granisian of the Temple of Light would have sensed this dark disturbance as well and immediately informed the Supreme Granisian, he knew it would be the excuse Sodric and Tycond would be looking for to persuade Mary for further action against Drakkaidia. While he rode with all speed through the days and nights back to the north, he sensed another surge of dark energy even closer to Grandaria days after. Baffled at what could be responsible for the explosions of power he was sensing, all he knew for certain was that he had to get to Galantia before Mary was forced to make a decision he knew they would all regret.

Four days later an exhausted Warrior of Light finally tore through the worn streets of the fourth and final tier of Galantia leading to the Golden Castle, praying to Granis he had not arrived too late. Blasting into the massive courtyard of the castle and hurriedly dismounting from his steed to run into the Grand Vestibule leading up into the higher levels of the ornate edifice, Tavin tried his best to make his perspiring, tattered and drained form presentable after riding for four days straight. As he made his way higher into the beautiful Golden Castle to the arching hallways leading to the staircase of the Supreme Granisian's throne room, two sentries before the closed double doors raised their hands for the haggard figure to halt, obviously not recognizing him.

"State your business here, man," one of them barked from behind his ornate golden helm. When the Warrior of Light realized they were speaking to him he raised his impatient blue eyes to meet them with a frown, struggling to speak through his heavy breathing.

"Do those helmets really impair your vision that much, soldier?" Tavin asked raising an eyebrow. The sentry grit his teeth for a moment before at last recognizing the weary figure as the Warrior of Light. His eyes widening and gulping, he bowed and stood aside.

Trial of a Maven

"My sincerest apologies, Sir Tieloc," he managed quickly, slurring his words. "I did not recognize you. The Senior Council has been in emergency session for hours and—"

"Then I really need to get in that room, don't I young man?" Tavin cut him off, moving to open the doors himself. The sentry flinched and nodded quickly, aware he should have heaved the doors open the first moment he realized the man's identity. From inside the illustrious throne room, the Supreme Granisian atop her beautiful throne shifted her attention to the massive doors at the end of the chamber lurching open with Tavin behind, powerfully stepping in to find the other members of the Senior Council assembled before her. Watching their eyes, the rest of them turned to face Tavin striding forward and breathing hard. He was obviously exhausted from his long ride, a stubble beard set in on his usually clean face. As he marched passed the aureate columns of the chamber along the white marble floor, he looked up to find the Supreme Granisian the weariest he had ever seen her. Even high atop the staircase where her throne sat, her regal appearance looked drained and at its end. Before he could make it to the line of other men before her and bow, she sighed with relief at his presence and spoke.

"You sensed this disturbing occurrence to the west as well, Tavin?" she asked hurriedly. The Warrior of Light nodded yes as he attempted to collect his thoughts and respond.

"Yes, Your Eminence," he returned shortly after. "I rode back for the capital as fast as I could immediately after to provide my council." There was a troubled sigh from down the row of men, prompting Tavin to look down with heated eyes toward General Sodric, turning to face him.

"Your effort is appreciated, Warrior of Light but the Supreme Granisian has already made a decision on how to respond to this Drakkaidian attack," he informed flatly, running a rough hand through his short grey hair. Tavin narrowed his eyes at once, throwing the ends of his blue and golden cape over his shoulder.

"Unless you know something I don't, this occurrence can neither be confirmed as Drakkaidian nor an attack, general," Tavin spoke not missing a beat and turning his head back to Mary. "Your Eminence, I don't know what you've decided in my absence but I implore you to hold until you have heard what I have to report."

"We have a report from the Granisian of the Temple of Light, Sir Tieloc, and any information you have to offer this council is obviously inaccurate if you are suggesting this attack was not caused by Drakkaidia." Realizing her council was about to explode in argument once more Mary raised her pink gloved hand for silence with a look of intolerance on her smooth face.

"That is quite enough from everyone," she sounded as powerfully as her delicate voice would allow. "I will have order among my Senior Council or you will be removed from it." Turning to face Tavin, her focused eyes locked onto his. "Tavin, I wish to hear your perspective of this latest disturbance as well. As I understand it there was a surge of dark power in the Border Mountains four days ago and another yesterday. Is this what you felt?" The Warrior of Light collected himself once more as he turned his attention back to the Supreme Granisian to nod yes.

"That is correct, Your Eminence. As I was traveling with Ril I sensed a massive explosion of dark power to the north. I can't say for certain because the Border Mountains are a very big place but if I had to guess I would say the source was around the portal to the void where the Sword of Granis now rests. The second that I felt yesterday was much closer to home, somewhere around the Battlemount."

"Yes, this is what the Granisian of the Temple of Light informed me as well," she nodded in agreement. "What I need to know is what caused this display of power? Is it possible that the God of Darkness has escaped the void?" Tavin immediately shook his head no.

"No, Your Eminence, I don't believe so," he assured her quickly. "As long as the Sword of Granis remains to lock the seal in place, Drakkan is trapped inside the void. If his power was loose on the world, trust me when I say we would know it. This is not the work of Drakkan." Mary looked at him with uncertain eyes, searching his for the confidence she so desperately needed to ascertain the truth of what had happened.

"Then what is responsible for this occurrence, Tavin?" she pressed, a hint of desperation in her voice. Tavin breathed deeply, shifting his weight between one leg to the other.

"I sensed something that I'm sure no one else here could," he began slowly, "but I need everyone to hear me out before stopping me so no one jumps to any hasty conclusions."

Tavin glanced to Sodric, already eyeing him distrustfully. "As I said, the Sword of Granis remains at rest over the portal to the void, but after the surprisingly potent detonation of power there I could feel something out of place. My connection to the sword has been off ever since and I fear something is wrong with it. I can't tell you what caused either of the disturbances we felt because I don't know, but I tell you now, there is no reason and no evidence from what I felt to suggest that Drakkaidia was responsible." With an audible huff of vexation, General Tycond stood forward to speak straight to Mary.

"Your Eminence, the Warrior of Light is beating around the bush here," he spoke callously puffing his chest until the buttons over his elaborate uniform threatened to burst off. "It's simple logic: the only origin of dark magic in the world is Drakkaidia. It they were not responsible for this disruption of elemental order then who was? There can be no other suspect and therefore no other culprit. We must assume this was direct action to instigate conflict."

"If it was, then you're playing right into their hands, general," Tavin spoke impatiently. "No other culprit, you say? As any Elemental Warrior will tell you, general, elemental order is disrupted more often than not by natural causes. There is an entire world of forgotten and lost magic out there. Assuming this disturbance was caused with intent by Drakkaidia just because you don't know where else it could have originated is not only reckless but foolish as well." Sodric rolled his eyes and raised the tone of his voice.

"The only foolish thing to do here would be to wait for another of these dark 'explosions,' as the Warrior of Light puts them, to strike again. He himself confirms that the second disturbance was closer to Grandaria than the first—would he have us wait for the next to occur at the gates of Galantia? No word has been received from the Battlemount yet—for all we know these explosions of power could be destroying everything around them."

"And for all we know they may be nothing," Tavin chimed in, stepping forward to garner Mary's attention. "The bottom line here, Your Eminence, is that we *don't* know. For all our bickering, none of us do. So before you act against Drakkaidia for something it may have had nothing to do with, let us investigate. Send me to the portal, me alone so I get there faster, and I'll personally see what is amiss. I know the Sword of Granis better than anyone—let me inspect it to see if something is wrong." The chamber went quiet then, all eyes turning up to the Supreme Granisian, staring at Tavin intently. She breathed deeply and looked down to her hands as if running all the facts at her disposal through her mind. After an agonizingly long minute for Tavin she at last nodded and brought her gaze back to the men before her.

"So be it," she decreed softly, to which Tavin loosened with relief. Seeing the frustration flush to the faces of the generals ready to challenge her decision, she spoke to preclude another argument. "And while Tavin is inspecting the portal to the void, Sodric and his recently returned patrol will depart for the Battlemount to inspect it." They fell silent then, satisfied for the moment. Mary let a large huff of vexation out, staring through the faces of the seven men before her. She could see dangerous dissonance down the middle of her council greater than the divide they had been dealing with in Drakkaidia for years. "All of you are right in respects. There is no concrete proof to link these disturbances to Drakkaidia so we will not jump to that conclusion, but common sense states we should be on edge with our dark neighbor to the west. Tavin, I will rescind my previous decision to prepare for immediate battle at the Wall of Light until you return with your report, but you are to make haste in doing so. If another of these disturbances is detected closer to Grandaria by the Granisian of the Temple of Light my previous order will stand. What you do not consider in your argument, Tavin, is that if this has nothing to do with Drakkaidia as you hope then Verix Montrox and the High Priest Zalnaught will be sensing these disturbances as well. Surely they will be as unnerved by this as we are and that may spark further unrest in the rogue troops in the war zone."

Mary stood then, her regal authority emanating from her every word.

"Whether we wish it or not, I believe we stand on the brink of conflict. I will not make a move that will lead us to war when we can resolve our differences diplomatically, but I will not stand by as Drakkaidian troops continue to build and threaten our borders. Tavin, I suggest you hurry to the portal at once." Somewhat taken aback at Mary's uncharacteristic burst of authority, the Warrior of Light slowly bowed.

"I take my leave then," he stated rising, holding the Supreme Granisian's gaze for another moment. Though he could tell she was trying to display resolute confidence in her decision, he saw the insecure desperation mirrored in her eyes. She was frightened. She carried the weight of the world on her back through her actions and for the first time she could feel its hulking mass threatening to crush her if she faltered. Though Tavin could sympathize from his experience in the Days of Destiny, as he turned to make his way back to the Gate Yard and the portal to the void he felt a pang of fear tugging at him in the back of his mind. If the situation did spiral out of control, Mary would not be strong enough to lead Grandaria at war. It would fall to him, the Warrior of Light, to assume her power. He breathed deeply as he exited the throne room and started back down through the Golden Castle. As he did in the days before his final stand against Drakkan all those years ago, he could feel a wave of inevitability crashing through him like something was coming he could not escape. He had to get to that portal fast.

Chapter 12

<u>Embarking</u>

Zephyr stood on the highest branch of a towering pine tree amidst the many others that rose from the rocky terrain along the eastern border of the Iairian Mountain Chain, a focused and serious expression mounted on his beaked face. It was a beautiful sight even in the cloudy afternoon in which he found himself. Beyond the rocky basin of the mountains, rolling green fields drew on before him as far as his acute purple eyes could see. Just beyond lay the southern border of Grandaria that led into the eastern half of the Southland—someplace he could not believe he was about to go. After what happened to both him and Edge years ago they had promised themselves they would never return for any reason, yet now they marched toward it with resolute speed as sure as the sun would set that evening.

The little sprite shook his head as the thought bounced through it once more. He still couldn't believe the situation he found himself in. It seemed like only yesterday that he and Edge were wandering the northern regions of the Southland scrounging for work, yet now here they were a week after the incident at the Grandarian Battlemount on a mission from a dead Mystic Sage to save the world with a girl harboring the spirit of the God of Darkness in her and a party of sorcerers from Drakkaidia after them. He wanted to yank out his tail feathers just thinking about it. They were walking straight into trouble on more fronts than he could count and both he and Edge knew it. Remembering the consequences of failure and the opportunity this job presented for his partner, however, Zephyr relaxed and nodded to reassure himself this had to be done. It was a chance for Edge to gain control of his life—to finally confront it and stop it from happening. Edge was his only friend in the world and he had to be there for him through whatever was in store for them. The

Maven would need him now more than ever. Zephyr knew his partner almost better than he knew himself and he had known from the beginning it wouldn't be easy for Edge to cope with the fact that he was supposed to be something other than a Maven. It was the only thing he knew anymore and all this Scion of the Order of Alberic business wasn't going to be an easy pill for him to swallow.

As he wrapped up his thoughts, Zephyr detected the faint sound of feet moving through foliage beneath him and opened his bright purple wings to leap off the branch he was perched on. Scanning the rocky basin he found his two human companions walking past the base of the tree and lofted down to their level. Edge, walking steadily ahead of Kaylan who always kept several steps behind, eyed his winged partner as he appeared through the branches of the pine and wordlessly broadened his right shoulder to allow him a place to land. Kaylan jumped in silent surprise as his tiny figure touched down on the Maven's black clad form. They had been strenuously marching south toward the eastern Southland for a week now but she hadn't grown accustomed to him descending out of nowhere to drop down in front of her face. She repositioned the pack slung over her back full of the provisions she and Edge had gathered after hurriedly disappearing from the destroyed Battlemount and the final disappearance of Zeroan. They had not wanted to remain there any longer than necessary after the sage's warning that Zalnaught's minions were upon them already, and took little time in fleeing from where the girl named Kaotica had appeared. She shuddered at the thought of the name and the dark power that now slept inside her answering to it. Kaylan had not been the same since learning of her possession by Drakkan's power. She felt dirty and unworthy of calling herself a Grandarian with the soul of their enemy festering inside her. Kaylan lowered her head to the bumpy earth she traversed and fought to resist the urge to cry yet again. She had wanted to every second since they retreated from the Battlemount that morning, trying to stay strong for the journey now before her to put all this right and save herself from the darkness inside.

Looking back to the blond haired Grandarian as she put her head down once more, Zephyr observed the grief encompassing her visage and tried his best to smile.

"Good news, you two," he started merrily from behind his wide beak. Kaylan came back to her senses upon hearing the sprite's voice for the first time since morning and forced herself to snap out of her depression, lifting her head to face him. "You can't see it from here but we're coming up to the southern border of Grandaria. If we keep on like this we ought to be there by tomorrow evening. It's out of the rocky mountainside and into the easy rolling hills for a while." Kaylan did her best to return the Sky Sprite's smile and nod.

"That is good news," she returned quietly. "My feet are already starting to get sore from all these rocks." Both of them heard a sigh from the other member of their trio and eyed him peculiarly.

"There is a lot worse ground we have to cover than this," he stated mechanically, dismissing her complaint. "What's the bad news?" Zephyr turned to frown at his partner, once more dismayed at his tactlessness to the poor girl.

"I didn't say there was any, Edge," the sprite recoiled unhappily. Edge kept his gaze focused ahead of them but responded immediately.

"Good news without bad news is just news, isn't it?" he stated quickly. "The bad news is that storm you saw that's been building ahead is going to pour on us later tonight. We'll have to stay close to the rocks and the trees for cover until it passes." Kaylan sighed deeply at this, her feigned smile fading to a frown. It was as if he purposely spoke to turn whatever hope she had around and show her the negative. Biting her tongue once more, she pressed on through the silence putting her head back down to the earth. Zephyr shot his eyes back to Edge with a look of intolerant impatience burning through them. When the Maven only kept his gaze ahead on the road before them, Zephyr sighed loudly and wordlessly lifted off to keep scouting ahead.

The trio kept on at Edge's demanding pace for the remainder of the day until the sun sank at last behind the peaks of the Iairian Mountain Chain to the west, blanketing them in a heavy veil of darkness. They made camp amid one of the last groups of thick pine trees before the rugged basin turned into the flowing hills of the border. To Zephyr's spiteful delight, the storm Edge anticipated moved past them in the late afternoon and the starry sky was nearly revealed in it's entirety through the towering pine branches. Edge collected wood for another small fire and set to work warming some rations for their dinner while Kaylan swept away a patch of foliage to place her bed for the evening. As they finished their meals in silence once again, Zephyr dropped out of the branches to land on a log next to Kaylan. Edge eyed him emotionlessly, noting his fatigue. The sprite outstretched his small feathered arms and yawned, his wide beak gaping. Kaylan couldn't help but spread a small smile down to him as she finished a bite of bread from their meager meal.

"Somebody's tired," she observed cheerfully. The sprite finished his yawn and met her gaze with half open eyes and drooping wings.

"You try flying up and down pine trees trying to dodge freak branches all day and see if you fair any better, miss," he returned with a soft smile, scratching his white feathered chest. Kaylan giggled a little, brushing a lock of her golden hair away from her face and behind her ear.

"I can only imagine," she said wistfully. "It must be so amazing to fly. I know it's not the same as with you but my father always told me stories about how thrilling it was for him in the Days of Destiny." Zephyr nodded but shrugged as well.

"It's more a way of life for me, but then I'm usually on the job when I fly these days so it can be a workout sometimes." He shot a playful glance at Edge, who returned it with an inert look that said he missed the humor. Kaylan shifted her eyes to Edge as well, noticing the weariness in his pale eyes.

"Well how about I give both of you a break tonight and take the first shift of watch," she offered, speaking to Edge. "You and Zephyr do it every night—why don't you let me help?" Edge folded his arms and exhaled softly, the worn blue tunic under his black vest swaying in a passing breeze.

"I'm supposed to be protecting you, not the other way around," he informed her quickly. She frowned at this.

"That doesn't mean you have to deprive yourself of rest. You look as tired as your partner—why don't you try to get some sleep for once?" The Maven at last met her gaze and tightened his frame, struggling to formulate what he had to say.

"I don't sleep around people, Kaylan," he informed her at last. She cocked her head uncertainly at this with an incredulous look on her face.

"What does that mean?" she asked with an offended tone in her voice. "My eyes work as well as yours, Edge. Let me help. We're in this thing together until the end—you're going to have to learn to trust me."

"Zephyr and I keep the watch, Kaylan," he returned impatiently. "And I don't sleep around people." Kaylan shook her head incredulously and stood.

"Why are you being this way?" she grilled, all the built up frustration from his dismissive and insulting manner toward her since they met culminating in her voice. "Why can't you just let me help every once in a while, Edge? I'm not some helpless little girl that you have to baby-sit; I can take care of myself the same as you! If you're going to treat me like I'm inferior and useless on this entire quest we won't succeed!" Edge rose to meet her at this, anger flaring in his eyes.

"First off, the only way we're going to succeed is that you recognize you *are* inferior to me when it comes to keeping us out of harm's way and in making decisions about our safety. I know the real world and what's out there hiding in it ready to snatch the life right out of you that you've only heard stories about from your parents. Second, when I say something I mean it. I can't sleep around people so don't tell me I can. There are things about me a sheltered little celebrity like you can't possibly understand—things that you should pray to Granis you never find out." The Maven suddenly stopped short, realizing a faint red mist of energy was bubbling to life around him. Kaylan saw it as well and cut off what she was about to retaliate with. Edge exhaled deeply and loosened his body, restoring the impassive visage that usually rested over his face. The palpable mist around his body dissipated quickly after. When he opened his pale gray eyes once more, Edge faced both Kaylan and Zephyr staring at him uncertainly. He sighed and turned, marching out of the camp. "I'll be keeping watch. Get some rest."

Watching as the coarse boy disappeared into the darkness of night, Kaylan couldn't believe her ears. She stood astounded for a long moment, before at last taking a seat next to Zephyr and burying her head in her hands. The sprite didn't have much experience dealing with this kind of emotion particularly from a human girl and wasn't sure what to say, but scooted himself to her side to put a miniature hand on her arm. Before he could think of anything Kaylan spoke, trying to suppress tears.

"I can't do this, Zephyr," she told him trying to fight back emotion. "This is going to be hard enough without having to deal with him the entire time. I don't know what to do. Why does he hate me? What did I ever do to him?" Zephyr looked up through the mess of hair draped in front of her face to see tears rolling down her cheeks. He exhaled deeply and took a seat beside her, his small frame dwarfed by hers.

"Kaylan, I think it's time I told you something about Edge," he said quietly. The girl forced herself to stop and look down at him, interest replacing her frustration. "Because at this point if he hasn't told you I don't think he's planning on it, and you need to know to be around him as much as you're going to be." Kaylan put her arms back around her sides and stared down expectantly, waiting. Aware he had her full attention, the sprite began. "You saw that red light around him just then, didn't you?" She nodded and replied yes, her curiosity taking hold. "You know from the spirit of that Zeroan fellow that he's got a power inside him but you have no idea what it is or what it's capable of." Zephyr broke his gaze from Kaylan and put it on the fire before them. "Well I do, and trust me, you never want to see it in full effect. Edge is a troubled young man, Kaylan. I didn't meet him until a few years back when he saved me in the eastern Southland but I've since learned about his past. Edge wasn't always the person that he is today. He isn't a Maven because he wanted to become one—it's the only way he knows to keep himself under control. You see, Edge was born in a little village in the forests around Windrun City. ...A village that he destroyed when he was just a child."

"Destroyed?" Kaylan repeated worriedly, to which the Sky Sprite nodded once.

"When Edge tells you he can't sleep around people it isn't because he doesn't trust you, Kaylan, it's because he's concerned for you. Edge has a power that reflects and reveals itself with his emotions. When he's happy and at peace nature blooms and animals follow him around; when he's sad it starts to rain; and when he's angry or under too much stress... bad things happen. Rocks shatter, the ground tears open around him, animals, people, or anything else around him... dies. The very air around his body explodes. This first showed itself in his childhood when he started having a dream every night. Every time it's the same. In his dream Edge is tied up in some giant building where he's beaten and thrown into this pool full of shimmering water. He always wakes up after that but whenever he has this dream his power comes alive in his sleep and... horrible things happen. That night when he was a child the dream was so strong that he leveled his village and killed everyone in it. He ran away overcome with grief until he was taken in by a party of Mavens that found him living alone in the forests. They trained him to be one of them and how to control his emotion to keep the power from appearing. He took to it quickly and over the years has earned a reputation among his colleagues as one of the best in the business. That's where he got his handle—he strikes like the edge of lightning.

"But after a while the Mavens he ran with turned from Blue to Red so he broke away from them and hooked up with me. Ever since Edge has been the way he is. He stays emotionless and objective to keep himself focused on the task at hand and away from his emotions. He tries to rest as often as he can but he never truly sleeps unless we know for certain that we're far enough away from people that if he had the dream and the power came out with it no one could be hurt. Otherwise he makes me watch him while he rests to be sure he never really falls asleep. It's a hard life but that's the way he thinks it has to be. There have been times even with me when he'd rather be dead than alive, but his power won't let him take his life. It's kept him alive when he should have died several times—some by his own hand. We never knew what the power was or where if came from until now, if what the sage said was true. All he knows is that he's killed too many innocent people for him to be reckless with his emotions and let them get the best of him, so he keeps them in check. He never gets close to people because he won't ever risk his power comprising their safety. So while it may seem like he just doesn't care and he's full of hate, he acts that way because he does care. That's why Edge is the way he is, Kaylan. I'm sorry I didn't tell you the truth until now but I was hoping he would do it himself." There was a long silence after the little sprite finished, with Kaylan staring into the slow burning fire before them.

"Thank you for telling me, Zephyr," she at last spoke, "but I still don't know what to do. If he doesn't trust me enough to tell me this how are we supposed to do this together? If he won't open himself up at all how can I rely on him to be there for me? The only hope we have of overcoming all we have before us is working together. If we don't trust each other we don't have a chance. What should I do?" She turned down to face Zephyr, already staring up at her with searching eyes. He kept his rich purple eyes fixed on hers.

"Advice is what you ask for when you already know the answer but wish you didn't," he said abruptly. "I don't know what to do to get through to him, Kaylan, but whatever it is you're going to have to do it." She raised an eyebrow uncertainly with obvious confusion tearing through her. Zephyr lifted off the log to hover in front of her. "I've already talked to him about this but he won't listen to me. The bottom line is, Edge has been through a lot and change is not something that comes easily for him. I've been trying to open his eyes to new things and other possibilities for years now but I never make a dent. But when I see him look at you, another human that he's responsible for and knows he's going to be around for longer than anyone else in years, I see an opportunity for you to make a difference. I know you have enough to worry about on your own and this isn't fair of me to ask of you, but he isn't going to open up on his own. You're going to have to help him do it. Remember, I know it seems backward but he's being this way because he cares. He just doesn't know how to express it because he's never had reason to before." Kaylan held his gaze for another moment, observing the sincerity present within.

"You really care about him, don't you Zephyr?" she stated more than asked. The Sky Sprite let a little smile spread across his wide yellow beak.

"He's my partner," he confirmed loyally. "Trust me, it's a hard exterior to break through but once you do you'll realize there's a truly thoughtful boy inside." Watching the little creature hover before her Kaylan couldn't help but smile as a small wave of understanding washed over her.

"Thanks, Zephyr," she stated again, rising from her seat on the log. "I'll try my best to do what I can. Maybe I'll try to get some sleep." Zephyr nodded and smiled, thrusting his wings to propel his miniature form into the sky to keep watch for the night.

Chapter 13

The Woods

    Edge knelt on the forest floor surrounded by a thick collection of dense trees, intently staring down at a broad brown root protruding from the earth. He let out a dissatisfied huff of irritation as he mumbled something to himself and quickly seized a small knife from one of the numerous black pouches around his waist.
    "Spore traps," he mouthed to himself, shaking his head. Lowering the small blade to the base of the root he flicked his wrist up to slice through it, revealing a viscose purple liquid oozing forth from either side. The boy let out another breath of annoyance before sheathing his blade and drawing the much larger one strapped to his back. "Poison, spore traps," he corrected himself. Rising amid the dense forest shrubbery with his flowing blue scarf falling over his shoulder, he took a sweeping look around his position to locate the three large bulbs nestled into the rich forest soil. Reaching over with the tip of his blade to swiftly tap the one closest to him, all three instantly burst upward from the ground and split in their middles to reveal mouths agape with rows of razor-sharp teeth jutting out for him. The head like bulbs were bolstered up by thin but sturdy stems that sprang from the sharp flowering leaves where the bulb had once waited for its prey to arrive. Swinging his blade in a perpendicular arch to the ground the Maven caught the first of them through its long stem, severing the otherwise impenetrable head from the body instantly. Quickly sidestepping to his right he avoided the stream of spraying purple liquid from the wailing severed stem and dodged the second attacking plant rearing out for him. Seeing the third of the trio about to lunge for him as well, Edge leapt and rolled over the green earth toward the second spore trap still struggling to reach out to him. As the third opened its gaping jaw to latch onto Edge and stream

its poisonous venom into him, the second attacking plant turned to where the Maven had disappeared past it and put its thin neck directly in the other's path. Clamping down on its kin's stem, the third spore trap severed the bulb from the body as Edge had to the first. Recoiling in surprise, the last of the deadly plants attempted to withdraw back to the flowery shelter in the earth but was cut short by a small throwing knife jetting through its stem to thud into a tree trunk behind it.

Softly exhaling and watching the poisonous purple liquid bleed from the last stem, Edge rose and placed his worn broadsword behind his back once more. He casually tossed his blue scarf behind his back and walked past the trio of decapitated spore traps to wrench his knife out of the thick tree trunk, carefully avoiding the pools of purple blood soaking the flora around his footing. No sooner than placing his gloved hand over the miniature hilt of the embedded knife, however, the sweeping sound of an object bursting from the forest floor behind him caught his attention. Edge's eyes burst open, guessing he must have missed one of the spore traps hiding underneath the foliage. As he was about to wheel around and dodge the incoming bulb before it could latch onto him, another sound echoed into his ears—the slashing of steel into the organic assailant. Finally spinning around with his knife free from the tree trunk ready to be thrown, Edge found Kaylan with a short sword in hand standing over the fourth spore trap, its bulb severed from the rest of its body. Edge raised an eyebrow as he stared at the Grandarian girl in surprise. She stood in a relaxed but honed battle stance lowering her sword, her shining blond hair cascading over her shoulders. Flipping her head back to clear it away from her face her beautiful blue eyes and the rest of face came into view, moving to meet his temporarily stunned gaze. She faintly smiled as she grabbed a nearby leaf to wipe away the purple liquid on the edge of her blade.

"When your father is the Warrior of Light you learn how to use a sword," she smiled faintly, breaking the silence. Edge forced the stunned look from his face and gave a single nod.

"And how to deal with spore traps, it would appear," he replied placing his throwing knife back into one of the silver buckled pouches around his waist. Kaylan nodded as she tucked her short sword that she had managed to keep concealed from him up to this point back inside her gear. As Edge was always dressed in his black Maven garb Kaylan was always adorned with a light blue traveling tunic and form fitting white pants covered at their base by thick blue hiking boots much like the ones her father used to wear in his travels. The large bag slung over her back looked heavy but she had yet to complain about it. Brushing another lock of her golden hair behind her ear, Kaylan at last replied.

"There are spore traps in the wooded area to the north of Eirinor Village," she returned. "We only see them in the summers but you have to know how to deal with them or risk a poisonous bite." Edge held his gaze on her for a moment longer than he should have, once again studying the girl that continued to surprise him time and again, but at last looked down to the gear around his waist and spoke.

"Well there might be more in woods as thick as these here in the eastland so keep your eyes peeled," he spoke before turning to begin his trek once more. Though it was no thank you for possibly saving his life, Kaylan could tell by the tone of his voice he knew she had and she faintly smiled to herself. Leaping past the dead spore traps to catch up behind him, the girl remembered Zephyr's advice from their last conversation back in the borders of Grandaria a few days ago and decided to press him for conversation.

"So Edge," she began getting his attention once more, "where are some of the places you've traveled to over the years? I bet being as a wandering Maven you get to see a lot of different landscapes." Edge looked back and shot her a quick glance but let out a small breath and repositioned his sword over his back.

"When I travel my mind is usually on a job, Kaylan," he answered briskly. "I don't really take in the scenery around me too much." Kaylan did her best to smile and find the most out of his response.

"Oh come on, I'm sure you and Zephyr have had some interesting experiences somewhere exotic before," she pressed. Edge cocked his head.

"I've had plenty of experiences, Kaylan—most of them I don't care to remember," he rejoined, obviously uninterested in where she was leading the conversation. The smile on Kaylan's face slowly faded as she nodded to herself.

"Are most of your memories unhappy ones, Edge?" she asked quietly. The boy kept his gaze out into the forest before him.

"I'd say about all of them are, Kaylan," he responded after a long moment. "And none of them would make very good conversation, especially with a girl like yourself, so..." Kaylan brought her gaze back up to face the back of his head once more. Though she realized he didn't want to let this subject go on any further, she decided he needed to know her feelings if he was ever going to come around. Hurrying her steps she walked beside the boy and looked up to his hard face.

"You know, Zephyr told me a little about your past, Edge," she told him softly. "He told me about your power and how you've struggled with it through your life since you were a child. About you being taken in by Mavens and trained to be the way you are now..." The boy obviously heard her but kept silent. Kaylan broke eye contact but forced herself to continue. "I just want you to know that I'm sorry you have to live as something you have to be because of the burden of your power and not what you might want to be, but I understand you act the way you do because you care. And I know you do. The first time we met you saved me and the boys that day in Eirinor without even knowing who we were. If you were the heartless guy you make yourself out to be you would have walked right past us but you went out of your way to help. That tells me there's a good person inside you, Edge. I appreciate the fact that you don't want to get close to people because you're concerned for them but you don't have to pretend to be something you're not around me. It's only wasting of the person you are. I understand where you're coming from now and I'm not going to judge you based on something you can't control—just as the person you choose to be."

Edge kept moving forward at the same pace but at last glanced down to the girl, again staring up at him with sincere eyes. Seeing him at last respond she smiled.

"And it would be a lot easier for me if the person supposed to protect me would open up a little," she smiled. "If my bodyguard is as grave as the quest we're on I'll lose my sense of humor completely. What do you think?" Edge shot her another surprised glance with an uncertain look harbored in his pale eyes, obviously taken aback at how up front and forgiving this girl could be. He had never encountered anyone that would treat a Maven, especially one as abrasive as he knew he could be, like a real person. Letting the faintest of smiles escape from one side of his mouth, he answered her.

"I think my partner has a big mouth," he responded struggling to hide his smile.

"Beak!" was the shrill exclamation from far above them beyond the tree tops. Edge let a silent chuckle escape from his throat as he raised his head to yell.

"Shouldn't you be using those perceptive senses of yours for tracking?" he called through the forest, causing Kaylan to actually giggle. Hearing her laugh, the Maven rotated his head back to her to roll his eyes and quietly laugh as well, slightly embarrassed. As his eyes fell upon her, however, they instantly morphed from relaxed to the utmost seriousness. He halted at once, his body tightening. Seeing the boy's abrupt transformation, Kaylan stopped as well, almost walking into him in shock. Before she could ask what was wrong he spoke. "Why is it doing that?" Unsure what he could be referring to, Kaylan followed his eyes down onto her midsection. Her face turning uncomfortably red from having him stare at her torso, she at last realized what had captivated him. The pouch in her tunic that contained the Granic Crystal was glowing. Narrowing her eyes she reached in to find the weak crystal flickering. When she just stared at it, Edge spoke once more, urgency in his voice this time. "Kaylan, what's wrong with it?" She shook her head uncertainly, watching as the sputtering light seemed to reach out and shine in a beam behind them. Following the light, she responded as best she could.

"It's pointing," she observed quietly. Edge raised an eye brow.

"At what?" he returned disbelievingly. Kaylan shook her head in uncertainty again. "I don't know but..." She trailed off, forcing Edge to ask her once again. "Well, my father used to tell me stories of the Granic Crystal pointing to warn him about things. Things he couldn't see himself." Edge eyed her tentatively for a moment but at last sharply exhaled.

"I'll believe just about anything anymore," he told her looking around. "I'll backtrack where it's pointing and check it out." Kaylan lowered the crystal and met his gaze with determination of her own.

"I'll go with you," she returned, to which the boy shook his head.

"I can all but disappear in the forest if I want, Kaylan, but only if I'm by myself," he informed her. "I'll do it faster and more efficiently alone. You stay here and hide in these rocks. Keep that crystal close and I'll be back soon." Though she was about to contest his order, Edge quietly leapt back through the trees and was gone from view in a matter of moments. Letting out a sharp breath, Kaylan decided to do as she was bid and crouched down behind the rocks above the ravine they had worked themselves into. Taking a seat with her back to a boulder, she opened her hand with wonder and watched as the Granic Crystal continued to flash and point in the direction Edge had disappeared. As the minutes passed by, she could see the crystal slowly moving the steady little beam of light from where they had come to the ravine behind her. Her curiosity getting the better of her, Kaylan closed her fingers around the crystal and slowly raised her head over the boulder she knelt behind to peer down into the ravine. There was a barren gap in the trees exposed enough to yield a straight path with a wall of rocks on her side and the towering trees jutting into the sky on the other.

Scanning the ravine for several long moments, a slow movement from the left behind the trees at last caught her attention. The girl's eyes opened wide and her body tightened as view of a single rider draped in black robes trotted onto the path between the trees and rocks. Its steed was midnight black as well, doing little to subtract from the figure's foreboding appearance. Though its hood was raised to mask his face, the figure slowly swept the ravine with its eyes, obviously taking care to note every detail. Opening her fingers to reveal the Granic Crystal in the silence, Kaylan saw it was pointing directly to the horsemen below. She swallowed hard, nervously wondering who this person could be to warrant a warning from the Granic Crystal itself. Guessing she didn't want to find out, she slowly sunk her head back behind the boulder before her and turned her attention back to the crystal. Closing her eyes to whisper a prayer to Granis for Edge to make a swift return, she didn't notice the light from the Granic Crystal intensify and slowly rotate behind her in the opposite direction. As the seconds ticked by with her eyes shut, the luminous stone grew lighter and lighter until at last Kaylan was forced to open her eyes to observe the glow below her. Worriedly following the new trail of light leading behind her, Kaylan's heart rose into her throat. It was as if the Granic Crystal itself was panicking. Slowing turning her near trembling head around, Kaylan's aghast eyes blasted open and she threw her back against the wall of the boulder.

There was another dark rider, hooded and cloaked in black robes streaked with crimson mounted not ten feet away from her, staring down with masked eyes. It sat motionless for what seemed like an eternity but at last descended from its steed with its armored boots clamping down on the rocky earth beneath them. Turning toward her and motioning for her to stand Kaylan instinctively drew the short sword hidden behind her back and rose to wordlessly point it out at the figure. He did not speak but laughed and made a gripping gesture with his open hand. Kaylan was shocked to find her weapon ripped out of her grasp and cast aside far to her right with a sweeping motion of the figure's arm. A wave of fear suddenly overcoming her, she tripped and painfully fell back to the rock behind her, watching as the figure drew near. It was then that she realized what the figure was. It was just like in her father's stories from the Days of Destiny; a dark clad figure with power like that of a Mystic Sage.

It was a Dark Mage of the Black Church of Drakkan.

The ones Zeroan had warned then about—warned them to avoid at all costs. Now one was standing mere feet away from her with a twisted smile on his face. As he reached down for her Kaylan threw forth her fist to slap his arm away but something happened then she had not expected. The second she threw her hand forward and made contact with the figure, the Granic Crystal burst alive and violently shined its light forward, forcing the Dark Mage back screaming out in pain. As the light faded the next moment, Kaylan stared awestruck as the mage grasped at his arm, dripping with blood. The next moment she could hear the other dark figure below in the ravine coming to attention and driving his horse forward. Terrified as the Dark Mage before her spun his head to face her and throw his burned hand down, she raised the Granic Crystal again defensively.

"Oh I won't be making that mistake again," the mage spoke with malice dripping from his voice as it raised a hand to make a gripping gesture once more. This time it was not an object on her person that was seized but Kaylan's very body itself. Feeling the air rushing from her lungs as her entire form slowly rose into the air, she dropped the Granic

Crystal and tried to grasp at something choking her that wasn't there. Desperately fighting for air and struggling to be free of the mage's constricting telekinetic grip, Kaylan watched in incredulity as a large dagger flew from behind her to land straight in the mage's middle, knocking him off his feet and onto the ground. Kaylan dropped out of the air to land on the rock with a thud, oxygen rushing back into her lungs. Before she knew what happened Edge leapt from behind her boulder, his long blue scarf trailing behind his every movement. He hurriedly took hold of her arm and pulled her to her feet, giving her a moment to catch her lost breath. With the stunned girl in tow, he raced to the downed mage to vengefully twist the blade in his middle before wrenching it free. Practically throwing Kaylan up to the horse behind them, he screamed at her to mount, seeing another rider appear from the ravine and two more from behind the hill they had just climbed after killing the spore traps. Leaping onto the horse himself he yelled for her to hold onto him and kicked the animal forward, blasting into the trees with three Dark Mages trailing behind.

Chapter 14

Evil Angel

  After downing one of the Dark Mages of Drakkaidia in the forests late that afternoon, Edge and Kaylan rode on in the woods through the evening and into the night with their remaining pursuers just out of visual range. Though their horse was burdened with two and an ill tempered beast being Drakkaidian bred, Edge managed to maneuver it through the forests in clever patterns taking twisting routes that left the three trailing mages frequently confused and guessing where they had gone. Edge had whistled for Zephyr to return to them as the chase began, instructing him to keep a close eye behind and ahead of them for any traps or tricks the dark magicians might employ. After nearly two hours of darting through the dense forests of the upper eastland, it was pitch black and their horse was clearly tiring of carrying two. With the Granic Crystal beginning to shine brighter once more, Kaylan shouted ahead to Edge.

  "They're getting closer, Edge!" she exclaimed, looking back and expecting them to appear any moment. The Maven did the same, gritting his teeth and nodding.

  "I know," he replied loudly. Running a collection of ideas through his head, only one seemed plausible to get them out of this situation. Pulling to the side of a large oak tree with huge twisting roots jutting up around it, Edge pulled back on the reins for the horse to stop. He wheeled back to Kaylan, staring at him incredulously.

  "Why did you stop!?!" she asked disbelievingly.

  "My little trick routes will only keep working for so much longer and then this horse is going to die on us. We can't both keep riding so I'll try to distract them on the horse while you hide here. Hopefully I can outsmart or outrun these things in the night with a few tricks I still have up my sleeve and I can backtrack to you by morning." Kaylan stared him down with skeptical eyes.

"Edge, you don't know who these men are," she stated worriedly. "It doesn't matter how skilled you are with a sword—they can kill you with a flick of their wrist." Edge's face twisted with impatience, hearing the steadily growing sound of hoof beats behind them in the night.

"Dammit, Kaylan, we don't have time for this!" he shouted in a whisper. "Remember what I told you before—I can disappear and lose them but not when I have you with me. Trust me—I'll come back for you." Hearing their pursuers encroaching on their position, Kaylan furiously shook her head and leapt off the horse. Before she knelt down to hide under the massive twisting roots she reached into her tunic pocket and extended her hand to the Maven.

"At least take the Granic Crystal," she begged, desperation in her voice.

"If something happens to me that will be your only protection," Edge refused, pushing her hand back to her. "I've never botched a job yet, Kaylan. I don't intend to now. I promise I'll be back." She stared at his gray eyes locked back on hers for a long moment, wanting to say something. Before she could figure out what it was Edge kicked his horse forward and motioned for her to hide. Watching him disappear into the night, Kaylan at last shook off her distress and crawled into the roots of the oak. Carefully concealing the light of the Granic Crystal in her hands, she listened as the three Dark Mages approached from another path and raced past her.

As Kaylan lay nestled in the darkness of the night, Edge catapulted his steed on through the myriad trees until reaching a knoll that could be seen from the distance. Turning the exhausted animal and drawing his sword to raise over his head he screamed and reared the horse back to make as much noise as possible to draw the attention of the mages. When he could finally see them racing down a hillside after him, he yanked the horse to turn it and kicked it off down the knoll toward another of the forest ravines below him. He knew the horse was tired but as long as he could draw them off of Kaylan long enough for her to make an escape he could disappear into the night and find her the next day.

The Dark Mages would allow no such thing. Though they were slowly gaining on him and they might have been in range for a blade in the next several minutes, Edge forgot to account for the range of their darkly empowered magic. Looking back to check the distance between them, the Maven witnessed the closest of them raising a hand and pointing at him with a crimson flare of light suddenly flashing around it. The next instant Edge was lifted off his horse and blown into a patch of forest foliage, painfully landing on his front. Struggling to rise and reaching for his sword he had dropped, he realized he would not have time to grope through the dark for it with the mages already on top of him. Reaching behind his back to summon his crossbow, the Maven opened it and heaved back its string to loose a steel bolt into one of the mage's hoods, dropping it instantly. Before he could so much as stand to reload another bolt the other mages were on him, leaping off their horses to seize him with their telekinetic power. Forced to relinquish his weapon to grasp at his neck like Kaylan had earlier in the day, Edge watched as the mage lifted him off the earth to dangle before them in the air. Slowly walking forward to stare through his hood with vengeful eyes, the mage spoke.

"Where is the vessel, boy?" he grilled threateningly. Though Edge was about to tell the mage he should try looking up his backside, he was suddenly awestruck to find the mage he had drilled in the face with a bolt from his crossbow rising. The man holding him followed his eyes to his comrade and darkly chuckled from deep in his throat. "Simple steel will not stop us, boy. Now tell me where the vessel is before I crush your bones inside you." Battling for breath, Edge brought his gaze back to the foe before him and tightened his face to spit in the other's. The mage recoiled and summoned his other hand to take hold of Edge as well. "If you wish to die then so be it, but die with the knowledge that we will find her before the sun rises." With that, the mage tightened his fingers in the air before him, pressing Edge to the point where he could feel his very bones ready to snap from the force.

He could feel it starting to happen. The inevitability of death surrounding him again, a boiling sensation burning his blood began to build around him and the faint red mist formulated around his skin. Before the mage even noticed what was happening to his prisoner before him, however, he abruptly froze as if something had just struck him from behind. Just when the world was about to go completely black around him and his power emerge, Edge heard a loud explosion from beyond the knoll he had just passed over. The mage loosened his grip on the boy and spun his head around, looking back to the source of the disturbance as if he had felt something in the air itself. Then, through the night's silence, a black mass of smoldering robes came flying down over the knoll to land just beyond the group in the ravine with a loud thud. Turning his eyes down to observe it, Edge saw the body of another mage—lifeless. He narrowed his eyes in disbelief. It looked like he had been shot out of cannon. When one of the mages at the other side of the ravine looked over the figure and turned back to mutter something to the others in an ancient Drakkaidian dialect, the mage holding Edge foolishly loosened his grip to the point where Edge could slightly move. Rearing his legs back to gain momentum, he threw them forward to kick his attacker back into the ground. Reaching to his sides to pull forth duel daggers in either hand, he prepared to make what stand he could before his power exploded.

He quickly discovered that the Dark Mages were far more preoccupied with the mounting power level on the horizon to worry about a Maven. As the seconds ticked by, a dark purple light shone brightly over the knoll until a speeding figure at last flew over it to careen to the ravine, splitting the earth around it as it landed. As the figure rose and the light from its body began to fade, Edge recognized the pair of jagged glowing wings of purple light radiating off its shoulders, shaped like those of a bat. The Maven let out a breath of disbelief upon seeing the dark form of Kaotica rising and letting the wings behind her fade into the night in a black mist. Looking around with a charming smirk, she eyed him as well and raised an eyebrow.

"Well hello there, cutie," she spoke teasingly, walking forward with hands on her hips. She appeared exactly as she had the last time they met at the Battlemount. An intricate black and white tunic and short purple skirt tightly were pressed against her slender body with long black boots and draping black hair flowing down her back. As she drew closer her rich purple eyes faintly shone with glimmering purple light. "I told you I'd see you again. You just can't believe how rude some people are. What's his name back there won't be making that mistake again though. Hey, looks like you've been busy since I saw you with my eyes last. I mean, look at you..." she trailed off with a laugh, running her fingers along the blade of his dagger as if they were toys. Edge pulled them back and grabbed her to pull her away from the advancing mages, uncertainly staring the girl down. Kaotica raised an eyebrow as she stood behind him, resting her chin on his shoulder. "Ah you get protective, huh? Well you should be—I'm worth protecting you know." When Edge merely shot her an incredulous glance and told her to be quiet, she giggled with glee and clapped her hands before her chest. "Fun, fun, fun!" Finally noting the other men clad in black moving toward them, she raised an eyebrow and let her smile dissipate. "And just who are these morons? Not your friends, I hope?"

"You must come with us, girl," one of the Dark Mages said then, reaching out his hand to her as he slowly crept forward. "You are the vessel of Lord Drakkan. Your place is with us." Kaotica raised her eyebrow higher and looked at Edge confused.

"What is this idiot talking about?" she grilled. "'Vessel' makes me sound like some boat or something, when I'm obviously a beautiful woman." Watching as she ran her fingers through her long hair, Edge quickly shook his head and forced her to step back with him.

"They're trying to kill us, girl, so would you just shut up and—"

"I have a name, you know," Kaotica cut him off standing on her tip toes and jutting her face before his. "And it wouldn't kill you to tell me yours either, Edge. Oh wait, I had to find that out for myself because you're so rude you wouldn't tell me before." Before Edge could react one of the Dark Mage's finally leapt forward with a flash of bleeding red energy appearing before him. It blasted Edge off his feet and shone around Kaotica for a moment but appeared to bounce off her body like it was nothing. She spun around to the men in black beyond her with a deep rooted scowl appearing. "Excuse me, we were trying to have a conversation here, jackass. Wait your turn or get lost." With a flick of her instantaneously electrified wrist the closest mage to her was catapulted off his feet to land on his back next to the smoldering one. As she turned her back on them for Edge, struggling to rise once more, another of the mages began muttering a deep chant in the back of his throat and extended his arms toward the girl to completely surround her with crimson energy. Though she stopped in her tracks at first, Kaotica wheeled around with a furious expression on her face.

"What is your problem!?!" she shouted like a child not getting her way. "Are you trying to tickle me or something? Get your filthy grip off me, sicko." When the other two mages joined in trying to take hold of her and the red light around her body only grew, Kaotica's face twisted with rage. "Oh *that* is it. If you guys want to hurt somebody, this is how you do it." Focusing her energy, a purple flash of light exploded around her and the jagged wings of dark light appeared once more. Leaping forward, she blasted across the ravine inches above the ground toward the mages. Moving so quick they could barely see her, Kaotica threw her electrified arm up and ran it through one of the men to cut him in half at his middle. His body detonated with dark light as his halves landed over the earth. Spinning around she rammed her other fist into one of the mage's back, blasting him to the ground. With her open hand, a wave of intense purple energy exploded to life beneath it to turn the ground where the mage lay into a crater. Having seen the girl destroy all three of his fellow mages without breaking a sweat, the final one took an uncertain step backward in terror.

When Kaotica at last turned to him, she touched down over the earth and scowled.

"Boo," she said flatly, expecting the exact reaction she got. The last Dark Mage wheeled around and sprinted as fast as he could back up the knoll and away into the night. As he was disappearing, Edge, having watched the destruction thus far realized they couldn't let any of them escape and shouted out to her.

"Kaotica, go get the last one!" he bellowed. She let the glowing wings on her back disappear along with the electrified light crackling along her body and turned to him placing her hands on her hips once more.

"Now Edge," she spoke dramatically, "I thought you didn't like it when I killed people. Remember what a fit you threw at that place with all the buildings that we were playing with?" Edge grit his teeth at the girl and marched over to her.

"This is different, he's our enemy," he spoke sternly. "If you let him go they'll send more after us faster." Kaotica rolled her eyes and threw her head back to shake off whatever he was feeling for him.

"Oh who cares?" she replied ambling forward. "And if they come back it's just more fun for me. Where are we anyway? Is there anything to do here? I want to have some fun—I'm already bored." Edge was beside himself with anger, not able to believe what a childlike mind she had.

"Listen to me!" he shouted at her. "Can't you pay attention for one minute? The world does not exist to be your little play thing. I couldn't care less about what you want to do and I couldn't care less about you! Turn back into Kaylan right now!" Kaotica stared at him with a confused and hurt look in her suddenly delicate eyes for a long moment. It was as if he had just told a child she couldn't have the toy she wanted and just like a child her temporary sadness turned to a temper tantrum. Scowling in his direction, she rushed up to him and pushed him back with such force he flew off the ground into a tree trunk.

"Fine, you jerk!" she yelled, balling her fists. "You can be such a killjoy sometimes! I don't even know why I like you—you're not *that* cute. I just want to have a little fun and what do you say? You couldn't care less about me and you just want to be with blondie. Fine! Take little blondie back—see if I care! But I'll see you soon and you had better be in a better mood or so help me we won't be friends anymore. Geez..." With that, Kaotica turned her back on him and crossed her arms, an aura of deep purple light forming around her figure. After a few moments the electrified bursts of black and purple light swirled upward together into a field of bright gold that slowly faded to reveal Kaylan falling to the ground, asleep once again.

Chapter 15

Doubt

Despite the fact that Tavin had resurrected the entire populace of Dalastrak with the power of the Holy Emerald after the Days of Destiny when they were killed by the demon horde Valif Montrox had loosed upon them, few of the revived Drakkaidians had returned to their capital city. It had been utterly destroyed from the explosion of the Netherworld upon it, scarred with gaping fissures that ripped through the city to swallow entire portions of it whole. Everything from the plebian slums on the outskirts of town to the royal castle itself had been leveled and what remained were makeshift ruins at best. Even after all the reconstruction over the years by the Loyalists to the Throne, they had done little to restore the city's former dark glory. It still looked dead. The only locale bustling with activity on a constant basis was the expanding military base at the foot of the lone peak that once played host to the royal castle. These days all that remained of it was the gate yard at its base that the Loyalists had christened as the provisional fortress to guard the throne and the Netherworld Portal quietly resting high atop the ruins of the old castle.

Verix Montrox let out a long huff of aggravated fatigue and shifted his weight in front of a window looking down to the ravaged the city. He folded his bulky arms and breathed deep, the chilling wind from outside the provisional citadel in which he stood waving past him to rustle his long red hair in front of his face. He was quietly staring down at the city with a blank look about his usually focused eyes. As he frequently reminded his Loyalists, the city was a solemn reminder of misuse of power and the terrible consequences of continuing down the path his father or Zalnaught would have them travel toward more destruction and death. The prince tightened his face as the latter name entered his mind. His enmity for the manipulative egomaniac to the north had exploded with new life upon their last meeting, aware that if left unchecked the High Priest and his New Fellowship of Drakkan would eventually spark war with Grandaria and his Loyalists. The High Priest's words to him in the Cathedral of Dalorosk echoed through his thoughts constantly—if Verix had any real power Zalnaught would have stopped breathing years ago. There was nothing the prince wished for more, but he had the prudence to predict what would happen if he was to remove the High Priest by force. There was no way Drakkaidia could survive a civil war in its current crippled state. His hands were tied.

Verix closed his penetrating red eyes and lowered his head as more of his confrontation with the High Priest seeped through his thoughts. There was a troubling detail Zalnaught had forced into his mind that he could not dispel. The disturbance at the portal to the void weeks ago still lingered in his mind, unsettling him more every time he thought about it and the cause of which Zalnaught had tried to convince him. Would Tavin really try to remove the Sword of Granis holding the seal over the void world? The possibility made no sense at first, but the more he found himself thinking about the display of dark power that had exploded there the more he found himself obsessing over the idea. There was no other explanation. The level of power he had sensed there and days later further south in the Border Mountains was far beyond Zalnaught or his Dark Mages— even beyond him. The only explanation was that something had tampered with the sword. Verix grit his teeth in fury for even thinking of buying into Zalnaught's story when he was most likely feeding him lies, but the thought would not leave him. Only the Warrior of Light could affect the seal holding Drakkan at bay.

As the prince ran the idea back and forth through the confines of his mind, he heard the large doorway behind him opening. Coming back to his senses, Verix turned with his gray and crimson cape twisting behind him to find his favored captain striding toward him from the now open doorway of his makeshift throne room. He was a large man, not nearly as muscular as Verix himself but foreboding all the same. Upon Verix's return to Dalastrak after the Days of Destiny it was this man, Celztur, who greeted him as the next in line for the throne of Drakkaidia and supported him through all his speeches to the people about the truth of what happened in the Days of Destiny. Celztur was an unflagging patriot to his nation that looked to its long term interests over the biases and unfounded hatred for Grandaria that most harbored. Because of his unflinching loyalty and wisdom to accept the truth that Verix imparted, he was promoted to the newly created position of Captain of Dalastrak. He commanded the city and the small Loyalist forces in Verix's absence and advised the prince directly on matters pertaining to their interests.

Celztur strode forward with his usually grave expression strapped across his battle hardened face, respectfully bowing before Verix as always.

"My liege," he greeted reverently in his deep, rich voice. Verix motioned for him to rise and began to slowly walk toward the door of the compact chamber, ducking his head to avoid passing through Drakkaidian flags of old draped from the ceiling. Celztur followed beside him, getting the impression that the prince wanted a frank discussion as two men and not as a captain and royalty. "I take it you achieved little from your visit to the Cathedral of Dalorosk." Verix let out a long breath of frustration and swept a hand through his thick red hair as they made their way out of the small throne room to a spiraling staircase leading down into the rest of the fortress.

"If anything the tension is compounding further," Verix spoke quietly. "You should have seen the looks we got from the populace while we were riding in. I'm surprised there wasn't an assassination attempt." Celztur grunted as they turned out of the staircase to make their way into a dark hall leading out to a thick protective wall of the fortress facing the city.

"The New Fellow-sheep talk big in their superior numbers and claim the throne is the past but they haven't forgotten who you are, sire," he stated. "They know you are your father's son. They believe steel would bend and shatter should it strike your body." Verix shot his captain a quick glance and shook his head.

"Being my father's son is not the mentality I want them to keep, Celztur," he reminded. "If they are ever going to accept the truth and rejoin us as a united Drakkaidia they can't see the throne as an oppressive force that embraces the hatred Zalnaught fosters behind his lies."

"With respect, sire, they can't see it as weak either," Celztur said softly so as not to let any of the passing Loyalist soldiers around them on the wall hear. "The lies that Zalnaught is feeding them are painting us and the throne as feeble and powerless." Verix breathed hard as they turned down a staircase on the wall for the base of the large courtyard around them.

"Zalnaught is only able to feed them those lies because the people are so hungry they'll eat anything. They merely want the meal that will go down easiest and taste the best to their starving bellies. Accepting the truth is not an easy thing to do." Celztur shook his head, a suddenly frustrated tone lacing his voice.

"If the people are so damn hungry why don't we only give them one story to eat up, sire?" Verix looked to his captain slowly, aware of what he was getting at. Seeing the prince's eyes on him, Celztur pulled closer to harshly whisper in his ear. "Why is that lying maggot not yet rotting in the Netherworld? If Zalnaught is in the way of uniting our country it is our responsibility to remove him. You could single-handedly penetrate the entire Fellowship army and break the miserable vermin in two with your bare hands." Verix shook his head and shot Celztur a glance that told him to hold his tongue.

"We've been through this a hundred times, Celztur," Verix spoke in a whisper, darting around a regiment of passing soldiers. "Our country is not as it once was. Things are so unstable I swear I can feel the ground beneath us shifting at times. If I was to simply kill the High Priest as my father did with such disorder and chaos around us we would never get control back. It would come to civil war and you know we cannot prevail with the numbers we have. Drakkaidia would implode in chaos. I must win back the hearts and minds of the people first." Celztur nodded and broke eye contact from the prince.

"Yes I know, my liege," he admitted. "My apologies. I speak out of place." Verix put a hand over his broad shoulder as they arrived at the gates of the fortress leading into the broken city below.

"You speak your heart, Celztur, which is more than I can hope hear from most of my advisors and generals," Verix told him earnestly. "That is why you are my Captain of Dalastrak. You serve your nation first, not just me. You

Trial of a Maven

watch over the city well, which you must now do once more." Celztur raised an eyebrow.

"You are leaving again so soon, sire?" he asked bemused. Verix nodded as he called to a stable boy that had been watching them to fetch him a horse.

"Yes, captain," he stated. "There was another disturbance of dark power like the one at the portal to the void that I sensed on my way back from the Cathedral of Dalorosk. I am having doubts about the Grandarians. Zalnaught could not in fact have had anything to do with these disturbances because the power I sense is beyond him and his feeble tricks. I need to see for myself just what is going on. If something abroad is out of place that could provide Zalnaught an excuse to spark conflict without directly ordering it himself, I need to contain it. I ride to inspect the portal to the void where I sensed the first of these disturbances, so you will remain and take command in my absence. Be wary of the New Fellowship, Celztur. I can tell Zalnaught is up to something. Guard the fortress and the Netherworld Portal well, my friend." Celztur nodded as he watched Verix mount his horse.

"We will, my liege," he confirmed with a bow. "I wish you speed and success on your journey." Verix bowed his head in acknowledgement and kicked his steed off through the gates of the fortress, speeding down the roads to the remains of his ruined city.

In the mammoth Cathedral of Dalorosk to the north, the High Priest Zalnaught swiftly strode down the halls of the highest levels leading to the small final staircase ascending to the enormous roof at its top. He had just received word from a servant that his Voss Stone was active in his chamber, obviously receiving a message from the Dark Mages deployed to locate the vessel. Rushing to collect it and speed to the open roof of the elaborate cathedral to receive a clear communication, he blasted his way up many levels of the building with the simple wooden staff in his grasp bolstering him up as he climbed. Finally rising through the final stairway of the cathedral, the High Priest emerged through a trap door in the roof and stepped through; his long black and crimson robes flailing in the tempestuous

Drakkaidian winds. Zalnaught looked around the massive roof and slowly walked to one end to peer down over the side to the sprawling city far below him. The huge roof of the Cathedral of Dalorosk was a rounded platform engraved with an ancient Drakkaidian emblem similar to the crest of darkness found on the Netherworld Portal itself, designed to be marveled at from a distance in the sky. Though its sharp beauty was wasted on the people that lived below the towering structure, it was arguably the most illustrious and amazing edifice in all of Iairia.

Turning his anxious attention back to the vibrating object within his robes, Zalnaught pulled forth his luminous crimson Voss Stone deeply shining with electrified light. As the seconds ticked by an audible hum began to echo outwards until it transformed into coherent speech.

"Your Excellency," a voice sounded from within the stone, the red light emanating outwards with every word it uttered. Zalnaught breathed deeply with a pang of relief and spoke.

"What is happening down there?" he boomed at the stone, his anger and impatience from the day before restored. "I sensed another appearance of the vessel yesterday. Have you captured it?" There was a long pause but at last the voice from within the stone sounded again.

"I'm afraid not, Your Excellency," it trembled. "The vessel has already grown too strong to manage. It appears to have a dormant form, however, so I can capture it—"

"What do you mean, 'you?'" Zalnaught grilled, furious at the report. "Where is the rest of your number?"

"The vessel and a Maven traveling with it killed them, my lord," the voice responded, to which Zalnaught's grip on the stone grew so hard he feared he may shatter it if he could not calm down. After gritting his teeth for another long moment with only the whipping winds to break the silence, he collected himself as best he could and brought the stone to his dry lips.

"Pay very close attention, mage, because I have not waited this many years to be so close to my goal only to have it delayed any longer by Dark Mages incapable of handling one being of incomplete power. You are to get to the Mystic Tower and alert the others still there to this latest failure. Take them and go find the vessel again. Capture it in its dormant form and contain it with shadow binding, then bring it back to me. After your failure to control the vessel's power Verix and the Grandarians will be aware something is wrong. I don't want my war starting before I am ready. Am I perfectly understood?"

"Yes, my lord," the voice sounded one last time. "It will be done." With that, the red aura of light inside the stone began to fade and disappear until inert once more. Placing the Voss Stone back in his robes, the High Priest Zalnaught looked down to the staff in his hands and writhed it between them. A look of fury sweeping across his face, he threw one side of the staff into the roof, cracking and slitting the stone several yards in every direction.

Chapter 16

The Empyrean Peaks

Kaylan woke the next morning in a crude bed of messy blankets under a small alcove of rock in the dense eastland forest. Like the first time after her dark twin had disappeared, a throbbing headache was there to greet her upon getting up, her body feeling sore and rigid. The sensation quickly dissipated when Edge and Zephyr found her awake and explained to her what had happened. Though the thought of Kaotica emerging through her again caused her skin to crawl, Edge reluctantly admitted that without her they might have been captured or killed by the Dark Mages. After giving Kaylan the morning to recuperate her strength, the trio pressed on to the south once more. While Kaylan slept that night Edge rounded up two of the black horses belonging to the defeated Dark Mages, at last providing a quicker mode of transportation. Moving into the east with renewed speed, the group penetrated through the upper forests and down into the fields leading up to the rugged terrain near the thin but towering collection of mountains on the horizon.

As they traveled Zephyr was happy to notice his two human companions finally in better spirits with each other. Though he had reserved his worries that his coarse partner would continue to squash Kaylan's attempts for friendship and keep her at a distance for the duration of the quest, ever since the day in the woods she had finally broken through to him the Maven had slowly been opening up. What she said to him that day must have somehow done the trick, as he was now comfortable speaking with her whenever she felt like talking and even initiated a little conversation of his own when observing her occasionally sink into depression over the ever-present darkness she could somehow sense building inside. The girl's spells of sorrow seemed to reveal themselves less as time drew on, however, and Kaylan's usually fervent spirit slowly returned. She could see that despite having difficulty expressing himself, Edge truly did care about what they were doing and his charge to protect her. Late at night when the Maven thought she was asleep Kaylan would occasionally glance from the corner of her eye to find him staring more at her seemingly sleeping form than the night beyond camp.

Within the week they arrived at the base of the Empyrean Peaks, the renowned mountains that accommodated two of the most distinguished exclusivities harbored by the east: the Sky Sprite colonies and the Temple of Wind. Though Zephyr's fears about traveling so close to the peaks, having been banished from them forever, made the amiable sprite uncharacteristically nervous, Edge convinced him that they would save time and shake anyone pursing them by cutting through the rugged winding roads at the base of the mountains. Leading the horses into the craggy growth around the peaks, they began their trek through the commonly traveled pass on the western edge. Giving their horses a break on the rough roads, Edge and Kaylan dismounted to walk them for a while. Swooping in behind them from his patrol, Zephyr caught sight of Kaylan's blond head sweeping back and forth around her staring up in wonder as she had been since first laying eyes on the monstrous peaks in the distance days ago. Spreading his wings to drop down he gently perched on her shoulder, instantly startling her. Seeing the shock in her visage as she spun her head to face him, the sprite was blasted in the face with a bundle of her flowing hair wheeling around with her. Nearly knocking him to the ground with her golden tresses, Kaylan realized it was just her Sky Sprite companion and let out a slight giggle, reaching out to help him back on her shoulder.

"Yank my tail feathers, I drop in to say hello and I'm attacked by your hair," he sputtered, spitting a few stray hairs out of his beak. Kaylan giggled again as Edge looked back with a smile himself, shaking his head and looking back to the road ahead.

"I'm sorry, Zeph," she apologized trying her best to sound sincere. "You just show up so quick you still surprise me sometimes." The miniature creature tucked his rich purple wings into his back and eyed her with a smirk.

"I wouldn't worry about being snuck up on if I had hair that doubles as a weapon," he teased sarcastically. "How's life on the ground today?" Kaylan shrugged, looking back up to the rising huge columns of rock around her.

"Not anywhere as amazing as the view from above, I bet," she commented in awe. "How high are these peaks?" Zephyr smiled and raised his tiny arm as high as it could reach.

"To the top of the world!" he returned with glee. "The Temple of Wind is at the highest point of the Empyrean Peaks, miles above us. Haven is only about a third of the way up the mountains above the usual cloud base but you can't get a good perception today because the clouds are far lower than usual." Kaylan raised an eyebrow curiously.

"Why are they lower today?" she asked bemused. The beaming smile from the sprite's face began to slowly dissipate. Before he could respond, Edge turned back to speak.

"Today is the ceremony, isn't it Zeph?" he asked quietly. Zephyr nodded and remained silent. Kaylan frowned and tilted her head in confusion.

"What's wrong, Zephyr?" she repeated, puzzled. "What's he talking about?" The sprite gently shifted his talon like feet on her shoulder and turned to face her.

"It just makes me a little nervous being here today, Kaylan," he said with his spirit drooping. "You know Edge's story but I never did tell you mine. There's a reason I'm the only Sky Sprite in the world not living in Haven with the rest of my kind."

"Haven?" Kaylan interrupted, still confused.

"Haven is the village that we Sky Sprites live in, Kaylan," he filled in for her. "There's a flat plateau jutting off the biggest of the peaks where we nest above the clouds." When Kaylan narrowed her eyes in obvious confusion, Zephyr smiled again and shook his head. "I'm sorry I'm getting ahead of myself, aren't I? You see, we sprites have very particular needs to live in large groups. Our number has been shrinking over the years because of the wyverns—predators that, well, eat us—that live inside the caverns in the Empyrean Peaks. Haven used to stretch for miles over the tops of the peaks but now we've been pushed back to the plateau. The plateau is special because it's the only place in Iairia where you can find Dew Drops."

"Dew Drops are enchanted blue flowers that the Sky Sprites use to make clouds," Edge chimed in from ahead of them. Kaylan squinted hard at this, disbelief encompassing her visage.

"How do the sprites make clouds?" she inquired, tickled at the very idea. "And why would you want to do that?"

"Well the wyverns are a superstitious lot that are afraid to fly above what they can't see," Zephyr continued. "If we keep a constant cloud cover below Haven we don't have to worry about them attacking us. We make the clouds by plucking the soft blue petals off the Dew Drops and dropping them into clouds already floating by the mountain below us. The moment they loft inside they expand until they break apart and create enough moisture to form huge billowing clouds. It's amazing how much just one petal can create but there aren't that many Dew Drops up there so we have to take good care of them. That's why I was banished..." he trailed off, staring down once more. Though Kaylan was sensitive to the fact she had brought on memories he would rather have forgotten, she had to say something.

"I'm sorry I brought that up, Zephyr," she said regretfully. The little sprite shook his head and shrugged.

"No you didn't do anything, Kaylan," he stated dismissing her apology. "We're all being honest with each other here so I guess it's my turn to lay my cards down. You see, when I lived in Haven I was one of the few selected by Triune to keep watch over the Dew Drops. It's a long story but the short version is a patch of them on the cliff I was supposed to keep safe somehow caught fire. We lost the entire cliffside along with the seeds. I was sleeping on the job when the fire started and by the time I woke up it was too late to put the blaze out. So the Triune took my Lift Power and banished me from the Empyrean Peaks. As I was leaving a group of angry sprites attacked me and threw me over the cliffside." When the sprite finally fell silent, Kaylan's face was overcome with distress.

"Zephyr, that's horrible," she spoke with empathy. "You may have made a mistake but that's complete overkill for them to have hurt you like that. You could have been killed." Zephyr just shrugged again and gave her a single nod.

"Well, I probably would have died there if Edge hadn't come along when he did," he told her earnestly. Kaylan smiled and looked ahead toward the black clad Maven ahead of them, already staring back at her.

"Well it's a good thing someone with such a big heart found you, huh?" she spoke almost playfully, obviously trying to reinforce the point she had been trying to make for days. Zephyr just laughed, to which Edge rolled his eyes and turned forward again. "But you lost me again on something—what is Lift Power, Zephyr?" The sprite contained his laughter and smiled up to her.

"Oh, I thought you knew about that," he said. "All Sky Sprites are born with the power to temporarily lift objects of pretty substantial mass off the ground and move them around. You see me fly with my wings but most of time sprites don't use them. We fly by invoking Lift Power on ourselves. Usually our wings only spread when that gets tuckered out."

"So how did this Triune thing take a power you were born with from you?" she puzzled, trying to remain as sensitive as possible.

"The Triune are our leaders and have twice the Lift Power of any normal Sky Sprite. So much in fact that they can take it from other sprites. That's what they did to me." Keeping his gaze ahead, Edge spoke to his partner once more.

"So now that Kaylan is up to speed, are you going to answer my question?" he cut in.

"And that was...?" Zephyr mused raising a finely feathered eyebrow.

"The ceremony. You think it's today?"

"Looks like it, I'd say," he observed looking up to the large peaks covered in low clouds.

"I don't get it," Kaylan queried again. "What is this ceremony and how can you tell it's today just by looking around?" Zephyr spread his wings and rose off her shoulder to hover in front of her once more.

"You see how low those clouds are?" he asked, pointing upward, to which she nodded yes. "The Triune orders the cloud level brought down on the day the ceremony takes place to be extra sure the wyverns are pushed inside their caves and can't interfere. The ceremony takes place once a year every year. It's a visit that the Triune makes to the Temple of Wind with a party of Windrun Warriors to inspect the cloud seal holding Wyrik." Kaylan stared at him wordlessly for a long moment, expecting him to continue. Seeing her stare blankly, the purple sprite beamed and rolled his eyes. "Geez, you've never even heard of Wyrik?" Kaylan giggled and shook her head no. "Yank my tail feathers, what do they teach you Grandarians up there? Wyrik is a massive wyvern creature that once terrorized the east. It used to live in the low caverns the wyverns do now, leading us to believe it was Wyrik that created them. In any case, he used to prey on both Sky Sprites and humans alike so one day centuries ago we teamed up to lock him away inside the Temple of Wind. There is a small indentation at its base just big enough to fit Wyrik within so they lured him inside and a former Triune used their combined Lift Power to create a unique wall of cloud that sealed him inside the temple. Every year the Triune and a party of Windrun Warriors go all the way up to the temple to add more Dew Drops to the wall of cloud to strengthen the seal and be sure Wyrik can't escape. Seeing as the clouds are unusually low today, the Triune must be going to the Temple of Wind to check on the seal."

"Which is why I suddenly regret coming this way," Edge spoke coldly. Zephyr turned to fly toward him and perch on his shoulder, confused.

"Why?" he inquired puzzled. "The ceremony won't affect us down here."

"No but it means wyverns that are forced to fly extra low today will be closer to us than I would like." Zephyr shook his feathered head with a smile.

"Don't worry, partner, I'll protect you from the big bad wyverns," he teased. "Come on, you know they never attack passing humans. Only Wyrik has that reputation and he's locked up so you don't have to worry about him."

"Do they ever let this Wyrik thing out to stretch or anything?" was the female voice from behind them. Zephyr kept his gaze ahead of them but raised his eyebrow as he responded.

"No, it would be way too dangerous to ever let that monster out," he answered.

"Well how mean is that? Would you like to be all caged up for that many years? You little sprites are a bunch of jerks!" the girl ripped at him harshly. Puzzled why Kaylan would say something so out of character, both turned their heads back to shoot her a puzzled glance. As their eyes fell upon the figure behind them, however, both were shocked to find the voice they had just answered to didn't belong to Kaylan. The dark figure walking exactly where Kaylan had been just a few moments before was Kaotica, a confused expression over her face. Edge instantly froze in his tracks, his heart dropping to mesh with his guts. This was not what he needed right then, he thought to himself. Watching the pair gawk at her, Kaotica halted as well. "What's everybody staring at? I know you think I'm beautiful, Edge but please. You'll make me blush!" She brought a hand up to playfully cover her mouth as a giggle escaped from it.

"How did you know what we were talking about?" Zephyr asked her befuddled. "You just appeared—you couldn't have heard anything about what we were saying." Kaotica made an impatient face at the purple figure.

"Please birdie," she spoke belittlingly. "Haven't you two brilliant guys figured this out yet? Everything that your little Kaylan sees; hears; feels; whatever—so do I. I may not see things with my own beautiful eyes but I can see through hers." Edge's brow furrowed, beleaguered with frustration at this revelation.

"If that's true why can't Kaylan see through you?" he grilled her. The dark girl threw her head back with an overdramatic laugh before staring him down once more.

"I can't help it if blondie's an idiot and hasn't figured me out yet, duh..." She trailed off, dropping the horse reins in her hand and walking toward them. "I know everything she does. Anyway I hope you're in a better mood today, Edge. If I didn't know any better I'd say you didn't want me around the last time you saw me." The Maven grit his teeth and drew his sword.

"How many times can I tell you this?" he asked harshly. "I *don't* want you around. You're a troublemaker and threat to everything around you. If you can hear everything Kaylan can don't you realize the whole reason I'm even with her is to kill you?" Kaotica cocked her head and gave him a look that said she was unconvinced.

"Please, Edgy—you wouldn't do it," she spoke mockingly yet the most mature he had ever heard her. "I know what you're trying to do but you never will. You may not appreciate me yet, but once you get to know me you'll be falling all over yourself to keep me around." She took another step toward him until her body softly rose to fold into his, slowly narrowing her eyes and leaning her smiling face toward him. "You just haven't given me a chance yet. You have no idea how much fun we could have together." Momentarily stunned by the admittedly striking girl so suddenly in his face, he abruptly remembered what she was and stepped back.

"I'm not playing your game, Kaotica," he spoke intolerantly. "Bring Kaylan back and do it *now*." Kaotica let out a huff of defeat and put her hands on her hips but contained the temper Edge expected to rise out.

"Fine, mister serious," she spoke eyeing him impassively. "If you don't want to play with me, I'll find someone who will. This Wyrik guy sounds like he's more fun than you anyway." In the next instant a flash of purple and black energy blasted to life around her, her electrified glowing wings appearing over her back. "I'll be back later." With that, she beat her jagged wings and kicked off from the craggy earth, blasting upward into the sky. Though Edge tried to scream out for her to wait, by the time he could summon his voice she had already punctured the dense layer of clouds above them. The Maven stared upward in disbelief for a long moment before at last tightening his body and kicking a large stone at his feet into the rock wall beside them.

"That dirty, self-righteous... ahh!" he cursed as loud as his lungs would allow. In his anger, the red aura suddenly streaming around his skin rippled to life, causing the ground he stood on to tear and crack under his feet. "Now what am I supposed to do!?!" As the Maven continued to curse under his breath, Zephyr's expression turned grave.

"Edge, what is she planning to do?" he worried out loud. "You don't think she's strong enough to break the seal holding Wyrik do you?" The Maven forced himself to cool down, noticing the fervent red mist boiling around his body. Cooling off in the silence that followed, Edge exhaled slowly and met his partner's nervous gaze.

"If there's a way for that girl to get into trouble, she'll find it," he affirmed resolutely. Shaking his head incredulously, he knew what he had to do. "Come on, Zeph. We have to protect Kaylan and right now that means getting up to Haven to find Kaotica before she destroys it or the Temple of Wind itself. If anything happens to her, Kaylan will pay the same price for it. Let's move." The purple sprite shrunk back then, gulping hard.

"Edge, I don't know if you want me in on this one..." he trailed off slowly, remembering the last time he was in his former home. The dark boy shifted his gaze back to his partner with a disarming expression over his face.

"Don't think like that, Zeph," he said waving his hand. "We're all facing our pasts these days—maybe it's time for you to do it too. I'm definitely going to need my partner on this one." The Sky Sprite took in a deep breath and slowly nodded, facing what he knew he had to do. Nodding to reply yes, Edge told him to stay close until they passed through the clouds and began their trek up the road leading higher into the Empyrean Peaks.

Chapter 17

<u>Sky Sanctuary</u>

    Climbing hard and fast for hours with eyes peeled for any roaming wyverns under the low cloud cover, the duo finally broke through the dense white billows and emerged on the high path leading up to the plateau that held the Sky Sprite sanctuary of Haven. The darkly clad Maven had practically sprinted up the steep mountain trails, fierce determination vexing his tense body and propelling it forward. The very thought of this entire situation infuriated him. He was letting—of all things—a girl toy with him, playing with his life and Kaylan's in the process. Having seen what Kaotica had done in the past he knew her power was potent enough to undo the seal holding the creature Wyrik at bay. If that happened, she, Haven and the entire eastland would be at risk. Though Zephyr was slow to follow his partner up the peaks, nervous of returning to the home he had been banished from, every second Kaotica was loose upon the peaks was another that she could be using to find the Temple of Wind. They had to press onward as fast as they were able.

    Emerging from the last moist vapors of the clouds and trekking up the steep pathway of rock leading to a massive plateau stretching out away from the largest of the peaks above them, the ground slowly began to develop from barren rock to green flora, signaling their approach to the Sky Sprite shelter of Haven. As the narrow pathway gradually expanded into the trail Windrun Warriors used to enter the village, Edge slowed his grueling charge and carefully swept his eyes around for better concealing cover, aware a Maven and a banished sprite would not be greeted warmly in an isolated place like Haven. Darting into the swaying grass to his left that stretched taller than he, Zephyr quickly lofted in after him, again mumbling he should have been born a Cronom. The plateau where the once sprawling village now

Tales of Iairia

lay in seclusion was of singular beauty on the Empyrean Peaks. Long flowing grass like the kind the duo raced through toward the outskirts of the village surrounded its border, perpetually swaying to and fro in the continuous winds. As he penetrated further through the grass, Edge at last felt the ground level out and eyed a sign back on the road adorned with colorful feathers reading "Haven." Shooting Zephyr a quick glance the nervous looking sprite motioned for him to continue on but slowly.

Creeping through the thinning grass and crouching closer to the earth, Edge could make out the sounds of activity ahead. Parting the long strands of grass before him just enough to peer out, the Maven finally found himself in Haven. Though Zephyr had told him what the small sanctuary looked like before, seeing it up close gave him an entirely new appreciation for how amazing it was. It was surprisingly green for a settlement so high in the peaks. Shorter grasses and shrubbery covered the base of the plateau. Blue flowers commonly grew in bunches around the large nests tucked against the protective vertical wall of rock at the other end of the village, obviously providing shelter for the precious Dew Drops. There were no buildings or shelters apart from the many shallow caves in the rock wall that Edge could see, but there were several elaborate structures stretching throughout the central city. Beautiful bridges composed of light blue stone connected different levels of the vertical city to the others, obviously constructed with the help of the sprites' Lift Power. There was extravagant railing around the gardens of Dew Drops further down the road toward the end of the plateau, with statues of sweeping featherlike designs similar to those found on the crest of wind rising from the centers. Sweeping his gaze through the central city street, Edge noticed several of the miniature Sky Sprites jetting back and forth from their nests in the caves toward the higher levels of the city. He couldn't help but let out a smile as he watched them soar by and interact with each other. They looked exactly like his partner but for their various vibrant colors. Looking back to Zephyr he caught him staring intently as well, longing in his rich eyes.

"How's it feel to be home, Zeph?" he asked in a whisper. The miniature figure shook off his feelings and returned the boy's stare blankly.

"It's not my home anymore," he replied bleakly. "I still can't believe I'm staring at it again. It was just that patch of Dew Drops way down there at the end of the plateau that I used to guard..." Edge gave him a single nod and tried his best to smile understandingly. Turning back to the Haven, he caught sight of another edifice he had yet to see father up. Following the stone bridge atop the village's highest level on the cliff wall were several columns of the blue stone rising into the sky. Squinting uncertainly at the structure, Zephyr saw him puzzling and hovered closer to whisper in his ear.

"That's where we need to get to," he stated with renewed purpose in his voice.

"What is that thing?" Edge mouthed quietly.

"Our only chance of stopping Kaotica," he returned gravely. "In the center of those columns is a portal the first Triune constructed millennia ago. It leads directly to the base of the highest peak and the Temple of Wind. It would take us days to climb up there and without Lift Power I don't think it's even possible, but if we can get to that portal it could teleport us right to the base."

"So all we have to do is penetrate through a wide open sanctuary filled with flying creatures who have eyesight as sharp as yours and power that could magically take hold of and throw us off this plateau," Edge stated sarcastically. "Well this should be easy." As he shook his head in frustration and looked down to check the satchels containing his gear, Zephyr leaned in to add to their troubles.

"And we've got another problem," he said worriedly. "The portal can only be activated with Lift Power—of which I have none. Even if we somehow got up there how are we going to use it?" Edge continued sorting through his silver buckled satchels for a long moment before slowly freezing, staring back up at the columns atop the village.

"What's the Maven credo, Zeph?" he suddenly asked, catching his partner by surprise.

"Turn your problems into solutions," he stated slowly, his brow furrowing. "Why?"

"How close do you sprites have to be to something to use your Lift Power?" he asked still staring up.

"Well the Triune can use them at about any range but a normal sprite..." he trailed off thinking, "has to be at least a few meters away to lift something." Edge let a smile materialize across his lips as he looked to the side of the village wall and started pulling a grapple out of his satchel.

"Then here's what we're going to do," he decreed. "You stay here to give me whistle cover while I sneak across the street at its narrowest point down there. I'll climb the segment of rock wall in shadow to the second level and drop onto the bridge connecting it to the third. Once I get on the bridge I'll make a run for the top level." Zephyr shot him an incredulous look.

"The plan was good until that last part," he imparted anxiously. "You'll get spotted for sure. If they see you appear out of nowhere running for the portal they'll use their Lift Power and heave you out of Haven!" Edge turned to him, his pale eyes alight with knowledge.

"Exactly," he returned with confidence. "When I get to the portal I'll stop and lure them to me to activate their power over the portal. Then we can jump in and get to the temple." Zephyr stared at him hard for a long moment before running a hand over his beaked face and shaking his head uncertainly.

"I don't know about this one, partner," he spoke quietly. "What if they catch you before you make it to the portal? They only have to be within a few meters to send you plummeting to the ground."

"Then I'll have to be sure to stay a few meters ahead of them, won't I," Edge returned. "It's our only chance, Zeph." The purple sprite exhaled sharply and nodded, agreeing but telling the boy to be careful. With that, the Maven crouched and dashed to his left through the concealing grass toward the narrow point of the central street of Haven, leaving Zephyr behind to keep whistle watch.

Creeping through his cover making sure to watch and listen for passing Sky Sprites merrily jetting through the gusty air above him, Edge peered out from the point in the long grass. Maneuvering closest to the massive vertical wall of rock stretching up for as high as he could see, he precisely plotted his path up the wall in the shadowed portions and where he could safely leap onto the beautiful stone bridges on the higher levels of the village. Taking a sweeping look around him and listening for the warning that did not come from his partner, the Maven tightened his body and leapt from the grasses to roll over the ground and up again to sprint to the oblique side of the rising rock wall. Pressing his back against it and scanning his eyes around the village to be sure no one had seen him, he lifted the duel grapples in his hands and spun around to begin climbing up the granite surface. Finding good footing to help bolster him up, he quickly and silently ascended the monstrous wall of rock for the second level of the city, praying he would not be spotted until the opportune moment.

Silently staring in nervous apprehension from his spot in the tall grass, Zephyr watched as his partner climbed up to the second level in the shadows with his blue scarf flying behind him in the mountain wind. At last moving as close as he could to the rising stone bridge below him and slowly turning his head to look for any passing sprites, Edge kicked off the wall and lunged from it to skillfully land with only a small thud of his equipment touching the stone. Coming out of his surprisingly quiet roll he bounded back up to his feet and began tearing up the intricately weaving bridge between the second and third level. Hearing a shrill whistle from far below him, the Maven rushed to duck behind a towering statue of a collection of stone feathers rising from a dais on the third level. Watching intently as a bright orange sprite aloft in the air wafted past him, he still heard no call of alarm and let out a nervous breath of relief. Edge turned his head upward with his black hair swaying in the wind, noting the remaining distance between he and the portal to the Temple of Wind far above him. He would have to ascend two more levels of the city's twisting bridges with minimal cover. If he was noticed before he got there the sprites would send him on a one way trip down the peaks to a brutal death.

Realizing he was running out of precious time, the boy took in another deep breath and let his determination take over. Leaping from his cover to sprint up to the next level of the city he took a sweeping gaze downward. The Sky Sprites were obviously a race that wasn't perturbed by heights. He was already a hundred of feet above the blue and green plateau below him racing over thin stone pathways devoid of railing of any kind. One misstep could send him plummeting down to his death. Crouching and pressing his back against a gazebo structure on the platform overlooking the western side of the Empyrean Peaks, the Maven stopped to momentarily catch his breath. As he sat breathing hard, a slight movement from above him caught his attention. Throwing his head up in shock, he found a single sprite covered in brilliant yellow feathers almost blending in with its golden beak sitting on a flat rock protruding from the rock wall behind the gazebo, obviously obstructing Zephyr's line of sight. The Maven swallowed quickly as he held the creature's uncertain gaze for a long moment, motionless. Watching as the uncertainty in the sprites yellow eyes filled with anxious inevitability, Edge realized he was caught and thrust his black form off the cylindrical column of the gazebo he rested on, his flowing blue scarf trailing behind him in the wind.

Instantly coming alert, the yellow Sky Sprite summoned a semi transparent sphere of energy around his miniature form and shot off from his seat on the rock wall to sweep down into the village. As Edge tore up the last long remaining bridge for the much larger platform at its end he could hear a small single voice from below screaming out there was an intruder in the sanctuary. Looking down he could see several of the small sprites lifting off with surprising speed for the top level of Haven and more coming alert around him in the rock wall. Pressing forward as fast as he was able the Maven neared the last stretch of the long bridge only to find a single sprite soaring over the top platform for his position. Realizing it would be all over if it was able to grasp him with its Lift Power, the Maven grew bold and charged toward it. Remembering Zephyr's trend of lifting up and swooping in on him, the Maven waited for the sprite to get within range to use his power. Lifting a few feet in the air before extending its small feathered hand out for him, Edge smiled and rolled once more, shrinking down just enough to pass under the confused sprite an inch too far away for its power to take hold on him.

Sprinting past the surrounding rows of rising columns onto the solid purple portal at the center of the final platform, Edge spun around to find himself virtually surrounded by Sky Sprites appearing over the border. Positioning himself in the center of the portal engraved with the sweeping crest of wind, the Maven raised his empty gloved hands and slowly placed them behind his head, waiting.

"All right, you have me," he stated dryly. "Take me away." A solid blue sprite with tiny gauntlets strapped across its forearms glared at him and pointed.

"Once you step off that portal you're on," he announced angrily. "Move back to the bridge." Edge frowned, guessing they knew what he was trying to do. The Maven remained motionless.

"I'm afraid you'll just have to oblige me here," he said trying to rouse them further by lowering his hands to pull forth the twin daggers strapped to his thighs. The sprite who had spoken looked to his kin around him and motioned with his head for them to move back. All of them clearing the platform to hover around it instead, he pointed his feathered hand forward and narrowed his eyes.

"Nice try, my human friend," he started caustically, "but whatever your game is it won't work. We have to be over the portal to activate it but I can still grasp you from here." Tightening his fingers in a fist before him, the sphere of barely visible energy around him transferred to surround Edge, slowly lifting him off the ground. As the blue sprite was about to turn and throw Edge away from the platform back down to the bridge, however, another sprite from behind him came flying into his back to force him forward. Edge smirked to find Zephyr throwing his arms around the blue sprite and pulling him over the portal, instantly activating it with his Lift Power. Aglow with life, the crest of wind in the platform began to radiate purple light that quickly spread over the three figures above it, lifting them into the skies and accelerating them at an incredible velocity. Before any of the sprites knew it they were gone, blasting into the skies for the top of the world.

Chapter 18

<u>Beast at the Peak</u>

Flying through the gusty air at impossible speeds to one of the highest points atop the Empyrean Peaks, Edge, Zephyr and the blue sprite that had inadvertently transported them there blasted onto a circle of carved boulders situated around it, the soft purple glow encompassing their bodies quickly dissipating. Gently touching down onto another portal exactly like the one atop the highest levels of Haven, Edge immediately crouched and snatched the blue sprite just coming to his senses before him into his grasp, holding his beak shut to preclude an outburst. With the sprite contained in his gloved hands, Edge quickly leapt to take cover behind one of the boulders surrounding the portal, unsure if anyone had seen them arrive or not. Already one step ahead of his tense partner, Zephyr swept down from another boulder to perch on his shoulder and lean into his ear.

"It's a good thing this portal doesn't make any noise when in use because it's a miracle they didn't see us," he stated, motioning with his eyes for the boy to turn and look past the boulder he sat behind. Struggling to keep the captive sprite in his hands from wriggling free, Edge rotated his head to scan what lay beyond the portal. His eyes instantly widened; sheer amazement of the view engulfing his mind. There was a steep basin of rugged rock stretching ahead for over a hundred yards, leading up to a massive solitary spire jutting into the sky. It was the object atop the lone peak that drew Edge's attention. Sitting at the highest point in the world stretching up to touch the end of the sky with its single thin tower was the majestic Temple of Wind, blowing unremitting gusts of air in all directions. Beyond was a sky of endless blue seeming to reach into infinity. Though Edge had never stopped to try and picture what the Celestial World might look like, as he sat atop the Empyrean Peaks staring at the magnificence of the top of the world he guessed it couldn't be much more beautiful than this.

It was the movement of the party of humans ahead of him that reminded Edge it was in fact the mortal realm. He had almost missed them in gaping at the towering Temple of Wind but focusing once more the Maven fixed his gaze on the party halfway between his position and the single peak harboring the temple. There were five humans all dressed in green and purple tunics with light armor pressed tightly against their chests, along with two Sky Sprites at their side. Edge immediately noticed the difference in their appearance to the average sprite he had seen, flaunting feathers much longer than most and draped in loose fitting cloths that covered their small torsos. When Zephyr saw him eyeing the group staring up to the temple, he whispered into his partner's ear once more.

"That's the Triune and their party of Windrun Warriors," the sprite informed him. Edge's brow furrowed as he looked back to his purple friend.

"I thought there were three sprites in your Triune," he puzzled. "I count two." Zephyr nodded and pointed up the Temple of Wind.

"Your eyes can't see it but the third is on his way up the spire for the temple," he stated with urgency entering his voice. "That means the ceremony is about to begin." Giving Zephyr a single nod of acknowledgement Edge turned down to the blue sprite in his hands fighting to be free. The boy brought it up to his face to stare into his bright blue eyes .

"Listen to me, little sprite," he spoke in a whisper. "I'm not here to hurt you, we just needed a ride up the peaks. My partner and I are looking for someone but I can't have you making any noise to rouse the others already here. So I'm going to have to tie you up for a minute but we'll be back when we're done—" Before Edge could finish the blue sprite managed to squeeze his right arm out of the boy's grasp and extend it toward him. The next instant a semitransparent sphere of energy surrounded Edge. Feeling gravity fail around him, the boy was blasted from his seat on the rocky earth into the sky, forced to release his grip on the captive sprite. As soon as he was free the sprite shifted his Lift Power from the boy to himself, dropping Edge back to the hard earth with an audible thud. Though Zephyr tried to lift up to the other sprite to preclude him from making any more noise, he could not reach him in time to stop him from crying out to the party before them.

"*Help!*" he bellowed as loud as his miniature lungs would permit him. "*Intruders!*" His words echoing across the windy peaks, the party of men and sprite wheeled around in surprise to find the blue sprite wildly waving his arms in alarm. Edge flipped from his back to his feet in a crouch on the earth, angrily gritting his teeth for letting the troublesome creature get the best of him. Watching as one of the Windrun Warriors drew a nimble blade and ordered the other four in his number over to the portal, Edge resumed his position of cover and drew the broadsword from behind his back. Trying to find his focus and clear the emotion from his mind to be ready for what he now had to do, the Maven waited for the sound of incoming footsteps to queue his strike. When the men were virtually on top of him Edge threw a knife in his free hand to his left, breaking into another boulder with a clear cracking sound. The four men behind him instantly spinning their heads toward the distraction, Edge leapt up to throw the hilt of his weapon up into the man closest to him at his chin, instantly knocking him out cold in surprise. The others wheeling on him, Edge jumped onto the top of the boulder he stood by and then off it as one of the Windrun Warriors slashed out their blades for his feet. Flipping over the man's head Edge extended one of his boots back to knock the blade from his hand. Landing in a crouch to avoid a sweeping horizontal slash where his head would have been, the Maven stretched out his leg and made a sweeping kick to trip the second attacker to his right.

Rising to meet another two rushing toward him Edge lifted his blade to parry one of them away. Delivering a spinning kick to use the man's momentum against him he was sent careening into one of the boulders, out of control. The fourth man still charging from behind stretched out his blade to thrust at the Maven's middle but was surprised to find him leaping back to nimbly dodge it. Edge quickly swatted the man's smaller saber downward and threw his knee up to catch him in the gut and send him falling to his back as well. Looking down to find the second Windrun Warrior he had felled on the ground grasping a blade to stab out for his legs, the Maven jumped to evade it but then clamped his boots together to twist the weapon away and out of the man's grasp. Following with a kick to the man's head

Trial of a Maven

to knock him out as well, Edge quickly scanned over the Windrun Warriors to make sure all of them were temporarily downed but still breathing.

Though they all appeared to be defeated the Maven heard a shrill whistle from above him cut through the air as if panicked. His taut frame alert, the Maven wheeled around just in time to catch duel sabers slicing forward toward his neck. Twirling his blade up to barely parry the attack of the fifth Windrun Warrior now leaping toward him, it was all he could do to brace himself and try not to lose his balance as he tumbled back over the rocks and downed bodies. Aware he was going to topple over if he didn't do something, the Maven dropped his sword and used his falling momentum to his advantage, opening the palms of his hands to back flip off one of the boulders behind him and land on his feet over the portal to Haven once more. When the fifth of his attackers merely lowered his defenses and the thin blades in his hands, Edge knew something was wrong. The next moment he felt why, the two sprites that had been hovering alongside the Windrun Warriors minutes ago appearing behind the leader to grasp him with their Lift Power. Frozen in place by two members of the Triune, Edge could only watch in aggravation as the Windrun Warrior slowly walked toward him with resentment in his eyes. The man was older than all the rest but still in excellent shape with a lean physique. As he looked Edge over distrustfully, he breathed hard and raised one of his duel blades to his neck.

"What business could a Maven possibly have atop the Empyrean Peaks?" he spoke, his words biting with the annoyance and intolerance Edge was accustomed to hearing from most people outside his profession. "Speak now or the consequences of your actions here will be far direr." Edge let out a long breath of frustration before replying.

"I know this is going to sound crazy," he started slowly, "but I'm here looking for someone." The Windrun Warrior raised an eyebrow to this and eyed him peculiarly.

"Looking for someone?" he repeated skeptically. "No one is ever permitted past Haven beside this party of Windrun Warriors and Sky Sprites or the Warrior of Wind, young Maven. Who is it you seek and why?" Edge shook his head with annoyance, aware there was no way this man would believe him.

"Like I said, this is going to sound ridiculous but you have to stop this ceremony right now," he imparted with urgency. "There's a girl somewhere up here with demonic power who's going to release Wyrik from its prison unless I can find her first. You have to let me go right now." The Windrun Warrior stared at him for a long moment, his brow furrowing once more.

"You have tremendous skill with a blade and a healthy imagination, young man, but please don't take me for a fool," he spoke irritated. "Now I don't know how you managed to get all the way up here but..." Before he could finish a purple sprite the man had never seen before swept in front of him to come between his blade and Edge.

"He's telling the truth," Zephyr spoke, turning to face the two sprites holding his partner in their grasp. Both members of the Triune stared at the purple sprite hard, a look of amazed remembrance washing over their faces.

"Zephyr?" one of them spoke at last. The amazement in the sprite's faces slowly warped to supreme fury. "Zephyr, you were banished from these peaks years ago! And now you return with a human trying to bring further damage to our home? You have sealed your fate, this time." Though the purple sprite before him swallowed hard, the Windrun Warrior lowered his blade from Edge's face and eyed him peculiarly.

"I don't know what either of you think you're doing up here but I will not fall for..." The man trailed off once more, this time cut off by the sprites behind him suddenly shouting with alarm and staring up to the Temple of Wind with incredulity. The man spun around to look up to the temple high above them, squinting to find a figure much larger than a Sky Sprite moving around. "What's going on up there?" It was Zephyr who answered the question, turning to Edge to nervously shake his head.

"She's at the entrance to the temple, Edge!" he exclaimed worriedly. They continued to watch as Kaotica began laughing and reached out to take the Dew Drop petals in the sprite's hands to gingerly place them in her dark hair. The Triune was horrified to see her slap the sprite out of her way and raise a hand to charge a large ball of electrified dark energy around her clenched fist. At this point Edge and the Windrun Warrior could see the dark display as well and watched helplessly as she raised the surging dark light above her head to throw it back down onto the wall of enchanted cloud at the front of the temple. The ball instantly detonated with power, the force of the explosion reaching out to rip through the group at the portal hundreds of yards away. Terrified at what had just happened, the Triune released Edge and turned to exclaim to each other their kin had been killed. Gathering his broadsword and placing it behind his back with a dissatisfied huff of anger, Edge stood tensely as the dark aura of power finally cleared to reveal an open entrance to the Temple of Wind.

The entire group watched in horror as a large movement from within slowly trudged out, revealing the mammoth form of the lumbering creature called Wyrik. Edge's eyes widened in shock as the beast came into full view, rearing three dragon-like heads back to scream out into the tempestuous air. It was at least ten times the size of any normal wyvern which was only a little bigger than a horse. Thick hues of blue and green scaled its thick body and legs with a lighter patch of fine scales over its belly and the three long necks jutting from above. As the fearsome creature swept its multiple pairs of eyes around it and spied the group far below by the purple portal in the rock, it at last spread its massive feathered wings and abruptly launched into the sky for the first time in millennia. Sweeping upward with surprising speed, the two remaining sprites of the Triune turned with terror in their eyes and screamed out for the group to run. While they took off soaring for what cover they could find behind them, Edge and the Windrun Warrior exchanged glances knowing they had to collect the men the Maven had knocked out and get them to safety as well.

"We can't carry them all to cover!" Edge shouted, lifting one into his arms. The Windrun Warrior shook his head as he began pulling two of them onto the portal.

"We don't have to—we must teleport back to Haven!" he returned watching as the winged beast in the sky continued to rise. Edge shook his head as he placed the one in his arms next to the others.

"You go back if you have to but I'm staying here!" he spoke with resolve.

"Young man, you'll be killed!" he shouted, grabbing the last of his men and placing him on the portal. "This beast is a survivor of the ancient world of magic—it can't be killed by any tool of your trade."

"I told you—it's the girl I'm looking for. I have to get to her to put this right!" The Windrun Warrior stared him down uncertainly for another quick moment but saw Wyrik above virtually on top of them and nodded, looking up to Zephyr hovering over him.

"You—sprite!" he called. "Activate this portal and take these men back to Haven.

"He doesn't have Lift Power," Edge answered for him, spinning around to the blue sprite ready to evacuate as well. "You! Do it!" All too happy to return to his sanctuary down the peaks, the blue sprite nodded and hovered over the portal to activate his Lift Power and the portal. As the soft purple light consumed them and teleported them away, Edge and those remaining in his party shooting their heads upward to find the beastly form of Wyrik descending on them in a vertical dive. Screaming for the Maven and his sprite partner to follow him, the Windrun Warrior sprinted forward toward an alcove of rock the two sprites of the Triune had hidden in behind the portal. Running as fast as their legs would carry them they tore over the rough summit of the peaks with the winged monster in the sky screaming out of all three heads as it plummeted toward them. With Wyrik barely a hundred feet away, Edge and the others leapt forward to dive into the small opening of rock that led into the alcove. No sooner had they landed inside, a massive crash that seemed to shake the entire mountain sounded from outside, accompanied by earsplitting screams of anger from the three heads trying to bite through the wall of rock protecting the group tumbling back and forth in the alcove. After several terrifying moments of waiting for the creature to penetrate their stronghold and clamp its enormous jaws around them, they listened as it gradually withdrew to beat its massive feathered wings and thrust into the sky once more, its thickly scaled tail whipping at the ground as it took off. Listening as it seemed to disappear, Edge released his grip on his chest; his heart beating so heavily he thought it would break free of his chest any moment. Scanning the faces of the others in one corner of the alcove, he found the Windrun Warrior beside him staring incredulously. Edge shifted his frustrated gaze to meet the other's.

"I won't bother saying I told you so but you're going to have to trust me now if we're going to get out of this alive," he spoke solemnly, to which the man stared him down uncertainly for a lingering moment but at last nodded.

"I don't believe this," he stated out of breath. "What just happened out there? Who are you really?" Edge shook his head and turned to peer out of the opening of the alcove to sweep the skies for Wyrik. He could still hear the beating of its wings far above but couldn't see it.

"It's trying to lure us into coming out," he spoke softly. The Windrun Warrior peered out into the skies as well, following Edge's gaze up to the Temple of Wind to see a single figure sitting atop the entrance. "That's the girl I was trying to tell you about. I don't have time to tell you my story right now but her name is Kaotica and she's my responsibility. She's immensely powerful but she's on a rampage and I have to get her under control. She's the only one strong enough to deal with the wyvern beast." The Windrun Warrior shot him a skeptical glance but it was one of the sprites in the Triune that spoke for him.

"He told you that it can't be killed, Maven," he reminded again. "I believe this girl of yours possesses power after what I just witnessed but Wyrik is a creature from another age—it can't be killed by anything in this world."

"Regardless, I have to get to Kaotica," Edge returned. "Believe me, for however dangerous Wyrik is that girl is twice the threat. I have to get to her."

"Then what are we going to do about Wyrik?" the Windrun Warrior pressed, adjusting the duel sabers at his sides. "Can we seal it in its prison again?" The sprites looked at each other briefly but shook their heads no.

"Gulsair was killed by this girl so the power of the Triune is undone," they replied. "Even if we could somehow lure Wyrik back inside his prison, we would need a third sprite to cast the spell to seal it behind the wall of cloud. Edge stared at them hard for a moment, before slowly looking to the purple sprite beside him.

"Here's one," he offered suddenly, to which his partner stared up at him nervously. "Could Zephyr help you?" The two sprites of the Triune scowled at the boy.

"Zephyr was banished from the rest of we sprites," one of them spoke acidly. "His mere presence here is an insult to our kind. Now you wish for us to grant him clemency and anoint him as a member of our most sacred establishment of order and power? You are out of your mind, boy." Edge tightened his face and he glared them down.

"Listen, I'll look past that you banished him over an accident that could have happened to anyone but if you don't seal Wyrik before it escapes from the peaks, where do you think he's going first? Your precious Haven will be leveled in minutes and all of your kind will die. I'm not asking you to grant Zephyr clemency, I'm asking you to do what you have to do to save your people." There was a long silence then, with only the whips of wind and the faint beating of Wyrik's wings far above to fill the air.

"I agree with the Maven, Triune," the Windrun Warrior spoke. "I implore you to let this one detail slide in order to serve the greater good. More than Haven rests on this—it's the entire eastland at risk now." The two sprites stared at each other hard for a long moment but eventually nodded and looked to Zephyr, waiting with anxious eyes.

"It appears we have no choice, then," one of them agreed. "We will grant Zephyr our power to help us create the seal once more but his fate will be decided later. Even with the power of the Triune, though, we still have to get Wyrik to return to his prison for our power to have any effect." Edge shot a glance back to the Temple of Wind and the girl sitting atop its entrance, playfully swinging her legs back and forth with her hands in her lap. He narrowed his eyes and spoke.

"Leave that to me," he declared resolutely. All four shot him uncertain glances as he turned back to face them, waiting for him to elaborate. "The Triune can use their power from any range, right? So lift me up to the Temple of Wind to get Wyrik's attention. I'll lure it inside and once it is you can create the seal again." Zephyr was the first to voice his concerned objections, rising to hover in front of his face.

"And what about you, Edge?" he grilled. "What if something goes wrong or you can't get out?" Edge shook off his concerns and pointed up to the temple.

"You know I always have a final trick up my sleeve to get me out of hairy situations, but I'll have her up there too. Hopefully I can get her to help me out."

"I don't like the sound of this either," the Windrun Warrior spoke from beside them. "There are too many risks. At least let me come with you."

"It's our only shot as far as I can see," Edge returned, standing to tighten the silver buckled straps across his chest

Trial of a Maven

securing his sword. "And we need you here. Keep watch over the Triune while they're using their power to make sure nothing interrupts them. Kaotica will only respond to me anyway." Though the Windrun Warrior looked discontented with the plan, he rose and nodded, extending his hand.

"I still feel like I don't know what's really happening here but I'll trust you, young man," he stated. "What is your name?" Edge reluctantly accepted his hand and shook it, replying it was Edge. "Well, Edge, I wish you good luck. I'll keep them safe here but you be careful up there. I'm called Kohlin Marraea, First Captain of the Windrun Warriors. When you return I'll be eager to hear the rest of your story." The Maven nodded and turned his attention to the three sprites reluctantly grouping together near him. Slowly, the two remaining sprites of the Triune lifted their arms for Zephyr and engulfed him and the sphere of Lift Power. Unlike normal, however, the light did not merely hover around his miniature form but seeped inward to penetrate his feathered body and soak into it. When the light faded, Zephyr's purple feathers seemed to glisten with new light—longer and brighter than before. The sprite slowly looked down to stare at his hands for a long moment then turned back to Edge with a wide smile beaming across his beak. Before he could say anything another of the Triune spoke with urgency in his small voice.

"We will lift you toward the temple as fast as we can, young man but Wyrik is sure to see you and will be hot on your trail. When you arrive at the portal you will need to find one of the Dew Drop petals the other of the Triune held before his death and place it before the entrance to the temple. Once it is in place and Wyrik is inside we will focus our power and create the Shield of Cloud over the entrance again. Do you understand?" Replying yes, they told him to move outside the alcove so they could take hold of him. Winking goodbye to his partner worriedly staring at him, Edge hurriedly stepped outside the alcove into the windy air of the Empyrean Peaks. Though looking around nervously, he could not see Wyrik anywhere. Grouping together inside, the new Triune wrapped their Lift Power around the boy and slowly lifted him inches above the ground. With flaring energy forming around their hands, the boy was suddenly catapulted forward for the Temple of Wind with incredible speed.

Instantly, Kohlin Marraea heard the screeching cry of three heads from above and watched as Wyrik appeared from a ledge behind them, turning to hurl itself forward after the Maven. As he blasted through the turbulent air Edge heard the massive wyvern screaming for him as well and looked back to find it furiously beating its feathered wings mounted on its back with ravenous claws seeming to reach out for him. He would arrive well ahead of the beastly creature but would only have a few moments to find one of the Dew Drop petals and get into position inside the temple, presuming Kaotica did not disrupt the plan with her "fun." Careening forward with his hair and clothes rustling wildly in the wind, Edge at last neared the temple and began to slightly slow. Still at the mercy of the sprites guiding him forward he was flipped upright and forced to the base of the towering edifice with a bone grinding landing. Shaking off the pain and surprise as he stumbled forward the Maven found his balance and hastily shot ahead looking to the top of the entrance of Wyrik's prison at the base of the temple. He grit his teeth once more as he swept the base of the tower for Kaotica—her dark figure nowhere to be found. Aware Wyrik was right behind him and moments away from slamming into the base of the temple, Edge forced her from his mind and wheeled around to desperately scan the recently scorched ground for one of the blue petals he had been instructed to collect. Spinning in all directions praying he could locate even one, he finally spotted a small blue object near a pile of rocks blown apart by Kaotica's attack on the seal. Dashing over to heave the rocks away from the delicate petal as the sound of wings beating the air behind him grew louder, Edge gingerly took hold of it and bolted back for the elaborate staircase leading to the indentation in the temple below the entrance that had served as Wyrik's prison over the years.

    Rushing up the staircase as the winged creature screamed so loud he could feel it directly above him, the Maven leapt into the temple as it crashed into the stairs and extended its center head to clamp down where he had been a second before. Rolling and dashing into the large space in the temple too far away for Wyrik to reach him without actually entering itself, Edge halted and wheeled around to stare it down. Wyrik did not move but slowly swayed its three necks back and forth, returning the boy's stare. Puzzled at why it would not follow him in, Edge drew his crossbow and took aim, screaming to get its attention. The small bolt jutted into the beast's front left leg but it did not react. At last, Wyrik took a step back and growled from deep in its throats, slowly taking a seat on the stairs and holding the boy's gaze. Edge narrowed his eyes at the creature.

It knew what he was trying to do.

There was no way the creature was going to enter its prison again—not for anything. It had made that mistake millennia ago. It was going to wait him out. Edge grit his teeth in fury. Now he was as trapped as Wyrik had been up until today. His mind racing for an idea, he knew there was nothing he could do himself. Even his power would not respond to him unless the direct and immanent threat of death hung over him. Desperate for an idea, he finally groped onto the only thing he could think to do.

"*Kaotica!*" he bellowed suddenly, so loud he strained his voice with each word to come. "Kaotica! Where are you! It's Edge, Kaotica! I need you! *Kaotica!*" He continued shouting her name for several long minutes with Wyrik staring at him unyielding the entire time. After he was sure his voice was going to fail the Maven realized she could not hear him. She had probably already abandoned the Empyrean Peaks altogether to find her fun elsewhere. Virtually collapsing with dread on the stone temple ground he placed his head in his gloved hands and massaged his eyes with the heels of his gloves. He wasn't going to get out of there. The Triune could do nothing to move the Wyrik and even with his partner part of their number the other two would be too scared to try. There was no one else.

As the inevitability of his doom began to sink in, the boy looked up to find Wyrik still staring at him, unmoving. Holding its resolute gaze, he noticed a faint movement from behind it. Squinting his eyes and tilting his head as he focused in, Edge's face burst alive with hope as he found Kaotica creeping up on the massive form of Wyrik with a tickled smirk on her face. Though he didn't want to give her away to the mammoth creature he began motioning with his head and desperate eyes for her to either come to him or attack it. She just smiled at him as he made funny faces at her, eventually laughing out loud in glee.

"Oh fun, fun, fun!" she giggled. "I heard *somebody* needs my help. Who could it be Edgy?" she mused making a dramatic face and lifting her hand to her chin. As she spoke, Edge stared at her mortified. Wyrik's right head looked down to the source of the giggling and spotted her instantly. "I told you that you'd be desperate to keep me around once you got to know me. Now what do you want—" She was cut off as the winged monster beside her pushed its body around and thrust its right head down to clamp its jaws down on her, taking hold and swinging its head back to swallow her whole. Edge's eyes burst open, terror filtering through his taut body. He couldn't believe what he had just seen. Kaotica's childishness had just killed both she and Kaylan. With her gone there was truly no hope at all. Rising in crazed desperation the Maven drew his broadsword and charged forward out of the prison consumed by his rage. Wyrik saw him coming and rose once more, preparing to snap out and consume him as well.

As the Maven charged forward an unbridled layer of crimson mist began to formulate around his body and swarm over him. Jumping out of the prison with all his strength, the boy met Wyrik's center head with his sword slicing down toward it. Though he was knocked back into the prison as the creature snapped out for him, Edge's power detonated to life on impact and tore through the beast's center head to send it reeling backward, bleeding profusely. Rising enraged, the creature beat its enormous wings to thrust if off the ground and onto the radiating boy inside the temple. Though Edge tried to roll away, the creature's first clawed foot caught him and pressed its prodigious weight onto him. Though it felt as though every bone in his body was crushing inside, Edge could feel himself tearing apart from the inside with his fury that desperately called to be released. Giving into it, the dense layer of barely visible energy boiling beneath the red aura of power detonated with force like never before, splitting the stone stairway around the temple and burning into Wyrik, his very scales and skin disintegrating into the air. Falling back and screaming out in pain, Edge watched it retreat into the only place it could find—the temple.

Rising with his rage still not satisfied, he could see Wyrik convulsing in pain and confusion, its right neck suddenly bulging. His power calming as his anger turned to amazement, Edge watched the creature's swelling neck exploded in a flurry of electrified purple light. Shielding his eyes from the dark display and the chunks of flesh falling around him, he felt a familiar power emanating with life once more. Lifting his head back to face the bloody creature falling over itself in anguish, he found the darkly empowered figure of Kaotica slowly levitating down from the air with an irritated look on her face. Edge eyed her incredulously as she slowly touched down before him at the entrance to the prison, letting her dark wings fade from her back and sweeping a drop of blood from her otherwise unvarnished person despite having been swallowed minutes before.

"Blech, gross," she sputtered shaking off the discomfort of being in the creature's throat. "Now I know why this guy doesn't get any playtime." Aware Wyrik was still far from defeated, the boy pushed her aside for the moment to contend with it rising in fury for the two humans standing before it. Noticing the Dew Drop petal still in Kaotica's hair that she had stolen from the sprite she had killed, he reached up and plucked it out, stretching it upward and looking down to the peaks where he had left Zephyr and the others. Kaotica raised an eyebrow as she watched him standing there raising the flower up. "Are you trying to give me flowers or what, Edge?" Though nothing happened at first while the infuriated winged colossus lumbered forward, all at once the petal lifted out of Edge's hand and rose in front of the massive entrance to the prison. As if aware what was about to happen to it once more, Wyrik suddenly cried out from its remaining heads and attempted to dash forward. But it was already too late. As soon as the soft blue petal arrived in the center of the entrance a sphere of Lift Power enveloped it and the petal rapidly dissolved into a thick layer of cloud like substance spreading to cover the entire indentation in the Temple of Wind. Grabbing Kaotica and leaping back down the stairs with her, the pair watched as Wyrik screamed once more before being sealed inside its prison a second time.

Breathing hard as he released her in the silence, Kaotica turned to Edge uncertainly. Seeing the boy only stare at her with a dumbfounded look on his tense face, she beamed and leapt forward to hug him.

"You saved me, you big manly man! I knew you cared about me, Edgy. It just took you a while to—"

"Care about you?" Edge finally returned, all the mounting frustration that had been building inside him since that morning when she had disappeared into the sky compounding and releasing. He pushed her away and threw his sword down into the earth, the blade fragmenting the rock around its tip. "Care about you, Kaotica? Do you have any idea what you put me through today? Do you know how much you put at risk because of your selfish fun? If that creature would have escaped it could have killed thousands of innocent people!" Kaotica gave him a puzzled look, placing her hands on her hips.

"Well you just wanted me to kill that thing, how is that any different?" she asked frustrated. "You want me to let things live, you want me to kill them—make up your mind!" Edge didn't miss a beat coming back to jump down her throat.

"Would you just shut your mouth!?!" he bellowed indignantly. "I can't believe how shortsighted and self-centered you are! I risked my life coming after you against Sky Sprites, Windrun Warriors and *that thing* all day long and all you can think about is yourself!"

"But, Edge," she said much softer, "I just—"

"I don't want to hear it, Kaotica!" he cut her off shouting in her face, the ground below her tearing open from his power active around him again. "Now do what I told you this morning and give me back Kaylan!" The dark girl before him stared at him hard for a long moment, confusion and pain flooding her face. After a long moment of holding his heated gaze, she threw her head forward, balling her fists.

"I just did all that so you would come save me like you save Kaylan, Edge!" she cried, obvious emotion in her voice for the first time. "I just want you to like me! But fine, take back Kaylan if she's all you want! I…" she trailed off then, falling to her knees over the ground. Edge looked down to her with worry, his power sealing off. She wasn't overcome with emotion but stricken with something. Edge slowly leaned down to look her over and make sure nothing was wrong. At last she slowly sat up and fixed her penetrating purple eyes on his, a single tear falling from one. "I'm tired," she said softly, shaking her head. "Why am I so tired, Edge?" The boy exhaled softly and shrugged, trying to remain hard.

"You've been out of Kaylan for most of the day—way longer than ever before," he guessed with a blank look on his face. "I'm sure you're out of energy." She nodded softly, looking down in defeat. For the first time seeing her vulnerable and thinking back to what she had just told him, Edge saw a glimpse of the humanity inside her that he never had before. She was the vessel of the God of Darkness and seemingly superhuman every time she appeared but he could finally see that at heart she was just a naïve girl as well. Breathing hard she looked back up to him.

"I'm sorry, Edge," she said softly. "I..."

"You need to rest, Kaotica," he spoke quietly. "It's time to bring back Kaylan." She looked at him for a long moment but at last let her eyes slip shut and the aura of dark purple light flared around her, gradually transforming into golden light. As the luminous field of energy slipped away, Kaylan appeared before him in the exact same position Kaotica had been. Her blue eyes were open this time and she was awake. Staring at her uncertainly, Edge watched her look around, unsure for a moment, but finally return his gaze.

"I..." she started virtually inaudible, "saw everything..." Edge nodded slowly and took a seat beside her, staring off into the endless blue before them over the base of the Temple of Wind. He leaned down with only his elbows to prop him up in his fatigue, just sitting next to the girl.

"I know, Kaylan," he replied softly. "I know."

Chapter 19

Recuperation

As soon as they had sealed Wyrik back into the Temple of Wind with their combined Lift Power, the Triune and the Windrun Warrior Kohlin Marraea leapt out of the alcove they had been hiding in to jet up to the Blue Maven called Edge and the blond girl now sitting beside him. Though Kohlin and the two sprites were confused at her altered appearance from what they had first observed, Zephyr informed them it was too long a story to explain then and that his partner and the girl needed their rest after such an ordeal. Gathering up the humans with their power the Triune ferried them back to the portal and warped to Haven. Upon their arrival the entire sanctuary was in pandemonium over the news from the blue sprite that Wyrik had been released, but the Triune was quick to allay their concerns and impart to them that the crisis had been averted thanks to the Maven they had encountered earlier and his familiar partner. Though Zephyr was not sure how the rest of Haven would react to his sudden return, he was greeted as a hero after this news and welcomed into his former kin's embrace. Edge couldn't help but let a wide grin spread over his face watching his partner finally find home once more.

Looking to Kaylan's health first, the boy asked Kohlin if there was any place fit for humans to rest in Haven. The other two members of the Triune were happy to remind him it was a sanctuary for all and pointed them in the direction of the end of the plateau near the Dew Drop gardens. There was a small stone building on the second level of the village there constructed centuries ago for visiting Windrun Warriors. Though not very large it had soft beds and food standing by. Thanking them earnestly and leaving his men to be attended to by the sprites, Kohlin led the younger humans to the opposite side of Haven and the house. Though Kaylan insisted her energy was restored after Kaotica's most recent appearance as she marveled at the Sky Sprite village, halfway to the end of the plateau she became dizzy and stumbled while walking, prompting Edge to pick her up and carry her in his arms despite her claims she was fine on her own. The girl blushed as he lifted her off her feet without a word, no longer leaving her protests open for debate.

 At last arriving at the end of the plateau, Edge and Kaylan stared in amazement as the green earth and Dew Drop gardens beneath them suddenly dropped off, replaced by the dense sheets of clouds below the unending sky. The cozy little guest house before them at the end of the second level bridge was crafted from the same stone as the curving bridges around the sanctuary, multiple windows and flowing feathers wafting in the wind on each side. Kohlin opened the door for Edge and quickly asked if he could be of any assistance for the moment. When Edge replied he would take care of Kaylan and get some rest himself that night, Kohlin respectfully bowed and replied he would return the following morning to hear the rest of their story. Closing the door, Edge turned to lay Kaylan in one of the four beds in the bright room and instructed her to try and get some sleep. She wanted to stay awake and talk to him as she lay down, but telling her there would be time later the Maven pulled the sheets up to her head and watched her fall asleep so she would feel safe with him nearby. Stepping outside the house as night began to darken the unending blue skies to black, he ambled to the back of the dark gardens. With a deep breath he stared out at the sea of stars glimmering above him before at last trying to rest as best he could without actually falling asleep. Zephyr had come to meet his partner for the night as always, merrily greeting him as a hero. Edge merely smiled as he lay down against a grassy knoll in the garden and told him the glory belonged to his gallant partner.

 With his friend to keep an eye on him as he slept in case the dream appeared, Edge fell to sleep for the night, away from Kaylan for her own safety, and rose early the next morning to clean and wash himself in the pond miraculously gathered from waterfalls further up the peaks. Refreshed once more, the Maven and purple sprite made their way back up to the small house on the second level of the city. As usual, Zephyr took to the skies to scan the area for anything unfavorable that could have been out there. Finding Kaylan

Tales of Iairia

still fast asleep as he entered, Edge silently closed the door behind him and unhurriedly draped himself over a chair beside her. Resting his chin over his folded arms bolstered by the back of the chair, he patiently watched the beautiful girl breathe and waited for her to wake on her own. When the rays of light from the luminous orb in the clear skies finally seeped their way onto Kaylan's soft face, she slightly stirred. Edge forced himself out of his daydreaming and nervously pulled away a few feet to increase the space between them. Her brilliant blue eyes opened slowly to find the dark boy glancing at her, pretending to look around the room not noticing her wake. Though she seemed confused at first, a wave of remembrance washed through her and she slowly sat up with a gradual smile growing in his direction, locks of golden hair tumbling over her shoulders as she rose from the white sheets.

"Good morning, Edge," she spoke sleepily, her smile widening. "Please tell me you got some sleep too." The Maven nodded as he let a small smile escape from the corner of his lips as well.

"I did," he confirmed. "How do you feel?" The girl replied she was fine but that she would like to wash up, feeling a little grimy. Informing her about the pond of clear water outside in the gardens, he let her wash and waited outside the house while she groomed herself for the day inside. As she was finishing up, Edge caught sight of the Windrun Warrior Kohlin Marraea turning the corner of a bridge for the guest house. He seemed like an honorable and respectful man from what little interaction he had with him the previous day; something he wasn't accustomed to from any Windrun Warrior he had ever encountered before. Thrusting his back off the doorway of the house he rested on with folded arms, the Maven slightly tipped his head and outstretched his hand in greeting. No sooner than they released hands Kaylan opened the door to tell Edge he could come back in, surprised to find the man from the day before with him. Smiling and inviting them both in, they entered and sat around the various beds and chairs in the room. As Edge moved to his chair from earlier he found himself holding his breath as he watched the beautiful blond Grandarian take a seat on the bed next to him. Though she had only washed her face and refreshed her hair from the day before she looked more beautiful than ever in the rays of fervent light shining onto her glimmering hair. She shot him a quirky glance as he stared but the Maven quickly came back to his senses and looked to Kohlin, his face slightly going red. Taking a seat on one of the beds himself the Windrun Warrior smiled to Kaylan.

"Are you rested, my dear?" he asked her sincerely. Kaylan nodded yes with a beaming smile and thanked him for his generosity and concern for them. "Oh nonsense, young lady. It's the Sky Sprites you should be thanking, but after yesterday I think they'll just want to be thanking you two for whatever you did atop the peaks." The smile on Kaylan's face slightly faded as she shook her head.

"I didn't have anything to do with saving anyone, sir," she replied humbly. "It was Edge that saved me as well." She turned to the Maven with a smile but he didn't say anything. Kohlin nodded, his face growing curious.

"Yes, well, speaking of yesterday," he started with his hands on his knees, "I was hoping the two of you could clarify what exactly happened for me and who the both of you are." Kaylan looked to Edge uncertainly at this, not sure how much of their story they should relate to the man or how much he already knew. Seeing the hesitancy and confusion in her expression, Edge leaned up to answer.

"Well it's a very long story, Kohlin," he began trying to hint with his voice it was not possible for them to explain it all. "Like I told you yesterday, you would probably think we're insane if we told you what we're doing but—"

"Wait," Kaylan suddenly interjected, bursting alive with shock abruptly running through her. "Your name is Kohlin?" The Windrun Warrior nodded his head with a smile.

"First Captain of the Windrun Warriors, Kohlin Marraea at your service, my dear," he replied, to which the girl's blue eyes widened. She slowly rose and brought a hand to cover her mesmerized face. Edge looked to her uncertainly, wondering what was wrong.

"Kaylan, what is it?" he asked her quickly. She turned to him with a small smile over her face.

"Edge, we can trust this man. We should tell him everything," she said suddenly, catching both of them off guard. Edge's brow furrowed.

"Why? You act like you know this guy," he said perturbed at why she so suddenly trusted the man to hear their entire story. She turned to face the confused Windrun Warrior then, taking a step toward him.

"Well I don't," she started with her warm smile growing, "but my parents do." The man squinted his eyes at this, trying to place her in his mind as someone he had met before. "I can't believe we're meeting like this, sir, but my name is Kaylan Tieloc. You traveled with my parents Tavin and Arilia Tieloc in the Days of Destiny." Upon hearing these names fall from the girl's lips the expression over the man's face suddenly turned blank, astonishment filling his wide eyes. He slowly stood and stared at her hard for a long moment before at last letting a wide smile overtake his face.

"It's true," he mouthed softly, looking her over. "You're the mirror image of Ril..." he trailed off. Taking a step toward her he laughed and opened his arms to ask if he could hug her. Though taken aback at his heartfelt reaction, she giggled and stepped forward to hug the man revealed to be someone she had heard stories about for years before going to bed. After releasing the girl with a smile, Kaylan turned to the confused Maven sitting and staring at her to tell him this man was one of her parents' companions on their journey in the Days of Destiny. Though Edge could barely believe it at first, from the way Kohlin seemed transformed before him he guessed it had to be true. With this newest revelation, Edge agreed they could trust him and let Kaylan tell him what they were doing. Kaylan started at her parent's marriage years ago and briefly related everything that they had been up to since, including her birth.

When she got to what she was doing with a Maven and his Sky Sprite partner in the Southland away from home, the two of them teamed up to relate the incredible tale of their journey to the portal to the void and the Mystic Sage Zeroan's charge for them to save the world. At the end Kohlin could feel the air in his lungs escaping into the high mountain atmosphere, almost unable to believe it was true. All they had battled for in the Days of Destiny was being undermined by this new Drakkaidian High Priest and his schemes.

"I just can't believe it," he spoke softly, staring at the ground. "After all we fought for with your parents and others, it's all at risk again." Kaylan silently nodded, waiting for his shock to dissipate.

"I wish as much as you it wasn't but it's all too true," she confirmed somberly. "We've already had an encounter with Dark Mages from Drakkaidia on the way here and more are sure to be behind us after Kaotica displayed her power for them to sense yesterday. Edge and I have to get to the Mystic Tower as fast as we can to find the location of a new Granic Crystal to put all this right. We'll need to be leaving this morning." She looked to Edge, who gave her a single nod from the chair in which he sat. Kohlin stared into space for another long moment before at last nodding to himself and bringing his eyes up to hers, determination within.

"Then I'm going to grant you what help I can," he stated powerfully, catching them both off guard. "If anything, I owe Tavin my life many times over. The least I can do to repay him is to aid his daughter in her own quest for the safety of the world. And I assure you I can definitely be of assistance to you. There have been reports of strange activity in the Mystic Tower for years now. If you're going there I can get you in and lead you where you need to go inside. I was once a guardian there before I left for Galantia in the Days of Destiny." Kaylan looked to Edge hopefully to find the boy already staring at her. Though she knew he preferred to keep their number as small as possible while traveling they could use all the help they could get and this sounded too good to pass up. He nodded to her approvingly, at which the girl beamed and rose from her bed once more.

"Thank you so much, Kohlin," she said gratefully. "We would be happy to have you with us." The seasoned Windrun Warrior rose with a smile himself and nodded.

"Very good then," he replied. "There are horses that my team left at the base of the Empyrean Peaks. Since our business is of the utmost urgency we will take them and be on our way whenever you are ready. The Sky Sprites would be happy to replenish your supplies as well."

"That's wonderful," she confirmed, turning to face Edge. "All we need is Zephyr and we're ready to go then, right?" Edge let his smile slightly fade as he took in a deep breath.

"I'm not sure if Zeph will be coming, Kaylan" he stated softly, to which the girl's brow furrowed. "He's finally got back what he lost years ago—his family and his home up here in Haven. I think he's going to want to stay with them now that he's got them back."

"Well you'd better think again, buddy," a fourth voice sounded from one of the windows beside them. All three humans in the room turned to find a purple sprite standing over the windowsill with a smile on his yellow beak. He formulated a semitransparent sphere of light around his body and lifted off to hover before the boy. "You think you can get rid of me that easily, partner?" Edge frowned and stared at him hard.

"Zeph, you know you're the only friend I've got but don't you remember what you first said to me years ago?" he asked. "I saved your life so you said you would stick with me until you repaid the debt. Well you have about ten times over—not including yesterday—so you're free. This is your home. Wouldn't you rather be here with your family than out risking your life with a lure for danger like me?" The little sprite eased his Lift Power and landed on the edge of the bed facing him.

"This is my home, partner," he started with a smile, "but there comes a point in your life when you realize who really matters, who never did, and who always will. After all we've been through and all we're doing now I couldn't abandon you even if I wanted to. It doesn't matter that we're even now—that just makes us true partners. And partners don't split up. I'm with you until the end, buddy." Edge looked at him hard for a long moment before at last letting a smile pass over his face in thanks to his best friend. Zephyr shot into the air again, turning to Kaylan. "Besides he wouldn't last two second on the outside without me to watch his butt anyway!" Kaylan giggled while Edge playfully swatted him away and rose from his chair, tossing his blue scarf over his shoulder. The purple sprite soared over to Kaylan who swept him up in her arms and kissed him on the forehead. "And how could I ever survive without this beautiful girl doing things like that to me? I can never leave now!" With that, the trio of humans and their Sky Sprite companion gathered up their supplies and thanked their hosts for their generosity once more. Departing down the slopes of the Empyrean Peaks, all of them felt a new burst of vitality and energy giving them the new hope they needed to press on for the Mystic Tower.

Chapter 20

Old Friends

With his Lavlas Rock clenched tightly in hand, Tavin Tieloc gazed up through the blizzard of snow raging around him and let out a deep breath of relief. He could see the summit of the southern glacier near the portal to the void just above him. He was almost there. After volunteering to personally inspect the source of the dark disturbance near the mighty Sword of Granis that had wrought the Supreme Granisian's Senior Council with tension nearly two weeks ago, the Warrior of Light had traveled with all speed for the Border Mountains. Bypassing the southern pass at the Battlemount to save precious time he cut straight through the mountains in the east, following a path he and Jaren Garrinal had discovered years ago in their travels across Grandaria that led straight to the peak containing the portal to the void. With the warming Lavlas Rock in his grasp, Tavin had penetrated through the unyielding snowfields in under a week, finally arriving exhausted at the steep slope he had once ascended over twenty years ago.

As the Warrior of Light reminded himself he was almost there once more, his determination took hold and drove him up the last stretch of the snowy glacier with the fierce wind blowing his brown hair and blue cape back into the frigid air. With the snow yielding at his coming thanks to enchanted Lavlas Rock, Tavin at last made it to the summit breathing hard and lifting his head to gaze upon a familiar sight. The portal to the void that Drakkan had created to seal Granis away after the Battle of the Gods eons ago lay before him, now containing the dark god himself after the Days of Destiny. Sweeping his anxious eyes around for any sign of trouble, Tavin slowly relaxed as he found the portal exactly as he had left it the last time he was here. Nothing seemed out of place or disturbed in any way. Though the

Warrior of Light allowed a massive wave of release to wash through him, he remembered he had not come this far merely to stare at the portal from afar and began to trudge through the summit snow once more.

After making his way across the long white peak for the gargantuan stone platform somehow clear of the falling snow perpetually coming down, he looked down to the illustrious portal surface and slowly stepped on it, expecting a familiar sensation of warmth to instantly sweep through his body as it had in his youth. As he planted a thick blue boot onto the stone platform, however, Tavin was gripped by the complete inverse of what he had expected. Instead of the usual sensation of warmth radiating into his body a malicious field of cold ripped through him, biting at his being the second he touched the platform. The Warrior of Light narrowed his eyes uncertainly at the abnormality, clearly revealing something was indeed out of place. Shifting his suddenly worried gaze back out to the center of the massive platform hundreds of feet away, he began nervously walking forward toward the object lying at rest far ahead. Steadily making his way closer to the mighty talisman jutting from the center of the platform, Tavin's eyes squinted with concern once more. He could not see the perpetual brilliant hum of the golden Granic Crystal as he should have. Picking up his pace even faster in his anxious state, the Warrior of Light found himself sprinting toward the pedestal holding the Sword of Granis in place.

Finally arriving within twenty feet of the pedestal Tavin forced himself to halt, feeling his heart sink to mesh with his guts. He shook his head in disbelief, distraught at what lay before him. The Sword of Granis lay tilted over the pedestal with a dark shroud of mist hovering at its base. Walking slowly toward the damaged weapon, he peered down aghast to find the usually brilliantly shining Granic Crystal vanished. He painfully shut his eyes and rolled his head back in anguish. It was his worst fear come true—something had happened to the Sword of Granis that had drained its power completely. Even from afar in Grandaria Tavin could always feel it's presence alive in the back of his mind but now standing mere feet away not so much as hint of its energy shone forth. It felt dead, and the powerful seal over the portal with it. His mind wheeling with what could have happened to cause this and what it now meant, he looked down to the faint mist of darkness hovering around

Trial of a Maven

the base of the pedestal. His eyes narrowed with distrust and suspicion. Something like this could not have occurred randomly or by natural cause; the Granic Crystal could not have disappeared by itself or the Sword of Granis fallen to its side diagonally without intervention. Someone had done this on purpose. Tavin's grief slowly morphed to anger as he remembered the words of the generals back in Galantia. This had to have something to do with Drakkaidia. There was no one else to point a finger at.

No sooner than this dangerous notion passed through his mind the silence atop the pallid summit was broken by a voice calling directly behind him.

"What is going on here?" It forcefully pounded through the chilled air. His eyes going wide with surprise, the Warrior of Light wheeled around to find a familiar figure standing barely fifty feet beyond, his thick gray cape flapping in the winds behind him along with his long crimson hair.

It was Verix.

The two apprehensively stared each other down for a long moment, fear and precarious volatility mirrored in each others' eyes. A million thoughts racing through his shaken head, Tavin did not respond except to slowly reach down for the hilt of his sword. Observing the move, Verix's face tightened and he shouted out again.

"You should be still right now, Tieloc," the Drakkaidian prince advised harshly, taking a step forward over the freezing portal. "Answer me! What are you doing?" Tavin kept his heated gaze on the prince but protectively took a step closer to the Sword of Granis behind him.

"A little far from home, aren't you Verix?" he responded with another question, still inching toward the sword. His eyes passing down to the dark mist radiating around the Sword of Granis at the Grandarian's feet, Verix instantly knew it had to be the malevolent power within the portal seeping out.

"Answer me!" he bellowed, his impatience getting the better of him. "What do you think you are doing? Are you such a fool you would toy with the key that locks the ultimate evil away?"

"Verix, I don't know what this is but I want the Granic Crystal now," he commanded, stretching an open hand out for the Sword of Granis. Seeing him within range to touch the mighty blade, a red mist of foaming light appeared around

Verix's hands, dissipating to reveal a savage broadsword resting in his hands that instantly rose for Tavin.

"Step away from the sword, Tieloc," he commanded vigorously. Seeing the Drakkaidian prince draw his sword for him Tavin leapt in front of the mighty talisman behind him and drew the blade at his side.

"You have no right to tell me what to do with the Sword of Granis, Montrox," he stated matching the other's intensity. "This is a Grandarian talisman and I am going to put whatever is going on here right. You can either help me or get out of my way, but I am going to get to the bottom of this." Verix grit his teeth and shouted out over him once again.

"I don't believe this—Zalnaught was right! If you think you can play with the fate of the world just because you are the Warrior of Light you are sadly mistaken. Now I said step away from the sword, Tavin!" he bellowed.

"I'm not moving!" he blasted back.

"Do it now!"

"I'm not letting you through!" As the two continued shouting over each other with their tempers soaring Verix saw Tavin twist back. Assuming he was trying to move the Sword of Granis again the prince threw his hand forward with a blast of electrified crimson energy exploding forth from nowhere. Sensing the attack coming, Tavin readied his own and summoned enough elemental power of light around his blade to swat the blast away as it came careening into him. Stronger than he had expected, the dark energy temporarily knocked him off balance. By the time the Warrior of Light resumed his fighting stance he found Verix only a few feet away with a furious aura of crimson energy radiating off his muscular body. Kicking forward to meet the Drakkaidian's charge, Tavin's elemental power of light burst alive around his body to illuminate the pallid portal with golden light.

As the two powerhouses' blades met, an explosion of power ripped through the air around them sending waves of energy blasting off in all directions that cleared the snow flurries above them and pounded into the trembling portal. So great was their momentum that both Tavin and Verix were forced to take another step past each other after their blades met to halt with their capes both whipping against each other's faces as they passed. Wrapping both hands around the hilts of their swords the two wheeled around then and sent them clashing against each other with another detonation of throbbing energy blasting out from the impact. Finally facing each other with powers alight, the veteran combatants let their warrior instinct take control and began dexterously clashing their blades through the frigid mountain air, agilely leaping and dodging the other's attacks or powerfully parrying them away. With their elemental powers to enhance their honed fighting skill the speed and strength of battle was beyond anything a common swordsman would ever have been able to contend with. As the battle raged on over the sprawling stone portal for several short minutes they worked their way to its western edge. Pushing Tavin back with a swift jab to his chest from his elbow, the Drakkaidian prince screamed and savagely swung his blade down with an arching wave of crimson energy leaping from it as it came down. Leaping to roll to his right Tavin barely dodged the electrified power as it sliced into the portal to tear a gaping fissure through its ornate designs and continue into the bank of snow beyond to divide and blast it upward. Instantly leaping back up to raise his sword and thrust outward for Verix, Tavin stabbed with such force that a golden aura formed around his blade to push Verix back and throw off his balance the same way he had done to Tavin at the start of their clash.

Seizing on this momentary advantage as his foe stumbled backward, Tavin rose and funneled his elemental power downward into his weapon. Flipping his blade downward he stabbed at the portal to release a blinding flash of light that illuminated the entire mountain summit. Bringing a hand to his eyes to shield them from the stunning display, Verix stood dazed and immobile as Tavin came rushing forward to pepper him with a burning fist of golden energy that sent him flying back through the air with his signature broadsword flying from his grasp. Though stunned and bleeding from his forehead, the veteran prince grit his teeth with purpose in his descent and flexed his crimson power alive around his body once more. Flipping himself over right before he touched down he landed in a crouch over the portal, fragmenting it beneath his feet under the weight of his power. Instantly rising, Verix clenched his fists and crossed his forearms before his chest, concentrating a swelling field of power around them. Realizing what Verix was about to do, Tavin dropped his sword beside him and balled up his own fists to charge them with golden energy at his sides.

Within seconds Tavin could feel Verix's strength peak and watched him thrust his arms forward to open his fists and blast a careening beam of dark energy forth from his palms, exploding out to meet his foe. The next spilt second Tavin opened his own fists and threw his arms forward to let a beam of flowing golden energy blast from his open hands of equal size and power to Verix's. Rushing to meet each other with impossible speed, the two beams of opposite energies collided with a thunderous clapping of power on power. The two held their ground and power for almost a full minute, mustering every ounce of strength they could to hold each other back. After standing firm against the black beam of intense energy for so long Tavin realized Verix's power was only rising and he could feel himself losing ground. His face tensed as the dark beam began to slowly push his counter attack back, weakening by the second. Though Tavin's command over the element of light had once matched Verix's sway over the dark blessing he had received from his father, Tavin had not had occasion to use it to this degree in years while Verix had maintained his power virtually everyday. Without the Sword of Granis, the Warrior of Light knew he did not have the strength to best Verix in a straight clash of power.

Holding his ground as best he could, Tavin listened as Verix let out a dominating scream and revealed another layer of power streaming out to blast into Tavin's failing beam of light. So quick came Verix's new energy that Tavin never had a chance to evade the blast that blew him off his feet and into the air in a massive explosion of darkness and flame over the portal where he had been standing. Though his circulating field of radiant power saved him from being incinerated he landed with a painful thud on his back far behind, stunned and immobile. As Tavin lay trying to rise with his ears ringing from the potent detonation, Verix dropped his arms and turned his head to find his sword lying on the other side of the portal behind Tavin. Raising his arm as if to take hold of it from so far away it disappeared into a cloud of red foam only to reappear in his open hand a moment later. Rearing down to build his power once more, the Dark Prince leapt off the portal to soar into the air with his power boosting his height. Reaching the peak of his jump, Verix looked down to find Tavin below him and flipped his sword point to extend it down.

Finally catching sight of the prince plummeting down for him with his weapon reaching for his adversary's chest, the Warrior of Light barely managed to roll away as he pounded into the portal with his blade piercing its surface and crushing it to a crater where he had been. Spotting his own sword blown beside him by Verix's last attack, Tavin kicked a single boot up into Verix's head and reached out to grab it, knocking the prince back. Rolling over and leaping back up to meet Tavin with his sword arching down for him once more, the Drakkaidian flared his power around him and threw his own sword out with both hands to meet it. Their blades locked and their powers flaring, both warriors knew this would be their last stand. They were each putting all their strength into their grips on the swords and only one of them was going to walk away from this final exchange of power. Their fields of radiating strength grew by the second, expanding over the entire surface of the portal.

Eventually Tavin's fear from their previous battle of power reappeared, sensing the Drakkaidian prince overpowering him. Screaming out once more, Verix's sword shot electric bolts of crimson light down its edge and pressed into Tavin's so hard that the Grandarian's blade shattered in his hands, forcing Tavin to stagger back in pain. Charging forward, Verix thrust up the hilt of his sword to ram it into Tavin's chest and forcefully drop him to his backside. His expended power leaving him, it was all the exhausted Warrior of Light could do to lie struggling for breath over the scarred and torn portal now weakened and dying without the power of the Sword of Granis to maintain it. Trying to rise, Tavin was stopped short by Verix's boot on his chest ruthlessly shoving him back down. Standing over him and breathing hard with his crimson power radiating around him, the prince locked his heated red eyes onto the blue ones staring back at him apprehensively. He raised his large broadsword and set its tip at the Warrior of Light's neck, holding it there for several long moments.

Though Tavin saw his life flash before his eyes the moment the cold steel touched his vulnerable skin, after a long final second of staring each other down Verix withdrew the weapon from his neck and rested it back at his side. He narrowed his irate eyes and silently shook his head, preparing to softly speak.

"Because of what you did for my country and who you once were," the prince spoke gravely through his heavy breathing, "you will leave this portal alive." Tavin eyed him uncertainly in the lingering silence as the wind slowly brushed the Drakkaidian's cape to and fro and his aura of power faded around his body. Tightening his grip around his sword, Verix leaned closer to the downed Grandarian and spoke almost inaudibly, his voice obviously choked with emotion. "But the next time we meet, I will provide no such mercy." With that, the Dark Prince powerfully lifted himself erect once more and turned in one fluid motion to begin marching back across the portal and to the snowy earth at its base beyond. Watching from the ravaged portal as Verix Montrox disappeared into the endless white beyond them, Tavin lay regaining his breath in disbelief of what had just happened and what it now meant for Iairia.

Chapter 21

Uninvited Guests

Edge, Kaylan, Zephyr and their new guide Kohlin Marraea arrived on the outskirts of the Sage's Valley containing the Mystic Tower as night sank in to blanket the world in darkness, the dense wooded area they had passed into now only illuminated by the full moon staring down from the heavens. They had traveled swiftly from the towering Empyrean Peaks on horses provided by Kohlin and his party of Windrun Warriors, bypassing the bustling Windrun City to cut right into the hills surrounding the Sage's Valley. The party had ridden hard for two days but arriving outside the valley that night, Kohlin brought them to a halt and instructed them to dismount. Though Edge insisted they continue being so close, Kohlin was hesitant to proceed through the night with all the recent rumors of strange activity within the Sage's Valley. None of his Windrun Warriors had been permitted inside since the fall of the sages during the Days of Destiny and no one else who had entered the valley had come out in years. It had become forbidden ground. Confident that they could use the cover of night to their advantage should they encounter anything unfavorable lying in wait for them, Kaylan agreed with Edge and pled for Kohlin to lead them inside at once. The Windrun Warrior obviously reserved his doubts but seemed to put much faith in the young Tieloc's confidence. Agreeing on the condition they leave the horses outside the valley to maintain their stealth he told them of a gap in the hills they could use to lead them into the valley.

Having loosely tied the horses up to a massive tree branch downed by the high powered winds that consistently swept through the valley, the party silently passed through the hills and into the heavy woods below. Though the Sage's Valley was one of the few places Edge had never been before he could feel a familiar sensation seize him as they passed through the gap to the woods, flashes of déjà vu seeming to strike out at him every few steps he took that threw off his concentration. Shrugging them off to focus on the task at hand, the Maven thought about what the spirit of Zeroan had told him before disappearing in the Battlemount. The answers he needed about his past and future would be within the tower. Though eager to finally account for his unbridled inner power and to find a way to control it, a nameless dread hung over him at what he was about to do. This Scion of the Order of Alberic business hardly sounded like something destined for a troubled soul like his. All he knew was being a Maven and whatever extraneous power dwelled inside him was just something he wanted to suppress and forget about. This fate Zeroan spoke of was not for him.

After quietly passing through the thick forest of the valley for nearly an hour, Kohlin silently called for the party to halt and drop into a crouch. Lifting his head to scan ahead of him around a bend in the road, after a long moment he turned and crept beside his younger companions.

"At the end of this path the forest abruptly ends and the small plateau where the Mystic Tower rests will appear," he whispered through the darkness. "No one has been inside since the attack of the demons in the Days of Destiny that left all the sages dead, yet there have been reports coming in to Windrun City ever since of activity within." Kaylan turned to shoot Edge a knowing glance of dread, guessing the source of that activity.

"Zeroan told us that Dark Mages infiltrated the Mystic Tower right after the Days of Destiny," she whispered back to Kohlin. "I doubt they ever left."

"Well there's one way to be sure," Edge affirmed from beside them, cupping a hand around his mouth to make a strange cooing sound like that of a bird. Kaylan eyed him peculiarly for a moment but looked up to find Zephyr descending out of the trees to spread his wings back and perch on the boy's shoulder. Feeling his talon like feet gently touch down on his frame Edge turned to face his partner. "I need you to recon the tower ahead of us, Zeph. Keep your distance but look for anything out of the ordinary—any activity whatsoever. If you see anyone try to get close enough to get a good look but make it fast." Wordlessly, the purple sprite lifted back off into the night air and disappeared through the branches of the trees above them. Waiting as the Sky Sprite made his reconnaissance Kaylan marveled at how skilled and efficient the Maven and his partner were on the job, making her feel all the safer with them watching over her. After a few short minutes Zephyr dropped back out of the trees to latch onto Edge's shoulder. His finely feathered face was wrought with discomfort, obviously shaken about something.

"There's definitely something in there," he spoke unnerved. "There wasn't any obvious activity from what I could see or anything in plain view but as I passed up the levels of the tower around the windows I could see faint movements appear and disappear like ghosts. A human eye could never pick it up in the darkness because I barely could, but there is unquestionably something odd going on in that building." Edge shook his head and let out an inaudible huff of vexation as he turned back to Kaylan and Kohlin.

"This has got ambush—and Drakkaidia—written all over it," he alleged quietly. "Even if we get inside undetected this sounds like a trap."

"Well if there's anyone you want to spring a trap with in the Mystic Tower it's me," Kohlin spoke up from beside them. "I know first hand how dangerous the Dark Mages are but if we can avoid them they won't be a problem. I know secret passages in this tower from my time as a guardian here that someone could pass by everyday and never notice. If you still want me to get you in I'm confident we can penetrate unseen to the master library." Kaylan looked back to Edge once more, noting the doubtful expression on his face.

"We don't have a choice," she spoke to the Maven, who silently accepted she was right and nodded. "Take us inside, Kohlin." Having their approval, the Windrun Warrior nodded as well and slowly rose, motioning for them to follow him. Still in a crouch he stepped off the beaten path and led them into the tangled trees, carefully avoiding ensnaring foliage as he crept through the darkness. Eventually he halted before a sunken stump half submerged beneath the forest floor and reached inside with his right arm, groping for something. At last pulling his arm back he turned back to them with what looked like a small leaf in his hand. Moving to the large tree trunk Edge knelt beside, the Maven and Grandarian girl stared in awe as he lifted a panel of bark from the tree and inserted the leaf into a small slit where the bark had been. Rotating it to his right in a circle a small popping sound echoed from behind the tree. Kaylan stared at the trunk in amazement as half its surface gave way and Kohlin pushed it aside like a door, revealing a hollow passage inside leading underground.

Turning and motioning with his head for the others to step inside, Kaylan uncertainly nodded and rose to lift her foot through the tree. Before she could step onto the ladder leading down Edge put on hand on her shoulder and pulled her back. Questioningly staring at him as he motioned for her to wait, the boy moved past her and stepped in first, one of his twin daggers in his gloved hand. Before disappearing into the darkness he instructed Zephyr to remain outside to keep an eye on the tower in case they needed to make a quick escape, to which the sprite lifted off the boy's shoulder in a ball of Lift Power once more. Sliding down the ladder to land at the surface of an underground tunnel nearly twenty feet below them, Edge looked up to find Kaylan following after him one rung at a time. Climbing down to the base of the ladder the Maven helped her to the ground, hearing her nervously breathing through the darkness. Watching as Kohlin followed closing the door of the tree behind him, he stepped down to grope behind them at the base of the ladder and quietly lift something from the wall.

At once an illuminating flame burst awake in a torch the Windrun Warrior held. Seeing Edge and Kaylan stare at him uncertainly, Kohlin vaguely informed them that many simple talismans around the Mystic Tower were enchanted to come alive at will and that they had to follow him closely in the tunnels with the many pitfalls ahead. Taking his word for it the band pressed on into the narrow underground tunnel, carefully following after Kohlin through what turned out to be a veritable labyrinth of passageways. Inspecting them as best he could in the weak light, Edge noticed many of the paths looked less than solid or stable—obviously the pitfalls Kohlin had mentioned.

After an agonizingly long journey through the dark musty tunnels Kohlin at last came to what looked to be a dead end of solid dirt. Reaching into his tunic pocket to pull forth the leaf-like key he had pulled out of the stump on the surface he gingerly placed it in the torch. As they watched it burn up like any leaf would, Kaylan and Edge's eyes slowly widened as the red light from the flame began to burn green. As the light changed, so did the walls of the tunnel around them. The once solid dead end of dirt before them had vanished as the green light fell on it, revealing a chamber of stone beyond. Stepping through the passageway into the room, Kohlin set the torch into a holder mounted on the wall. The moment he did the enchanted fire died away but a slow grinding sound to their left sounded through the stale air. The dark chamber was instantly lit by the faint light from a much larger chamber beyond, into which Kohlin motioned for them to follow him. Stepping through the open doorway in the wall, Edge looked around to find himself in a wide chamber filled with weapons and armor.

"This is a secret armory under the Mystic Tower once used by its guardians," Kohlin quietly informed them, leading them past tables and racks of swords and shields to the other side of the faintly lit chamber. "It leads to various parts of the tower through secret passages concealed by decorations and magic like the tunnel we just passed through." Stepping up a small row of stairs to a higher level of the chamber Kaylan and Edge noticed three doorways revealing spiraling staircases within. "The stairs to the left lead up to a room outside the meeting chamber on the third floor, while the one on the right goes to a passage outside the Draught Chasm hidden behind what looks to be a stained glass window. We'll be taking the middle staircase that leads directly to the first level of the master library on the first floor. I want you both to remember this armory well because if we encounter something that forces us to retreat out of the tower we will fall back to this position." Seeing Kaylan and Edge nod in approval, the Windrun Warrior told them to be quiet as they traveled up the stairwell as they would be entering the tower.

As Kohlin turned to make his way into the stairwell Edge abruptly froze, the déjà vu blasting awake in his mind once again. The images flashing through his mind were not of simple memories past but of the dream he had lived with since childhood. Gritting his teeth in sudden alarm, the Maven forced his eyes shut attempting to erase the images from his mind. Turning back to find him immobile and his face wrought with tension, Kaylan's expression turned worried as well and she shot back to extend her hands to his shoulders.

"Edge, are you alright?" she whispered distressed. Feeling the girl softly grip him Edge forced his eyes open, the flashes of his dream subsiding. He breathed deeply for a long moment but at last wordlessly nodded, straightening his body and motioning for her to release him and be on her way up the stairs. She did so hesitantly, aware something was troubling him. Leaving the armory and ascending up the compact stairway that seemed to spiral upwards forever, the trio at last came to another dead end. Kohlin turned back to them and pressed a finger against his lips to signal the utmost need for silence. Slowly rotating his head back to the wall he put his head up to it until it touched the surface. Edge and Kaylan stared in awe as he pushed it through the outwardly solid barrier with the false stone rippling like water. Shooting each other astounded glances, the pair waited for Kohlin to eventually bring his face back through the fake wall to give them a single nod, indicating their path was clear.

With that, the Windrun Warrior gradually extended a leg through the rippling wall until his entire body had vanished. Though hesitant, Kaylan slowly followed and pushed through, followed by the black clad Maven behind her. As the tail end of his flowing blue scarf fell out of the false barrier, Edge turned back to find a stained glass window where he had just emerged. Extending his hand to it he pushed the tips of his gloved fingers through, a disbelieving smile briefly spreading across his lips. Hearing his Grandarian charge gasp in front of him, Edge wheeled around to face whatever had caught her attention. Stretching for hundreds of feet before them and three floors above was the master library of the Mystic Tower, filled with thousands of books over its myriad selves. The Maven could feel his jaw drop at the vastness of the knowledge contained in the chamber, virtually the entire history of Iairia lying before him. Remembering their task at hand, a thought struck him and a frown crossed his face.

"So where do we start?" he whispered to no one in particular. Kaylan's eyes widened with his question, a blank look falling on her expression. She turned back to him with a doubtful look in her blue eyes and shook her head.

"I have no idea," she returned clueless. "Zeroan just said we would find the location of a new Granic Crystal inside the Mystic Tower. He never told us where..." Trailing off with incredulity entering her expression, she realized it would take them a lifetime to peruse all the texts around them. Any of these books might hold the location of the Granic Crystal; looking for it aimlessly was like trying to find a needle in a haystack. She looked to Kohlin hopefully but the Windrun

Warrior merely shrugged back to her, reminding her only the sages were permitted to read the ancient texts of the libraries. He was as much in the dark as either of them. Realizing they didn't have time to waste in the tower with Dark Mages and Granis knew what else lurking around, Edge breathed hard and spied a huge book resting on a cylindrical table in the center of the room.

"Well we've got to try something," he stated frustrated. "Why don't you two go open that big book over there—maybe it's a reference guide for the material in this place. I'm going to sweep the chamber to make sure we're the only ones in here." Kaylan nodded approvingly.

"All right but be careful, Edge," she spoke with sincerity, still worried something was vexing him that he was not sharing. He nodded wordlessly, holding the Grandarian girl's gaze for a moment longer than he anticipated and turned to weave his way into the towering shelves of books. With the Maven gone for the moment, Kaylan and Kohlin crept across the first floor of the library to the lone table in the center of the room holding the massive brown leather-bound book sitting at an angle atop. Kaylan grasped it softly, wiping away the layer of dust that had settled on it over the years. Slowly opening it to reveal the first page, the girl hopefully widened her eyes. The cover page read "Iairian Almanac of the Eighth Generation." As she flipped through its hundreds of pages, however, the girl narrowed her eyes in confusion. All the pages were blank. Getting a closer look at the book himself, Kohlin's face seemed to come together with a knowing expression.

"Oh I remember what this is," he whispered suddenly. "This is an enchanted book supposedly crafted by Alberic himself that records all the history for a certain period of time all on its own. The pages erase themselves after that measure of time is done and starts over." Hearing this, Kaylan let a wave of disappointment wash through her. That didn't make any sense; there wasn't one page of text in the entire book except for the cover page. Even if a new age of time had just begun something would have to have been recorded. Thinking back to the title of the book, however, she remembered something Zeroan had told her before. The eras of the Mystic Sages were measured in generations of Master Sages over the years and they were now in the eighth one. It had to be because of Edge. He was supposedly the next Scion of the Order of Alberic destined to begin the sages anew but he wasn't the Master Sage yet, so technically the new generation had not yet begun.

Frowning and closing the almanac before her, Kaylan let out a deep breath and slumped in defeat. She was no closer to finding the location of a new Granic Crystal and she still had no idea where to look. As her head drooped to the floor a faint light from inside her tunic caught her attention. Narrowing her eyes in perplexity, they shot open the next instant realizing the Granic Crystal was flashing inside her pocket once more. Fishing it out she laid it in her open hand and watched in amazement as a weak but steady beam of light shot out to point to the other side of the library chamber toward a large shelf of books. At first worried that there was a threat nearby as it had warned her in the woods to the north, as time slipped by with no danger appearing she realized it was merely pointing her in the right direction once more.

Her hope restored, the Grandarian let a small smile appear from the side of her face as she turned to look up to Kohlin Marraea, staring at the golden crystal as well. As she was about to start forward where the Granic Crystal was pointing, however, a loud snapping noise echoed into her ears from directly behind her. Jumping with fright, she spun around expecting to find Edge having worked his way back to them. Although she found the Maven standing there as she predicted, there was another man behind her as well that forced her to jump back. Loosely hanging in Edge's stranglehold grip was another figure covered in light black armor with sharp crimson emblems decorating it, now lifeless with his neck snapped. Kaylan brought a hand to cover her mouth in horror while Kohlin instinctively brought a hand to the hilt of one of his duel sabers. Edge eyed them both with a frustrated look on his face and shook his head.

"It's a good thing I snuck up on this one before he snuck up on you because if I had noticed him slip through one of the bookcases behind you a second later you'd both be dead right now," he spoke in a harsh whisper. He broke off his aggravated gaze and drug the man behind a shadowed aisle between two rising bookcases to silently lay the lifeless body out of visual range from the doorway. In shock, Kaylan at last dropped her hand and shook her head incredulously.

"Thanks, Edge," was all she could manage to get out at first, to which the Maven merely let out a disturbed huff once more and gave her a single nod. "Who was he?" Kohlin released his grasp over the hilt at his side.

"Judging from the armor, a Drakkaidian soldier," he spoke gravely. "If he managed to sneak up on us in here there are bound to be more under the leadership of a Dark Mage." Edge nodded.

"And if he was on patrol he's going to be missed eventually so we're running out of time," he finished hurriedly. "Did you find anything?" Coming back to her senses, Kaylan raised her hand containing the faintly shining Granic Crystal.

"I think so," she confirmed with a hopeful smile. Not sure how the Granic Crystal could help them find the location of the book they needed but remembering the nature of its magic worked in mysterious ways, he nodded and began following her as she strode toward a large bookcase perpendicular to the rows on the right side of the chamber. The light from the miniature crystal vaguely intensifying as she grew closer, Kaylan stopped in front of the shelf and followed the light from the crystal onto the spine of a worn white book tightly squeezed in between the others. Reaching out to lay her fingers on its pallid surface the crystal fell silent again. Guessing its work had been done she tucked the golden gem safely back in her upper tunic pocket and pulled the ancient book from the shelf, blowing the dust from the edges of the pages. As she opened its cover and flipped through its first pages, she found a list she guessed to be a table of contents and swept her finger down it looking for anything that might relate to the Granic Crystal.

Carefully perusing the long list she eventually came to something that struck her eye. A heading halfway down the second page read "Miracle Gems." Squinting her eyes to backtrack to the main heading she found the word Godsmark emboldened on the page. Running it through her mind to try and remember anything from her history of Grandaria that linked to this word, she was suddenly interrupted by the sound of an opening door from beyond them past the rows of shelves she sat behind now. Throwing her head up in fear, she looked to Edge and Kohlin already on their way around the bookcase motioning for her to get down. Peering through an opening in the shelves, Edge narrowed his eyes to spot a black figure looking around in the shadows.

"Looks like another Drak soldier," he whispered almost inaudibly to Kohlin. "I'll take care of it." Drawing a small blade from one of his silver buckled satchels, the Maven crept around the shelf staying in the shadows. Waiting in the silence for her guardian to return Kaylan was immediately horrified to see him suddenly flying off his feet into a bookcase, knocking it over to land in a pile of books toppling over him. Staring at the motionless Maven in horror, she rose and attempted to rush to his side but was held back by Kohlin, silently grabbing her and mouthing for her to remain quiet. He quietly positioned her behind him and wrapped his hands around the twin sabers at his sides, waiting. Listening to the menacing footsteps draw near, the Windrun Warrior tightened his face with resolve and spun around the corner of the bookshelf to heave forth his blades and jut them into the dark figure before him. As it fell to its knees dying, Kaylan felt a wave of relief wash through her. She rose from the floor with the white book tightly gripped in her arms, staring down at the bleeding figure. More closely inspecting the body of their dispatched attacker, however, Kohlin narrowed his eyes to find it was just another Drakkaidian soldier. Noticing this for herself, Kaylan screamed with horror as another movement from the aisle of the library adjacent to them leapt forward with dark robes flying up. Appearing out of nowhere the second figure threw its right hand toward Kohlin, forcing him to drop his blades at his sides and reach up to his throat as if choking him to death. Instantly realizing what was happening, Kohlin brought his eyes up to the girl before him one last time and managed to articulate a single word.

"Run," uttered virtually inaudibly. The next moment Kaylan watched helplessly as his eyes closed shut and his hands dropped numbly to his sides, dangling. With a swiping gesture of its forearm, it cast the lifeless Windrun Warrior aside, smashing him into the cylindrical table in the center of the room with the wood splintering from the force of impact. The Dark Mage quickly turned to her with his dilapidated robes swirling around its large figure, a twisted smile on his face. Kaylan was frozen still for a long moment, disbelief that the legendary Windrun Warrior had just been murdered in front of her filling her tearing eyes. Watching as the Dark Mage took a step toward her she forced herself to drop the book in her hands to try and reach into her tunic pocket to pull forth the Granic Crystal. Having seen the light in her chest pocket the mage raised his hand to take hold of her before she could even get her fingers inside. Tightening his telekinetic grip around her, Kaylan could rapidly feel the breath escape from her lungs. The last thing she remembered before blacking out was being tossed over her other unconscious companion lying in the pile of books beside her.

Chapter 22

<u>Awakening</u>

Edge opened his eyes slowly, his head throbbing as it lay motionless on the stone floor he was draped over. Perplexed at the images and activity slurred together in a mess of light and sound around him, the Maven forced his pale eyes open and focused them until they were at last clear. Slowly moving and attempting to rise, he felt cold bonds of metal on his hands and feet constricting his movement. Looking to his arms and legs he found himself chained to the floor of a cylindrical chamber of stone illuminated only by the ominous glow of a faint white light in a hole in the floor beyond them. Slowly lifting and turning his head to inspect the rest of the room his eyes widened to find Kaylan hovering before him over the wide lighted hole in the floor, tears in her eyes as she called his name. His hearing finally returning to him as he watched her lips move, the Maven narrowed his eyes to find bonds of dark light slowly churning around her hands and feet, keeping her suspended in the air and stretched from limb to limb. Remembering what had happened to him in his final moments before blacking out in the master library of the Mystic Temple, a deep rooted frown enveloped his face and he turned to find four dark robed figures making their way into the room from the small passageway to his left. Staring in alarm his mind was rapidly bombarded with déjà vu once more, familiar images flashing before him of being there before.

As the four Dark Mages strode through the chamber toward Kaylan and the deep well of light in the floor, Edge grit his teeth in enmity and rose to his knees to thrust his body toward them as hard as he was able before his chains took hold and drew him back. Seeing him rise one of the mages turned to him and flicked its wrist with a flash of crimson energy around it, forcing the Maven to forcefully slide back and land against the wall behind him. The other three stood around the girl hovering before them, observing her struggle against the dark bonds of magic holding her in place.

"You are bound by shadow, young one," one of them informed her as it stepped forward, staring into her blue eyes. "You cannot break free but we will let you go unharmed if you do as we ask."

"You killed Kohlin, you murdering Draks!" she screamed as loud as her emotionally taut voice would allow.

"His death was swift and without suffering," the mage told her quietly, "which is more than we will grant you if you refuse to cooperate. You realize where we are, don't you? This chamber is the Sage's Chasm, where their precious enchanted draught is kept. If a human was to merely touch it they would be incinerated instantly, I'm afraid. So with this in mind, we need you to summon the vessel of Drakkan." Both Kaylan and Edge shot the mage confused glances, guessing they were talking about Kaotica.

"Summon?" Kaylan at last repeated. "Even if I could she would just destroy you like last time. She can't be controlled." The mage in the center of the three standing before her let out a disappointed huff before raising his hand and spreading his fingers wide. Simultaneously, her bonds began to stretch farther apart, a trail of dark energy smoking off of them as they extended apart from each other. Kaylan screamed out in pain as her limbs were pulled with fierce strength, to which Edge shot forward again shouting out for the mages to leave her alone. The mage standing beside him again pushed him back against the wall with his power, the crushing force threatening to break his ribcage. As the boy lay pressed against the wall the maddening déjà vu abruptly stopped when Edge finally realized what was happening.

It was exactly like his dream.

He was bound in a mysterious building with evil men and a girl being beaten and held back. It was playing out exactly like his dream. The Dark Mage at the center looked to the boy causing the ruckus beside him and then back to the girl screaming above. Finally easing his grip, the shackles of dark power returned to where they had been and Kaylan was left limply dangling in the air again, fresh tears welling in her terrified eyes.

"Now summon the vessel," the Dark Mage commanded her again, his patience wearing thin. Kaylan shook her head hopelessly, begging for it to listen to her.

"I told you I can't," she pled desperately. "I don't know how..." Trailing off as the mage lifted his hand toward her once more, Edge violently shot forward with a fervent red mist of power boiling to life around his body. Watching as the dark figure took hold of her bonds and prepared to stretch her again, he stood with a semitransparent aura of force erupting from his body, shattering his chains and blowing the suddenly horrified mage beside him off his feet. Edge rose at once grasping at his side to find his gear completely stripped from him. Charging forward in rage nonetheless, the other three mages spun to face him in surprise and threw their hands out to him to catch him in midair and lift him off his feet. The mage in the center of the three eyed him peculiarly for a long moment before at last raising his other hand to ease Kaylan's shackles once more.

"I was not aware this boy possessed any kind of power," it spoke uncertainly. "You boy—the vessel saved you before in the woods. Summon it out now." Though his power still blared with life around him, it was held in check by the grips of the three Dark Mages holding him down.

"She's telling the truth!" he managed, his breath constricted by the mages' telekinetic grasp. "Kaylan can't summon Kaotica at will! Neither can I! She appears when she wants to..." The Dark Mage let out another vexed huff of aggravation as he shook his head at the boy.

"Then we don't need you, do we?" he asked rhetorically, swiping his arm to the side toward the gaping hole in the chamber floor. Jerked in the same direction, Edge felt the mages' grips on him failing but with no floor below, his eyes opened wide as he descended in free fall toward the final stage of his dream. A pool of shimmering white liquid lay beneath him, its brilliant light reaching out and burning into his flesh as he plummeted toward it. Hearing Kaylan scream his name one last time, the Maven plunged into the shimmering liquid headfirst, splashing the normally dormant surface upward with the light bursting awake the moment his body touched it.

Trial of a Maven

Everything and nothing. That's what Edge could see as his eyes slowly opened, floating aloft in an ocean of slurring images jetting around him like fleeting gusts of wind. His vision seemed to stretch for eternity in every direction—even where his eyes where not looking. Slowly struggling to focus his mind amid the overpowering display of vibrant scenes and voices voraciously swirling around him, he remembered he had been thrown into the Sage's Chasm full of the enchanted but volatile liquid they called draught. His brow furrowed in confusion at this. Shouldn't he have been killed, he though to himself as a flaring image of armies meeting on a battlefield jetted past him followed by another of a woman quietly preparing a meal inside a small house. Looking out to his outstretched hands wafting in the lack of gravity, he noticed a familiar aura of transparent force boiling around his skin. The myriad depictions looked to be live events from across the realm of Iairia, but with so many enfolding before him he couldn't concentrate on any one for more than a moment. The sounds from the pictures echoed directly into the confines of his mind, overwhelming his senses. The Maven desperately brought his hands up to cover his ears to try and block all the noise out. It continued ringing through his ears as if all the chaotic images were taking place inside his mind. Edge reared his head back to scream out in terrified bewilderment.

Lofting motionless as the flashes of events passed before his eyes, all the various sounds from each of them began to flow into one coherent voice originating within. Trying to block everything else out to listen to the cryptic words, Edge shouted out for anyone to respond to him.

"Who are you?" he hollered spinning around. "What is this?" The voice continued speaking until the rest of the noise finally died down to a dull roar and his words became audible.

"... and as the scion comes so shall the next age of the order, reviving the principals of old that drove our number in our first age," the voice continued from whatever it was saying before. Though blurred and masked by the other sounds alive around him, Edge could barely make out the suddenly familiar voice as Zeroan's. "A generation fraught with peril now stands before you, scion. The sages are no more, the Elemental Warriors decline, Drakkan stands ready to be loosed upon the world and our most precious talisman is stolen by his minions. Here in this well of our draught, this lifeblood that sleeps within your veins, you will find everything. Our entire history lies before your fingertips, as does your power over it." With that, all the images slurring around him and the sound echoing out of them abruptly shone with blinding light and accelerated past him with hundreds of images flashing before his eyes every second. Though Edge painfully tried to shrink away from the overwhelming information blasting into his head it penetrated through and buried itself inside him. As if observing Edge trying to reject everything bombarding his body and mind Zeroan's voice spoke once more. "Do not let yourself be besieged by all that is yours to uphold and to know, scion, but accept it. It has fallen on you, child conceived from the power of the draught, to carry on with the heritage begun by Alberic himself in the time after the Ancients. You must reclaim his legacy to maintain the order now weakening across the world. Within this enchanted draught, awaken to what you were born to be and become what once was."

As the voice of Zeroan faded into the back of his mind, the images flaring around him intensified again, pulling Edge into them as if he were there himself. Feeling the bombardment blast the life out of him by the second with each passing blow, Edge retreated deep within himself in the most desperate effort to escape. Staring at his soul, the boy was confronted with what he had buried inside since becoming a Maven. Inside the core of his being staring in the face of the monster that was his power, he could feel two choices burning within him. He could submit to what lay inside and let the barrage continue until it killed him as it surely would, or he could push it deeper still and pray all this would disappear. As he looked on through the images of past, present and future jetting past him, he saw one that stole his attention away from all others. It was Kaylan, still hopelessly dangling in the clutches of the Dark Mages in the tower.

Realizing her torture was taking place right above him as he lay in the draught, all other images and realities faded from significance. There was only one choice to make—get out of this draught and save her no matter what the cost or consequence. The swelling, transparent field of force building around his body began to swell with volatile aggression beyond anything he had ever felt before. Ignoring the choice he still had to make with his own fate, the boy clenched his fists as power ignited around his body, driving the images away from his mind for as long as he could.

Dangling over the Sage's Chasm bound by shadow, Kaylan screamed once more as the mages stretched her limbs so hard she could feel them ready to dislocate. Having seen no sign of the vessel they sought, the Dark Mages grew impatient and growled at her to summon it or die. As the one in the center warned the girl her final chance to cooperate was at hand, the one at the right slowly shifted his gaze to the deep well she hovered above, noticing the light from within slowly intensifying. Taking a curious step forward, the mage's eyes widened as its normally still and silent surface far below began bubbling and rippling. As he turned to alert the other mage's of the strange occurrence, the Sage's Chasm suddenly erupted with an explosion of thunderous power. Its potent draught blasted up to the very mouth of the well at the mage's feet. Releasing Kaylan from its grip in shocked horror, the mages watched as a black figure dripping in the mystical liquid landed burning at the surface of the chamber with the stone floor fragmenting beneath his boots.

Kaylan looked to her side in awe as Edge stood before her once more, stumbling off balance with a savage aura of throbbing force engulfing his destabilized body. Fierce determination radiating from his glowing red eyes the boy raised his arm and threw it forward with violent power surging forth, tearing a fissure down the floor and ceiling of the room and blasting two of the four mages off their feet. They soared into the wall behind them so hard they punctured the hard stone and continued flying into the room beyond, maimed and broken beyond recognition. The other terrified Dark Mages instantly threw up their hands to take him into their grasp. Their power knocked the boy off balance and sent him toppling over himself to the ground, the nearly invisible waves of power blasting off of his every movement. Rolling over and tightening his face with resolve he lifted himself back up groaning with pain and screamed out, expanding his chest and clenching his fists. The tiled stone on the floor before him instantly blew up like the shingles of a roof in a windstorm along with the mages standing on them, forced into the wall behind them with an audible shattering of bones.

With the mages gone, Kaylan spun her head to the boy painfully stumbling back to lean against the wall behind him, awestruck.

"Edge," she called astonished, "can you get me down?" The Maven kept his eyes tightly shut but lifted off the wall and stumbled toward her, falling every few steps with the floor cracking beneath his savage power. Eventually he reached her and brought his radiating hands up to rest on her middle section, slowing drifting up to her chest. Though Kaylan's eyes uncertainly widened in confusion as his hands slid up her body, he eventually reached inside the pocket high in her blue tunic and pulled forth the Granic Crystal. She watched in amazement as he lifted the crystal to each of the four shackles of dark power holding her in the air, its dim but steady light quickly dispelling them. Kaylan could tell by the tension in his shaking face he was putting all his energy into withholding the power around him to keep it from hurting her as he worked. When the last one disappeared she dropped into his arms, once more causing the obviously disoriented boy to crash to the ground. Kaylan gazed at him with worried bewilderment, wondering what could have happened to him to trigger the violent explosion of power apparently beyond his control. "Edge, are you alright? What happened?" He merely let her go to bring his hands up to his ears and tightly pressed against his head as if to shield himself from some noise she couldn't hear. The girl rose terrified and helped him up, propping him over her shoulder.

As she collected the ailing Maven and draped his left arm over her shoulder, her head shot toward the entrance of the chamber and the sound of dozens of feet racing up the stairs with swords being drawn. Looking around in panic, the Grandarian girl spied one of the holes in the wall Edge had created with his power and the room that lay beyond. Hoisting him over her and forcing him to walk alongside her they passed through the makeshift doorway for the dark room beyond. As Kaylan looked back to find Drakkaidian soldiers darting into the Sage's Chasm after them, she yelled out to the boy fumbling to stand next to her.

"Edge what are we going to do?" she shouted desperately. Opening his distraught eyes and lowering his right arm from his head to drop it to his side with a detonating flash of power leaping off it to inadvertently crash into the wall beside them, Edge fixed his gaze on the circular window at the end of the hall. Pointing out to it the boy tried to focus his groans of pain into speech.

"Through there," he yelled slurring his words. Kaylan followed his pointing arm to the window hundreds of feet above the plateau beneath them.

"Are you crazy?" she asked disbelievingly. Hearing the Drakkaidians notice them and begin rushing toward the hole in the wall, Edge's face tightened with purpose once more. Trying his best to keep his balance, he took hold of Kaylan and began rushing toward the glass wall at the end of the hall. Kaylan's eyes went wide and she screamed with terror as the boy threw his shoulder into it, power exploding off his frame to shatter the glass before their bodies even touched it. Falling through the window Kaylan latched onto his radiating body, plummeting downward through the night air toward the rapidly approaching ground. Watching the earth and her death near as she fell, from the corner of her eye the girl suddenly caught sight of a small movement swooping down toward them. As she searched past Edge's body above her for its source, a sphere of semitransparent energy abruptly wrapped around them and instead of falling downward they began to soar forward above the trees away from the tower. Staring up with incredulity, Kaylan saw Zephyr flying above them with his hands stretching down to hold them with his Lift Power. Letting out the deepest breath of relief she had ever felt in her life, the Grandarian girl held onto Edge as they soared away from the Mystic Tower into the night beyond.

Zephyr held the two humans below him with his recently restored Lift Power for several longs minutes, trying to get as far away from the tower as possible. Though he might have been able to ferry them all the way out of the Sage's Valley, holding onto Edge with his power erupting below them destroying anything it reached out for proved to be too difficult a feat. Eventually Edge threw his hand up above him reaching for his head, once more sending a wave of invisible throbbing force colliding into Zephyr, throwing his miniature figure away into the sky. With his grip on them gone, Kaylan and Edge dropped into the treetops uncontrollably, painfully falling through the branches until they landed in the foliage on the forest floor.

Slowly raising her spinning head from the soft flora around her, Kaylan shook off her dizziness and rose to wildly scan the dark ground for Edge. Hearing a massive tree trunk snap in two and land in a vale of shrubbery behind her, the girl spun around to find Edge groaning in pain lying in the dirt next to the stump he had just uprooted. Rising hesitantly for fear his power might do the same thing to her, Kaylan's courage seized control and forced her up to rush to his side, aware something was horribly wrong. Power was exploding off his body with his every movement beyond anything he or Zephyr had described to her before. Though she could see he was obviously in a great deal of pain, she had no idea what was causing it or what she could do to help him. All she knew for certain was that if she couldn't figure out something he was going to die. Though cautious about placing her hands on his body for fear his volatile power would sear her at her mere touch, she placed a hand on his chest and one on his burning face.

"Edge, what's happening?" she inquired trying to get his attention. He merely pressed his hands over his ears tighter, groaning as if his skin was being torn off.

"They're everywhere!" he managed to shout. "I can see it all!" Kaylan fearfully flinched as the very sound of his voice seemed to make the earth around them tremble and quake.

"What can you see, Edge?" she returned doubtfully, not even sure if he could hear her.

"*Everything*!" he bellowed back, squirming over the ground. "It won't stop! It won't leave me alone! I don't want any of this—I just want to be left alone!" With this he angrily threw his fists to the ground, the energy blasting from them pounding the earth and knocking Kaylan off her knees to fly back into the trunk of a tree. She rose slowly, her back aching from slamming into the wood so hard. Not giving up, she mustered all her fortitude and inched back over to the Maven writhing in pain.

"Edge, please," she begged. "I just want to help you but you have to calm down first!"

"I can't!" he blasted back as if trying to lift his voice above noise from something else. "It won't let me! It's awake inside me and it won't disappear this time! *I can't push it away*!" Aware he had to be talking about his power, Kaylan guessed falling in the draught had somehow triggered its most potent and dangerous level. It was the only explanation of how he had survived to emerge from the liquid that would have incinerated anyone else. Remembering what Zeroan had once told them about his power, Kaylan knew what she had to do and shouted down to him as well.

"Edge, you can't push it away anymore," she told him fervently, grasping his clenched right hand. "It's awake for good and you have to acknowledge it. Can't you feel it killing you? You have to accept it or it will destroy you!" Edge violently shook his head and grit his teeth, sealing his eyes as if trying to hide from her words.

"I don't want it!" he screamed back to her, the bark on the trees around them splitting off the trunks. "I don't want any of this! I can't handle it!" Kaylan determinedly shook her head as she thrust her face near his, the violent power swelling from his body burning her skin. Though Kaylan saw the small frame of Zephyr land beside them to her right she maintained her gaze on Edge.

"Yes you can, Edge," she refused for him, "you have to! This is who you are—you can't run from it any longer. It's your fate, Edge. If you don't accept it you'll die here tonight, and that means so will I because I'm not leaving you. You promised me you wouldn't let any harm come to me when we started this journey, Edge. You promised! Don't break it now after saving me as many times as you have!" The boy's power seemed to blast with new turmoil at this but he remained silent, opening his glowing eyes to stare into hers, passion and purpose beaming back at him. "Please, Edge. I can't do this without you. Let it in." The Maven twisted, burning force leaping from his body as his eyes shut once more. Watching it violently surge over his frame for the next long moments Kaylan was sure it was going to consume them both. Right after it blasted the earth the most violently she had seen it all night the boiling energy began to slightly wane and withdraw, shrinking away as if soaking into Edge's body. Holding onto his burning skin for another moment the girl could feel his white-knuckle grip slowly ease until his hands lay open on the forest floor, grasping at the dirt beneath them.

After several long minutes that stretched on for an eternity for Kaylan, the last remnant of Edge's violent power faded and disappeared into the night air, wafting away and dissipating like a quiet summer breeze. The Maven was motionless for several long moments, his hand limp and cold. Leaning down to look for any movement whatsoever, Kaylan

Tales of Iairia

leaned in to hover over his silver buckled chest praying to Granis for him to just breathe. Ready to close her eyes with tears welling inside, the girl jolted up to see Edge's eyes slowly lift open, a new layer of tranquility glistening from their watery surface. Kaylan couldn't help but let out a smile of deep relief pass over her lips as his newly blue irises locked onto hers, searching. Neither said anything for a long moment, not sure what had just happened.

"I..." he trailed off, unable to find the right word to express himself.

"Yes?" Kaylan smiled, a tear falling from her eye. Edge held her gaze for another long minute before squinting uncertainly and giving her a single nod.

"I feel bushed," he replied at last. Kaylan could only giggle, too exhausted and emotionally worn out to do anything else. The two could hear another soft laugh from beside them and slowly turned to find Zephyr hovering toward them with an incredulous look on his beaked face. He didn't say anything but Edge knew what he was thinking as he stared into his rich purple eyes.

"Are you alright?" Kaylan finally managed, helping the boy rest his back against the stump of the tree his power had lifted out of the ground minutes before. He stared into space for a long moment at this, a vague look hovering about him.

"For the first time in my life, I think so," he replied cryptically. Shifting his gaze, he raised his gloved hands to look them over. Kaylan and Zephyr stared at him uncertainly for a lingering moment before he nodded to himself to confirm what had just happened. Staying silent for a long moment he at last brought his gaze up to Kaylan, a look in his eyes she had never seen before.

"Thanks, Kaylan," the boy at last managed. As he spoke, she identified the unknown look he was giving her as one of sincerity. She merely smiled back, wiping a tear away from her eye with the sleeve of her beaten tunic.

"You saved yourself, Edge," she replied modestly. Edge shook his head slowly, holding her gaze.

"No, Kaylan, you... were right," he returned. "I... I couldn't bring myself to face what was inside me, even when I knew it would consume me if I didn't. All my life I've been suppressing it and hiding it inside. Even at the end when I knew—I *knew*—I was going to die if I didn't accept it, I wouldn't do it. I've hated it for so long I couldn't forgive myself

Trial of a Maven

for being what I am and the things I've done because of it. But over all the voices and all the images exploding around me from the draught, I could hear yours the loudest. You saved me, Kaylan." The girl didn't know how to reply, never having heard him speak this way before. Though she could feel her face reddening, she modestly smiled and gave him a single nod.

"That's what friends are for," she beamed softly. "I'm just glad you're okay. I couldn't do this without you, you know." Edge silently laughed in spite of himself and nodded, slowly blinking his eyes as he rested his head against the tree he sat behind. Though Zephyr would have loved to let his partner and the girl continue talking as he had never seen him look so at peace, he forced himself to speak up, rising to hover with his Lift Power active once more.

"Well I'm glad everything turned out alright but we are still in the Sage's Valley, you two," he reminded them. "I know you're both exhausted but there's just no way we can stay here for much longer. The Drakkaidians are probably already on their way out of the tower on horses looking for us." Edge's expression focused once more, nodding and looking to Kaylan.

"He's right, it won't be safe here for much longer," he responded sounding like himself once more. Surprising both the girl and his partner the Maven leapt to his feet, stretching out his limbs and tossing his torn blue scarf behind his back.

"Edge I know we can't stay here but you are in no condition to travel after all that," Kaylan spoke with careful concern pouring form her voice. Edge rotated his head around his neck and popped it from side to side, turning to meet her gaze with a smile.

"No offense, Kaylan but you don't have any idea what condition I'm in right now," he said calmly. The girl eyed him peculiarly, unsure what he meant but noting the unusually tranquil expression in his eyes. His movements looked to be full of energy and life despite his being so close to death minutes before. Though he could see the reserved doubt in his companions' eyes, the Maven held his small smile. "Trust me." Slowly returning his smile, Kaylan nodded as well and told him she did. "Zeph, do you think you have enough energy to get us the rest of the way out of the valley to those horses we left on the way in?" Zephyr shrugged with a smile before turning to Kaylan and rolling his eyes.

"See? Flying's just a workout when I'm on the job," he stated again, recalling one of their earliest conversations weeks ago in Grandaria. Instructing them to stay together, the purple sprite dropped his hands to form a sphere of Lift Power around them and lift them out of the trees toward the edge of the Sage's Valley once more. As they soared through the night air with Kaylan tightly holding onto Edge as she had earlier, she raised her face up to his.

"Edge," carefully wording what she head to say, "I'm glad you're alright but what are we going to do now? We escaped in once piece but we didn't get what we came here for; we still have no idea where we can find a new Granic Crystal." The Maven slowly looked down to her, closing his eyes for a long moment, obviously focusing within. Kaylan uncertainly waited as the seconds ticked by but eventually his new blue eyes opened once more with a nod of assurance.

"We couldn't find it in a book but we've got all the clues we need," he answered with confidence. When Kaylan eyed him skeptically he paused, trying to formulate what he had to tell her. "I don't know how to say this, but when I fell into the draught I saw... everything, Kaylan. Everything the sages know. Not in any detail whatsoever but enough that I caught glimpses of certain things—one of them being the location of the Granic Crystal." Kaylan's eyes widened, incredulity mirrored within.

"You know where the new Granic Crystal is?" she questioned astonished.

"Not exactly," he returned plainly, "but I know where we have to go now." Staring at him with renewed hope and curiosity in her eyes, Kaylan Tieloc smiled through the night as they soared over the treetops out of the Sage's Valley.

Part Three
The Third Holy War

Chapter 23

Mobilization

Since the attack of the mysterious demonic girl on the Battlemount several weeks before, General Ronus had his hands full repairing and restoring the Grandarian base with what forces he had left. Many of them were killed in the wake of the dark onslaught. Though he had dispatched messengers to Galantia the next day to inform them of the irregular assault, he had received no acknowledgement of any kind from the capital city. Growing impatient in the silence, Ronus was surprised to find support finally arriving in grander scale than he could have possibly fathomed. Scouts sighted the ill-tempered commanding general of the Wall of Light, General Sodric, marching on them with a battalion of reinforcements from Galantia, apparently under orders to distribute them not to the wall but the Battlemount itself. Though the support from the golden capital had arrived unacceptably late, Ronus let out a deep sigh of relief upon hearing of their number approaching his demolished mountain stronghold still in desperate need of repair.

While Ronus allowed himself a momentary release of his worries upon seeing the reinforcements flood his gates, Sodric was less than pleased when as he rode into the devastated base to find entire segments of the perimeter wall and all its watchtowers obliterated to rubble. Debris and weapons were scattered around the gorge that rested beside the base, with the road that lead up to it torn up and filled with craters from the dark explosions of power that had ricocheted out of the sky. Immediately summoning Ronus to debrief him on what had happened, the besieged general informed him of the bizarre attack several weeks prior and the devastating toll it had taken on the base and the men guarding it. Sodric was furious, screaming to himself that the Drakkaidians had indeed concocted some sinister plot to destroy them despite Tavin's reservations. Convinced beyond a shadow of a doubt that war was upon them, Sodric turned his anger to Ronus and his command over the Battlemount. Blaming him for allowing a single Drakkaidian to cripple their age old mountain stronghold when they needed it most, the short fused general assumed control of the Battlemount until it was repaired to his standards. Though Ronus tried to impart to him there was nothing they could have done to stop the impossibly powerful onslaught of the mysterious dark girl and repairs were going as smoothly as possible, Sodric was not in the mood to listen and revoked his command until additional reinforcements from Galantia could arrive so he could move on to the Wall of Light.

In the days that followed, Sodric began strenuously repairing the Battlemount with the battalions of troops he had brought with him, keeping the disgruntled Ronus beside him only as an advisor. Though they made significant progress in repairs to the outer defenses, it was obvious reconstruction of the wall and guard towers to what they once were would take years. A week into the friendly occupation, Sodric's staff began planning for what augmentations they could make to the mountain fortress before moving on for the Wall of Light. Ronus sat in a chair in the corner of his former conference chamber, his arms crossed as he listened to the irascible general reject idea after idea from his underlings trying to brainstorm a suitable makeshift defense for the west side of the wall that had been leveled by the dark girl. Though Ronus knew the base he had been in command of for years better than anyone and was aware there was no way to protect the Battlemount's perimeter from siege without the wall, he also knew Sodric would never listen to his advice and remained silent as he fumed around the table littered with maps of the base. Eventually there was a knock at the door to the long chamber, prompting a sentry to open it and speak to a single messenger Ronus knew well. Finding Sodric too consumed in his anger to notice him, the general motioned for the sentry to let him through. The messenger quickly strode to Ronus, leaning forward to listen to whatever report he had. As the messenger whispered into his ear, Sodric finally spied him and narrowed his hard eyes warily.

"If you have a report to deliver you may do so to me, soldier," he loudly snapped from behind the opposite side of the table, straightening his wide armored frame. The messenger nervously came to attention and fumbled over himself, trying to formulate the words to speak. Before he could, Ronus rose from his seat and unfolded his arms with a hopeful look on his face.

"I've just been informed the Warrior of Light has arrived in the gate yard, sir," he answered confidently. "Alone. He has asked for my presence." A look of contorted rage swept over Sodric's face at the mere mention of this man and immediately cast away the plans and maps before him.

"He can ask for anyone he wants but I will be the one to face him today," he stated furiously, already marching for the door to the chamber. Shooting an uncertain glance to the messenger, Ronus let out a deep huff of frustration and strode out of the chamber after Sodric and his staff. Passing through the stone hallways and staircases of the command headquarters in the innermost building of the Battlemount, the generals strode into the central courtyard and around the annihilated Medic Quarters for the gate yard beyond. As they marched through the bustling roads of the fortress in the dim afternoon light cut off by banks of rolling clouds above, units of soldiers stopped what they were doing to watch Sodric blast by them, noting the furious expression on his hardened face. Any soldier who knew anything about Sodric could always tell when he was about to explode and they could all see it in his volatile eyes as he marched into the gate yard.

Following closely after him, Ronus at last spied a group of soldiers massing around a well beside what was left of the perimeter wall. As word spread through them of Sodric's coming, they quickly came to attention and began parting to reveal a single figure sitting next to the well taking a long gulp of water. Ronus smiled as he recognized the man as his old friend Tavin Tieloc, the fabled Warrior of Light himself. Hearing the commotion of Sodric and his staff marching toward him and the muffled voices of soldiers commenting on what was about to ensue, the veteran Elemental Warrior slowly rose from his seat on a wooden crate and began walking forward to meet them. Eyeing him up, General Ronus' smile slowly faded. The Warrior of Light looked severely beaten. His attire and usually long stretching cape were torn and sullied as if they had nearly been ripped off his bruised body. Deep cuts in his face were crusted with blood and had stained the dim golden cloth around his neck collar. He ambled forward with a limp and the shattered sheath to his sword loosely dangling at his waist. Something horrific must have transpired for a warrior as powerful as Tavin to be so trodden, Ronus thought.

Ronus did not have much time to infer what his old friend had been through as Sodric plowed up to him furiously raising a finger to point at his face. The Warrior of Light remained calm and unflinching as the short fused general abruptly stopped with his staff doing the same behind him.

"I told you, Tieloc," he snarled quietly, obvious anger in his every word. "I told you the Draks were up to no good and you would not believe me. Now look at the Battlemount! Look what happened here!" Sodric irately shot his right arm out to point at the destroyed perimeter wall beyond them and the rubble still lying around it. "If we had acted to reinforce the Battlemount and the Wall of Light sooner this all could have been avoided, but now this fortress is so damaged it will take years to repair! And what in the name of Granis happened to you? It looks like you just came from war yourself!" Tavin was quiet for a long moment, obviously struggling to maintain himself in the face of Sodric's biting words but at last responded in a calm and controlled tone.

"Now is not the time for bickering amongst ourselves, Sodric," he replied. "There is indeed something amiss here and I am trying to get to the bottom of it, so I don't need to be blasted by your anger the second I get here. I need to speak to Ronus—"

"You will speak to me, Tieloc," Sodric returned folding his arms in defiance. "I have assumed control of the Battlemount and Ronus' authority here until it is repaired as best it can be in the wake of this Drakkaidian attack on our own soil." Tavin's eyes narrowed at this.

"This is not your arena, Sodric," the Warrior of Light returned. "General Ronus can take care of the Battlemount— you need to get this additional battalion you brought with you to the Wall of Light immediately where you are needed."

"I am in command here and I will decide for myself where I need to be, Tieloc," he snapped quickly.

"Sodric, we don't have time for this squabbling," Tavin leapt back in his face with newfound frustration entering it, causing many of the surrounding soldiers to slowly stop what they were doing and watch the volatile scene before them unfold. "You need to get these reinforcements to the Wall of

Light fast before it's too late for them to be of any use." Sodric raised an eyebrow uncertainly at this, his body loosening.

"What do you mean 'before it's too late?'" he questioned slowly. "What happened at the portal, Tieloc?" The Warrior of Light let out a deep breath and paused before collecting himself once more and softly continuing.

"It's possible you were right, general," he answered slowly. "When I arrived at the portal to the void I found the Sword of Granis had been tampered with. I still can't believe it but Verix Montrox appeared soon after and attacked me. Though I do not wish to declare war over a possible misunderstanding, I fear conflict on a much larger scale might be on the horizon." Sodric let his head drop with frustration and slowly shook his head, the entire Battlemount seeming to go quiet as he did.

"I told you, Warrior of Light," he spoke at last. "First the Drak troops invade the war zone, then their mages destroy the Battlemount and now their prince is attacking you on *our* ground. We all knew this was coming, yet you would not accept it and now as war looms over our heads we are not as prepared as we should be. I will not wait any longer for another Drakkaidian attack to strike closer to home. I am returning to the Wall of Light and taking this fight to them." Tavin was instantly stepping forward and voraciously shaking his head no.

"Sodric, you aren't listening to me," Tavin reiterated. "We need to get to the wall to be prepared for anything that may be coming but we cannot start open war beyond it. We may yet be able to salvage this situation diplomatically."

"Diplomatically?" Sodric repeated aghast. "Diplomatically? You've lost your mind, Tieloc! The Drakkaidians have provoked this conflict; they have attacked us on our own soil and killed our men with dark magic from mages to the north."

"General," Ronus spoke up form behind them stepping forward to face him, "while you have continually dismissed it as an insignificant detail I believe it is important that you distinguish what really attacked us from Drakkaidian Dark Mages. It was some sort of demonic girl, not a mage. As I stated in my initial report to Galantia, while she was empowered with dark strength she did not display any sign that she was Drakkaidian."

Tales of Iairia

"Spare me your reservations, Ronus," Sodric cut him off, shaking his head with annoyance. "If the girl was not Drakkaidian what could she be? This was a Drakkaidian attack just like their prince's clash with the Warrior of Light after he sabotaged the Sword of Granis, putting our entire nation at risk of Drakkan himself!" Though Tavin was about to try and calm Sodric once more, he looked uncertainly to Ronus as his story passed through his mind again.

"Ronus, you say it was a girl responsible for the attack here?" he inquired confused.

"Or something like one, Sir Tieloc," he confirmed vaguely. "It was no ordinary girl—she had power enough to destroy entire buildings and stop our forces cold."

"That makes no sense—the only person left alive with access to the kind of dark power I sensed is Verix," Tavin returned skeptically. "Is it possible this girl was his daughter?"

"I wouldn't know, Tavin," Ronus returned with a shrug. "I never actually saw her and most of the men who did perished. I was more concerned about the threat of a siege and your daughter resting in one of our Medic Quarters when the attack began." Tavin froze at this, his blue eyes bursting alive with urgency suddenly radiating out. He took an uncertain step toward Ronus, raising a hand for silence from Sodric as he did.

"...What do you mean my daughter?" he asked quietly. Ronus raised an eyebrow in confusion, staring into his focused eyes.

"I mean young Kaylan, of course," he returned. "She was still here with the boy during the attack. They were fine but left the next day without a word..." The Warrior of Light could feel his heart rising higher into his chest with each passing second at this, disbelief and sudden dread filtering into his eyes. Ronus and Sodric both stared at him uncertainly as they watched his body tense. "You didn't know she was here, Tavin? I thought you were the one who sent her."

"...I left her with her brother in Eirinor months ago," he returned almost inaudibly, everyone around him instantly falling silent. His worried eyes sweeping uncertainly to the generals and their staff, Tavin abruptly shot forward inches away from Ronus with distraught urgency pouring from his voice. "You're telling me my daughter was in the Battlemount during this attack?" Ronus nodded fearfully, noting the terror and confusion ripping through the man before him.

"Yes, she and the boy requested a Lavlas Rock from me to ascend the mountains," he answered delicately. "They returned days later but Kaylan was unconscious in the boy's arms so I put her in the Medic Quarters. I went to check on her the day after the attack but they were both gone. Tavin, I thought you knew..."

"Who is this boy?" the Warrior of Light grilled, sudden wrath stabbing from his every word.

"I don't know, Tavin—I never learned his name," he returned tentatively. "He was dressed in black and carried an assortment of weapons with him. I took him for a Maven at first but I wasn't sure by the way he acted. He arrived with her in tow a few days before the attack and returned the day of, but they were gone soon after and I haven't seen them since." The painful confusion mirrored in the Warrior of Light's eyes slowly morphed into horror as the seconds ticked by and he shifted his gaze from Ronus to the ground below him, wildly staring into space with his mind reeling. He couldn't believe what he had just learned. His daughter was being towed around the Border Mountains by a mysterious boy dressed in black? Right as both the disturbances had erupted to life? Something was horribly wrong. Though the Warrior of Light had been trying his utmost to look past Verix's attack hoping it was some sort of misunderstanding, this newest revelation could not be disregarded as an unrelated incident. The scene that he had found at the portal to the void spoke for itself, and now hearing that his daughter could be caught up in this, in danger with a Drakkaidian agent using her and her potential power for some dark end, loudly conveyed the truth of all this as well.

With the thought of his only daughter somehow at risk because of Drakkaidia, all other thoughts and judgments dissipated in his suddenly clear mind. The truth could not be ignored any longer. Tavin's face slowly tightened with anger once again, his biting eyes looking up through the silence to Ronus and Sodric once more.

"You're sure of this beyond any doubt, General Ronus?" Tavin asked with quiet vehemence in his voice. The general slowly nodded and replied yes, aware something was terribly wrong as well. Tavin nodded once and swallowed hard, locking his gaze onto Ronus. "General, though I wish it were

Tales of Iairia

not so, it is my judgment that there is a Drakkaidian plot in motion to destroy Grandaria. The events of the past few weeks can lead us to no other conclusion. At this point war could be inevitable and we must take the necessary steps to defend ourselves. We have to get this battalion to the Wall of Light immediately and strengthen it for any coming attack."

"Finally," Sodric mouthed more to himself than anyone, letting his arms fall to his sides in relief. "Very well then. We will proceed as I previously ordered. I will take these troops to the wall as soon as we are ready while the Warrior of Light returns to Galantia to report on this matter to the Supreme Granisian—"

"No, Sodric," Tavin cut him off, ice hanging from his words. As he opened his mouth to speak once more, he emboldened his voice to boom it throughout the entire gate yard, already eagerly listening to them speak. "All of you are witnesses to what is about to transpire today so listen carefully. I am proceeding from this point forward with the mentality that this is an emergency situation to the entire nation of Grandaria. To answer the mounting threat of Drakkaidia, I, Tavinious Tieloc the Warrior of Light, am assuming my emergency powers delegated to me by Supreme Granisians Corinicus Kolior and Maréttiny Kolior. Henceforth I am taking control of the Grandarian military and acting in the Supreme Granisian's stead to make decisions for the greatest good of Grandaria until this crisis has abated." There was a long pause of dead silence throughout the gate yard for several long moments, all the soldiers and commanding officers staring at the Warrior of Light in shock. The silence was at last broken by General Sodric, stepping forward with an intolerant look of rage in his burning eyes.

"You cannot simply assume command of all Grandaria when you feel like it, Warrior of Light," he mouthed heatedly but in control of his fury. "General Tycond is in command in Galantia and *I* command the Wall of Light." Tavin shifted his equally focused gaze to Sodric, fortitude enveloping him.

"Not anymore, Sodric," he stated sternly. "Command of all the military will shift to me as I deem necessary in this emergency. Until this situation is resolved you must respect my judgment." Sodric abruptly leapt forward, his face bursting red and saliva exploding from his mouth as he widened his jaws to blast out at him.

"I do *not* answer to you, Tieloc!" he exploded with rage, breaking discipline in front of the men. "You have closed your eyes to this building conflict for years when we could have done something about it and ignored all the vicious attacks on our country up to this point—and you expect me to follow you now? Never in my life will it be so, Tieloc! The only reason you act now is because your precious daughter has been sucked into it! I say you are not fit to lead!" Sodric then drew the sword at his side and pointed it out for the Warrior of Light threateningly. Having already abandoned discipline himself, the moment Sodric mentioned Kaylan Tavin grit his teeth and swung one of his arms covered in a gauntlet out to swipe Sodric's blade away. In one fluid motion, Tavin threw his opposite fist forward to sail it into the crazed general's face, dropping him to the ground. Ronus' eyes widened as he watched Sodric fall unconscious to the cold earth and nervously looked back to Tavin. The Warrior of Light cooled himself in the silence that followed but eventually turned to shout out to the soldiers around him once more.

"Grandarians, many of us have been divided over the years on the situation in Drakkaidia," he began taking a step ahead. "Many of you have heard the truth I have been trying to tell you about what happened in the Days of Destiny twenty years ago. While what I said was true, that our history of hatred for Drakkaidian cannot continue with the revelation from Lord Granis himself that they are our forgotten brothers, we have been thrust into conflict with them once more. There are power hungry tyrants that rule Drakkaidian who would seek to destroy us no matter what desires for peace we may wish with them, and we cannot let them have their way. Powerful forces of dark magic are harbored by our enemies and we must stand as one to repel them as we could not do here at the Battlemount. Though I wish it was not so, believe me when I say that we face peril now that only I know how to deal with. I ask for your trust. I ask you to trust my judgment and power as an Elemental Warrior in this time of emergency as the Supreme Granisian does. Follow me, and we will defend our nation."

There was another long silence as the Warrior of Light finished his speech and scanned the faces of the hundreds of soldiers around him. Though no one spoke for a long moment, there was one voice directly behind them that sounded first.

"I will," it boomed throughout the gate yard. Tavin turned to find Ronus stepping forward, confidence in his expression. Tavin gave him a single nod of acknowledgement as another of his staff stepped forward to reply yes as well. As the seconds turned into minutes more and more of the soldiers stepped forward and shouted their approval for the Warrior of Light until the entire Battlemount was cheering in his favor. Standing still and silent as the plaudits and battle cries sounded through the brisk mountain air, Tavin remained focused and hard. He wheeled around and ordered Sodric's staff to carry the downed general back inside the command headquarters and put him to bed. Turning to Ronus, Tavin breathed deeply and shook his head. Despite his powerfully rousing words moments ago, Ronus could see the same lingering worry for his daughter in his eyes that had been there upon first learning of her being there.

"I'm so sorry, Tavin," Ronus spoke in his ear through the soldier's cheering. The Warrior of Light swallowed hard again and gave him a single nod of acknowledgement.

"Ronus, I'm appointing you the new commanding officer of the Wall of Light," he announced quietly, changing the subject. "I need a general with me I can trust. Leave one of your captains in command here to brace it for further hostilities and make the best repairs you can. Send a messenger to Galantia to inform the Supreme Granisian and the Senior Council of my actions here. Prepare your staff and the men to depart in the morning." Turning to walk toward the center of the mountain fortress, Ronus shook off his surprise and forced himself to speak.

"Where are you going, Tavin?" he asked as his staff heaved the bulking figure of Sodric off the ground. The Warrior of Light continued forward without looking back.

"I... need a little time, general," he spoke just loud enough for his voice to carry back to him.

Chapter 24

<u>City by the Sea</u>

  Rounding up the horses they had left at the entrance to the Sage's Valley, Edge, Kaylan and Zephyr had made it across the eastland in four days to the largest city on the coast of the Eastern Sea—Acquanautta Port. After the trio had escaped the proximity of the Mystic Tower and the Drakkaidians in the vicinity, they had rested for the night concealed in a small forest vale. Though they had failed to procure the location of a new Granic Crystal from the libraries of the sage's fortress, Edge told Kaylan he had learned where they would find it nonetheless. Though Kaylan was mystified at how he could have discovered any clue as to the whereabouts of the crystal when he was either unconscious or consumed by his newly awakened power raging inside him for most of their time in the tower, she trusted that he had indeed learned something and patiently waited for him to impart it to her later that night. To the Grandarian girl's disbelief, Edge related to her his experience in the Sage's Chasm filled with the enchanted draught. He told her everything it had done and shown to him. Amidst the barrage of images and sounds igniting around him of all the collective knowledge retained by the sages, he had seen a glimpse of an ancient cliffside fortress filled with shining golden crystals in the center of an island surrounded by fog. Though he admitted the flashes he saw were fleeting at best, Kaylan could tell he was sure beyond any doubt of what he experienced and truly believed in what he had seen. It was all they had to go on so they were left with little choice but to trust Edge's sporadic vision.

  Though Kaylan had faith in the Maven she was quickly besieged with further doubt. Edge's lifelike hallucinations had revealed much but they raised more questions than answers. They had no idea where this island was or how to find the fortress holding the Granic Crystals even if they somehow managed to get there. Mulling over their options for the night, Edge decided their best bet of finding the mysterious island was simply to get to the ocean and look for it with the hope the dim and nearly dead Granic Crystal still in Kaylan's pocket would point them in the right direction once more. Agreeing it was their only option, Kaylan and Zephyr set out with the Maven for the largest port of the shores where they could surely find a ship to ferry them into the expansive waters of the Eastern Sea.

Before they began their trek across the rest of the eastland Kaylan insisted they do something to remember their fallen comrade lost to them in the Mystic Tower. Though she had wanted to send word to Windrun City that the First Captain of the Windrun Warriors had fallen, Edge insisted there was no way they had time and it was too dangerous for them to try to recover his body inside the Drakkaidian controlled tower anyway. For now they had to leave him be. Kaylan still couldn't believe he was gone. She had heard stories about Kohlin Marraea's skill and bravery for years from her parents, and now when she finally met him and witnessed it for herself it had cost him his life. The girl tightened with resolve as they mounted their horses to travel away from the tower and his body, silently vowing to return and honor him as the hero he was by taking his body back to a proper burial place in Windrun City.

As the party traveled across the forests and fields of the eastland toward the coast, both Zephyr and Kaylan could see a striking change in their third companion. Though he remained the same tensely focused and objective leader he had always been, keeping his gaze ahead and his thoughts to himself, his usually emotionless visage had been slowly filling with one of curious energy and verve. For the first time since she had met him weeks before Kaylan could see the boy smiling for no apparent reason as he rode, his new blue eyes mirroring a silent contentedness never before present. Since he had finally accepted the power inside him that night in the woods it was as if he had finally found some measure of inner peace that had so long eluded him. Though she could tell he was very uncertain about his new power and that it was far from under his will to control or even understand, there was a newfound air of self confidence and assurance the boy had begun to exude that told her he wasn't afraid of it anymore. To Zephyr's supreme shock he actually allowed himself to fall completely asleep in the same campsite as Kaylan. Though a seemingly insignificant difference to the Grandarian girl, Zephyr appreciated how substantial the change was for the reclusive Maven that had never trusted himself within a hundred yards of anyone else at night for years. All Kaylan knew was her once course and terse protector was finally allowing his humanity to gradually shine out, putting a renewed smile on her face as well.

With the entire party in the best spirits they had been since departing from Eirinor Village they at last drew near their new destination four days later, riding up a ridge above Acquanautta Port at a lively gallop to view the sprawling waterfront city below them in the warmth of the beautiful afternoon sunlight. Finally rising over the peak of the high ridge a beaming smile of wonderment escaped from Kaylan's lips as she caught sight of the extensive harbor below them on the shoreline of the massive Eastern Sea, sparkling blue into the flat horizon far beyond. The Maven ahead of her casually rotated his head back to find her smiling down at the city with her shimmering golden hair reaching up to caress her smooth face in the salty sea breeze.

"Don't tell me you've never seen the sea before," he mused curiously, a smile materializing from the corner of his mouth. The girl shifted her mesmerized gaze to him, slightly embarrassed at how captivated she must have appeared.

"I've been to the Gulfrin Bay in Grandaria with my parents before, but this..." she trailed off letting her gaze fall back onto the vivid seaside once more. "It's just so magnificent from up here..." Edge's smile broadened at the girl's awe and tossed his head back to the sky sprite sitting behind him over the pack on his back.

"Why don't you go see what's down there, Zeph?" he asked cheerfully. The purple sprite widened his beak with a smile as well as he launched off from his partner to soar into the blue sky with a sphere of Lift Power enveloping his body. Watching Zephyr descend into the airspace around the city, Edge and Kaylan kicked their steeds forward with renewed vitality as well, quickly winding their way down the increasingly busy roads of the ridge into the dusty streets leading into Acquanautta. It was a large port town nearly half the size of the Southland's capital city of Torrentcia on the opposite side of the Iairian Mountain Chain to the west, but boasted the largest harbor of ships of any coastal town on the shores of Iairia. The largest river pouring from Lake Torrent and the Elemental Temple of Water at its center flowed across the plains of the Torrentcia territories and underground in a vast natural aqueduct beneath the mountains that allowed it access to the sea. The mouth of the river cut right through the center of Acquanautta, dividing the city and the port in two with a massive stone bridge connecting the north and south sides.

As the two horses carrying Edge and Kaylan galloped into the heart of the city near the harbor district they stepped down into the outskirts of a colorful bustling marketplace decorated with flapping blue flags and crusty seashells ornamenting shops and inns along the large courtyard overlooking the harbor. Deciding they wouldn't be needing horses anymore the pair sold them to a caravan of rangers on their way back to Windrun City. Placing the satchel full of their only funds into one of the silver buckled pouches along his waist, the Maven motioned through the commotion of the busy market for Kaylan to follow him to a quieter side of the courtyard near the massive bridge connecting the two sides of the city to each other. Kaylan rushed to the blue railing of the walkway near a single wooden bench and gazed down onto the harbor, the massive ships and their billowing white sails resting peacefully at dock or hastily coming and going to and from the open waters beyond. It was only in the past century that the Southland had begun to look past its conventional borders to the groups of small islands beyond in the shores of the east to begin settling on them. Ever since port towns like Acquanautta had been bursting with new life.

Seeing the girl gaze with rapture out at the bustling harbor, Edge let out a faint smile once more and tossed the tail of his flowing blue scarf behind his back in the direction of the breeze.

"Now comes the tricky part," he stated staring out at the rows of ships as well. The girl looked back to him with an eager smile over her lips, waiting for him to continue. "Finding a ship with a captain crazy enough to help a Maven and a Grandarian girl find an island that could be anywhere out in that endless blue salt."

"But you have a plan," she stated more than asked, her optimism shining through his qualms. Though nothing concrete seemed to blast alive inside his mind, the Maven found her spirit contagious and merely nodded away his doubts.

"Where there's a will there's a way, I suppose," he mused, to which the girl beamed at him. Edge placed his black gloved hands on his sides and took a deep breath, collecting his thoughts. "So here's what we'll do." The Maven threw two fingers up to his mouth to let a shrill whistle sound through the busy air. After a few moments of staring into the sky, the pair watched a purple bullet shoot over a nearby building and plummet down onto the boy's shoulder, moving fast to attract as little attention as possible.

"It's a blustery day up there," the cheerful sprite reported, tucking his wings close to his back. "But otherwise nothing out of the ordinary. Most of the ships in the harbor look to be merchant transports out to the nearby islands with a few fishermen adding to the mix."

"We're going to need to get a hold of a captain, not a ship I think," Edge concluded. "Zeph, forget the harbor for a while. We're going to rest up here for a night anyway so instead of going ship by ship interviewing captains, we'll go to a place we can find them all at once."

"And where does your seaworthy intuition tell you this place would be, Captain Edge?" the sprite sarcastically played with him, to which Kaylan let out a giggle.

"You don't have to be a sailor to know where to find them on shore," he replied dryly. "Sweep the city for a tavern where crews congregate at night. The grittier the better I'm sure." Nodding his long feathered head, the sprite shot into the sky once more with his new task in hand. When his partner was gone the Maven found Kaylan's eyes on him once more, skepticism within.

"Don't you think we should try to gather some more clues as to where we're actually going before we recruit a ship to take us there?" she questioned raising an eyebrow.

"We'll kill two birds with one stone," he replied confidently. "The men who live on the waters of the Eastern Sea know them intimately better than any book in the Mystic Tower. If anyone will have any clues about the whereabouts of this island we're looking for it'll be a veteran captain who's seen it. But for now there's a little inn on the other side of the bridge here that we can rest in tonight. Why don't we go get some rooms for the night and come back and get some supplies here in the market while we wait for Zephyr?"

"Or we could kill two birds with one stone and you could go get the room while I get the supplies," the girl answered in a lighthearted tone. The Maven frowned at her and furrowed his eyebrow.

"I thought we agreed a long time ago that for me to do my job you have to stay with me," he stated flatly. Kaylan shrugged and smiled knowingly.

"And I thought we agreed you have to trust me and let me help out every once in a while," she returned with a smile. "I may need saving from Dark Mages on occasion but I hope you know me well enough to know I can take care of myself in a little market, Edge. I am a girl after all—let me handle the shopping." The Maven stared at her uncertainly for a long moment, sometimes forgetting the powerful spirit she harbored. He at last silently chuckled to himself and smiled, nodding yes. Agreeing that they would meet back on this segment of the bridge next to a decorated wooden bench so Edge could help her carry back the supplies after he had procured their rooms, he gave the Grandarian girl half their satchel of Seir and left her to tend to the shopping. Hastily making his way across the long arching bridge connecting the stone streets of Acquanautta Port to lessen his time away from his charge, he quickly came upon the first building to his left with a flowing blue banner of cloth bolstered upright and a pair of enormous seashells fixed to the building. Stepping through the wooden door of the inn he had passed through before on other jobs, the Maven found the innkeeper standing behind a wooden counter coming to attention. Nodding in acknowledgment Edge took out what Seir he had left and dropped it on the counter, stating he needed a pair of rooms for the night. Though the innkeeper eyed him hesitantly for long a moment noting the blue scarf around his neck, he eventually nodded and accepted the currency in trade for two room keys.

"I assume you'll leave your business outside my inn. Any troubles I should know about, Maven?" he asked watching the boy place the keys in a pouch along his waist, to which Edge merely raised his blue eyes impassively.

"I don't bother telling my troubles to people—most don't care and the rest are glad I have them," he stated turning for the staircase to his right.

Stepping back outside into the rich afternoon air after inspecting the rooms on the second level of the building,

Trial of a Maven

Edge began to walk back over the wide bridge for the other side of the city and Kaylan. Hustling back to where he had left her, the boy couldn't help but smile as thoughts of the Grandarian girl rippled through his mind. Though he had purposefully tired to push her as far away as possible when they first met, he had to admit that having her around was a constant breath of fresh air that he had never experienced before. It was a gradual sentiment but he had come to appreciate and even admire the girl's cheery fortitude and desire to contribute despite all her reasons for sorrow. As Edge arrived back near the wooden bench besides the railing overlooking the harbor where they had parted he swept his gaze through the thinning crowds for Kaylan, nowhere to be seen. The Maven let out a huff and took a seat on the bench, guessing she was just taking her time in gathering all the supplies they might need. As he crossed his arms over his chest and turned his head to look out on the busy harbor while he waited, the cool breeze gently swept his dark hair to and fro like soft grass swaying in the fields outside of the city. Staring at the blue waves slowly lapping against the wooden docks below him while occasionally looking over his shoulder into the market for his beautiful female companion, the Maven found the seconds turning into minutes and his impatience morphing to unease. Slowly turning to the shops and carted vendors beginning to close with the approach of the evening, the boy's expression hardened. Even for a girl this was taking too long and Kaylan wasn't one to doddle or delay anyway.

Though trying to dispel his worries Edge couldn't help but amble into the market to begin looking for her. Scanning his eyes up and down the wide road he could find no sign of her anywhere. The Maven grit his teeth nervously, his fear slowly growing. All the supplies they needed could be found right on the street; there was no reason for her to have disappeared into any of the other shops or buildings around the market. Wheeling around to find the bench where they were supposed to have met up still vacant, Edge tightened his frame and called her name into the crowd. Though he drew a little attention from the passing civilians around him, no reply came and he soon found himself marching down the street shouting for her. The boy cursed himself for letting her out of his sight even for a moment, remembering that evil pursued them that could get to her anywhere. If anything had happened to her the blame would rest solely with him for ignoring this and letting her out of his reach.

As he continued pushing his way through the streets of the market checking over every shop and vendor with his the utmost anxiety he eventually spied something lying in the middle of the street that stole the breath from his lungs. Grinding to a halt, the Maven's suddenly terrified eyes opened wide as he slowly leaned down to pick up a faintly glowing golden crystal lying in the dirty street. Staring at it in disbelief Edge felt his heart drop inside his chest. If there was one thing he knew about Kaylan it was that she would never let the Granic Crystal slip out of her possession. Dread welling into his mind, the boy felt panic taking over and he shouted Kaylan's name into the streets as loud as he was able. Having no idea what to do other than start asking townspeople if they had seen a young blond girl pass by he noticed a dim glow shining from the Granic Crystal. Loosening his grip around it until it lay flat in his palm, the Maven curiously followed its beaming light as it stretched out to point to his right. Aware it was somehow trying to communicate with him as it had before with Kaylan he shot his gaze to the right to stare at a rare flower stand with an old woman sitting next to it. Quickly striding toward her, Edge closed his fingers around the luminous gem in his hand and placed it in one of the satchels along his belt.

"Excuse me, have you seen a blond girl wearing a blue tunic pass by here in the last few moments?" he asked quickly, getting the elderly woman's attention. She ran his question through her head for a lingering moment before shaking her head.

"I'm afraid I haven't, young man," she replied slowly. "But wait... there was another young lady just here who mentioned she was looking for a young Maven. Are you the one she was talking about?" Edge raised an eyebrow at this, his frame tightening once more.

"What did this girl look like?" he inquired quietly. The elderly woman raised her head as if trying to remember her appearance but suddenly burst awake once more, pointing to Edge's right.

"Oh, well..."

"She's beautiful with silky smooth hair and shining purple eyes. Oh and she wears the cutest outfit everywhere she goes," a third voice suddenly cut the old woman off from beside Edge. Spinning around in surprise, Edge's shocked blue eyes burst open as he found Kaotica standing before him, a coy smile on her face. Before he could react in any way, the girl outstretched one of her hands from behind her back and presented a rich blue flower like the ones the woman was selling. "I got this for you, sweetie. It matches your scarf, see?" Still stunned by the dark girl's abrupt appearance Edge found himself unable to move as she inched closer to gently set the stem of the blossoming flower to a tear in the black vest over his tunic with a smile, staring up into his eyes with a knowing look in hers. "I missed you too, Edgy..." Feeling the girl clutch fistfuls of his tunic in her hands as she continued to pull toward him, the Maven burst out of his stunned state and seized her arm to pull her away from the old woman, marching her down the street back to the end he had come from.

"Kaotica, what do you think you're doing?" he whispered vehemently. "I really don't feel like dealing with you and you're trouble right now." The girl slowed her steps and forced him to release her, momentary frustration flashing across her face.

"Well if you'd calm down for a measly second I have something to tell you," she snapped impatiently, to which the Maven sharply exhaled but slowed to match her pace as well. Seeing she had his attention, Kaotica beamed once more and placed her hands behind her back while she gently pushed into him. "I'm... sorry for making you mad last time. I know I caused some trouble but I just wanted to have some fun with you." Edge rolled his eyes and tried to pull away from her again.

"You have a pretty twisted idea of fun," he returned heatedly. "Now bring back Kaylan." Kaotica stopped where she stood and balled up her fists, throwing her heel down into the stone street.

"Are you kidding me?" she practically shouted, drawing attention from around them. "I just find you after being all cooped up in little-miss-goodie-good for like a week and you want me to leave? What's the deal with you? Do you hate me or something?" Noting her escalating voice and the attention she was drawing to them from the passing crowds, Edge collected his anger and stepped closer, motioning for her to calm down.

"Kaotica, don't make a scene here," he whispered irritated. She raised an eyebrow at him, looking around to the shoppers and vendors staring at her.

"Then I guess you'd better not give me reason to, Edgy," she whispered mockingly. "You're stuck with me until I get tired, so I suggest you keep me entertained until then or I'll go find something else to do. Come on—I promise I won't cause any trouble. Please?" Edge's frown deepened at this. It was pointless to argue with her and if he angered her again she would just fly off and force him to chase after her like she had at the Empyrean Peaks. Remembering how emotional she had been the last time he exploded on her at the Temple of Wind he decided it would be easier to just let her have her way. He didn't have any choice but to tolerate her until she tired out or grew bored.

"If I let you stay around for a while you have to promise me you won't use your power and you do what I tell you," he breathed with ice hanging from his words. Kaotica's face lit up with glee at this and she rapidly clapped her hands.

"Oh, fun, fun, fun," she giggled. "I told you you'd come around once you got to know me, didn't I?" The Maven merely shot her an impatient glance, steeling himself for the most likely long few hours he was in store for. As he was about to tell her to follow him back to the inn Edge heard a sharp whistle. Looking up to find Zephyr circling above, he whistled back and told Kaotica to follow him. Making his way out of the busy city street and into a smaller alley between two larger buildings Edge looked up as Zephyr dropped out of the sky to perch on his shoulder, immediately stiffening with alarm upon seeing Kaotica.

"How long has she been here?" he asked nervously, to which the girl glared at him.

"Unless you want to become a cooked delicacy you should watch your mouth, birdie," Kaotica snapped caustically. Edge merely shook his head impatiently and turned his attention to his partner.

"What did you find?" he asked, changing the subject.

"Well, there are a few little taverns where sailors and merchants tend to get together but there's one big one in the higher levels of the harbor that sounds to be exclusively for seamen. A few of the captains I saw in the harbor were either heading that way or talking about it. Might be the place we're looking for." Edge nodded in response, agreeing that was the place they would find their transportation to the sea.

"So we're going to mingle with the sailor-boys, huh?" Kaotica asked playfully from beside them, placing her hands on her hips. "Sounds like an adventure already." Edge breathed deeply, holding her penetrating gaze.

"Don't make me regret this, Kaotica," he spoke sternly, stepping past her. The girl merely smiled and followed after him, running her fingers through her smooth black hair.

"I wouldn't dream of it, Edgy," she replied willfully.

Chapter 25

Harbor

It was dusk by the time Edge and Kaotica arrived at the harbor tavern Zephyr had located for them. The sprite led the humans back down to the docks they had been staring at earlier, taking care not to draw any unnecessary attention that could provoke the dark girl following behind Edge with a pert bounce in her step. Though Edge feared her wandering eyes would surely catch sight of something that would lead her to trouble, she merely trailed after him wordlessly taking in everything around her with sparkling curiosity. The tavern Zephyr had found was a small building nestled tightly between two rows of the high docks with the wall of another level of the city behind it, sulking in disrepair. Loud music coupled with the sound of mugs slamming against tables echoed out through the purposefully hidden entrance, men from the docks stumbling in and out every passing moment. Though the windows were difficult to see through from the rows of barrels he hid behind with the other two members of his party, Edge could tell the tavern was packed to the gunnels with drunken sailors. Watching unaffected as an intoxicated sailor was thrown from the entrance onto the wooden dock outside, Edge nodded to himself in confirmation that this was indeed the place they were looking for.

Turning back to Zephyr and Kaotica he found the dark girl staring with an eyebrow raised at the drunken man falling unconscious on the dock beyond them.

"You sure know the best places to take a girl, Edge," she stated shifting her tickled gaze to him. The Maven rolled his eyes as he looked down to his waist to prepare the tools of his trade for whatever they might be required for inside. As his eyes fell upon his belt he quickly remembered virtually all of his weaponry and tools had been taken from him in the Mystic Tower and all he had left was the sword on his back. Letting out a breath of frustration, Kaotica rose from her crouch behind the barrels they hid behind to peer into the window of the tavern and scrunch her face together in disgust. "What a dump. This entire place is germ ridden and breathing disease—do you really expect me to go in there?"

"No," was the curt reply from Edge, grabbing her wrist to pull her back down to a crouch beside him. When she returned his gaze in confusion, Edge turned to Zephyr perched on a crate to their right. "Zeph you stay here with the girl and keep her out of trouble. Don't let her move from this spot and don't let anyone see her."

"Excuse me, no," she chimed in revolting at the idea. "You want me to sit just here? Bor-ing."

"The first step you took through that door I'd be up to my waist in trouble, Kaotica," Edge declared resolutely. "You're not going."

"Hey—I promised I would behave didn't I?"

"Kaotica, mayhem gravitates to you as it is," Edge stated flatly. "The last place I want you to be is surrounded by a room full of drunken sailors who haven't seen a woman in months." Kaotica's irritated expression quickly turned to a knowing smirk and she set her arms on either side of Edge's crouched body to lean up to his face.

"Ah, you just don't want any other guys looking at me, do you?" she whispered mischievously. "You get so cute when you're jealous..." Once again caught off guard by the striking girl's abrupt advance into his personal space, Edge froze uncomfortably for an instant before thrusting his body upright to distance himself from her. Watching him rise with his eyes still on her Kaotica's smile broadened and she wheeled around to take a seat on a crate beside Zephyr, lifting one of her exposed legs to cross it over the other. "Fine. Since you're so concerned for my well being I'll wait here with birdie. Just hurry back." Edge let out another deep breath of annoyance before telling Zephyr to keep her out of trouble and turned for the entrance of the raucous tavern.

Passing through the torch lit doorway into the tavern's bar, the Maven scanned the room to survey what lay before him. There was a mob of drunken sailors causing the most noise at the left end of the bar, taking shots of their favorite spirits and virtually inhaling a keg of dark ale. Beside the bar were several round tables with another raunchy cluster of sailors singing and a party of others passed out behind them. To the right were several darkly lit booths housing the calmer crowd within. Slowly walking past them taking care not to hold their gaze long Edge spied groups of older men casually talking, lone harbormasters sitting in silence and even another Maven intently looking over a satchel of Seir in his grasp.

Deciding to migrate toward the opposite side of the bar where a group of bearded men sat watching the younger ones make fools of themselves, Edge took a seat beside one of them and called out for a drink to the already overwhelmed bartender. Turning in bewilderment to the boy suddenly sitting beside him, a gruff man downed the rest of ale in his mug and slammed it on the bar counter.

"You're in my seat," he barked, the smell of alcohol pouring from his breath. Edge raised an eyebrow, looking the man over.

"This is your seat too?" he asked unwavering.

"This whole bar is my seat, you little weevil," he replied furrowing his brow. "What do you think you're doing in here?"

"I'm looking for a ship," he replied easily, breaking eye contact to find a few of the men in the booths across from them staring in his direction.

"I may be drunk, boy, but I'm pretty sure you aren't going to find one inside a bar," the man returned, extending his mug to the end of the bar to have it filled up again.

"Then do you know where I could find the captain of one who knows the open waters?" Edge finally asked, bringing his eyes back to the other's.

"That depends on which waters you're looking to find," he replied. Edge gradually leaned in closer and rested his elbow on the bar as the other raised his mug to take a swig.

"I'm looking for those that are shrouded by fog," he spoke just loud enough to be heard. The gruff captain jerked his mug to a stop before it reached his lips, slipping some of the contents over his thick beard. The man slowly grinded his head to face the boy, fixing his eyes onto him.

"The fog?" he returned almost inaudibly. Edge nodded once, holding the man's gaze. "Boy, I don't know what you think you're doing speaking about the fog but if you value your life you'll never bring that up to a man that makes berth on these docks again. Now get your hide out of my seat." Seeing the quiet fury emanate from the captain's eyes as he spoke, Edge reluctantly leaned back and withdrew to preclude an unfavorable encounter. Sweeping his gaze throughout the rest of that side of the tavern he saw several uneasy faces turned in his direction murmuring under their breath. Deciding he had somehow struck a sensitive nerve, the Maven prepared to turn back for the opposite side of the tavern when a familiar whistle sounded over the drunken calls and laughter around him. Wheeling around to a window behind the booths Edge found Zephyr hovering on the other side with a panicked expression over his beaked face. His face morphing with dread, Edge heard a sudden roar of shouting from the drunken men at the entrance to the tavern. Wheeling around he quickly eyed the mob that had been at the left of the bar drifting to the doorway and the slender figure standing there conversing with another sailor eyeing her up and down. Edge grit his teeth, shooting forward through the crowds to try and get to Kaotica before anything happened.

"So you sit on a boat and look for fish?" the girl's voice eventually reached out above the crowd as he drew closer. "Who's holding the knife to your neck to make you do something like that?" The man seated in front of her tilted his head as he replied with a drunken smile.

"Well do you have something more exciting you want to do to me, honey?" he asked. Kaotica smiled and raised a hand with a quick flash of purple electricity shooting over her fingertips.

"Somehow I think your idea of fun and mine might be different, sailor boy," she answered flipping her hair behind her back and turning to wade into the advancing crowd of men gathering around her. Trying his best to cut his way through the thick crowds of stumbling sailors to get to her, Edge was too late to arrive before his fears were realized and trouble found her. As she stepped away from the seated man at the entrance her eyes suddenly flared open as she felt the hard smack of his hand along the backside of her tight purple skirt. The entire crowd laughed at this and began groping forward once more. Her deep eyes momentarily flashing with pulsating light, the girl's smirk faded as she spoke.

"Oh is that funny, boys?" she asked them with dramatic flare. "Do you want to see what makes me laugh?" Spinning around with her dark hair flying up behind her, Kaotica outstretched her right hand for the man that had slapped her, a wave of electric energy bursting forward to bind him in place. Forcing the man to drop his mug, Kaotica turned with a smile and flipped her hand to her right, sending the man flying from his seat into the air across the entire room landing squarely on a table where a group of four sat passed out in their chairs. Plummeting onto it with a scream of confusion his weight smashed the unsteady wood in two. As the dust cleared from his ungraceful landing the entire tavern went quiet, all eyes staring at the darkly smiling girl. "Anyone want to try that again?" The faces of the men remained still and silent, some taking a step back. As the mob at last began to separate and disperse, the black clad Maven in the back at last managed to push his way through them and stride toward the girl with an intolerant look on his tense face.

Kaotica merely smiled upon seeing him and pushed a lock of her hair behind her ear. She turned to one of the men staring at her with his jaw agape and raised a hand to cover one side of her mouth.

"I'm in trouble now," she whispered with a giggle as Edge pulled in close to furiously whisper in her ear.

"*What in the name of Granis do you think you're doing?*" he breathed irately. Kaotica shrugged and made a theatrical expression of regret.

"I missed you," she replied trying to suppress laughter. "Did you find us a boat yet?" Realizing every second they remained in the tavern was another that a more volatile scene could explode around them, the Maven took hold of her wrist and began to pull her after him for the doorway. However, as they were about to pass through it into the evening air once more a voice from behind them sounded through the breaking silence.

"Hold on a moment, Maven," it called over the crowd. Edge quickly reached behind his back for the hilt of his sword and turned with Kaotica behind him. Watching the crowd disperse to get back to their drinks and put distance between them and the girl, a single old man pushed his way through them to stand before the pair with a mug in his hands. A thin white beard jutted out from his haggard face, revealing his numerous years. He was covered in a worn blue coat with the lapels pointing off his surprisingly large body. One of his eyes was concealed by a small patch with the other intently staring at Edge. His expression remained hard as he took a step forward but his voice was soft.

Trial of a Maven

"You won't need that," he spoke watching Edge reaching back for his blade. The Maven kept his hand where it was and curiously spoke back.

"What do you want?" he replied tersely.

"I may be able to help you, lad," he returned after a long pause. "Come sit with me." He turned then, his long blue coattails sweeping the ground as he walked and turned to sit in one of the dark booths at the end of the room. Edge remained motionless for a long moment but at last released Kaotica and turned to whisper in her ear once more.

"Stay beside me and don't say or do anything," he instructed her heatedly, to which the girl wordlessly raised an open hand in the air and closed her fingers together, signaling her promise. Edge held her gaze with distrustful eyes for a lingering moment but at last walked over to the booth where the old man sat and tucked Kaotica in to the wall with him on the outside. As he took his seat the man finally smiled and tipped his head to the girl with respect.

"Thank you," he spoke in his raspy voice, taking hold of another two mugs of ale beside him and sliding them to the others. "Thirsty?" Though Kaotica reached for hers curiously, Edge quickly grabbed it from her hands.

"The last thing you need in this world is alcohol," he murmured more to himself than her as he slid it to his opposite side. Shifting his gaze back to the old man staring at him, he prepared to speak but was cut off by the girl beside him leaning her elbows on the table with a puzzled look on her face.

"What's with the black thing on your eye?" she inquired in her usually frank tone. The man smiled at her, lifting a hand to flip up the patch over his right eye. Kaotica's brow furrowed at what she saw, or the lack thereof.

"Lost it on a fishing voyage to an outskirt isle in my youth, miss," he announced. "Taught me the great lesson of my life—even facing death the prey can become predator."

"You lost your eye fishing?" Kaotica returned disbelievingly.

"No, I lost my eye catching," he replied. "Damn Jagged Pike—the nastiest fish in the waves—hooked my eye with a tooth after I thought it was dead on the deck. He nicked me but I got the blaggard stuffed and he's been hanging on my wall ever since." Kaotica raised her eyebrows and lifted her elbows off the table to turn and face Edge.

"I think this one's been away from land a little too long," she spoke sardonically, to which Edge merely ignored her and tried to bring them back on topic.

"What did you mean you can help me?" he asked with his voice quiet. The burly man flipped his patch back down and nodded, his serious expression returned.

"I couldn't help but overhear your conversation at the bar before," he returned quietly. "I'm Captain Maxraeil Brathrad. You can call me Max, as most do. I know the waters you're looking for." Edge could feel his body tighten up on hearing this, letting a long pause hang before responding.

"Well that isn't exactly the response I got from captain 'weevil' over there," he returned skeptically. "He made it sound like the place I'm looking for is forbidden."

"It is," Max responded sternly, not missing a beat. He leaned in toward Edge, taking a look around to be sure no one was looking at them. "The island of fog has claimed more ships and crews than the pike or Vorkoise itself. No one who has passed through the fog has ever made it out alive. Make no mistake—what you're talking about is dangerous beyond anything you can imagine, young Maven. Probably suicide."

"If so then why would you possibly be interested in helping me get there, Captain Max?" Edge grilled distrustfully. "What would you have to gain for risking your neck?" The seasoned captain shot his eyes to the table then, slowly spinning the mug in his hands.

"There might be mutual benefit for us to work together, Maven," he spoke staring into space. "For me to undertake a voyage so perilous I would of course require great compensation on your part. By the looks of you, more than I would venture to guess you possess. But there might be a way for you to repay me around Seir." Though his suspicions of the old man grew with each word he spoke, Edge was compelled to keep his calm and respond.

"And that would be?" he pressed.

"I had my doubts at first seeing as you are only one Maven, but after witnessing what your friend here can do there is no doubt in my mind you could help me," he stated confidently. "You see, I captain one of the fastest ships in the Eastern Sea but, well, it's not exactly ready to sail at the moment." Edge let out a huff of irritation and sat back against the cushioned booth, folding his arms.

"What does that mean?" he replied impatiently.

Trial of a Maven

"...It's my damn crew," Max finally answered with a hint of resentment in his voice. "They got drunk in another tavern when we returned to shore last week and caused a ruckus up in town. Long story short is they all got locked up and are awaiting trial from the local magistrate. The *Halcyone* is a very big ship—it takes a large number to crew it and I'm shorthanded as it is. I've even got the new explosive powder cannons on board. Recruiting an entire new crew would take weeks and if I'm not out of the port by tomorrow the harbormaster has threatened to impound my ship. I need those men back tonight.

"So you want me to break your crew out of jail?" Edge summarized incredulously. "What makes you think I'd be able to do something like that?"

"You're a Maven, aren't you?" Max returned. "And this young lady you're with seems to know how to take care of herself." Kaotica beamed at him.

"How true, Edge," she said turning to face him. The Maven merely shot her an unappreciative glance but was cut short by Max once more.

"If you do this for me I'll owe you a great debt. If you wish I will even take you to the island of fog despite the risk."

"What reason do I have to trust you, Max?" Edge pressed. "How do I know you won't betray me if I was to free your crew or that you even know where the island of fog is? If no one has ever returned alive how do you know where to go?"

"You forget my ship, young Maven," he replied coolly. "The *Halcyone* is the fastest ship in these waters. It's survived encounters with Jagged Pike on more than once occasion, which is more than most captains can boast. I've never actually seen the island said to be inside the fog but I've made it through the outlying mist once. I'm one of the only men to have ever seen it and I guarantee no one else in this port could find it even if they were brave enough to try. If you really need to get there so badly I'm your only option in this port. That you can believe beyond any doubt."

Edge remained still and silent at the end of the old captain's speech, running the plan through his mind. Observing him struggle between his hopes and doubts Kaotica rhythmically tapped the tips of her fingers on his shoulder.

"Come on, Edge," she pressed him with a faint smirk. "We could do this easily. This is what you were looking for, right?" The Maven shot her an uncertain glance, remembering what he was trying to do by getting to this island and what it would mean for the dark girl if he accomplished his mission. Putting it out of his mind, Edge at last exhaled slowly and turned to face Max.

"All right, you've got a Maven," he answered.

Chapter 26

Jailbreak

Having agreed to spring Captain Maxraeil Brathrad's crew from the custody of the local Acquanautta magistrate in the humble detention center in which they were jailed, Edge with Kaotica, still bounding with dangerous energy and excitement, departed the sailors' tavern for the massive ship known as the *Halcyone* silently resting on the docks. Inspecting it for himself for final assurance that Max was indeed capable of fulfilling his promise to ferry them across the Eastern Sea, the Maven quickly drew up his plan with the captain. Max informed him the prison was on the opposite side of the port adjacent to the local magistrate's office. Though he stressed there would be several ranks of guards and provisional soldiers keeping watch over the docks under their authority Edge was confident he could penetrate any guard with the cover of night to aid him. While Max trusted that the Maven could indeed break his men free he was not so sure about the escape plan. Even if they made it clear of the docks, if they were detected the harbormaster would realize who the fugitive crew belonged to and order the *Halcyone* seized or destroyed immediately. They would have little time to get the crew back to the ship before the rows of cannons along the top wall of the harbor walls opened fire on them.

With the knowledge that the entire plan rested on their speed and stealth, Edge instructed Max to prepare the ship to sail as best he could and wait for their return. Though aware Kaotica would be a liability to the entire mission if he brought her with him, he knew it was far more dangerous to leave her behind unsupervised. If left to herself she would either follow him anyway and blow his cover or wreck havoc elsewhere on the port. Keeping her with him under his watch was his only option.

With the roguish girl and his Sky Sprite partner beside him, Edge departed from the *Halcyone* and swiftly made his way south over the docks of Acquanautta Port toward the magistrate's office and the nearby jail. As he silently darted over the damp wooden docks with only the faint moonlight and occasional torches to illuminate his way the Maven was surprised to find Kaotica obediently following behind him taking care to conceal herself as well as he. Occasionally glancing back to observe her slender figure trailing him as they ran through the night he couldn't help but look at her in a different light than before. Though he knew the enormous threat she posed to the world and the terrifying things she was capable of, as the girl ran behind him with an excited look on her beautiful face nearly identical to Kaylan's he could almost see her purely as what she appeared to be— an adolescent girl craving the same love and attention any other so desired from the world. Every time she had revealed herself through her Grandarian twin, Kaotica had never conveyed any desire for purposeful evil—just fun. Though resolute to his purpose of destroying her to save Kaylan, for the first time the Edge felt a pang of hesitation in taking her life to save another.

His doubts quickly dissipated as they came upon the border of the high docks looking down on the lower ones around a bend in the shoreline that revealed the magistrate's office and the perimeter of guards around it. Slowing and ducking down behind a row of old wooden crates Edge motioned for Kaotica to do the same and softly whistled into the night air. Waiting with only the gentle lapping of ocean waves against the docks beneath them to break the silence, Zephyr finally dropped out of the air to swoop in and perch on Edge's shoulder.

"It's like Captain Max told us, partner," he began without having to be asked. "The magistrate's office is the big one in the center of the dock nestled up against the detention building on the other side. Not the most heavily guarded place we've ever seen but enough that they have just about every angle covered."

"Just about?" Edge inquired, guessing his partner had found something.

"The way I see it you can go one of two ways," he returned, brushing a hand through the long feathers rising from his head. "There are barred windows over a room

Trial of a Maven

holding a large group of men —I guess to be our crew—on the southern side of the building. The stone wall doesn't look too steady and I bet little-Miss-Explosive here could probably punch through pretty easy."

"You're too sweet, birdie," Kaotica sarcastically interjected with a sneer. Edge shot her a frown telling her to keep quiet. Before she could reject the idea, Zephyr continued.

"But seeing as my partner eats, breathes and sleeps stealth I figured I'd better find a more subtle approach. The weakest point in the guarded perimeter is there, near the unlit section of the wall." Edge followed Zephyr's pointed arm toward the eastern wall of the magistrate's office where only one guard sat on top of a barrel staring out to the ocean.

"How does a solid wall get me into the prison, Zeph?" he pressed skeptically.

"Not the wall, partner, what's under it," was the sprite's answer. "The planks behind the row of barrels the guard is sitting on are all rotted out. I punched through one of them and found a trap door under the building. Looks like it leads right up to the prison hallway." Edge nodded and let out a deep huff of breath as he turned and narrowed his eyes at the building before them.

"All right, Zeph. Take position on the roof above one of the barred windows of the prison and give me whistle cover. Kaotica and I will sneak to the eastern wall of the building and knock out the guard so we can get under the docks and up into the building. There is a walkway down there for us, right?" The Sky Sprite nodded.

"Yes but it looks pretty worn by the elements," he warned. "I wouldn't put more than a few bodies on it at a time once you have the crew." Edge silently acknowledged but was interrupted by the gentle clapping of hands from beside him.

"Oh fun, fun, fun!" Kaotica merrily whispered from beside him. "I never knew you could be such a bad boy, Edge. Are you sure you know how to do this?" The Maven rolled his eyes and positioned his blade on his back to one side ready to be drawn.

"In my line of work I'm no stranger to bending the rules now and again, Kaotica," he replied quickly, eager to change the subject. "I know what I'm doing."

"Maybe but you've never had me to help you before," she spoke alluringly with a bewitching smile over her lips. Edge instantly shook his head at this, a stern expression of negativity encompassing his visage.

"Kaotica, I don't want any help from you," he told her articulately. "If I take you with me you have to promise me you won't use your power under any circumstances. I mean for *any* reason at all. And you do what I tell you." The girl rolled her eyes and sat back on her heels, folding her arms.

"Uhg, whatever," she replied impatiently. "If that's what you want, fine." Edge narrowed his eyes at her, aware she didn't appreciate what he was saying.

"I mean it this time, Kaotica," he continued firmly. "This isn't some game we're playing here like you obviously think; this is real life with lives on the line. If you don't listen to me people could die here tonight. Promise me you won't use your power." Keeping her gleaming purple eyes intently fixed on his as if soaking up every word, she nodded in visible understanding.

"All right, Edge, you're the boss," she agreed with a smile. Praying she would actually keep her word this time, the Maven at last broke his gaze from her and rose to plan his next move. Eyeing a thick railway covered in darkness where the guard by the wall was staring, the Maven quickly crept up through the cover of night with Kaotica closely behind. Leaping to roll behind a large post in the railway he checked past it to make sure no one had seen them. Observing the guard sitting atop the barrels still staring blankly out to the endless black of the sea, Edge looked around to spy a loose plank beside him. Taking hold of it he loosely dropped it on the surface of the dock with an audible noise sounding into the night. The guard on the barrels quickly came awake, curiously turning to eye where the noise had come from. Seeing he had the man's attention Edge lifted and dropped the plank once more, this time harder. Listening through the night as the guard jumped off the barrel and slowly ambled toward them with his short sword raised, Edge quickly reached up to his neck to unfasten the frayed blue cloth around it. Staring at him curiously as the boy wrapped its ends around his fists and pulled it taut, Kaotica watched in surprise as the Maven quickly threw the midsection of the scarf up around the guard's face as he walked by them in the darkness. With his scarf over the man's mouth to preclude him from shouting for help Edge jerked him down to slam his head into the rounded edge of the massive post behind him, silently knocking out the guard.

As the Maven pulled his scarf from the man's face and fastened it back around his neck he glanced up to find Kaotica staring at him with an inquisitive sparkle in her eyes.

"There are ways to solve problems and get rid of people without killing them, Kaotica," he whispered through the darkness, to which she smirked and flipped a streaming lock of hair away from her face. With a portion of the magistrate's office exposed and unguarded, Edge and Kaotica shot forward and crept on through the night once more, quickly dashing up to the rows of empty barrels around a rotting section of the wood on the docks. Locating the small hole Zephyr had already made, Edge pulled free his broadsword and began quietly hacking away at the soft wood until he had worked away enough for a large person to easily slip through. Motioning for Kaotica to jump down first, he helped her through the hole and scanned the still quiet docks for anyone who might have noticed them. Clear, he leapt behind the dark girl and landed in a crouch on the wet docks below them, hovering right above the lapping water. There was barely enough room between the lower docks and the floor of the building above them to squat, much less stand. Following the pathway in the modest light from above that allowed itself through cracks in the boards and from the magistrate's office, they at last spotted the trap door which Zephyr had told them about.

Slowly lifting his hands, Edge gingerly cracked it open to peer through and survey what lay above. To his right was a wall and straight ahead lay what appeared to be the hallway down the center of the prison block with cells on either side. Though the boy could hear muffled voices of what sounded like guards further down the hall he was confident the trap door was hidden in some sort of indentation in the hallway and they would be safe to emerge unseen. Gradually lifting the door to set it on the ground behind them, Edge further lifted his head from the hole to find a spiraling staircase leading to another level of the prison behind them. Climbing into the room and helping Kaotica up behind him, the Maven motioned for her to remain silent while he peered around the corner of the wall to the right where the sounds of voices originated. There were two guards at the end of the hall sitting beside a table playing a game of cards with two of the jail cells beside them filled with men he guessed to be the crew. Withdrawing his head back to press it against the wall, he turned to Kaotica waiting beside him with her arms folded before her.

"So what's the plan, fearless leader?" she pressed raising an eyebrow impatiently.

"The guards in the hall have the keys we'll need to open the cell doors," he replied. "But there are two of them. We need a way to down them both at the same time or the other will blow our cover to the rest of the guards inside the office."

"And how are we going to do that?" she returned unconvinced.

"I'm not sure yet, so calm down and just wait there," Edge told her staring off into space to think. As he closed his eyes to contemplate the safest option to proceed, Kaotica let out an impatient breath of air and lowered her arms.

"All this sneaking around is boring," she whispered. "This is taking too long." With that, she stepped forward and entered the hall with her hands on her hips, slowly turning to face the two guards on the other side. Edge didn't realize she had even moved until he felt the wind of her passing stroke his face. By the time his eyes shot open in fury she was already on her way to the guards with the sound of the heels of her long black boots on the wooden floor getting their attention.

"Hey boys," she spoke as flirtatious as he had ever heard her, slowly ambling toward them. Though both guards dropped the cards in their hands and shot up in their seats in alarm, Kaotica raised her hands defensively with a disarming smile gracing her lips. "Calm down, boys, no need to get up for me."

"How did you get in here?" one of them asked preparing to stand. Kaotica let a seductive giggle escape from her throat as she placed her hand on the man's chest and pushed him back down, surprising them both.

"Oh I let myself in," she replied honestly, leaning in to extend her face before the man. "I was looking for some fun. How about you?" The guard glanced uncertainly to his partner, already staring at the attractive girl's exotic and revealing attire. From the way she was dressed, they both guessed she had been sent to provide them with a little entertainment for the night. Kaotica's smile broadened in the silence and she took a seat on one of the men's legs, crossing hers over each other and leaning back into his chest. Edge shifted nervously from his position behind the wall in the center of the hall, unsure what the dark girl was up to. She leaned in to one of the guard's ear to whisper inside, placing a hand on his chest as she spoke. As Edge watched her hand slide up the man's body to wrap around his neck he noticed her other slipping down to his belt to quietly pull forth a set of keys inside his pocket. At last letting a curious smile pass over his face in understanding, Edge shook his head with incredulity and continued staring as the dark girl rested the large key ring on the small purple bow behind her back. By this point the imprisoned crew had all noticed the beautiful girl and began calling and whistling for her attention as well. She rose then, seductively motioning with a finger for the two men to rise and follow her as she backed her way through the hall away from the inmates. "We should have our privacy, don't you think?" The guards looked to each other with knowing smiles and did as they were bid, ambling after her.

Swaying her striking curvature to and fro with every step, the girl at last came to one of the open cells and stopped, pointing inside.

"We're going to play a little game," she spoke flirtatiously. "Tonight you get to be prisoners too. Now in you go..." Shooting each other curious but excited glances, the two guards stepped inside the open cell as they were told. The moment they both turned around waiting for Kaotica to do the same, she took hold of the barred door and closed it shut, locking it immediately. The smiles on the guards' faces quickly disappeared at this and they stepped forward in surprise.

"What are you doing, girl?" one of them grilled. "Unlock this door right now." A dramatic look passed over her face as she stepped forward a mere inches from the bars.

"Sorry boys," she spoke tilting her head to one side with false sorrow. "I only said you get to be prisoners, not me." Reaching forward through the bars, she grabbed the backs of their heads and wrenched them forward with strength far beyond that of a normal girl her size to smack into the bars with a heavy ringing of iron. They dropped to their backs the next second, out cold. Turning and reaching behind her back

Tales of Iairia

to grab the keys she had hidden there, the girl tossed them to Edge still hiding behind the wall in the hallway with an incredulous look in his blue eyes. "Boys are all the same," she announced passively, reaching into her long hair to run her fingers through it triumphantly. The Maven merely shook his head and tried to hide the small smile behind his lips that was trying to escape. Dashing to the doors of the cells he began to unlock them, the crew bursting awake upon seeing him.

"All of you calm down," he ordered quietly, Kaotica coming to stand beside him with hands on her hips. "My partner and I have been hired to break you out of here by your captain but there are guards everywhere so you have to be quiet and work together if you want to get out of here and back to your ship." The Maven quickly explained how they would make their escape and opened the doors, telling them to get to the trap door and wait for him. As the crew began filing past him Edge was surprised to find Kaotica stepping into him with a broad smile once more.

"Ah, you called me your partner, Edgy," she told him, running two fingers up his chest. "Now aren't you glad you brought me along?" Edge held her gaze for moment longer than he should have, his eyes sweeping down to her body pressed up against his but before he could respond or pull away she put a finger on his lips and tilted her head knowingly. Releasing her finger she leaned up to place her lips on his to slowly kiss him for a long moment. Softly pulling back with her lips sticking to his, the girl smiled once more and turned with her black hair flying up behind her to make her way behind the crew racing for the trap door. Though stunned and baffled out of his mind as to why she had just done that, or more significantly, why he had let her do it, the Maven felt frozen to the floor for several long moments. His attention was at last brought back to him when he heard the shouting of several men beneath the floor. Gritting his teeth, Edge charged ahead to force his way to the staircase where crewmen were already jumping through the trap door eager to be free of the prison. Aware the old rotted pathway below could not hold so many at once, Edge forced the others to stay back and he whispered down to those below him to calm down.

By the time they turned to listen to him it was already too late. With over six of the burly crewmen on the pathway at once the worn dock loudly snapped, dropping them into the ocean water beneath them. Edge kicked the ground in rage as the sound of guards upstairs and outside began to come to attention and shout alarm to each other. Hearing Zephyr's whistle call from outside, the Maven looked back into the trap door to spy another dock at the end of the harbor that looked to be intact. Aware they could not escape out the front door of the prison with all the guards outside Edge ordered the crew to jump into the water and swim for the dock that would lead back to the *Halcyone*. Though hesitant, the sound of doors opening from the opposite entryway in the hall of the room sent urgency tearing through them and they did as they were told, one by one leaping into the water. Wheeling around to see guards rushing their position in the hallway, Kaotica raised her fists with electric energy charging around them. Seeing the purple light surge around her Edge heaved his sword off his back and shouted over to her.

"*No*, Kaotica!" he commanded loudly. "If you use your power the Drakkaidians will know where we are! Get out of here with the men and I'll catch up to you!" The girl was about to willfully protest but when the Maven charged forward to slash his blade past her into a guard's to parry him away from her she took an uncertain step back. Edge wheeled around and thrust his blade to the side to swat the guard away and simultaneously kick backward to catch another in his face with his boot. "I said *go*, Kaotica!" The boy's voice was so loud and brimming with emotion even Kaotica shrunk back in fear, conforming to his order. Spinning around she pushed the remaining crew into the trap door and leapt in after them, the water splashing up behind her. Seeing another four guards dashing into the cell block, Edge picked up one of the lighter short swords beside him and heaved it at one of the open doors to slam it shut and bottleneck them. Running to a wall to kick off and spin over two more guards coming down the stairs behind him Edge landed in a crouch and delivered a spinning kick to their feet that toppled them both onto their backs. Leaving his heavy sword behind, the darkly clad boy leapt into the open trap door as another wave of guards entered after him.

    Swimming through the lapping waves of salty water as hard as he could as the last of the crewmen made it up to the lower docks of the harbor and began running back to their ship, the guards above began firing arrows through the openings in the dock floor, jetting into the waters around him. Though making it all the way to the docks unscathed the Maven was eventually caught in the upper arm by one of the thin missiles. Though slowed by the water it still penetrated his skin and slowed him down, making it difficult to lift himself onto the dock. As the boy struggled to pull himself up he suddenly felt the grip of two hands on his good arm heaving him up and laying him out on the dock. Looking up he found Kaotica soaked from head to toe, yelling for him to hurry up. Rising and breaking the arrow shaft protruding from his arm, Edge leapt forward after Kaotica onto the lower docks that led to a small staircase up to the crates where they had first spotted the magistrate's office. Stumbling onto the top layer of the docks as fast as they could run after the rest of the crew, volleys of arrows began sailing around them once more. While Kaotica was about to spin around and fire a blast of dark energy from her open hands no matter what Edge told her the incoming missiles were swatted away by another field of enchanted energy surrounding them in spheres of light and pulling them off trajectory at the last minute. Turning back Edge found Zephyr swooping through the skies after them to lift them both into the air and carry them over the docks toward the *Halcyone* in the northern port.

Catching up to the crew already boarding their ship, the exhausted sprite was at last forced to set the humans down near the adjacent dock and perch on Edge's shoulder.

"I've got to rest for a while, partner," he spoke out of breath from behind his yellow beak. Edge nodded, telling him he had gotten them far enough. With the sounds of the pursuing guards still approaching in the distance, the burly form of Captain Maxraeil Brathrad standing over the railing of the ship shouted down to them.

"Hurry and get on board!" he bellowed as his restored crew began unfurling the sails and pulling up anchor. "We've got to get out of port before word spreads and—" Before he could finish the nearby blast of cannon fire sounded through the night air, accompanied by the whizzing sound of a spherical projectile passing by and landing in the waters beyond. Max spun to the top level of the harbor to see men rushing to man the other cannons facing the sea. "Hurry or we'll be torn apart before we ever set out!" Not needing to hear him again, Edge and Kaotica began dashing for the gangplank leading up to the ship and at the end of the dock with the sound of multiple cannons erupting to life behind them. The incoming shots immediately spread a wave of terror and chaos over the docks with the late night crowds coming in from their ships or making their way to or from the taverns running for their lives. While most overshot the *Halcyone* and either landed in the waters beyond or the tips of the docks, as they took aim in the second volley, more of the shots began nicking the railways and masts of the ship. By the time Edge and Kaotica finally sprinted to the gangplank and began charging up it, the *Halcyone* began to lurch forward with a strong eastern wind pushing them from behind. Leaping up into the ship Edge could hear the crying calls of a child below them standing on the splintered edge of the docks with a fishing pole in his hands and a man in the waters below whom the Maven guessed to be his father. Though he wished he could help him, his mission had to come first and he grabbed Kaotica from the gangplank before it toppled over into the waves.

    The dark girl landed with a thud on the hard deck of the ship, looking up to find Edge still holding her protectively. Another shot from a cannon behind them sounded through the night, drawing their full attention. Though Edge could tell it was going to miss them and land to their port side, Kaotica spun her head toward the incoming projectile and suddenly leapt to her feet. A dark aura of electrified power exploding around her, Edge watched in horror as the pair of jagged wings of purple light materialized on her back and she leapt off the ship's railing. Screaming for her to stop, he rose and flew to the railing to see the girl ignoring him and quickly building a charge of dark light in her hands to throw it forward and pepper the cannonball sailing toward her and the dock they had just escaped. As the light from the explosion cleared, the dock that would have been obliterated by the cannonball remained intact with Kaotica crouched down on its surface holding something in her arms. Peering down through the darkness illuminated only by the ominous power radiating off of her body, Edge's eyes widened as he found the object nestled safely in Kaotica's arms to be the crying boy that would have been killed by the shot if not for her intervention.

    Staring flabbergasted, Edge watched her tenderly pick the crying boy up and lift him to the higher levels of the harbor to drop him where he would be safe. Setting him down, the dark angel turned and threw another charge of dark energy into the cannon to obliterate it before soaring back to the *Halcyone* to land on the deck before the Maven, half the crew staring at her with jaws agape. None of them were as amazed by the girl's actions as Edge, however, staring at her in disbelief as the flaring power around her now dry body dissipated into the eastern wind blowing the *Halcyone* forward out of range of the remaining canons in the harbor. When the last of her power was gone Kaotica took a deep breath and let her form sink in fatigue.

"I feel tired, Edge," she spoke earnestly, kneeling down over the deck. The boy forced himself to overcome his amazement at what had just happened and stepped forward. He leaned down beside her, putting a hand on her shoulder.

"You just did a good thing, Kaotica," he told her softly, sincerity in his voice he never thought he would express for the dark girl. Kaotica merely smiled one of her alluring smiles and looked up to him.

"It's what you would have done, isn't it?" she asked, already aware of the answer. The Maven merely forced a faint smile of his own and wordlessly shrugged. Kaotica silently chuckled and nodded, telling him she would see him soon as an aura of darkness began to swell around her, signaling the golden light that would follow the next moment. As the radiant light dissipated around the girl's body another one was sitting before him with her blue eyes slowly blinking open and shut in momentary confusion. Seeing Edge leaning over her, Kaylan remembered what had happened and what she had seen through her dark twin's eyes. Though confused and unsure what to say with Edge and a crew of men staring at her in disbelief, she merely asked to be taken to a bed to get some rest.

Chapter 27

<u>Moving the Pawns</u>

It wasn't moving. It hadn't moved in over five centuries since the first Holy War when a group of Dark Mages once known as the Dégamar had absorbed what was left of its strength to pass it to the patriarch of the House of Montrox—Veriod Montrox. It was this creature's power that had created the Warrior of Darkness in the first place; the creature known only as Dalorosk. The High Priest Zalnaught lowered the Staff of the Ancients in his hands to set its tip back on the dark stone floor of the deep basement in the Cathedral of Dalorosk. Faint torch light steadily danced across the walls of the spherical chamber in which he stood, painting an orange glow on his frustrated face and that of the motionless head resting before him. The beastly form was easily fifty times bigger than his with black horns protruding from its thick, beastly cranium and rows of bloodstained teeth within. This room and the motionless beast before Zalnaught were the best kept secrets in Drakkaidia and perhaps all of Iairia. While most knew the legacy and origins of the Warrior of Light in the wake of the Days of Destiny, even most Drakkaidians still did not know how the Warrior of Darkness was anointed or where the first one had come from. Far underground the surface level of the Cathedral of Dalorosk and the Temple of Darkness lay a chamber built millennia ago by the ancient Drakkaidians to imprison one of the last remaining relics of the old world before the time of the nations. Dalorosk was a behemoth of mythic dark power that had somehow been captured and locked away underground where its energy could be extracted and utilized by the Dark Mages to fuel their purposes, particularly the Dégamar centuries ago that had taken the last of its strength to empower the first Warrior of Darkness.

Though Dalorosk had barely shifted its massive body under the enormous iron chains that held it down over the years in the building that bore its name, the Dark Mages still tended to it as their most prized prisoner in case they ever needed to reach into its regenerative strength once again. When looking for dark energy to empower the Staff of the Ancients, Zalnaught had attempted to coax what strength he could from the beast into his talisman but virtually nothing was gained. In the wake of the explosion of power from the vessel of Drakkan he had just sensed on the coast of the Eastern Sea the previous night, Zalnaught's impatience for gathering more power had grown insatiable and he had returned to the underground prison of Dalorosk to try and absorb it altogether. Though it would certainly bolster the staff's strength, the High Priest knew it would not be enough to matter so he lowered the staff once more and allowed his temper to cool, staring into the mammoth face of the creature before him weighed down by the heavy chains.

Zalnaught tightened his grip around the seemingly simple wooden staff in his hands, shifting his weight over the dark ground he stood on with his flowing black and crimson robes gently twisting around him. His minimal patience was all but gone in the wake of the Dark Mages' newest failure to capture the vessel. First they had missed her in the forests, the Mystic Tower, and now it appeared the vessel had escaped into the Eastern Sea with another figure that seemed to possess power of its own. Zalnaught's already taut body all but quaked with rage. If the vessel was fleeing Iairia it would take even longer to find and secure it. The war would start before he was ready. Zalnaught had sensed the colossal clash between Verix and Tavin at the portal to the void and knew both of them had the power to declare war on their own if they wished. Things had turned out better than he could have hoped but they were moving too quickly to be controlled. He needed that vessel now.

As the High Priest stood thinking in the massive chamber he heard the sound of the usually bolted doors opening behind him and turned to face a hooded and cloaked Dark Mage entering the room.

"I asked not to be disturbed," he whispered, following the mages' long tradition of keeping quiet in the presence of Dalorosk. The Dark Mage bowed and stopped before him.

"My apologies, Your Excellency," he spoke humbly in a hushed tone, "but I have an urgent report from General Nedross in the war zones. His scouts have detected Grandarian activity on the Wall of Light building beyond anything we have seen in years these past days. Scouts have learned of rumors that the Warrior of Light himself is marching on the wall." Zalnaught was still at this, slowly blinking as the words filtered through his mind.

"Then things are indeed accelerating," he murmured more to himself than the mage. Zalnaught raised a hand to rub the thick lines in his forehead, contemplating this new development. "Perhaps we can use this to our advantage. If the Warrior of Light himself is there to match Verix, our forces will be held at the wall in stalemate when the war begins. This will give us additional time..." The High Priest trailed off then, noticing a faint red hue suddenly painting the spherical wall of the chamber. His brow furrowing uncertainly, he spun around with his robes flying up behind him to find Dalorosk's dim crimson eyes open, staring motionless at them. Both Zalnaught and the Dark Mage stood unnerved before it for a lingering moment, unsure of what the massive creature was doing. At last the beast's enormous eyelids slid shut once more, a deep rumbling growl echoing out from its throat to vibrate through the entire chamber.

Though disturbed by the unusual awakening they had not seen for years, Zalnaught collected himself and slowly turned back to the mage.

"It's taken us millennia to whip this beast," he began in a whisper, "I don't want it growing bold again just because we haven't been using it lately. I have work to do—stay here and execute the runes." The Dark Mage's fearful expression widened upon hearing this, nervously shifting his weight.

"The runes, Your Excellency?" he repeated august. "He's barely even moved in decades. Is that really necessary?" Zalnaught's dark visage flashed impatience and violence as he stepped forward to harshly whisper with his grip hard around the Staff of the Ancients.

"Anything I order is *necessary* and you would do well to remember that or find yourself living down here with him, mage," Zalnaught spoke with acid dripping from his words. "Now get it done." Stepping past him the High Priest extended an open hand toward the heavy doors of the chamber and blasted them open with his telekinetic power, stepping through them to begin his trek up the long staircases leading up to the surface level of the cathedral. Pressing on for several long minutes Zalnaught at last arrived in a sealed off hall of the structure only the Dark Mage's were permitted to enter, then back to the sanctuary to which it led. Making his way back to his quarters to fetch his Voss Stone, Zalnaught traversed the dark passageways of the cathedral to a balcony adjacent to the second level of the Chamber of Statues housing stone busts of dead High Priests from ages past and kings of the House of Montrox blessed by the Black Church. Stepping outside onto the balcony beyond, Zalnaught tightened the large black hat covering his bald dome and reached into his pockets to pull forth his Voss Stone.

The High Priest gradually closed his eyes and began massaging the crimson rock in his hand, a faint red light from within beginning to pulsate outwards from the dark core. As the moments passed on with wisps of wind from the angry skies above passing by, Zalnaught began to speak in a monotonous tone of voice with his eyes still shut.

"Verix," he called softly. "Verix we must speak. You know you must speak with me, young prince. Answer me." Zalnaught stopped then, slowly opening his dark eyes once more and holding the glowing stone in his palm, waiting. He remained standing still for several minutes before a faint humming noise from deep within the stone began to resound outwards, slowly taking on the clear sound of speech.

"You haven't spoken to me through the Voss Stone in years, Zalnaught," a quick and biting voice at last responded through the silence. "What do you want?" The High Priest silently smiled to himself, eager to feed upon the anger in the other's voice.

"I sensed what happened at the portal, Verix," he began in a calm and contained tone. "I told you I had nothing to do with the disturbance. It was as I feared, wasn't it?" As he finished his words there was a long pause, huffs of air revealing obvious uncertainty on the other side of the stone.

"The Sword of Granis was lying almost on its side with dark energy hovering around it," the voice at last responded. "When I arrived he was there standing beside it."

"So you saw the truth of this sabotage and acted," Zalnaught responded for him. "Is this not so?" There was another pause before Verix responded with dejection in his voice.

Trial of a Maven

"I'm on my way back to Dalastrak," he responded at last. "I need to think this over."

"There is nothing to think about, young prince," Zalnaught interjected. "I have just received word that Tieloc is marching on the Wall of Light with the full strength of the Grandarian army brought to bear. This is not the time for indecision. You must act now before it is too late."

"What would you have me do, Zalnaught?" Verix responded aggravated. "If war is coming, thanks to you and your lies I have a divided nation to wage it with. My Loyalists are too few to march for battle against all of Grandaria and your twisted New Fellowship has been brainwashed against me."

"You forget, young prince," Zalnaught reminded him, "that the rogue soldiers in the war zone belonging to the New Fellowship of Drakkan. They will follow you if I... encourage them to do so." There was another exhausted breath of hesitation on the opposite side of the Voss Stone, followed by what sounded like Verix halting the horse he was riding.

"Then listen well, Zalnaught," Verix spoke resolutely, restored purpose in his words. "If it is war that we now face we do so as one. I am assuming control of the nation you robbed from me and uniting the people. I will send word for what troops we can spare in Dalastrak to march for the Valley of Blood with the war machines but I ride now for the war zone where your New Fellowship troops have gathered. Whether you relay your 'encouragement' or not, I am taking command and *any* who oppose me will face the same fate as any Grandarian foolish enough to provoke conflict. Do you understand, High Priest?" Zalnaught's smirk widened behind the Voss Stone as he raised it up to his lips.

"The survival of our nation is paramount," he responded approvingly. "Do as you must, Prince Montrox." With that the humming glow from the core of stone began to fade, the galloping hoof beats once more sounding from within disappearing into the gusts of wind around the Cathedral of Dalorosk. Zalnaught's face continued to twist with pleasure at how things had developed as he placed the Voss Stone in his robes once more. "That's right, Verix. Wage war on the Grandarians with my troops while I send the rest of my soldiers here to destroy Dalastrak and your precious Loyalists while you are away. Then, with the restored power of the Staff of the Ancients in my hands I will finish you and this Holy War in one blow." Zalnaught silently chuckled as he slowly turned and ambled back into the dark chamber of the Cathedral of Dalorosk high above the city below.

Chapter 28

The Halcyone

    Kaylan Tieloc sat alone in the large galley below the deck of the *Halcyone*, blankly staring at the steaming food on the plate before her. There was an assortment of broiled vegetables and cooked fish generously prepared for her by the ship's cook a few minutes before, but her usual appetite had diminished since their departure from Acquanautta Port over three days ago. The *Halcyone* was a fast ship for being so large. In the minimal time they had been at sail on the Eastern Sea they had already passed the small island chains settled by the Southland and were heading for the deep waters beyond. The Grandarian girl took a deep breath and frowned, pushing the plate away from her on the gently rocking table. She folded her hands in her lap as the creaking of thick wood on the hull of the ship echoed through the galley.
    Though she had to admit being on the sea for so long her first time frequently made her queasy, it was the qualm in the back of her mind ever since waking up as herself on the deck of the ship three days ago that had set Kaylan in a state of unusual dejection. Though she had always been unnerved after her dark half had come awake to take possession of her body, the most recent appearance of Kaotica had seemed to weaken her like never before. Like the second entity inside her, she could see and feel the world through Kaotica's eyes almost as if seeing it through her own. She had witnessed the dark girl's actions helping Edge in the prison and saving the boy on the docks and the effect it had made on the Maven. Kaylan forced herself to close her eyes and grit her teeth as the thought of Kaotica kissing him bounced through her mind. She couldn't drive the image from her mind; it was maddening. Realizing she was dwelling on it once more the girl exhaled in frustration and rose, clenching her fists in anger. Though not through her own eyes she had seen the

look in Edge's when he stared at the dark girl that night. Though he knew better it was as if Kaotica was fooling him into thinking she was a real person.

Why did she even care? Edge was with her to destroy Kaotica. It wasn't as if she had anything to be jealous of. Kaylan froze at this thought, amazed it had even crossed her mind. She stared blankly at the wooden wall in front of her for a long moment before dispelling these thoughts and breathing deeply. She ran a hand through her long golden hair and flipped it behind her back once more, one of the many traits Kaotica had adopted from her. Kaylan looked as fatigued as she felt. The shine that usually radiated from her eyes and smile felt diminished and diluted by the weight of the darkness hanging over her. Her bright blue tunic was frayed and ripped beyond repair so she had discarded it for a loose brown sailing shirt long enough to act as a skirt over her last white undershirt. Remembering his first priority of keeping her safe Edge had insisted she remain below deck while they sailed unless he was beside her. Though the crew was still scared half to death of the girl after seeing what her dark half was capable of in Acquanautta Port, the Maven didn't trust them around a girl as beautiful as she for more than a few seconds without him directly watching over her.

The more time that elapsed with the dark vessel inside her the more Kaylan could feel her presence and power growing stronger. It was as if she could feel Kaotica alive in the back of her mind, present in everything she did. She could feel her strength increasing every time she appeared which had been for longer durations with each emergence as well. If the trend continued Kaylan wondered how long it would be before she would someday surface and never disappear. She shook her head at his, driving such thoughts from her mind. She and Edge were going to find the new Granic Crystal and drive her away for good before she had that chance. As thoughts of the determined Maven rippled into her mind yet again all she could think about was Kaotica kissing him and the look on his face afterwards. Thrusting her back off the wall the girl let her arms drop to her sides in aggravation, desperate to be free of the haunting image.

"*Ah, looks like somebody's jealous,*" a voice suddenly sounded from directly beside her. Kaylan's eyes widened in surprise, wheeling around toward whoever had managed to sneak up on her. Shooting up to the other side of the room in fright, the girl was further surprised to find no one there. The galley was completely empty but for her. Letting her mouth slip open in confusion and unease she took an uncertain step back. *"What's the matter, Kay-Kay? You look confused. Not to mention a little weathered, shall we say?"* Kaylan spun around again, feeling the voice surrounding her from every direction. Though she had been sure someone was somehow playing a trick on her a feeling of familiarity seeped through her as she focused on the sound of the voice. *"What are you looking for, blondie? I'm right here where I always am."* Kaylan's frightful blue eyes softened with realization then, staring into space before her.

It was Kaotica.

Somehow she was awake inside her mind, speaking directly to her.

"Kaylan, this is the part where you say hi back, honey," the female voice pressed dramatically. *"What—do you think I'm talking to myself here? Or wait, am I...?"* Kaylan's brow furrowed at this, obvious resentment encompassing her view.

"What do you want?" she spoke coldly, looking around the empty room. Kaotica's voice sounded insulted as she let out a momentary gasp of offense.

"Oh come on, miss goody-good, no need to be like that," she retorted. *"It's bad enough that you're already jealous of me but you don't have to be all snippy about it."*

"Jealous?" Kaylan repeated amazed. "What possible reason would I have to be jealous of you?"

"Oh Kay, do I really have to say? You've been thinking about me and Edge for days straight now. We're in your dreams for crying out loud. I think somebody's just a little envious that he likes me better." Kaylan could barely believe the words echoing through her mind, caught completely off guard by what she was implying.

"What are you talking about?" she returned scornfully. "First off, I don't have anything to be jealous of, and second, don't you even realize what Edge and I are doing? We're on our way to kill you." Kaotica let out a dry chuckle that relayed the message she wasn't impressed.

"Please, sweetie, I already had this talk with Edge if you were awake enough to remember," she stated flatly. *"You may think he'll do it but your precious Edgy won't hurt me. Before*

this is over he'll be breaking his back to keep me around. You, on the other hand, are another story."

"Quit wasting your breath, Kaotica," Kaylan almost yelled back. "We both know what you are and we're not going to let you fool us. Edge knows as well as I do you're just a demon the same as any other."

"You're calling me a demon now? If you recall, little miss purity, I'm you. Your twin. I'm no more a demon than you are, which you actually could very well be with a nasty mouth like that. But why don't you go look for yourself?" Kaylan stopped at this, unsure what she was talking about. *"Go on—why don't you take a look at your beautiful self in the mirror if you're so sure you and I are so different."* She turned to the long mirror she had seen behind the open door to the galley on the opposite side of the room, facing away from her. Curiously stepping toward it the Grandarian girl closed the door shut to reveal the mirror and what lay inside it staring back at her. Kaylan leapt back in surprise, finding not her reflection but that of Kaotica, standing full length staring her back with a smirk on her glossy lips. *"Oh, look at you now. What's the matter, Kay? Don't recognize your own face?"* Kaylan stared at the girl before her for a long moment, too shocked to say anything. Apart from her revealing attire and the color of her hair and eyes she looked almost exactly like her. Her every idiosyncrasy was somehow familiar.

Kaotica let her dark grin grow as Kaylan began to inch away from her.

"Now this is how our body should look," she spoke raising a hand to run her fingers through her silky dark hair. *"I've been waiting to talk face to face with you for a long time now, Kay, so let me spell this out short and sweet so you understand. Edge is mine. Period. Don't try to fight me for him because you won't win."* Shocked at her dark half's words once more, Kaylan could barely formulate the words to respond.

"... I don't even—"

"Don't start with that," Kaotica cut her off. *"I know you—I see your entire mind and you think about him as much as I do. But he's mine, you got it?"* Kaylan shot back in anger at this, stepping toward the mirror on the door.

"The only thing I've *got* is that you aren't going to be around long enough for Edge to think twice about you because as soon as we get a new Granic Crystal on the Sword of Granis you're gone," she returned stooping to the girl's immaturity in her annoyance. "If Edge likes you so much why is he traveling with me to destroy you?"

"*He's only going to be with you until I take over, honey,*" she returned flatly. "*As soon as I do, Edge will never see you again. I suggest you get used to the idea.*" Kaylan could feel the girl's words tearing at her and desperately wanted to shut her up.

"Just leave me alone!" she screamed, ready to kick the mirror in. As she was about to charge forward to shatter the glass holding the image of her dark twin the door suddenly cracked open. Kaylan froze in place as the miniature face of her purple Sky Sprite companion popped through, staring at her uncertainly.

"Are you okay in here, Kaylan?" he asked, disturbed. The Grandarian girl wasn't sure how to respond, an embarrassed wave of red sweeping over her face. He must have thought she was crazy to be yelling in an empty room. Looking to the mirror again the image of Kaotica was gone, reflecting only herself. At last free of her Kaylan breathed deeply and silently nodded, the queasy feeling in her stomach returning. "Well Edge just wanted me to tell you that we've spotted the island of fog. Or at least the fog. If you want to come up and see you can." The Grandarian girl forced a smile from her mouth and told him she would be right up. Before the sprite could withdraw Kaylan stopped him and embarrassingly asked him not to tell Edge what he had just heard. Though hesitant and asking if she was alright once more, Zephyr agreed and pulled away back up to the deck. Kaylan stood motionless for a long moment in the silence, only the creaking hull of the ship sounding through the large galley. Though she knew the manipulative dark girl was trying to get inside her head as she had Edge, she couldn't shake off what she had said about the Maven boy. Was she jealous?

Doing her best to bury her confrontation with Kaotica and compose herself, Kaylan opened the galley door to step into a narrow hallway leading up to a row of stairs at the opposite end. As the girl started toward it she raised her hands to collect her flowing golden hair into a loose ponytail behind her, exposing the whole of her tired but beautiful face. Feeling chilled sea air seeping through the cabin door ahead of her leading to the deck she plucked one of the thick brown sailing shawls hanging over the wall to her right by

Trial of a Maven

the stairs to pull its comforting warmth over her. Taking a deep breath the Grandarian girl pushed the door open to step onto the long deck of the *Halcyone*. She was confused at what she found outside at first, the normally jaunty and noisy crew dead silent at the railing of the ship looking out past the bow. Kaylan ambled uncertainly from the doorway of the cabin through the moist air of the sea. It was a cloudy morning again. Making her way across the damp wooden deck she grabbed onto a thick line of rope running from the railing to the mast above her. She leaned her head out past the railing of the starboard side of the ship and gazed ahead with the rest of the crew.

Instantly she found the reason for their silence. Kaylan's mouth slightly dropped open as her mystified blue eyes locked onto a massive shroud of fog over the hidden waters ahead, stretching for several nautical miles to their port and starboard sides. Disbelief encompassing her mesmerized frame, she stepped onto the thick railing around the deck to lean her entire upper body over the ship to better her view. It was as if the overcast sky draped down from above over the sea like curtains hiding whatever lay beyond and above. Staring out at the seemingly motionless gray waters of the ocean where the fog silently sat for several more minutes a swooping sound of small wings behind her caught her attention along with the gentle feeling of something grabbing onto her right shoulder. Turning her head in surprise she found Zephyr perched there jokingly raising his arms to brace himself for the girl's hair that usually knocked him off balance when he surprised her. Recovering from her shock, Kaylan couldn't help but smirk at his attempt at humor as she leaned back to the ship to place both feet on the deck.

"Zephyr, you nearly scared me off the boat, you little feather duster," she joked seeing his smile.

"Well after all the times your hair has sent me tumbling we'd probably be even," he rejoined merrily. Though Kaylan silently giggled at this she quickly remembered her amazement from before and forced herself to focus.

"So we made it to the fog Edge told us about but now what?" she asked noting the ship was at a standstill with the sails collected above the masts. Zephyr shrugged and smoothed his white feathered chest as he motioned with his head for her to look behind him.

"Captain Max and Edge have been trying to figure that out since we spotted it," he replied. "It sounds like Max is having second thoughts about doing this but I think we both know Edge will, one way or another, persuade him to stay true to his word." Not liking the sound of that at all, Kaylan turned to the helm of the ship above the cabin to spot her Maven protector speaking with Max and two other men beside him, all with unhappy expressions visible on their faces. Observing the stairs that led to the top level of the ship the girl began striding toward them with Zephyr eyeing her uncertainly as she did. "Edge wanted you to leave this to him, Kaylan." The girl met his eyes with her usual determination emanating forth.

"So I will, but I want to hear this for myself," she informed him plainly. Zephyr's brow furrowed as she climbed the stairs toward his partner, noting the determined look in her eyes. The sprite lifted off to resume his spot on tip of the crows nest scanning the waters around them as she arrived near the helm and the men around it. Edge had his back to her with his arms folded before his chest but noticed Max's eyes drift behind him and turned to spot her for himself. Though she could see frustration in his face at her coming, the girl continued forward until standing beside him. Though Max paused from what he was saying as he tipped his head to the girl now before them with an expectant look on her face, he quickly placed the unsettling gaze out of his single eye on the Maven once more.

"It's not that I've forgotten my promise or that I'm changing my mind, young man," he began again, "I'm just trying to warn you what you're talking about here is insane. No one simply sails into the fog."

"You did," Edge returned, his voice laced with impatience. "We agreed on this at your tavern the night we met, Max. You told me you've navigated the fog before—that you were the only one who could do it." The burly seaman let out a deep breath of air and nodded more to himself than Edge, pushing away from the table and the maps spread out over it.

"Cutting through the outer vapors to escape from Jagged Pike is not the same as sailing right into the heart of it, son," he spoke with his voice weighted down with desperation, tightening his long blue coat around him as a faint breeze rustled past them. "I'm only saying that there might be a different way to approach this."

"The only approach I want to hear about is this ship approaching the island beyond that fog, Captain Maxraeil. That was what we agreed. I broke your crew from Acquanautta, risking my life and hers in the process," he said motioning with his bandaged right arm to the girl now beside him, "and now you're going to hold up your end. I don't care what your crew thinks about this—they'd all still be in prison right now if not for me." The other man beside Max with a crusty bandana around his bald skull leaned closer to his captain and quickly interrupted the boy.

"Captain this is madness," he said with a quivering voice. "Even the *Halcyone* is no match for whatever lies inside the fog. Whatever deal you made with this boy twas a fool's pact. We would be better off rotting behind the bars than sailing to our deaths out here." Max raised a hand in the air for silence at this, staring down at the wooden deck beneath his feet with his single eye.

"Edge, I am a man of my word but how can I proceed with such a plan of lunacy when you will not even tell me your true aim out here? My trust has been shaken ever since..." he trailed off, looking toward the blond haired girl across from him.

"Our business is our own, which is all you need to know to get us to where we need to go," Kaylan suddenly spoke up from beside Edge. The Maven raised an eyebrow and shot her an impatient glance but nodded in confirmation.

"So I suggest you unfurl those sails and get us moving again, Max," Edge informed him brusquely. "Our patience is far from endless." Max held his gaze for a lingering moment with a nervous look about him before his first mate leaned in to whisper in his ear. The Maven exhaled sharply and turned to Kaylan with a flash of warning in his eyes. Though unsure what was going to happen she could tell the boy was expecting trouble. "And if anything is going to be said here it will be for me to hear as well." Max and his first mate stopped and looked at him, both a fretful expression in their eyes. "Because I've been around enough spineless liars to know when I'm being betrayed in silence. Don't even think about it." Panic seemed to filter through the men around Max at this and they stepped forward placing their hands over the hilts of cutlasses and short swords at their sides.

"Give us an order, captain," the first mate pressed, staring at Max with alarm in his eyes. The burly captain moved his single eye to the two youths standing before him on the opposite side of the table and the helm, staring hard. Edge slowly raised his left hand toward Kaylan's thigh to gently push it, signaling her to get behind him. Holding strong, she stared hard into Max's single eye and realized he was deciding whether or not to rid himself of them. As the uncomfortable silence lingered with the tension thick enough to cut with a blade, the sound of a bell atop the primary mast suddenly echoed through the dead air in rapid succession. Shooting his gaze upward Max listened as the lookout in the crows nest screamed down to him in panic.

"Captain! Vortex on the horizon!" his loud voice carried down to them. "Starboard!" Max and the once silent crew on deck immediately came to attention at this, sprinting to the starboard side of the ship with new energy bounding to life inside them. Though easing his tense body as the situation about to explode before him passed, the Maven curiously followed the crew to the railing of the ship to stare out at a disturbance in the otherwise dead ocean surface almost too far away to see. Squinting uncertainly, he let out a shrill whistle for Zephyr, instantly dropping from the mast to plunge onto his shoulder.

"There's something strange out there, partner," he immediately reported. "Looks to be some kind of giant whirlpool but it isn't behaving like one." His confusion only compounding, Edge shouted above the cries of the crew to Max, trembling as he stared into the horizon.

"Max, what is it?" the boy yelled, moving beside him. "What's out there?" The captain remained motionless for another agonizingly long moment before at last whispering something to himself.

"It can't be," he trailed off in disbelief. "The odds are impossible."

"What is it!?!" Edge blasted, noticing the vortex appear to grow larger. The captain wheeled around at the Maven as he grit his teeth in fury to contain his obvious anger.

"...Vorkoise," he breathed.

Chapter 29

<u>Unfriendly Seas</u>

Edge quickly took hold of the flat bladed sword on his back he had acquired from the armory in the *Halcyone* and pulled Kaylan behind him as the crewmen around Captain Max hastily drew the cutlasses at their sides and extended them out for the Grandarian girl.

"Captain, the girl and her magic have marked the *Halcyone*!" the infuriated first mate shouted as the rest of the crew along the deck continued to shout out and point with increasing panic toward the massive whirlpool approaching them in the distance. "We must throw her to the sea so we might be spared!" Edge tightened his face with resolve and confusion at the chaos unfolding around them as the crewmen began to close in on them. Though he could tell the first mate was about to act on his own and charge ahead for them Max suddenly threw his clenched fist out to slam into the man's jaw and drop him to the deck. The rest of the crew froze at this and eyed him uncertainly. Max merely dropped his fist and turned back to the tense young Maven standing before him, his single eye radiating urgency.

"No, I gave them my word and it will be honored," he spoke quickly. "The vortex has already spotted us so it will be coming for us whether the girl remains on board or not." Max blasted his voice as loud as it would reach, extending it to the ears of all his crew on deck. "Our only chance is to try and lose the beast in the fog! Set sail and make way before it's on us! Run out the cannons!" With this, the entire crew immediately came to order and began hurriedly taking their positions around the ship to unfurl the massive white sails above them and get the *Halcyone* moving again. As the men around the helm where Edge and Kaylan still stood hopelessly confused at what was happening dispersed onto the lower deck, the vexed Maven slightly lowered his sword and looked back to Kaylan, already staring at him worriedly.

"Max, what is happening?" the darkly clad boy at last managed, moving to stand before the burly captain. Max continued shouting orders to his crew, personally manning the helm of the *Halcyone* but tried his best to respond, keeping his single eye on the rapidly approaching vortex on the horizon.

"Know you nothing of the sea, Maven?" he returned apprehensively. "The vortex signals the beast coming from the deep. It will probably surface in mere moments!"

"What is this beast, Max?" Kaylan shouted from beside Edge, her bewilderment threatening to consume her.

"There are tales of a gigantic sea serpent in the Eastern Sea called Vorkoise that preys on ships passing above it while it waits in the deep," he informed them as he watched the white sheets over the primary mast of the *Halcyone* tighten, the wind pushed them forward. "No ship that's ever encountered it has survived."

"But what does this Vorkoise thing have to do with me?" Kaylan pressed. "That man said it could sense me!"

"The sea is too large a place for Vorkoise to happen to appear before us now by chance, young lady," Max returned hastily. "The myth is that the beast is attracted to magic as it passes over the waves. Magic like yours." Edge worriedly looked to Kaylan hearing this and leaned into her ear.

"Even if that's true I thought you told me only active magic could be sensed," he spoke nervously. "Is the Granic Crystal calling it or something?" Kaylan quickly looked down to a satchel in her tunic where she was keeping the enchanted gem, prying it open to observe it lifeless. She quickly shook her head no. "Then how could this thing sense us? Neither of us are using any power." Though Kaylan was about to agree and guess it had just been chance, a fleeting voice sounded inside her head.

"*Forgetting about someone, aren't you Kay?*" the voice spoke in a mocking tone. Kaylan froze with dread, remembering how greatly Kaotica's power had been increasing lately. It must have been the dark girl that the creature could sense. Pushing her from her thoughts Kaylan tried to focus on Edge and Max as they continued to speak.

"So what do we do?" Edge grilled, noting the size of the vortex to their starboard side churning more violently than before.

"The only thing we can," Max returned. "Vorkoise is supposed to be a monstrous Jagged Pike. The pike are afraid to pass beyond the fog so I'm hoping Vorkoise will feel the same way. We have to make it into the fog before Vorkoise can take us down. I suggest you and the girl brace yourselves. Looks like you're going to get where you want to be after all."

"*Uh oh,*" the voice in Kaylan's head sounded once again. "*Sounds like it's about to get crazy out there. Want me to come out and help?*" Kaylan did her best to try and suppress the voice ringing through her mind, feeling Edge take hold of her forearm as he instructed her to follow him. Coming to her senses once more the Grandarian girl nodded and trailed after her Maven protector as he descended down the staircase to the lower deck and toward the cabin with his blue scarf gently flying up to caress her face. Before they could get far, however, the massive swirling vortex on the horizon suddenly went quiet, its turbulent currents fading. The crew of the *Halcyone* slowly halted what they were doing to stare in bewilderment, wondering if the creature had lost interest. As the seconds ticked by and their worries began to dispel, however, the last remnant of the swirling vortex abruptly exploded to life with a column of water blasting out of its center into the sky. Frozen in shock, Edge and Kaylan watched as a long blue body of scales rose out of the column to careen forward and dive back into the sea charging toward the ship like a torpedo.

Though its body had only been exposed above the water for a few moments the men and girl aboard the terrified ship saw more than they wished they had. Vorkoise was a snakelike monster almost twice as long as the *Halcyone* from bow to stern, covered in dark blue scales with long jagged fins behind its bulky head and thin tail. The serpent's head sported blank fish eyes and bulky gills beside its massive jaws that concealed rows of shark like teeth, easily large enough to tear a ship even as large as the *Halcyone* to shreds. As the serpent continued shooting toward them like an underwater bullet, Edge leapt to the railing of the deck to stare ahead at the wall of fog still far beyond them. Though they had a strong eastern wind to propel them forward the Maven knew as fast as Vorkoise was coming at them they would never reach it. Silently cursing their luck and turning to Kaylan, the boy shook his head.

"We aren't going to make it," he spoke irately, clenching his fists as several crewman running past midship to secure a fouled line. Kaylan wasn't sure how to respond at first, his forthright statement not leaving much room for debate.

"Correction—you aren't going to make it," the voice inside her head sounded. *"But I'll make sure Edge and I do. Ready for me to take over now?"* Not able to take the devilish voice tormenting her every thought any longer Kaylan sealed her eyes shut and tightened her besieged frame.

"No!" she abruptly bellowed into the gusty air, to which Edge stared at her uncertainly, curious at her unusual outburst. Seeing his eyes upon her, Kaylan embarrassingly shook her head and continued pushing Kaotica out.

"I mean no, Edge," she recovered, not wanting him to know Kaotica was toying with her. "I'm not giving up and you can't either. You're the only one here with the power to save this ship." The boy raised an eyebrow at this, his face beset with hesitancy.

"What are you talking about, Kaylan?" he returned impatiently. "Did you see that thing? How could I do anything to stop that?"

"You have to try, Edge," she returned forcefully. "You've been a different person since you accepted your power. Maybe now you can control it." Though sensing the desperate hope in her voice he didn't know how to respond.

"Kaylan, I still don't know the first thing about my power," he returned hopelessly. "And even I did do you really think I could ever hold off something like *that*?" The Grandarian girl took a step forward, her face hard and determined as he had never seen it before.

"All I know is you have a job to protect me, Edge, and I need you right now," she spoke with blunt passion and helpless distress intertwined in her shaking but strong voice. "You've never botched a job before and I don't believe you will when I need you most. Please." Edge doubtfully held her fervent gaze for a long moment, locks of her golden hair blowing into his face from the wind. Though the Maven had no idea what he could do to satisfy her, as he stared into her passionate blue eyes he found a nameless strength within that transcended all the odds of failure to give him new hope. Steeling himself

Trial of a Maven

with fortitude, the boy gave her a single nod and wordlessly pulled away to turn for the railing. He narrowed his eyes as the underwater behemoth continued closing the gap between them with incredible speed. Desperately brainstorming for any semblance of an idea, the Maven knew there was only one option that couldn't be put off any longer. Turning back to the deck of the *Halcyone* he scanned its surface until spying a crate beside him. Uncertainly extending his arm out for it, Edge closed his eyes and focused his discipline and desires together to quiet his mind, willing his wish into being. Though nothing happened at first with Kaylan silently pleading for a miracle as she saw the beast almost upon them, the crate suddenly jolted from the deck to slide to the left and slowly rise with Edge's open hand. Slowly opening his eyes he stared in wonder as he found the crate obeying his mental command to move. Though amazed at what he had just done, the Maven quickly let it fall and nodded to himself to confirm what he knew he had to do. He wheeled around to grab the arm of a passing crewman carrying a cannonball.

"Load the cannons and start firing as fast as you can," he ordered quickly, catching the man off guard.

"Who in the name of Granis are you, kid?" the man returned to which Edge grit his teeth.

"I'm the kid who's going to save your ass, so I suggest you do what the hell I tell you if you want to make it out of this alive!" he shouted heatedly. Though the crewman shrunk back surprised, a blank look of hesitancy still lingered.

"Well what do you want us to shoot at? We could never hit that thing..." he murmured.

"Just do what I tell you and trust me!" Edge returned, kicking his buttocks to get him going and running to all the cannons along the ship's railing with his blue scarf flying up behind him. "That goes for all of you! Just load those guns and start shooting! I don't care if the creature is on the other side of the ship or underwater, just keep shooting! Hurry!" As the baffled crewmen hesitantly did as they were ordered and loaded the cannons along the midship of the *Halcyone*, Kaylan uncertainly kept her gaze on the boy as he leapt up to the railing and took hold of a mast line stretching up to the beam above them. Watching with nervous eyes as Vorkoise drew near, the first of the cannons aimlessly opened fire into the sea. Throwing a gloved hand forward and tightening his grip in the air, he attempted to seize the blasting cannonball the same as he had the crate beside him. Taking hold of something moving away from him so fast proved to be much more difficult. The first few shots sped past Vorkoise with their trajectory untouched, falling randomly into the ocean. Though the crewmen paused seeing their little ammunition wasted, Kaylan kept her faith in the Maven and determinedly shouted for them to keep firing.

As the guns were being reloaded Vorkoise at last arrived at the *Halcyone* and reared its long back above the water before sweeping under the ship to nudge its hull and shake them all. Though temporarily thrown off balance, Edge grit his teeth and sprinted to the opposite side of the ship to find Vorkoise surfacing again. Though he expected it to charge back and tear the ship in two, the serpent began to turn and circle around the bow coming back for the stern. Curiously staring at it Edge realized it was creating another vortex to suck them beneath the waves. Focusing, Edge eased his mind and waited for the sound of cannons exploding to his right to sound through the air. Extending his mystic grip once more, the Maven fixed his mind on the speeding shot and forced it downward into the depths as the serpent passed. Though he missed completely, the crew noticed the bizarre change in the ball's trajectory as well and realized what he was somehow doing. Hastening their efforts on the cannons Edge waited for Vorkoise to pass again as the whirlpool forming around the ship began to take shape. The second he heard a cannon explode he willed the ball he was staring at to fall and pointed downward for the beast's head.

Though passing dangerously close to the serpents' hulking skull the shot missed once more, generating groans of agonizing desperation from the crew. Gritting his teeth with rage as the ship began to veer off course in the unnatural currents, the Maven leapt off the railing to the opposite side of the *Halcyone* to force his telekinetic grip around a shot before he even reached the railing. Again pointing downward into the churning water he set all his concentration on the passing beast and veered the cannonball blasting above it down into its back. A shrill cry of pain tore through the atmosphere as Vorkoise veered away from the *Halcyone* in anguish, the water turning red where the abandoned vortex slowly died. The entire crew shouted wild cheers as the beast descended back below the surface into the crushing depths, disappearing from view. Edge stood behind the railing breathing hard, in disbelief that his farfetched plan had worked. Letting his frame ease, he turned back to Kaylan who had a mesmerized expression on her soft face, equal incredulity in her eyes.

As a faint smile formed from the corner of her lips, however, the sea once again exploded upward as Vorkoise raised its long body vertically out of the water with blood flowing down its scaled neck. Wheeling around in surprise Edge could only watch in amazement as the creature reared its head back to spread its gaping jaws and vomit a beam of blasting water outwards that smashed into the rows of cannons along the midship of the *Halcyone*, tearing the deck up and blowing all the crewmen there off the ship to the opposite side. When the enormous jet of water ended Edge and Kaylan had been knocked off their feet with the rest of the surviving crew and looked to the ship's center to find the deck completely obliterated and the cannons gone. Though the hull was still intact and the mast unharmed, they were now defenseless. Seeing the crewmen it had blasted away from the ship falling in the waves behind the ship, Vorkoise leapt out of the water to careen through the pointed stem of the ship jutting off the bow and knock the remaining crew to their feet.

Captain Max watched in horror as the beast leapt on his crewmen bobbing in the waters and forced them into its open jaws by the mouthful. Commanding a crewman next to him to take the helm he leapt down the stairs of the cabin to what was left of the main deck. Rising and helping Kaylan up beside him, Edge took advantage of Vorkoise's temporary digression and spoke to Max.

"Can it still sail?" he asked hopefully, his purple feathered Sky Sprite partner landing on his shoulder after dropping what men he could save from the serpent with his Lift Power back on deck. Max shook his head as he deeply exhaled.

"She can still move forward but too many lines and beams are fouled," he replied. "With this many crewmen gone we can only move forward, provided it doesn't hit us again. I don't suppose you've any more tricks up those sleeves of yours, Maven?" Edge remained silent at this, glancing at Kaylan. Realizing that was a no, Max nodded and heaved one of his wounded crewmen to his feet. "Then hopefully we can get into the fog before it—" As if hearing the captain's words, Vorkoise suddenly spun around and dove into the water to resume its charge of the ship. Feeling his heart drop, Edge realized it wasn't going to let them get to the fog. The creature slowly raised its head out of the water as it came, its jaws dripping as they spread open once more. Realizing what the creature was going to do Edge looked back to find Kaylan staring at him despairingly, speaking with her eyes. Finding the same strength in her beautiful blue irises as before, the boy steeled himself with what energy was left to muster and raced to the rail of the ship to meet the incoming beast.

Focusing his will as he closed his eyes and brought his arms into a cross before his chest, the Maven readied himself for what he knew was coming. As Vorkoise grew near, its scaled neck shot upward and the blasting beam of liquid came, this time reaching out for the hull of the *Halcyone* to cut through and end the game it had been playing. As the monstrous jet came careening forward, Edge opened his fierce eyes and threw his open palms out as if to accept it. The moment the attack was about to splinter the wooden hull for the last time, it halted as if meeting another unseen wall of energy first with a thunderous clapping of the water colliding with Edge's power sounding through the air. The boy could instantly feel it pushing him back as if it was he the water was sailing into and not the invisible shield of his creation. Fighting with every ounce of his strength to hold the volatile liquid at bay as the vapors of the fog began to formulate around the *Halcyone*, the boy realized he would not have the endurance to hold Vorkoise for long. Scanning around him on the splintered deck the Maven found a single cannonball rolling past his feet that had not been fired. Spreading his fingers with his left hand to hold the water, Edge threw his weight behind it as he reached down with his right to slowly take hold of the cannonball below him.

Closing his eyes and trying to quiet his mind as he had with the crate, he slowly lifted it into the air while holding back the jet of water growing more powerful by the second. Focusing his thoughts around the ball an invisible layer of throbbing force began to materialize around its surface. When the semitransparent energy was almost as large as the ball itself, the Maven opened his mouth to scream out with resolve and throw his right hand toward the water. Obeying its master's command, the ball engulfed in the boiling energy flew from its place in the air before him. Careening into the beam of rushing water faster than anyone could see, the shot penetrated all the way through to the beast in less than a second, slamming through its gaping mouth and the back of its neck with flesh bursting outwards into the waters behind. Gripped in the agonizing pain done unto it by the boy and sensing the fog forming around it, Vorkoise at last cut off its watery attack and abandoned its chase of the *Halcyone*, slowly withdrawing beneath the surface of the water with blood trailing from the two punctures in its neck.

Watching as the defeated serpent fell back beneath the crimson waves around it, Max and the rest of his crew rowdily cheered out for the black clad boy still standing with his frame taut before the railing of the ship. Though shocked beyond all belief, Kaylan at last forced herself to run to her protector when he slowly collapsed on the wet deck in a heap. Sprinting down to lean to his side and hurriedly pick his torso up to rest in her arms, she was relieved to find him merely exhausted and out of breath. A broad smile overtook her face as she leaned down to ferociously hug him.

"Edge, you did it!" she exclaimed happier than she had felt in days. "I told you that you could do it! You saved me! You saved all of us!" Though still struggling for breath in her arms, the Maven let a faint smile overtake his lips and gave her a feeble nod.

"Yeah well, I'm not going to start botching jobs now," he replied, his fatigue from the expenditure of such amazing power for the first time showing through. Kaylan could only laugh, nodding with a beaming smile.

"Whatever you say," she smiled back. "But somewhere in there I think you really care." Edge blinked slowly and tried to raise his hands to rest them over his chest.

"Maybe," was the quiet response from behind his smile. As the two sat on the deck Captain Max and the remaining crew began to mob around them, offering their thanks and to help the Maven up. Though Kaylan appreciated their gratitude after being ready to betray them several minutes before, she insisted they let him be for a moment. Agreeing, Max quickly ordered his crew to the ready, reminding them they were far from out of danger. They had now passed into fog so thick they couldn't see from one end of the ship to the other and no one knew what lay in wait for them on the other side. While Kaylan tried to lift Edge to his feet as the minutes passed, all at once she curiously froze, observing the fog suddenly end and reveal an open expanse of water beyond. Staring past the damaged bow of the *Halcyone* her jaw dropped. She saw an open circle of water stretching for dozens of nautical miles before her but around the circumference was only more fog.

There was nothing inside the fog at all.

Shaking her head in disbelief, she turned down to Edge already raising his head to observe what had caught her attention. Staring uncertainly at what lay before them, or the lack thereof, his blue eyes slowly widened as he spotted something above them. Confused, Kaylan followed his baffled eyes into the sky until she too saw what had captivated him. Lumbering almost a mile over them, still and silent, was a mammoth landmass resting in the sky. Neither of them said anything at first, so distraught with what appeared to be hovering above them they couldn't find the words to speak. As the *Halcyone* continued to slowly trudge forward through the still waters inside the fog, the entire ship fell dead silent. The crew was as amazed as Edge or Kaylan, all staring up at the brown landmass levitating high above.

As they continued holding their gaze on the enormous object in the sky, a faint glimmer of golden light almost too distant to see caught their attention. It flashed for only a brief moment and was gone, but as the seconds ticked by Zephyr suddenly swept down from the tip of the mast he had been standing at to cry out in alarm. By the time Edge figured out what his Sky Sprite partner was screaming it was already too late. Narrowing his eyes, Edge found a golden beam of light firing down through the sky directly toward the ship. As it approached both Edge and Kaylan could tell the beam was over twice the size of the *Halcyone* and would completely engulf them. Before they could move, a sphere of semitransparent energy wrapped around them from Zephyr sweeping down to collect them in his grip and heave them off the deck into the open waters just as the burning beam of light came careening into the ship to blast it to pieces and virtually incinerate it instantaneously.

As the force from the exploding light pounded into the water to throw it into towering waves, the sheer power radiating from the beam ripped through the air to knock Zephyr off balance and blast him away, leaving the two humans in his grasp flying away from the light and plummeting into the sea. Feeling the cold waters sweep across her skin Kaylan

Trial of a Maven

instantly struggled to rise back to the surface to find the boy that had been in her arms a moment before. Taking a deep breath as she rose back above the water Kaylan wiped away a wet lock of her golden hair sticking to her forehead to scan the sea for the dark boy. She found him twenty feet away slowly sinking beneath the waves, obviously unconscious. Determined to get to him the girl drove forward through the chilling waters to where he had disappeared and dove downward to lift him up and heave him back to the surface.

Already strained and losing energy, the frightened Grandarian girl spun around to find Zephyr but his miniature frame had either been blown too far away or already disappeared beneath the waves. Struggling to tread water to keep both herself and the unconscious boy in her arms afloat, she looked back to where the *Halcyone* had been moments before to find nothing but steaming waves lapping back and forth with random segments of drifting slabs of wood floating where the golden beam of light had struck. Aware her strength was already nearly depleted she began swimming for the nearest piece of the hull she could find to drape Edge's motionless body over it and rest on its side herself. As she scanned around the massive expanse of empty water for a sign of anything that could help her, she realized they were alone. Trying to fight back her tears at the hopeless situation in which she found herself, the shivering Grandarian girl nestled herself next to the dark boy at her side more afraid than she had ever felt in her life.

Chapter 30

Unification

"You're a fool, Dax," a Drakkaidian soldier spoke with disbelief as he squinted his eyes into the distance of the plains in the war zone. "It can't be a rider. Who would be brainless enough to be riding toward over ten thousand soldiers marching through the war zone?" The other black armored soldier beside him shrugged but pointed his short sword back onto the empty brown fields of grass before them and the miniature black image far beyond that had caught his attention.

"I'm not saying he's sane but that *is* a horseman out there," he returned aggravated. "He's riding straight at us." As the seconds ticked by and the first Drakkaidian squinted his eyes past the rows of soldiers marching ahead of him, he noticed the black image on the horizon his friend had spotted moments before was in fact drawing closer. Though he couldn't guess what lunacy had possessed him to ride at a Drakkaidian battalion armed to the teeth and over ten thousand strong and building by the day, it had to be a rider. The New Fellowship troops that had been massing in the war zone over the past year on their own recognizance under the vague orders from their leader in the Cathedral of Dalorosk had recently been taken control of by General Nedross, a former captain in the army amassed by Valif Montrox himself. Ever since they had been steadily inching closer to the Border Mountains and the Grandarian Wall of Light by the day. Though they all knew war was coming many were confused at why the High Priest Zalnaught would not order a direct attack. They had done little in the war zone to prepare for war beside mobilize their forces. An attack on the Wall of Light would require siege towers, battering rams, and iron line guns to get them over the top—all of which they currently had none. Only the Loyalists had control of such weapons back in the Valley of Blood. Though confused and doubtful of their orders under Nedross, the general assured them the High Priest had something special in mind for the Grandarians that would ensure their defeat.

Behind the lanced rows of soldiers at the head of the army, General Nedross turned to face another horseman parting the ranks as he approached the main army with an urgent look on his face. Nedross coughed from deep in his throat and shifted his armor clad body over the decorated horse he sat upon, his cruel expression tightening as the messenger approached.

"General, several of the infantrymen have spotted a lone horsemen riding straight for us from the fields," he reported quickly.

"Affiliation?" the hard general returned.

"He's still too far off to tell but it can't be one of ours sir. All the scouts are in right now."

"Then assume it is an enemy scout and rid him from the land before he can return to the Wall of Light or the Southland," Nedross commanded, following by instructing the long bow archers to pick him off as soon as he was in range. Bowing his head in acknowledgement the messenger kicked his steed forward to relay the order back to the infantry commander ahead of them. A row of archers stepped forward from the ranks immediately, drawing arrows to their long bows and taking aim for the lone figure now close enough to clearly make out he was no Grandarian. Hesitant but obeying their orders, the archers tightened their arrows and let them fly, arching upward into the cloudy sky. As the missiles began to descend on the figure, the entire regiment of soldiers slowed to a halt seeing the figure raise an arm to send a flashing wave of electrified crimson energy from his forearm to catch the incoming arrows and incinerate them before they could get near him. Observing the unexpected display as well, General Nedross' eyes widened and he raised a hand to signal the main army to halt. Scanning the rider still charging toward them, Nedross realized he was dressed in Drakkaidian garb with a tattered gray cape flailing behind him as he came. It was not until the rider slowed to a trot and began passing through the ranks of infantrymen ahead of him that the general noted his fervent red hair and inhaled nervously, realizing who was now riding for him with focused eyes fixed on his.

Tales of Iairia

With the entire battalion now at a quiet standstill with only the gentle wisps of wind over the fields and the uncertain murmur from the lips of the men audible around them, the worn figure of the Prince of Drakkaidia parted through the final row of soldiers ahead of Nedross and stopped before him, his battle hardened face fiercely resolute. Both men could hear the slow drawing of swords from scabbards and the spiteful remarks toward the Loyalist leader circulating around them, yet both remained motionless. Though Nedross was doubtful of what the prince was doing there or what his intentions were he slowly tipped his head in greeting.

"Verix Montrox," he announced in his gruff voice, "what business brings you to the war zone?" Verix remained quiet for a long moment, staring the general down hard.

"When last I looked I was still the crown Prince of Drakkaidia, and you will address me as such, Nedross," he eventually snapped back in a low but dangerous tone. "I'll make this simple. You will relinquish command of this battalion to me now. As of today, I lead." The entire mob of soldiers attentively listening fell dead silent at this, amazement mirrored in each other's eyes. Nedross merely held his contemptuous gaze upon the other, unmoving.

"I think you forget that this battalion belongs to the New Fellowship of Drakkan, Prince Montrox," he returned mockingly. "These men are no longer loyal to the throne in its current state of decadence. It is no longer your place to lead." Montrox held his crimson eyes on the challenging general before him for several long moments as the silence hung between them, eventually taking a slow look at the bitter faces of the soldiers around him.

"Is this what you all believe, then?" he asked raising his voice so he could be heard far ahead and behind him. There was no direct response but for the continued murmurs and glares of hatred showing his way. "You all see the throne as 'decadent?' The throne that gathered you and trained you in the first place years ago under the rule of my father? I wonder—if my father were here sitting before you today instead of me—if any of you would dare to challenge him the way you challenge me now."

"You are not your father, prince!" was an anonymous cry from the ranks of soldiers ahead of him, to which mummers of agreement swept through the battalion. Verix

Trial of a Maven

nodded in confirmation, gradually turning his black armored steed as he spoke.

"He speaks the truth—I am not my father," the prince returned coolly, though his face tightened with wrath as he continued. "And for that you should thank Drakkan. For if Valif Montrox were here today instead of I your general would already be decapitated and half your number blasted to the abyss for having voiced the slightest hint of disagreement with his tyrannical rule. Many of you were forced into this army by my father's iron fist as children; you saw the carnage and horror with which he ruled. Was that the throne you consider strong?" Verix quickly turned to the ranks of infantrymen behind him casting off his words. "The reason the throne has fallen to decadence is because of Valif Montrox. It was he, not some Grandarian curse, that released the demons upon us to destroy our capital city and maim our families, and your lying High Priest sheltered in his cathedral to the north knows this as well as I. He is a man consumed by his lust for power, the same as my father was. His manipulative tongue has fooled you into believing Grandaria is the cause of all our problems when it is truly men like him and my father that weaken us. He has fragmented our nation and pushed it to the brink of civil war, but today I am here to unify it once more."

"Zalnaught is the High Priest!" came another voice from the mob. "Why should we believe you over him?" Verix continued turning toward the questioning man with steeled confidence.

"Why do you think I was absent from Drakkaidian during the Days of Destiny when the High Priest robbed me of my authority as king?" he asked them swiftly. "I was there at the Final Battle of Destiny along with Grandarians and Southlanders fighting to save our lands from the demon horde. And while I fought and bled defending him, Zalnaught hid in his Cathedral of Dalorosk turning truth into lies to fool you into granting him power. I have seen Zalnaught behind his closed doors and know the man he is. His only aim is to achieve greater power and he will do anything to accomplish this. Whether that be toying with the Netherworld Portal where the demons lie as he has been asking from me for years, or marching you all to die with no hope of victory. Why do you think you march on the Wall of Light without my siege towers or our war machines to bring it down? You are

Tales of Iairia

here to spark conflict so that he can use you as an excuse to make broader war on Grandaria." There was a long pause as the murmurs in the crowd continued, obvious doubt passing through their minds.

"What would you have us do, prince?" was the next question. "The Grandarians rally for war on their own!" Verix was slow to respond to this but at last nodded his head and turned his crimson eyes in the direction from which the comment came.

"I did not believe it until recently but this is true," Verix confirmed softly. "The stories Zalnaught has convinced you of may be false but it is true that behind their Wall of Light the Grandarians provoke us for battle." His voice escalated with uncharacteristic passion and fervor as he drew on. "And if it is war they crave, it is war they shall have, but if we are to defeat them and the power they possess we must be united! Drakkaidia has always been strong because we have fought together! From the Ogren Sieges in the world of old to the invasion of the barbarian cults in the north, we have emerged victorious and survived because we fought as one! If we are to match Grandaria we must be so again. So as your prince I ask you to follow me now. I extend to you my hand in brotherhood to fight alongside you, not my fist to beat you down in oppressive rule as my father did and Zalnaught would seek to do. See the truth of what Zalnaught is doing to you—he uses you as sheep, and without my power to aid you this battalion will be slaughtered as would any livestock. Today you must cast aside the pointless bickering and unfounded hatred for your fellow Drakkaidians and join with them to reclaim the power of our unity once more. War is upon us. There are no Loyalists and there is no New Fellowship—only Drakkaidia. Will you stand for Drakkaidia or not?"

There was great pause on faces of the ranks of soldiers around him at this question, with many looking to each other uncertainly. At last an angry voice from behind Verix broke the silence accompanied by the drawing of a sword. Spinning his head around the prince found General Nedross charging for him with his sword raised above his head ready to attack. Though Verix could have summoned his broadsword and parried his armored assailant away at the last moment, another sword suddenly swept upward as the general's came down to deflect the blade. As Verix's horse reared back in alarm the prince looked down to find a single infantryman

Trial of a Maven

standing beside him with his blade clasped tightly in his hands. Nedross furiously wheeled around and extended the tip of his sword for the solider that had deflected his blow.

"You dare to betray the New Fellowship for this lying Loyalist, you treasonous dog?" he boomed with spit flying from his lips. The soldier remained firm but obviously frightened as he could not summon the words to speak. Before the general could shout down to him again another soldier drew his blade and stepped in front of Verix's steed.

"It is you who betray Drakkaidia in trying to assassinate the prince, general," he answered. Nedross' irate face shone red at this as he kicked his horse forward.

"Then you will both die! Kill these traitors!" he blasted, raising his sword upward to slash down once more. Before he could bring his blade down to meet with the soldiers an arrow came flying past Verix to slam into the general's chest at a weak point in the armor, instantly dropping him from his steed to the earth. Verix wheeled around to find an archer holding his empty bow before him, breathing hard at what he had just done. Waiting for the man to meet his gaze, Verix silently nodded his thanks and turned to the rest of the men staring at the general coughing up blood on the grassy field.

"Such is the fate of those who clash against Drakkaidia," Verix shouted to the entire battalion, "and so shall be the fate of the Grandarians if they desire war as well. Will you stand as one?" Verix's question was immediately answered with the ardent shouts of all the men around him, slowly spreading into cheers for Drakkaidia all the way to the rear of the massive battalion. Standing amid his new Drakkaidian troops Verix Montrox remained hard. Motioning to the first soldier who had saved him, he promoted him to a captain on the spot and instructed him to spread the word to the rest of the thousands with them of the change in power and to prepare to march at once. They were going to the Wall of Light.

Chapter 31

A World Apart

The gentle bumping of the hard surface he lay on coupled with the soft grip of someone's hands on his shoulder was what prompted the Blue Maven Edge to wake from his deep slumber, his head throbbing with a headache as he slowly tried to lift it off the uncomfortable wooden surface it rested on. He opened his eyes at a snail's pace, the bright rays of light seeping into the small area he lay in blurring his vision into a wall of slurred watercolors. Focusing his senses as the moments ticked by, the Maven at last realized another figure lay before him gently nudging him awake. Widening his gaze on her, he found Kaylan staring at him with her bright blue eyes distraught. Sweeping his confused eyes up and down her dirtied and obviously exhausted but ever stunning form sitting in front of him, a thousand questions sprung from his mind ranging from how they had escaped the Eastern Sea to where they were now. He forced his eyes tightly shut and shook his head, trying to center his thoughts to speak. Kaylan beat him to the punch, placing her hands on his shoulder.

"Edge, just take it easy," she bid him in a whisper. "You've been out for hours." The boy opened his eyes once more at this, feeling as though he had been unconscious for days. As his eyes fell upon her soft hands on his black vest they immediately shot open in alarm, noticing they were bound in thick iron shackles. The Maven shot up and attempted to summon his hands from his sides only to find them bound beneath him as well.

"What's going on?" he grilled her worriedly. "Where are we, Kaylan?" The Grandarian girl hurriedly brought a finger to place before her mouth to signal the supreme need for quiet.

Trial of a Maven

"Calm down or they'll hear you," she whispered back, frenzied. Edge's eyes narrowed at this, slowly turning over to raise himself up and sit on his backside beside her.

"What are you talking about?" he pressed quickly, matching her quiet tone. "Where are we?" The girl held his gaze motionlessly for a long moment, struggling for the words to respond. At last she swept her eyes to the end of the wagon they sat in toward a cloth entrance at the front.

"I don't know, Edge," was the only answer he got as she turned back to face him, fear in her unusually vulnerable eyes. "Do you remember anything after you drove off the Vorkoise beast in the ocean?" The Maven paused, thinking back to his battle with the serpent creature before entering the fog. Though it was faint, he remembered a flash of light descending on the *Halcyone* before blacking out.

"A light," he recalled out loud, searching Kaylan's eyes for more. "What happened to the *Halcyone*, Kaylan? Where are we?" The girl slowly blinked her eyes as she temporarily broke eye contact from him to collect her thoughts.

"It's gone, Edge," she informed him quietly. "We barely made it off with our lives. After you wounded Vorkoise and we passed through the fog we came upon a wide open circle of clear water in the middle of the fog. Do you remember the enormous object in the sky where the light came from?" Edge slowly nodded yes, recalling what appeared to be a floating landmass above the sea. "Well I know this is going to sound crazy but... we're on it. That light that you remember was a beam of energy that blasted the *Halcyone* to shreds. We're the only ones that made it off in time thanks to Zephyr and his Lift Power that threw us off the ship before it was destroyed. He dropped us in the sea after the shockwave hit him and knocked him unconscious the same as you. I pulled you to some driftwood and tried to wake you up but you wouldn't. But just when I thought it was all over and we were going to die alone in the middle of the ocean they came." Edge raised an eyebrow curiously, clueless as to what she was talking about. "These men riding enormous white birds dropped out of the sky and picked us up from the ocean. We flew all the way out of the fog above the clouds to this, well, floating island."

"What?" Edge cut in incredulously. "You're telling me we were rescued by men riding birds on a floating island in the middle of the ocean?" Kaylan kept her gaze upon him, burning into his.

"I don't think 'rescued' is the right word, Edge," she corrected with a hint of dread in her trembling voice. "Once we got to the edge of the island they brought us to a caravan of wagons and bound our hands. They threw us in the back of one of them and we've been traveling inside ever since. It's been almost two hours since we were put in here." Edge kept his eyes fixed upon hers, obvious skepticism mirrored within.

"I don't believe this," he stated more to himself than her. Observing his doubt Kaylan motioned with her head for him to look behind him.

"Take a peek out that tear in the fabric and see for yourself." Edge turned around to observe a slit in the white fabric covering the top half of the wagon they sat in, slowly leaning toward it to peer out with one eye going wide. The Maven felt his jaw dropping as the expansive scene before him came into view. A green milieu of fields and trees lay to the road behind them, with one of the most amazing architectural feats he had ever seen sprawling out ahead. As the road widened the flabbergasted boy found a city of golden metal and stone rising from the tiled streets beyond, jutting high into the blue sky with white and gold banners flying from masts everywhere he looked. The more of the distinct environment he took in, the stronger the previously vague waves of remembrance of the images he had seen in the Sage's Draught swirling through his mind became. A haunting sensation of déjà vu creeping over him, the Maven quickly withdrew his head and placed his dumbfounded gaze back on the dirtied girl beside him. "What is this?"

"I told you I don't know," she returned uncertainly, "but I think we're going to find out soon. We've been coming into this city for a while now and I can hear the activity outside getting louder the farther in we get. Something doesn't make sense, though. I have no idea what this place is but the more I look at it the more it reminds me of home. Those flags outside are almost exact copies of the crest of light." Edge's brow furrowed at this, peering out at the extravagant cityscape once more to notice for himself the beautifully curving insignias adorning signs and flags around them which looked to be identical to any Grandarian emblem he had ever seen. As he brought his gaze back to Kaylan the wagon abruptly jolted and began to slow, the sound of several men jogging along the stone path outside the wagon echoing inside. Kaylan fretfully leaned into the boy beside her and set her anxious eyes on his. "I'm scared, Edge. What are we going to do?" The Maven slowly exhaled and tried to pull his tight metal bounds apart to no avail before staring back at her with what sincerity he could muster.

"It's going to be alright, Kaylan," he told her trying his best to reassure her. "Whatever happens try to stay with me but look to yourself first. Until I know who and what we're dealing with let's try to stay out of any more trouble than we're already in." The girl nodded quickly, her tangled blond hair falling over her shoulders. Leaning forward to protectively block Kaylan from the back of the wagon, Edge listened to the various men outside the rear gathering and halting. Waiting for them to make the first move, the sheets covering the back suddenly flew open letting rays of bright sunlight flood in. Edge and Kaylan squinted as they stared ahead past the opening to find several armed men standing before them covered in ornate golden armor. No one made a move for a tense moment but a single man at last parted the ranks of soldiers to stand before the wagon and stare in at the two youths huddled together. Edge narrowed his eyes distrustfully as the man extended a hand out for them, motioning for them to come out. He had a thick brown beard over his muscular visage and illustrious attire covering the rest of his large form. He wore a golden chest plate similar to the soldiers around him but the illustrious plates on his shoulders told Edge he was obviously a man of higher rank.

"Come out now, you two," the man instructed them plainly, his deep voice impassive. "You have nothing to fear. Come out." Deciding cooperation was their best and only option, the Maven turned to Kaylan and gave her a single nod. The pair slowly rose and crouched as they made their way to the exit of the wagon and dropped out onto the tiled stone street beneath them, soldiers taking hold of their bonds and linking them together with a light rope. As they exited the wagon and took a sweeping look around them Edge and Kaylan spied several more units of soldiers and passing civilians dressed in upscale city garb silently staring at them with hushed whispers carrying over the crowd. The large man that beckoned them to come out quickly took hold of the rope connecting the two prisoners and gave it a slight tug, instructing them to follow him. Though still willing to comply for the time being, Edge cleared his throat and opened his mouth to speak.

"Do you mind telling us who you are?" he asked civilly.

"Just follow me for now, boy," the large man answered, turning to walk toward a large structure ahead of the wagon with the Maven and Grandarian in tow. As they pressed forward, Edge noted the four guards that marched alongside him and Kaylan on either side. While he began to study the idiosyncrasies of their captors to glean any information that might be useful in the future, Kaylan stared up at the towering architecture around them, her mind reeling at how familiar the setting felt. They stood in the center of a massive courtyard contained by six tall walls, all flying golden flags on every side. Behind them was the bulk of the city they had passed through, incredible structures with architecture years ahead of the capitals of either Grandaria or the Southland strewn throughout. The immense structure before her was what drew Kaylan's complete attention, however, bearing an implausible resemblance to the Golden Castle in Galantia. Soaring spires of golden metal shining in the sunlight shown far into the sky with a massive circular emblem engraved into the face of their midsections almost identical to the crest of light. Several pairs of the large white birds adorned with wide saddles on their backs like those that had plucked her and Edge from the sea hours ago swept between the towers above them, their expansive wings casting large shadows on the lively courtyard below. Kaylan shook her head in disbelief at the scenery around her as they passed through two enormous double doors and into a golden carpeted hallway boasting crystalline furnishings of suits of armor and statues of robed scholarly figures within.

As Edge and Kaylan continued pressing through the halls and staircases of the castle for several long minutes with the armored guard surrounding and holding them at sword point, the Maven quietly leaned in toward Kaylan and spoke, keeping his gaze ahead as they walked.

"Where is Zephyr?" he asked almost inaudibly. Kaylan remained silent for a long moment and swallowed hard.

"Edge, I never found him after he saved us," she managed, emotion choking her voice. "I don't know where he is." Edge felt his heart sink at this, softly gasping and

Trial of a Maven

blinking rapidly to keep a thin layer of salty water from welling in his eyes. The Maven forced himself to shake off his feelings, aware his clever partner had worked his way out of worse situations before. As they continued up a wide staircase with statues of the large birds he had seen soaring around the castle on either side of the railing, he couldn't pry the thought from his head that his partner could be gone.

At the end of the staircase lifting through several levels of the castle, they at last penetrated all the way to a final open doorway leading into the most extravagant chamber yet. The composition of the room was a mix of rich white stone and shimmering golden crystal, boasting carved columns of a strange mineral rising on either side of the carpeted pathway they walked down and a ceiling harboring golden glass windows above depicting scenes from the past. Before them at the end of the arching and symmetrical chamber was a platform where seven men sat waiting in towering chairs all angling to one in the center, a brilliant stained glass window of gold and blue illuminating the room behind them. The men were dressed in curving white robes with circular gold cloth around their necks and shoulders embroidered with fluid sweeping designs similar to those found in the castle's regal décor. They were adorned with golden crown-like halos set gently over their heads shining in the light from the illumined window behind them.

All seven kept their solemn gazes fixed on the pair of bound adolescents as they continued walking forward to the base of the lofted platform where they sat, observing the large man before them bow as he neared. Seeing the guards surrounding them halt, Edge and Kaylan did as well, nervously inspecting the regal figures on the platform. The one in the center of the seven raised a hand from the arm of his chair and swept it to his right, motioning for the large man ahead of them to move to the side. He did so at once, rising and striding to his left to reveal the two captives to the robed figures. Edge and Kaylan stumbled forward as the soldiers behind them shoved the butts of their lances into their backs, anxiously waiting for them to say something. After an uneasy silence in the majestic chamber the man in the center of the seven at last leaned forward to narrow his intense eyes at the prisoners. Though all the men were aged with white hair and beards, the one staring at them seemed the youngest and most focused.

"*These* are the instigators, Bellinus?" he questioned doubtfully with a thick accent foreign to both Edge and Kaylan. "They seem rather young to have created such a stir." The bulky man to their left gave a single nod before placing his hands behind his back and puffing his armored chest to respond.

"They were all that survived the holy beam, Dignified Hierarch," he reported back in a reverent tone. "The rest aboard their vessel were destroyed." The man in the center nodded slowly and leaned back into his seat once more. Edge could feel Kaylan nervously inching toward him, her weary form slightly trembling.

"Do you have names, young ones?" the man asked them tilting his head with curiosity. Though Edge was unsure how to respond at first, he eventually decided to continue cooperating and quietly cleared his throat to speak.

"We do, but first I wish to know why we are bound and in the custody of those we do not know and have not wronged," he stated coolly with respect. The moment he finished his question the large man who had led him there seized the hilt of a large dagger at his waist and reached out to slam it against Edge's neck, dropping him to his knees in pain. Kaylan dropped after him and defensively put her arms around his neck, her taut body gripped by fear with the big man hovering over them.

"That will do, Bellinus," the man at the center of the robed figures softly spoke, motioning with his hand for him to move back to the side of the prisoners. Hearing him withdraw and sheath his dagger, Kaylan slowly lifted her head from Edge's back and eased her grip around him. The Maven raised a gloved hand to massage his throbbing neck and stood once more, his frown growing. "I apologize for our captain, young ones. Osric Bellinus is the head of our elite palace guard. He and his Fethiotts are the ones who rescued you from the sea. But you must remember that you are the instigators here and unless you cooperate, things will become difficult. Now, your names please." Turning to Edge once more, Kaylan could see the anger building in his face and decided it would be up to her to make sure they made it out of this alive.

"My name is Kaylan and this is my protector, Edge," she answered suddenly, catching the entire room off guard. The man in the center of the seven shifted his curious gaze

Trial of a Maven

to the girl stepping in front of Edge, her eyes uncertain but strong.

"And what was your purpose in coming here, Kaylan?" he asked. The girl turned back to Edge at this, unsure how she should reply. Though wanting to cooperate to assure their continued safety she couldn't tell them the truth.

"Or are you merely here to instigate?" came another voice from further down the line of the chairs. The white robed figures all placed their eyes to the older man at the far right, tightening his fist on the arm of this chair. "They cannot even answer a simple question, brothers. The dark one is trouble—we can all sense it. He must have been the one with the magic. It is the will of Gavanos we dispose of them immediately. The risk is too great."

"I agree," another of the figures spoke from the left of the center. "Whatever power it was that this instigator revealed can be of no use to us anyway. They are no reclaimers. To harbor them otherwise is foolish. Gavanos wills it." The figure in the center of the seven exhaled slowly and nodded, turning back to the large man called Bellinus below them.

"Then so is the will of the Hierarchs," he decreed. "Take them back to the edge of the island and discard of them, Bellinus. They are merely instigators after all." Instantly the soldiers around them came to attention and pushed Edge and Kaylan together, preparing to pull them back out of the illustrious chamber. As Osric Bellinus pushed them forward once more Edge angrily turned to Kaylan.

"Who are these people?" he whispered stumbling forward.

"Granis only knows," the girl replied under her breath. Not a moment after Kaylan uttered her last words the robed figure in the center of the other suddenly bolted out of his seat, energy racing through his every movement.

"*Wait!*" he bellowed, to which the rest of the seven men stood as well. Edge and Kaylan jumped in surprise as Bellinus and his guard wheeled them around to face the seven men turning to each other wildly. "Did you hear what the girl said?"

"The ancient name," the older man from the right spoke once more, mystified. "She could be a reclaimer yet!" The center figure spun around and shouted at the top of his lungs.

"Bring her back here at once!" he boomed. Kaylan fretfully swept her terrified eyes to Edge, struggling to kick his way free as Bellinus took her back to stand before the central man taking a small step toward her. "How do you know of the ancient name, young girl?" The frightened Grandarian uncertainly held his intense gaze for a long moment, her mind wheeling with what he could have been talking about.

"I don't understand," she mused fearfully. "You mean Granis?" The seven men spun to each other with mixed smiles of ecstasy and incredulity.

"She knows of the ancient name," another of the men spoke to the leader in the center. "Bellinus, get those shackles off of her!" The large man quickly leaned down to Kaylan to unlock her iron bonds with a key at the side of his thick belt. "We are sorry to have doubted you, young one. Please except our apologies." Though ecstatic to be free of the painful iron, she instantly wheeled around to Edge still locked up behind her then back to the white robed men before her.

"I will if you release my companion as well," she promised quickly. The man in the center eyed the dark boy before raising an eyebrow and staring back at Kaylan.

"Are you in union with this protector of yours?" he asked doubtfully. Though Kaylan wasn't sure what he meant she decided it could only ensure his safety and replied yes, to which the man in the center of the platform nodded to the guards at the rear of the chamber who quickly released the Maven in response. With his shackles removed the boy quickly strode back up to Kaylan to stand beside her with a distrustful expression on his face. The white figures slowly took their seats once more as they whispered to each other, shooting glances back to the girl before them as they did. At last the man in the center spoke again.

"I am sorry to have held you captive this long but we thought you were mere instigators," he informed her. Kaylan's brow furrowed at this, desperate to know what they were talking about.

"Sir, I'm not sure what an instigator is here but could I ask who you are?" she asked. "We don't even know where we are."

"Of course, I apologize again," he said bowing his head. "We are the Hierarchs of Godsmark Isle. I am First Hierarch Centrioc, the head of our number. It is our esteemed honor to have you here."

"Godsmark?" Kaylan repeated bewildered. "I'm afraid I've never heard of Godsmark before." The First Hierarch Centrioc smiled at this.

"Do not fret, young Kaylan, no one else from your world has either," he informed her to which both Kaylan and Edge stared at him in supreme confusion. Noting their bewilderment the First Hierarch continued. "Perhaps now is the time to shed some light on your uncertainties. But first, I must ask Kaylan how she knows the ancient name of Lord Gavanos." Kaylan paused for a moment, wondering why the Hierarchs were so intent on her knowledge of Granis.

"If you mean Lord Granis, he is the God of Light that watches over the land of Grandaria where I'm from," she spoke tentatively. The Hierarchs lit up once more at this, turning to each other with excitement mirrored in their eyes. "I don't understand—why does the name of Granis mean so much to you?"

"You are actually from the homeland," Centrioc spoke with rapture pouring from his voice. "Your people still call the God of Light by the ancient name but since the founding of Godsmark Isle we have referred to him by the second name of our oldest writings and the sacred vernacular in which it was composed—Gavanos. The fact that you have made it all the way from his homeland reveals to us you are no instigator." Kaylan exhaled sharply and raised her hands defensively.

"I'm sorry but all this talk of instigators and reclaimers is confusing me," she interrupted. "What does any of this have to do with us?" Centrioc shifted his weight in his chair before he continued.

"I suppose I should start from the beginning then, young ones, as the story of Godsmark is a long one," he stated gathering his thoughts. "Being from the homeland you both know its origins and subsequent history that has taken place and formed the rest of the world. Grandaria is the motherland from which all other nations have sprung over the millennia. The dark land of Drakkaidia to the west was formed by disgruntled Grandarians, as was the massive country of the Southland. But before either of these two factions of Grandarians decided to break away from the homeland the first separation took place at the dawn of the golden nation in ancient times before its record of history began. You see, when the people of Lord Gavanos first appeared to establish their dominion over the land that would become Grandaria,

Tales of Iairia

they were endowed with a great magic left behind by the God of Light after the legendary Battle of the Gods. It was the elemental power of light that they could manipulate to make their lives easier in the form of miracle gems.

"There were two great cites that stood from the land in the ancient times: Galantia and Godsmark. The smaller municipality of Galantia housed the Elemental Temple of Light, while Godsmark harbored the ruling council of the Hierarchs and the Shrine of Gavanos that contained the miracle gems that supplied us with the remnant power of the God of Light. As the years went on however, many of the Galantians began to resist the use of the magic Lord Gavanos left behind in Godsmark, claiming it was not meant for us to possess such power for the trivialities of daily life and that the true Source of Light was inside their temple at the heart of Galantia.

"Galantia's view began to spread over the rest of the land and the population came close to civil war over the issue, but Lord Gavanos granted one leader amongst the Hierarchs of Godsmark the great wisdom to see conflict coming. He decided to act to protect the miracle gems. Drawing on one of the gems at its full power, the Hierarchs used its energy to lift the city and the surrounding countryside out of the earth itself and into the sky. If the rest of Grandaria did not wish for the power of the miracle gems they would not have it. So to this day Godsmark has remained isolated from the rest of the world, floating hidden in the skies. That is where you now stand, young ones—the isle of Godsmark." Kaylan stared at the Hierarch for a long moment, her mouth slipping open in astonishment.

"So you've been floating over the Eastern Sea for all this time?" she asked aghast. "How have you survived for so long?"

"I already told you, Kaylan," Centrioc replied. "Look up through the window behind you." Both Kaylan and Edge spun around in wonder at this, looking up to find an open window revealing a bright glow shining high in the sky with brilliant arches of light spreading down on either side like a golden rainbow. Seeing the pair before him staring in wonder, Centrioc continued. "That is the miracle gem that the Hierarchs of old activated in the skies above Godsmark to lift it from the earth. Its power and the will of Gavanos have kept us above the world ever since. Utilizing our minimal sway over the power of the gem we Hierarchs were able to construct a new contemporary city as well as blanket the island in mist so no passing vessels can spot us from below. And in the event one does, we simply weaponize the gem's power into a beam like the one that almost ensnared you." Staring up at the shimmering light in the skies for another curious moment, a thought passed through Kaylan's mind and she slowly turned back to the Hierarchs while reaching into a small brown satchel at her side.

"Hierarch Centrioc, does your miracle gem in the sky look anything like this?" she asked with distant hope in her voice, pulling her hand out of the satchel to reveal the dim Granic Crystal within her open palm. The white robed figures before her all slowly leaned in, their eyes wide as they fell upon the golden object in her hands. Though Edge let out a worried breath as she revealed their precious talisman of magic to them, Centrioc slowly raised a hand for silence as he slowly opened his mouth to speak.

"Is that gem active?" he asked almost inaudibly. Kaylan shook her head and lowered the crystal to her side.

"I'm afraid it's almost dead," she informed them. "That's why we've come here, Hierarchs. I don't know if you are aware of this but in recent years the prophesy that Gavanos left behind was fulfilled and the evil of the God of Darkness, Drakkan, was defeated by the Warrior of Light." "Yes, Lord Gavanos revealed to us this epic struggle," Centrioc confirmed.

"Well I'm afraid the struggle isn't over," Kaylan continued. "Drakkan was sealed inside a void-world apart from this one by the power of the Sword of Granis, or Gavanos if you prefer, where he has been ever since. But dark magic from Drakkaidia has sabotaged it and this miracle gem that gave the sword its power. My protector and I have been charged to find a new Granic Crystal to restore the power of the Sword of Granis and prevent Drakkan from emerging into the world again."

"And your quest to find a new miracle gem has led you to us," Centrioc finished for her, drumming his fingers against each other before him. "We Hierarchs send scouts out on Fethiotts to the mainland to report on the affairs of the old world but we were not aware of this. The threat of the God of Darkness is a mighty one indeed. But why have you, a young girl, come and not the guardian who bares responsibility for the Sword of Gavanos? Do you possess the power to wield a miracle gem?"

"The guardian you sensed is my father, Tavin Tieloc," she returned stoutly. "He is busy with other matters so I have come in his stead." Centrioc slowly turned to look down the faces of the other six Hierarchs around him, already staring at him with wide eyes.

"She *is* a reclaimer," the Hierarch to his immediate left spoke in a whisper just loud enough to pass to Edge's ears. In the disturbing silence the Maven narrowed his eyes and swept them along the row of white robed men feeling like something was going on he and Kaylan were not aware of. At last Centrioc smiled once more and turned to face her, followed by the rest of the Hierarchs.

"Then for the sake of the homeland and the entire world we must aid you in finding a new miracle gem," he announced with poise, to which Kaylan finally allowed herself to smile. "It is not an easy task to acquire one but if you are indeed a descendant of a chosen line, it is possible. But for now you will require rest. You have traveled far and overcome much in getting here and we were less than hospitable at first. Please take the night to sleep and recuperate. Trust me when I tell you that you will need your full strength for the path that lies before you if you are to succeed in your quest. You will be our guests in the palace tonight. Osric, please take care of them and make sure they are comfortable." Osric Bellinus was still for a moment but quickly bowed and turned to motion for Kaylan and Edge to follow him out of the beautiful chamber. Before turning Kaylan quickly bowed in respect.

"Thank you so much for helping us," she told them gratefully.

"It is the least we can do, young Kaylan," Centrioc smiled graciously. "We will meet tomorrow to discuss what lies ahead. Until then may Lord Gavanos bless you." Bowing once more Kaylan turned to follow after Osric Bellinus who was waiting for them at the open doors to the chamber. As she passed Edge she turned with a slight frown to observe him merely standing like stone with a deep routed frown on his dirtied face, staring at the white robed figure of Centrioc. She reached out to gently pull his shirt sleeve after her but before she could, he turned and quickly began striding away, shooting her an uneasy glance. Though unsure what had him rattled Kaylan swiftly strode beside him out of the majestic chamber of the Hierarchs, leaving the white robed seven behind to watch them depart.

Chapter 32

Purging

After departing from the regal chamber of the Hierarchs in the towering palace at the heart of Godsmark, Edge and Kaylan's guide Osric Bellinus led the outsiders to an infirmary in the lower levels. He had noticed the wound in Edge's arm that he had sustained days ago in Acquanautta Port, agitated and bleeding once more after their rough treatment on the way to the palace. Though the Maven insisted he would be fine and he could take care of himself, Kaylan implored him to at least let the healers of Godsmark take a look at him. By the time the healer attending to him was finished the sun had begun to sink into the west, slowly dropping past the edge of the green floating island to usher in waves of orange and yellow into the sky. Walking away from the infirmary through the ornately decorated hallways of the Hierarch's Palace while following their quiet guide, Edge and Kaylan couldn't help but marvel at the perpetual light far above them as it appeared through windows and opening to the exterior of the citadel. The brilliantly shining glow of another Granic Crystal in the sky at the peak of the golden rainbow keeping Godsmark aloft above the ocean waves forced Kaylan to smile, realizing that despite all the obstacles that had almost ensnared them she and her Maven protector had indeed found the place they were seeking. There was a sense of familiarity radiating from the miracle gem as the Hierarchs called it, almost calling out to her like the nearly depleted Granic Crystal in her pocket.

Edge was in considerably lower spirits as he sauntered through the halls after Kaylan and their guide, fidgeting with the tight bandage on his arm. The sense of hope Kaylan garnered from the crystal far above granted him only suspicion. Their entire encounter with the Hierarchs had made him distrust this place more with every word they spoke. They had been all but ready to sentence them to death before Kaylan revealed who she was and now they were suddenly giving them royal treatment? Something seemed out of place. That and the Maven felt like a piece of his soul was gone without his cheery partner perched on his shoulder. Though he knew Zephyr could take care of himself in even the most dangerous of situations, they had never been in anything like this before and he had been missing for hours somewhere far below over the perilous ocean waves.

As the trio ascended a final staircase and entered a hallway with windows that looked down over the entire city far below, Kaylan smiled in amazement. It looked like Galantia from afar but somehow years in the future. Though not sure how the Hierarchs or the citizens of Godsmark employed the magic of the apparently many Granic Crystals on the island, she could tell they put them to good use in creating a world far advanced to the Grandaria she knew. As she marveled at the cityscape below them, Edge suddenly spoke up in a passive voice from behind her.

"So Captain Bellinus," he started to get the big man's attention, "your Hierarchs never answered our question about these instigators and reclaimers they kept talking about. Care to elaborate for us?" Osric looked back as he walked, scratching his thick brown beard.

"You should pose that question to the Hierarchs, young man," he answered plainly.

"I'm posing it to you," Edge returned curtly, to which Kaylan shot him an intolerant glance. "Aren't you supposed to provide us with whatever we need? Well I need an answer to that question." Bellinus raised an eyebrow and stared at the unflinching boy behind him for a long moment as if sizing him up but at last faced forward once more.

"We continue to live apart from the world for a purpose, boy," he snapped back. "Anyone who would seek to threaten our way of life or provoke us to act outside of the island is an instigator. They are dealt with swiftly with the power of the miracle gem."

"You mean executed with no questions asked," the Maven returned. "The crew aboard the ship you destroyed with that beam of energy were innocent men just helping us get here."

"Whenever the Hierarchs sense presence below us they assume it is an instigator," he replied. "For the safety of our people we cleanse the space around the island of that presence without question. The island is veiled in fog for a reason. But this time they sensed magic as well—from one of the two of you I suppose. Consider yourself lucky they dispatched the Fethiotts to inspect its source or you would still be floating in the water down there waiting for the sea to consume you."

"So if we're not instigators does that make us reclaimers?" he pressed. Bellinus slowed for moment at this, knowingly keeping his gaze ahead of him.

"Time will tell," he replied after an uncomfortable silence, stopping before a door in the hallway. "I suggest you do not dwell on such things. The only things you should be concerned about are the Trials that wait for you at the end of your journey."

"The Trials?" Kaylan repeated curiously. "There are Trials we have to go through?" Osric nodded and folded his arms across his armored chest.

"The miracle gems are housed in the Shrine of Gavanos at the opposite end of the island," he replied. "To access them one must first pass the Trials of the shrine. Only then can you reclaim a miracle gem and activate its power, if indeed you are able."

"What kind of Trials are these?" Edge asked shifting his weight and staring hard at Bellinus, to which the large captain merely took hold of a key at his side and unlocked the door beside him.

"That can only be answered by the Hierarchs, so I suggest you ask them tomorrow," he answered. "This will be your room for the night. I will be here to wake you in the morning." Edge raised an eyebrow at this.

"Only one?" he asked tersely.

"You told the Hierarchs you were joined in sacred union, did you not?" he questioned with a suspicious frown, to which Edge turned to Kaylan uncertainly. Remembering what he was talking about from her discussion with Centrioc earlier, she gulped and nodded.

"Of course, this will be fine," she said opening the door attempting to shake off her discomfiture. "Thank you, captain." Bellinus raised an eyebrow at the two and held the girl's gaze for a long moment but at last bowed.

"Rest well, then," he spoke turning to make his way back down the long hallway in the fleeting sunlight pouring

Tales of Iairia

in from the wide windows. As he turned the corner and disappeared, Edge turned back to Kaylan with a doubtful expression on his face.

"You told them we were married?" he asked incredulously. Kaylan slightly blushed red before opening the door and rolling her eyes.

"I was kind of preoccupied with saving your life at the moment," she returned defensively. "I would have said anything if it meant keeping you around." Realizing what she said, the girl froze and blushed again, awkwardly turning to step through the door into the room they had been given. Edge followed after her hesitantly, turning back to look down the hall for anyone assigned to keep watch on them. Seeing nothing but knowing someone was keeping tabs on them somewhere, the Maven tightly shut the door and locked it behind him. He slowly turned and pulled his tough black gloves from his hands to cast them on a table by the door and run his fingers through his tangled black hair, breathing heavily. As he stood mulling over his thoughts Kaylan took a look out the window in their room and faintly smiled.

"You were right, Edge," she said turning with thankful eyes, "this place was here. You got us to it." The Maven slowly brought his blue eyes to meet hers and dropped his hands back to his sides with a disheartened breath.

"I almost got us killed more times than I care to remember, too," he returned in obviously low spirits. "Don't thank me just yet, Kaylan. I get the feeling this is just beginning. I don't trust these Hierarchs as far as I could throw all seven combined." Kaylan frowned at this.

"They're going to help us, aren't they?" she returned moving past the window to pull the ponytail out of her dirtied hair to let it cascade over her shoulders. Edge let out a disgruntled breath once more.

"So they say," he replied dryly. "But step back and look at this objectively, Kaylan. Every word that Centrioc guy told you made me feel like he was feeding lies to us." Kaylan frowned as she took a seat on the cushioned chair beside a wooden dresser, relaxing her legs for the first time in what felt like an eternity.

"What makes you think that, Edge?" she asked. "All you have to do is look around at the customs and society here to know these people are the closest thing to Grandarians we could ever hope to find. They may have built their society around Lord Granis—or Gavanos—to an extreme but that means they know how dangerous Drakkan is and they have every reason to help us." The Maven shook his head as he put his hands on his hips.

"That doesn't mean they're telling us the truth about anything," he reminded her. "Think about all this, Kaylan—they were ready to throw us off this little island of theirs to our deaths until you mentioned you were a Grandarian. But what difference would that make if we were the threat they originally made us out to be? You told them something else that got them excited. I don't know what it was but I know they're using us for something. Whatever this reclaimer thing is they must think it's you because they wouldn't shut up about it in their little whispers."

"Edge, you can't go through life thinking everyone is out to get you or how can you ever trust anyone?" she asked suddenly. The Maven took a flustered step toward her at this, raising his voice to respond.

"The only reason I've survived this long is by trusting myself, Kaylan, not other people who would slice my throat for whatever Seir I might be carrying before they shoot a glance at me," he returned heatedly. "Don't lecture me about trust."

"Why are you yelling at me about it?" Kaylan burst, more in pain at his words than anger. "Would you have rather had me tell them I wasn't who I am so they might have killed us?" Caught up in his emotions, the Maven shouted back before he knew what words were coming.

"I'm just trying to do my job, and that means protecting you from enemies that attack you head on and enemies who do it from the inside by using you. I've already lost one partner, Kaylan—do you think I want to lose the only other person in the world who matters to me?" he asked, immediately realizing what he had said. They both fell quiet at this, holding each other's gazes in the uncomfortable silence that followed. At last feeling the weight of his words sinking in, the Maven forced himself to break her gaze and cast it upon the wooden floor. Not knowing what to do or say after unwittingly imparting his feelings, he mutely found his way to the soft cushioned bed in the center of the room, slowly dropping onto it. Letting the silence hang for the next several moments the boy lifted a hand to loosen the constricting bandage around the wound in his left arm. Seeing him stiffen in pain as he fumbled with the white cloth, Kaylan at last rose and took a seat next to him to wordlessly work her fingers inside and loosen the bandage. Though he held his eyes into the empty space before him, Kaylan placed hers on his troubled face and leaned in closer.

"I'm sorry, Edge," she spoke softly. "I know you miss Zephyr—I miss him too." The boy blinked at this, his eyes actually acquiring a transparent layer of liquid around them in the moments that passed. Seeing him react, Kaylan forced what emotion she could from her voice as she continued. "You don't like to say it but I know you think this way because you care. About what we're doing, and me." The boy slowly swept his eyes to hers and followed with his entire head turning to hers. "You do care about me, don't you." It was not a question posed from her mind but a statement of fact she could read from his eyes as they stared into hers. He didn't respond but held her gaze, to which Kaylan softened even further, aware it was his way of replying yes. Though she would have normally expected the closed off boy to retreat from her and his feelings, he remained still as if unsure what to make of the strange pang in his chest he had never felt before. The girl blinked, slowly nearing closer to his face and completely closing her eyes. As she sealed them shut and allowed her mind to drift, she heard a distinct voice resound from around her.

"*What do you think you're doing!?!*" it called angrily. "*He doesn't care one bit about you, you two timing little brat! If you think I'm going to sit in here and let this happen you've got a whole other thing coming, blondie!*" Kaylan shot back in surprise, her jolt forcing Edge back to his senses as well. Watching her painfully seal her eyes shut and shake her head, the boy narrowed his eyes uncertainly.

"Kaylan, what's wrong?" he asked quickly. "Are you okay?"

"*She's not if she thinks that was about to happen!*" the voice inside her mind sounded once more. Kaylan fought to ignore Kaotica's words as best she could, pretending she was fine.

"I'm alright, Edge," she responded raising a hand to her forehead. "I'm just feeling a little sick all of the sudden. Do you think I could be alone for a minute?" The Maven's brow furrowed at this, aware something was bothering her.

"Yes we really need some alone time, Edgy," Kaotica spoke scathingly.

"Are you sure you're alright?" he asked again. The girl merely nodded quickly and stood, moving to the window once more.

"I'll be fine, Edge, I just really need a second to breathe," was her cryptic answer. Assuming he had done something wrong to upset her in allowing himself to let his guard down, he slowly inhaled and rose from the bed to step toward the door.

"Maybe I'll go take a look down the halls then," he informed her awkwardly. "If you need anything I'll be close, okay?" The girl merely nodded and forced a meek smile as she turned to watch him step out the door. The moment he closed it behind him she wheeled around and pressed her hands against her ears as if trying to force the voice ringing through her head away.

"What do you want!?!" she winced painfully under her breath so Edge couldn't hear her as he walked away. Kaotica let out an arid huff of disgust.

"What I want is for you to get your eyes off of Edge, you thief," she started again. *"I thought I put this in black and white for you last time but apparently I need to say it again— he's mine, understand?"* Kaylan grit her teeth as she spun around the room, furious at of the dark presence lingering inside her.

"Would you just leave me alone?" she cried irately. "I hate you!"

"Well the feeling's obviously mutual but you don't have to worry long because you won't be around much longer anyway, Kay-Kay," was her mocking response. Ready to cry, Kaylan spied a long mirror mounted to the wall of the small bathroom beyond the main chamber she stood in. Marching in with a fierce expression of determination on her face she found Kaotica waiting there for her with an intolerant expression on her dark face. She rested her hands on her hips and frowned at the Grandarian girl as she approached. *"So you finally—"*

"Listen to me!" Kaylan screamed to cut her off. "I am through having you inside me! Take a look around, Kaotica— we're on the island where the Granic Crystal is waiting for us. Bright and early tomorrow morning we're going to get it and both Edge and I are going to kill you with the Sword of Granis. It's over for you."

"I'll be out of here before you ever make it back, so I wouldn't bet on it," she returned spitefully. *"If I wanted to I could come out right now and make sure you never came back."*

"Then why don't you?" Kaylan blasted at her, reaching into the satchel at her side to pull forth a faintly glowing object pointing to the mirror before her. "Go away!" With that, Kaylan gripped the Granic Crystal so tightly its sharp edges cut into her palms with blood dripping out and thrust it at the mirror with all the strength she had. The moment the crystal touched it in her fury it the mirror shattered and the crystal shone with new light that she had only heard of in stories from her father, forcing Kaylan to stumble out of the bathroom in pain. Surprised the talisman had actually reacted to her rash action in such grand scale she couldn't lift it away from her as it continued glowing brighter. As the seconds ticked by Kaylan opened her mouth to scream in pain but another voice echoed out alongside hers. The light from the Granic Crystal continued increasing until it filled the entire room with its golden rays, slowly burning into Kaylan's flesh.

Then, with an audible cracking of glass from below her, Kaylan managed to open her terrified eyes and watch as the crystal shattered in her hands with its golden light exploding through the room and out the window behind her. The next instant a wave of dark electrified energy detonated to life around her and a layer of shadow matching the exact curves of her body leapt off of her, filling and widening until an exact shadow replica of Kaylan's body flew from her figure through the air apart from her. As the dark mass took form it landed on the floor of the room with a thud, slowly materializing into compact tangible matter. The pain gone from her as she fell to a heap on the ground, Kaylan watched in horror as the dark contours of the shape began to fade and reveal a layer of skin with a familiar set of clothing appearing over it moments later. By the time the final wave of darkness disappeared over the developing body and the last electrified surges of dark purple energy faded, Kaylan sat in awe as Kaotica sat before her, her rich purple eyes wide open and staring back into hers. The two girls on the ground remained silent as they stared at each other, both equally awestruck at what had just happened.

Before either of them could say anything, the door to the bedroom slammed open with the darkly clad form of Edge lowering the boot he had just used to kick it in. Leaping through the door with fists raised to defend the girl he had left inside from whatever had caused her to scream, his body suddenly froze in shock as he found both she and her dark twin on the floor staring back up at him. The Maven let his fists unfold and drop to his sides, ultimate confusion entering his eyes. He couldn't believe what he was seeing—both Kaylan and Kaotica before him at the same time. After several long moments trying to find the words to ask what had happened, he took a step forward to try and make sure that what he was seeing was real. As he stood staring unable to utter so much as a word in his mystification, the sound of boots rushing up the stairs at the end of the long hallway abruptly echoed into the room and all three turned to face the door. Before any of them could react Osric Bellinus came charging before the doorway into the room with a unit of over a dozen soldiers behind them, all brandishing sword points.

Edge steeled himself once more, preparing for whatever was in store for them now. As the moments ticked by with the Maven and captain staring each other down, no one made a move until Bellinus at last stood aside when a white robed figure approached from behind. It was not Centrioc but another of the men from the left side of the chairs they had left the Hierarchs in earlier in the day. He dashed into the room quickly, his eyes falling upon the third member of the party of outsiders he had never seen before.

"What is the meaning of this?" the Hierarch fumed irately. "There has not been dark power in Godsmark in millennia! What is this treachery that you have brought with you!?!" Though Edge remained on guard he tried his best to respond.

"It's very complicated but this other girl is with us," he said to which both Kaylan and Kaotica looked to him uncertainly.

"It is surrounded by dark energy and cannot be allowed to live!" the Hierarch shouted in contradiction. "Guards!" Though Edge tried to talk the Hierarch down Bellinus and two of his guards charged into the room with blades arching downward toward Kaotica trembling on the floor. Gritting his teeth, Edge threw his leg upward to kick one of them away and take hold of the hilt of another as the solider passed, forcing him to flip it downward and release it in pain. In one fluid movement he threw himself forward to head-butt the second soldier and extend the tip of his new blade out to reach the neck of Osric Bellinus as he drew near Kaotica.

"If you value the life of your captain I suggest you back down now," Edge spoke menacingly, watching the Hierarch and the other soldiers freeze.

"You treacherous dog!" the Hierarch blasted at him. "You would allow the corruptive stain of dark power into our city?" Before Edge could respond another voice sounded from outside in the hall, cutting him off.

"Perhaps things are not as they seem, my brother," the familiar voice of the First Hierarch Centrioc sounded coming around the door to step inside the room and gauge the scene about to explode before him. "Is this the case, young man?" Edge held his heated gaze on them for a lingering second before slowly nodding.

"It is," he answered. "This girl may possess dark power but she is a good person. She's not a threat to you and is under my control. If you're going to help us this girl is not to be harmed." Kaylan stared at the boy in painful confusion, awestruck at why he would defend her wicked twin this way. The white robed figure cautiously held his gaze, then turned to the other Hierarch beside him and nodded.

"Very well then," he returned softly. "As long as this is the case there is no need for rash action. Are there any other surprises you have not informed us of, Edge?" The Maven shook his head and replied no. "Then I believe we are done here. I suggest you get your rest for tomorrow. If you require addition rooms for this evening we can provide." With that the First Hierarch turned with his regal white robes rustling around him as he snapped his fingers to signal the soldiers to follow him. Edge turned down to Osric Bellinus, still crouched as the Maven held the blade of his sword to his neck and slowly lifted the sharp edge away. The large captain rose and eyed him warily as he walked out, closing the door behind him. Alone once more, Edge lowered the blade in his hands and slowly turned around to the two girls still lying on the floor staring up at him.

Chapter 33

Commencement

The grassy plains immediately west of the nearly two mile gap in the Border Mountains were perhaps the greenest in all of Iairia, untouched by human activity for over a century. In ancient Grandaria the massive gap before the fields that revealed a path into the mountains and back home to Galantia was frequently used by Grandarians making their way to and from their home to the new world beyond. This all changed after Drakkaidians had found the pass and backtracked them to their capital city in the First Holy War to nearly raze the golden municipality to the ground. After the conclusion, the first Supreme Granisian had ordered the gap sealed to protect them from further invasion from their enemies to the west. Though the ambitious sovereign never saw his decree completed, over the next two centuries the Grandarians constructed arguably the greatest edifice ever built—the Wall of Light.

Stretching for almost a mile through the gap in the war zone to seal the mountain route to their homeland, it had stood firm for over three centuries through ten full scale battles and the Second Holy War. The wall was composed of heavy white stone forged from the mountains around it, bricked over twenty feet thick and fifty feet high. Next to the Gate Yard in Galantia the largest military base in Grandaria lay behind the wall, storing everything from barracks for soldiers to war machines kept at the ready in the event of a siege. The wall boasted several watchtowers and protective ramparts bolstered by thick bulwark shields on the wide walkway at its top, constantly manned by over a hundred soldiers from one side to the other. Serving atop the Wall of Light was the highest honor a Grandarian solider could hope to receive—to be charged with the first line of defense against aggression from Drakkaidia. Though the position had lost none of its significance to the men of the Grandarian Army in the calm that had endured since the Second Holy War over a century ago, many believed it was no longer a necessary task in the wake of the apparent peace that had lingered since the Second Holy War.

This perception maintained by many of the soldiers drastically altered upon the surprise arrival of the renowned Warrior of Light and his battalion of reinforcements from the Battlemount, bringing with him news of a Drakkaidian plot to assault the Wall of Light. Believing an attack immanent and inevitable, Tavin Tieloc immediately assumed control of the wall and ordered its defenses to their most ready state. Coming alive with activity that had not been present since the Second Holy War, the wall was augmented with a double watch at all times, increased rations and supplies to hold them in the event of a siege, and the disassembled catapults in the bunkers behind the wall reassembled and moved into position for immediate use. Under the impression the Warrior of Light had advised against mobilizing for war for the entirety of his tenure on the Galantian Council, the soldiers at the wall clearly knew something was indeed wrong and conflict was upon them.

During the days after Tavin arrived and began fortifying the Wall of Light with the additional battalion of troops he had marshaled at the Battlemount, he and his second in command, General Ronus, had been planning for as many scenarios of battle as they could come up with. Though the Drakkaidians had never made more than a dent in the thick wall in past sieges, under the leadership of Verix Montrox and the mysterious dark power Tavin had sensed at the portal to the void and the Battlemount, he was convinced they could no longer depend on the wall's girth alone to defend them and would need to prepare for every possible contingency they could imagine—feasible or not. As morning dawned on the western edge of the Border Mountains in his fourth day there, Tavin woke early and dressed in full battle armor as he had every day, imparting to the troops the seriousness in his claim of the utmost need to stand at the ready. The sky, seeming to grow darker by the day, had been enveloped in a dense cloud cover threatening to open up and release a torrent of rainfall since the Warrior of Light had arrived. Making his way through the tense courtyard to inspect the catapults recently assembled and aligned in a long line in the expanse behind the wall to cast boulders and flaming projectiles into the ranks of any enemy that dared gather outside, the anxious faces of attentive soldiers on duty watched him pass. He looked as commanding and legendary as his men regarded him, his new blue and gold cape mounted to the gilded armor plate over his chest and back majestically swaying in the breeze. Though he maintained his commanding and determined demeanor before the uneasy men, Ronus in particular could tell he was still silently suffering from the thought of his daughter in danger somewhere out of his reach.

As Tavin arrived at the command bunker tucked into a rock wall normally occupied by General Sodric, he found Ronus waiting for him inside. Greeting each other somberly, the two began to strategize through the morning once again. Tavin's staff arrived shortly after to present him with the tactics they had drawn up through the night to meet his demands for a fallback plan in the event of a breach in the wall. Laying them out before him, the Warrior of Light's face slowly morphed with impatient irritation as he flipped a paper down onto the table before him.

"This is the best we can do?" he questioned pessimistically, casting the final map of a retreat route into the mountains out of his hands for the floor. "This is the *best* you could come up with? This is only a map showing me a road back to the Battlemount!" A captain that had collaborated with the rest of Sodric's former staff eyed the Warrior of Light uncertainly, slowly formulating the words to respond.

"The Battlemount has always been the planned fallback position from the wall in the event of a... catastrophe," he answered. Tavin let out a deep breath and leaned forward on his arms to bolster himself up on the table.

"I thought I made it clear to everyone yesterday that conventional tactics will not suffice for this battle," Tavin stated with frustration. "If the wall falls the Battlemount is not fit to defend against a siege in its current state. It wouldn't hold for more than a day under the full pressure of a Drakkaidian attack. There has to be another point in the road through the mountains where we could force enemy troops into a bottleneck or something that could give us a fortified position." The captain remained impassive, a look of virtual disgust emanating from his eyes at what the Warrior of Light was suggesting.

"We have not needed a fallback position in centuries. It would take months of surveying the land to draw up a new defensive point. I'm afraid there is no other option in the Border Mountains," he stated flatly. "Our defense is the Wall of Light. Even if it is another Holy War we face, it has held firm through one before. The wall will not fail." Tavin tightened his fist at this and slammed it onto the table before him, shocking them all.

"Have you even been listening to me the past few days?" he shouted. "I don't know how much clearer I can possibly be yet you still seem to have no concept of what we face! When this begins it isn't going to be a little skirmish outside the wall that we can win by firing a volley or two of arrows into a single regiment of rogue Drak troops waving swords at us from the ground. The Drakkaidians will have muscle with them strong enough to blast through even the wall."

"We have beaten back the pitiful war machines of the Drakkaidians with ours for centuries without ever suffering a breach of any kind, Sir Tieloc," was the captain's aggravated response.

"I'm not talking about war machines, captain," Tavin lashed back. "The wall was built to hold back armies alone. What you neglect to consider is the Drakkaidians are going be led by Verix Montrox. Between him and whatever dark magic the Draks have conjured up that destroyed the Battlemount it is easily within their power to puncture this wall. And if that happens, I don't want to be on the run back to a decimated base in the mountains to make our final stand because you think we're invincible here. This wall is not composed of the spirit of Granis, captain—it's earth and stone that will crush and fall to rubble beneath the might of dark power such as Montrox possesses. And when he summons it we'd better have a plan to counter it and regroup or this army won't last more than a few minutes. Is that perfectly clear?" Before the flustered captain could open his mouth to respond the wooden door to the compact chamber abruptly burst open with the sentries outside parting to allow in a single armor covered soldier, sweating and stumbling into the room as he panted for breath. Tavin and the others instantly spun around to face him, tensing with concern at his unexpected arrival.

"Sir Tieloc!" he managed through his quick breaths, "We can see them! Thousands!" Though Tavin was about to tell him to calm down and repeat himself, the sudden ringing of several rich horns sounding from the wall began to fill the air with their unique timbre that was immediately followed by the rumbling of soldiers racing to attention outside, making his message clear. His eyes widening, Tavin wheeled around to collect his thoughts and stare over all the plans he had made the past days. Shooting his gaze upward, the Warrior of Light found Ronus staring at him apprehensively.

"Ronus, you and Marcum come with me," Tavin ordered quickly. "The rest of you remain here and await further orders. For all our sakes I hope your faith in this pile of bricks is as strong as you claim." Rushing for the door the Warrior of Light motioned for the anxious messenger to return to his post and quickly marched into the hallway beyond for the exit of the command building. Stepping through the doorway to the courtyard beyond, Tavin found it erupting with chaotic activity with soldiers running past armory stations to form ranks on the ground and make for staircases on the wall. Archers formed atop its surface ahead of the swordsmen rushing behind them drawing their blades and raising shields baring the crest of light on their chests. Though wanting to sprint up the staircases with them the Warrior of Light remained calm and swiftly marched through the courtyard with Ronus behind him, aware the eyes of his soldiers were on him for assurance that he was in control.

As he at last ascended the nearest stone staircase leading to the top of the wall, Tavin looked back to the courtyard and the vast expanse behind it to find their catapults drawing back and being loaded with large boulders. With nearly ten thousand suits of golden armor coming to attention around him and several thousand more lining the expanse behind the wall, Tavin nodded to himself to confirm they were as ready as they could be. Stepping onto the wall top, Ronus and his subordinate shouted for the soldiers lined up before them to make way for the Warrior of Light as he strode across the wall top bustling with soldiers racing to and fro distributing weaponry and taking positions behind archers. Stepping past the row of archers before the edge of the barrier atop the wall, Tavin's focused eyes went wide as he found what had caused the alarm.

Covering the fields on the horizon was a colossal black mass of soldiers slowly lumbering toward the Wall of Light through the morning air, trampling ground that had not been touched by human feet in over a hundred years. Tavin couldn't help but blink in fear as he studied the mammoth force marching toward them for the next few minutes, estimating them to be at least twenty thousand strong. Hushed whispers passed along on the lips of the Grandarian soldiers around him as they watched the black mass in the distance, disbelief passing across their faces at what they were finally seeing. As the foreign horde of dark soldiers drew nearer, Tavin uncertainly narrowed his eyes. Though their number was greater than he first guessed, he didn't see any war machines with them. Not so much as a single siege tower or iron shot accompanied them, only the men. The Warrior of Light quickly turned back to eye Ronus, so captivated with the view before him he barely realized Tavin was staring at him.

"General, you will return to the courtyard to command the catapults and the reserves," Tavin ordered calmly, getting his attention. "No solider is to fire an arrow or release a boulder until I give the command—is that understood?" Ronus nodded immediately, confirming his order. Wheeling around he at once ordered his subordinate and two of the passing soldiers to follow him back down the stairs. As the general departed Tavin turned back to the dark horizon beyond them, silently watching as the Drakkaidian troops continued forward with the faint sound of their feet trampling over the earth beginning to rumble.

"I can't believe this is actually happening," the voice of a solider from his right spoke to another beside him, obviously not aware Tavin was standing no more than a few feet away. "I never thought I would live to see a battle here, much less another Holy War." As he turned to find the Warrior of Light beside him, he instantly froze and bit his tongue in fear. Though Tavin kept his gaze focused out on the dark mass before them, he slowly opened his mouth to speak.

"Neither did I," he spoke loud enough for the soldiers around him to hear. Tavin slowly turned and began walking past the solider who had spoken, putting a hand on his shoulder as he did. "Courage is not living without fear. Courage is being scared to death and doing the right thing anyway. Stand tall, young man." With that the Warrior of Light continued

Trial of a Maven

down the wall keeping his gaze steadily before him. After powerfully striding down the rows of nervous soldiers with his regal cape flowing behind him, Tavin eventually came to the rampart at the center of the Wall of Light and stepped onto the short stone extension branching off from the main wall to stand before all his troops. As he folded his arms encased in metal gauntlets across his chest, the Warrior of Light patiently waited for the next agonizingly long moments for the approaching Drakkaidian battalions to draw near, the sound of their marching now thundering through the morning air.

Seeing his archers along the Wall of Light drawing their bow strings tight and loading them with arrows as the dark army came just outside of their range, Tavin instantly raised his arms to signal for them to hold. Word spreading down the wall for the soldiers to remain at ease, the Warrior of Light watched as the disciplined ranks of organized Drakkaidian soldiers at last came to a halt before them. As the echoing sound of their feet trampling the earth faded, a single voice shouted over the quiet ranks of darkly armored men. Though too far away to tell what the order was, Tavin watched as the Drakkaidians drew their lances closer to their bodies and lowered their blades in unison, falling dead silent. Tavin frowned, aware the army before him was no rabble of amateur rogue troops that Sodric had reported but skilled warriors amassed by the hand of the late Valif Montrox himself. Drakkaidia was a nation bred for war. In the moments that followed, another voice barked through the silence and the front ranks of infantrymen slowly parted down their middle, revealing a row of horsemen slowly drawing forward.

As the riders appeared from the front row only one pressed forward at a gallop within range of the bow, a gray cape flying up behind him. Tavin felt his heart begin to beat faster, instantly realizing the identity of the horseman. As the black steed drew closer to the wall, the fiery haired warrior below pulled back the reins of his horse to make it rear back and neigh for half of the entire wall to hear. As it dropped back down to the earth, the figure swiftly cocked his right arm back to throw it forward, mightily lobbing an object through the air right at Tavin. Though defensive at first, the Warrior of Light observed the object to be a small rock and reached out to his side to catch it in his gloved hands before it could fall to the stone walkway and break. Examining the stone closer in his gloved palms he saw it already glowing with a steady crimson light from within, pulsating like the heart beating in his chest. Though nervous at what the powerful warrior on the ground was up to, as he looked back at him he saw a second crimson stone in his hands close to his lips. Eyeing him uncertainly, Tavin was surprised to hear a faint humming begin to radiate from the core of the stone. As the seconds ticked by the low humming gradually took on a familiar tone of voice that Tavin knew all too well.

"There are two kinds of light, Grandarian—the glow that illuminates and the glare that obscures," the voice sounded with surges of electric energy forming around the stone with each syllable uttered. "Grandaria has strayed to the latter. These will be the terms. You will return to the portal to the void immediately and restore the Sword of Granis to its rightful place. Whatever damage you have done to the portal you will undo. If you do this within the next six days I will pull my army back to the higher war zone. We will withdraw only when I sense the seal restored. From there you and I will meet alone to negotiate further."

"Pull back, Montrox?" Tavin repeated skeptically into the stone. "And what happens then? You return the next day when I am gone to demolish the Wall of Light? Grandaria sees past your lies, Verix. It is our portal and our Battlemount that lie destroyed by Drakkaidian power. *I* will be making the terms here. Now pay attention closely because I will only say this once. I want the Granic Crystal back, these New Fellowship troops back in the Valley of Blood, and I want to know where my daughter is *right now*." There was a long pause of silence on the other side of the stone but as Verix's horse circled once more he responded.

"I'm through playing these games with you," he picked up monotonously. "You know me well enough to know I am no fool, Tieloc. You are the only one with the power to affect the Sword of Granis. If you continue upon this course of denying your actions and taunting the bull, you will get what you are provoking and find its horns reaching out for you. Do not make the mistake of testing my resolve here."

"The Wall of Light has held Drakkaidia at bay for centuries," Tavin began with mounting anger pouring from his voice, "and it will hold today. You don't even have your war machines with you; if you think you can single-handedly bring this wall down you are sorely mistaken, Montrox. Now answer me—what have you done with Kaylan? I swear to Granis if so much as a hair on her head is harmed—"

"The only thing I have been mistaken about is your sanity, Tieloc!" the other blasted back from the opposite side of the crimson stone cutting him off, abundant electricity surging forward. "If you assumed I would sit back idly as you toyed with the fate of the world unchallenged you are in for a painful surprise! If I have to I will see the Sword of Granis restored with my bleeding hand over yours but you will stay this madness. This is your final chance, Tieloc. One way or another you will set this right." Letting his emotions get the best of him the Warrior of Light raised the crimson rock in his hands above his head to throw it back down onto the stone surface of the Wall of Light, fragmenting it into faintly glowing shards that wildly danced around his feet.

"I want my daughter, Verix!" Tavin abruptly shouted with his voice sounding loud enough for the soldiers all along the entire central face of the wall to hear. "*Where is Kaylan!?!*" Verix remained still on his black horse below the wall for a long moment but eventually tossed the Voss Stone in his grasp casually over his back and turned his steed to gallop back into the black ranks of the silent Drakkaidians behind him. Breathing hard with his fists tightly clenched over the extension in the center of the Wall of Light, Tavin silently watched as the Drakkaidian army unanimously raised their blades and extended their lances once more, shouts echoing through the number barking orders to stand at the ready. While the Grandarians high atop their wall remained quiet, the ranks of Drakkaidians began rhythmically pounding their black shields with the hilts of their weapons, beginning to scream out war cries on every beat. Tavin couldn't believe it. The moment he had wished for countless nights as a young man that he never thought would come now stared him in the face like a wild animal ready to pounce. Though he had resisted the thought of what now marched toward him since the Days of Destiny, it was on his shoulders to protect his golden land from the forces of Drakkaidia once again.

Fierce determination overtaking his face as it had so many times before, the Warrior of Light spun around from the extended rampart on the wall to begin marching down the wide pathway at its top through the ranks of golden armored soldiers all staring at him doubtfully.

"Grandarians one and all, rise and hear me well!" he boomed as loudly as his voice would carry through the rumbling onslaught of marching drawing near from the fields before them. "Our country has not seen war of any kind for over a hundred years, meaning none of you standing here today have ever tasted the sting of battle before. Yet you were brought up to expect it, even desire it as was I. The glory of defending the golden land is unparalleled by any other destiny we aim for in this world. This is the credo by which generations of our people have lived and died. But over the past twenty years since the Days of Destiny you have heard a different story from me—that Lord Granis does not desire further Holy War against the Drakkaidians and that peace must reign. I realize now that while this may be the case, it is now fallen to us to protect our homes and people from forces of corruption that lead the dark nation to the west once more. I know that many of you are gripped by fear—shaken with self doubt—but I assure you this battle is ours to win! The forces of our enemy may seem daunting as you stare into their vast numbers, but no matter how fierce they have ever appeared or how many swords they have ever brought against us, this Wall of Light has never been penetrated, and it will not fall today!" As Tavin pressed on down the wall the soldiers around him loudly cheered and raised their arms into the sky, proudly bellowing out cries of glory. The Warrior of Light drew his sword and pivoted to make his way back to the center of the wall. "So stand tall and draw your swords for your home and each other! Whether we must hold this wall for a clean hour or a bloody year, I vow to you now that so long as there is breath in me I will stand beside you to the end. My power is yours and yours will be mine. Rise now, for Grandaria!"

The cheers intensified as Tavin stepped onto the extension beyond the center rampart of the wall, watching as the incoming Drakkaidians passed into range of their longbows. As he raised the blade of his sword perpendicular to his body the archers along the wall top tightened their bows once more and loaded them with the iron tipped missiles. Waiting for the Drakkaidians to move from a quick march to a slow charge over the grassy earth raising their shields above their heads, the Warrior of Light tightened his face and cast his blade downward signaling the first volley. Instantly the hundreds of archers atop the Wall of Light released their arrows to send a black mass of wood and iron arching into the air to descend on the approaching Drakkaidians now screaming war cries as they came in full charge.

The arrows cut into them with lethal accuracy, dropping virtually half of their first ranks to the ground. Ordering another volley, Tavin curiously narrowed his eyes to find the formerly concentrated Drakkaidian soldiers parting and widening as they came within range of the conventional bow, revealing several large wooden frames previously concealed by their number. His eyes widening in realization, the Warrior of Light shouted out for his troops to take cover as several oversized spears carrying ropes behind them were launched from the cleverly disguised iron shots in the center of the Drakkaidian army. The massive pikes easily punched into the top of the wall, blasting a few soldiers back but for the most part merely puncturing the stone below the pathways. Seeing several ranks of Drakkaidian forces suddenly lifting enormous ladders above their heads they began charging forward toward the ropes angling up to the top of the wall. Realizing they were trying to lay the ladders against the incoming ropes for passage to the top of the wall Tavin screamed out for the swordsmen to start hacking at them before the incoming Drakkaidians could attempt to climb them or place ladders over them.

As Tavin leapt to his right to slash down at one of the thick ropes that slammed into the wall from the iron shots earlier, the barrage of Drakkaidian arrows commenced falling into the wall and the courtyard behind it, creating a dangerous crossfire of missiles around him. Glancing toward the horizon to gauge the reserve Drakkaidia forces that were still arriving from the war zone he found a row of soaring siege towers rolling forward in the distance. Gritting his teeth as he savagely swung down to sever the rope beneath him the Warrior of Light shouted out for the catapults to begin firing. Turning into the swarm of black soldiers gathering beneath the wall he watched as a round of boulders and flaming projectiles began soaring from behind the wall into the Drakkaidians outside. The Warrior of Light grit his teeth as he stood tall amid the havoc of battle around him, his cape flapping in the incoming wind from the east. The Third Holy War had begun.

Chapter 34

Trio

Edge had slept poorly in his stay at the Hierarch's Palace in Godsmark. With the expenditure of so much power for the first time taking its toll on his beaten body, the disappearance and possible death of his longtime partner, being captive in a strange new world under the suspicious Hierarchs, his intimate moment with Kaylan the night before, and now the appearance of Kaotica as her own person apart from the Grandarian girl, the young Maven had never felt so besieged in his life. After discovering the separation of the twins and defending them from the Hierarchs' immediate response to the dark power exuded by Kaotica, Edge was quick to grill them about what had happened. It was immediately clear that keeping the opposite halves of his female charge together was begging for trouble, their hatred of each other nearly leading to conflict the second the Hierarchs left. Securing another two rooms from a sentry outside the hallway, Edge instructed Kaylan to stay put and settle down in their original room while he tried to talk Kaotica into submission and put her to bed for the night. Though anticipating a headache from the dark girl as she sought her "fun," after leading her into her room she proved to be surprisingly compliant to anything he asked as if childishly trying to impress him with her behavior.

The cooperation ended when he attempted to leave to check on Kaylan and to discern what had really happened. Stomping her black high heel boot on the ground in fury she blocked his way to the door and insisted she would not let him out of her sight so Kaylan could lie about her and have the boy to herself. His thin patience and worn temper slipping at her usual immaturity, Edge shouted for her to listen to him for once and promised to return. Though skeptical, the dark girl could tell she was upsetting him and painfully wheeled around with a huff, telling him to hurry. Rolling his eyes the Maven at last returned to Kaylan, huddled up in a corner of the floor in her room crying. Quickly rushing to her side to gingerly lift her from the ground and set her on the soft bed she latched onto him spraying tears. Fighting through her emotions she at last explained how Kaotica's rising power coupled with the last strength of the Granic Crystal had triggered a reaction that had somehow purged her from Kaylan as her own entity. Terrified she had inadvertently released Drakkan in her emotional attempt to rid herself of the dark girl, Edge comforted her by gently rubbed her back and telling her Kaotica appeared to be the same as always so the full power of Drakkan could not have emerged through her yet.

    Calming Kaylan down and telling her they would sort the rest of the mess out in the morning, Edge instructed her to rest and recover her strength for the coming day. Nodding in agreement, the girl hugged her protector goodnight and attempted to fall asleep while he returned to deal with Kaotica. The Maven found her wandering the dark hallway giggling as she removed decorative armor from the walls to curiously inspect it and either set it in a pile before her or toss it from the window if not to her liking. Quickly collecting her and pulling her back into her room, Edge angrily admonished her that if she wanted to stay with him she had to listen to what he told her. Though she merely laughed off his concerns as always and closed the gap between their faces, he pulled away and ordered her to get some sleep. Kaotica yawned at this, realizing she was indeed tired.

    By the time the boy had finally put both the girls to sleep and climbed into his own bed the wee hours of the morning had come and gone and his exhausted mind was too besieged with the situation he now found himself in to ever fall asleep. Used to resting little in his travels with his missing partner, the Maven rose with his mind troubled at dawn to bathe and clean his wound in the tub of warm water the servants of the palace had prepared for him. Replacing the frayed blue tunic under his thick black vest with a new silver one laid out for him by the servants, Edge pulled his black gloves over his hands and tied his dilapidated blue scarf around his neck once more. Stepping out of his room into the quiet hallway he peered into both of the girls' rooms to make sure they remained peacefully asleep.

Folding his arms and leaning his back against the stone wall behind him as the auburn morning sky slowly lit with the fervent rays of the sun to the east, he stared out at the sprawling city of Godsmark distrustfully. Something didn't add up about this place. If the people here were really the extremist Grandarians they claimed why did First Hierarch Centrioc allow the first dark power he had sensed in their city in millennia to survive the previous night? Though he wasn't sure if they would have been able to harm a being as powerful as Kaotica, it seemed obvious they would have at least tried to remove such a clear threat that had appeared out of nowhere. Why would Centrioc not at least question where she had come from? Though Edge didn't know the answer, he knew whatever it was had to spell trouble and he would have to keep up his guard.

Kaotica would make the situation more volatile. She was the unstable factor in every situation she wove her way into that Edge could not control. No matter how much he warned and admonished her to avoid trouble there was nothing he could do to make her listen. It was a miracle she had stayed in the Hierarch's Palace the previous night instead of spreading her bat-like wings to take off and search for "fun" elsewhere. Edge frowned at himself as her admittedly beautiful figure entered his mind and at the emotion that reared itself inside him as it did. The girl was a foil to her other half, reflecting the exact opposite personality of Kaylan. She was driven solely by her passions and desires with no thought to any long term goals or ideals. The world existed for her personal pleasure alone. It was as if she had been created with all of Kaylan's basic knowledge and experience but none of her maturity. The Maven shook his head slowly, dismissing this thought. Despite her outward veneer of selfish cravings and excitement for exploration of the world around her, Edge now knew there was more to the seemingly shallow girl than he had first thought. Though it came out rarely, he had seen her act on the behalf of another before. Thinking back to their escape from Acquanautta Port and how she had saved the boy that would have otherwise been killed by the cannon fire from the docks, he knew somewhere deep inside she had inherited some part of Kaylan's virtuous heart with a sense of right and wrong. This fact made it all the harder for him to continue on a quest to destroy her knowing some degree of her soul was innocent of the evil that slept dormant within.

Contemplating the dark girl and how her permanent presence alongside Kaylan would affect the duration of their quest as the sun rose, Edge at last came awake as the sound of the door to his left slowly cracked open to reveal Kaylan stepping out, dressed only in a loose gray nightshirt she had borrowed from the closets inside her room. It was obviously intended for a large man, the neck hole so wide it left one of her bare shoulders exposed as it draped down to her knees. Spying him instantly as her bare feet stepped onto the chilled palace floor she let out a deep breath of relief and ambled next to him to uncomfortably meet his gaze, fidgeting with her coils of blond hair. Noticing the uncharacteristic insecurity in her eyes, Edge groped for something to say.

"Did you sleep?" the Maven quietly asked through the morning stillness, tilting his head toward her. The girl's expression remained unnerved but she slowly nodded.

"Yes," she replied in almost a whisper. "Did you?" Edge exhaled and swallowed, shifting his weight on his feet.

"There are a few tubs of hot water in the room across from yours," he answered avoiding her question. "I'm sure you'll want to make use of them before Bellinus shows up again." Kaylan kept her deep blue eyes on his face as he looked to the room across from them in the silence that followed, searching. Feeling her eyes on him the Maven turned to face her again, watching her open her mouth to say something that would not come. At last she swallowed and took another step toward him.

"Did you mean what you said about her last night?" she asked suddenly, catching him by surprise. The boy raised an eyebrow, confused. "You said she was a good person, Edge. I know the way you talk... you meant it, didn't you?" The Maven remembered what she was talking about and let out a long sigh, blinking and shaking his head in frustration.

"I haven't forgotten what we're doing, Kaylan," he answered.

"That isn't what I asked, Edge," the girl returned quickly. "Has she really fooled you into thinking that? Why did you protect her from them? Why did you say that?" Edge thrust his back off the wall he leaned on to turn and face the Grandarian girl, meeting her intense eyes harboring some emotion within that caused them to tremble.

"My mission is to protect you, Kaylan," he told her. "Protect you from external threats and from the threat of your dark side unleashing Drakkan. This just means I have to protect two people now. We have to keep her safe with us until we get the new Granic Crystal on the sword or Drakkan might emerge through her before we can stop it. I can control her—"

"I don't want you to control her," Kaylan cut him off emotionally, surprising the boy. "You can't see it but I know her mind, Edge. She was inside me. I know she's trying to use you somehow—she's trying to trick you into saving her. It's the only reason she would be..." The girl trailed off there, still holding his gaze. Edge narrowed his eyes uncertainly at her.

"Kaylan, what's really bothering you?" he asked delicately, to which the girl's already vulnerable eyes softened further.

"I just," she spoke, unsuccessfully letting her words hang. "I just don't want you getting hurt, Edge. She's more dangerous than you think." The Maven held her gaze for a long moment, aware there was still something behind her words she wasn't telling him. Assuring her he wouldn't let any of them be hurt, he suggested she get herself ready for the day. Reminding her he would need her to be the strong girl he had come to know for the Trials Osric Bellinus told them about, Kaylan forced a smile and nodded, turning to gather her clothes from her room and wander into the bathroom across from her. As the Maven lingered in the hall listening to the Grandarian girl bathe and groom for the day, he heard footsteps approaching from the end of the hallway and quickly turned to the staircase to find the massive form of Osric Bellinus lumbering toward him with his golden plated chest armor gleaming in the morning sun. As he approached Edge folded his arms once more and strode to the center of the hallway to meet him with a somber expression over his face.

"Good morning, young man," the bearded Godsmark captain spoke as he approached. "Are you and... your company ready to embark?"

"Not quite," he returned. "One of them is bathing and the other one—"

"Is always ready," came a third voice from behind them as a door beside the bathroom swung open. Edge spun around in alarm to find Kaotica striding toward him with a mischievous smile on her lips. The girl was dressed in her normally revealing attire but for a white flower she had tucked into her hair that she had found somewhere in her bedroom. She stopped beside Edge and took hold of his arm merrily. "Oh you were right, Edgy, I feel much better after a little sleep. I was so lonely though..." The Maven quickly pulled his arm from her and flushed red, turning back to Bellinus staring at her uncertainly.

"Can you give us a few minutes to finish preparing, please?" Edge asked.

"The Hierarchs are waiting on the balcony of the seventh tower," he responded quickly. "They will not wait for long. Meet me at the bottom of the stairs when you are ready but be quick about it." With that, the large man turned to make his way back down the hallway and the stairs beyond. Edge turned to Kaotica as she exhaled with disgust and flicked her wrist for him to be gone.

"Is that the same idiot you had to deal with last night?" she asked bluntly. "I'd like to see him try that again—you were ready to whip him like a crying baby." The girl smiled at him and reached out to take his hand. "I told you that you'd be desperate to keep me around. And there you were ready to fight for me against three swordsmen. Ah, I knew you cared about little ol' Kaotica." Seeing him about to speak and pull away once more Kaotica raised her eyebrows and stepped closer. "That's why you won't do it, Edge. You meant what you said about me, didn't you?" The boy froze at this, staring into her penetrating purple eyes. "So that's why I'll still keep you company even if you decide to keep going to find your little crystal, because I know you'll change your mind before the end." Edge remained still and silent as her words seeped into him, curiously staring at her beautiful face as the moments ticked by. As he did, the door to the bathroom at last opened to reveal Kaylan, refreshed in new clothes with her curly blond hair shimmering once more. As she stepped out of the bathroom throwing her head back to cast her hair behind her back, she abruptly froze with the smile from her lips fading as she found the two standing so close together. While Edge hastily came back to his senses to force Kaotica's hand from his, the dark girl merely cocked her head back with her darkly painted smile restored.

"Ah, don't you look pretty, Kay-Kay," was her cheerful but mocking greeting as she rested her hands on her hips and looked her up and down. "Weird outfit as usual but not all of us know how to dress to impress, I suppose." Kaylan's frown deepened and she clenched her fists and opened her mouth to respond.

"Well I need to be dressed properly since I'm about to go find a Granic Crystal, don't I?" she asked sinking to her dark half's immaturity.

"Are you going to end up breaking that one too?" Kaotica shot back, to which Edge grit his teeth and jumped in front of the two to preclude their tempers from flaring anymore than they already had.

"That's enough from both of you," he commanded heatedly, raising his hands to put them in front of both girls. "If you think I'm going to sit here and stomach the two of you bicker like a couple of toddlers you'd both better think again."

"You tell her, Edgy," Kaotica chimed in spitting her tongue out at the blond girl. Edge wheeled around with malice in his eyes, locking them onto her.

"Do you not hear me?" he ripped impatiently. "Look, whether the two of you like it or not you're both stuck with each other right now and there's an impatient Maven right in the middle who can't stand stage shows like this is turning into. I'm still not sure how this happened, but beyond whatever is coming for the three of us at the end of this thing, we all have one common goal right now—getting off this island in one piece. These Hierarchs are up to something and whatever it is I'm going to need both of you to listen to me and work together for me to do my job of protecting *both* of you." Though still adamant that her dark half was gradually twisting the Maven around her finger Kaylan realized he was right for the moment and swallowed her worries as best she could, slowly nodding her head. Kaotica's brow furrowed as she folded her arms and lifted her nose into the air unmoved.

"As if I need protection," she murmured in a hush.

"I mean it, Kaotica," Edge pressed intolerantly, raising a finger before her face. "So help me Granis I..." Edge trailed off there, realizing the pointlessness of threatening her. Dropping his hand, the Maven collected himself and shrugged, stepping beside Kaylan. "Well, if you don't need me to protect you feel free to go. Kaylan and I will just go on by ourselves." With that, Edge gently nudged Kaylan to start walking down the hallway for the staircase at its end, his scarf trailing behind him. Though Kaylan glanced at him uncertainly knowing they couldn't afford to let Kaotica out of their sights, he continued forward confidently. As the seconds ticked by Kaotica narrowed her eyes and let her arms drop back to her sides, jealousy and distress filling her eyes.

"Hey! Where do you think you're going?" she shouted desperately from behind them. Edge looked back but continued striding forward, shrugging once more.

"I told you—*Kaylan* still needs me so she's coming with me to the Trials," he replied simply. "You can do as you please." The boy turned around unaffected, slowly shooting Kaylan a knowing glance as the sound of footsteps started racing behind them down the hallway. All at once Kaotica appeared beside him to latch onto his left arm.

"I need you too, Edge," she spoke desperately with a longing look in her rich purple eyes, to which Kaylan let out a huff of disgust but continued forward. Though glad his psychological gambit had worked, the Maven rolled his eyes impatiently realizing he was in for another long day.

"Then if you want to stay with me you follow my rules, understand?" he started. "First rule: what I say is what happens. No arguments. Second rule: you and Kaylan will work together and act like the ladies you are. That means no squabbling and no fighting whatsoever. And third: my arm is not a toy, Kaotica. Let go." The dark girl grinned at this and slowly released him to giggle as they came to the stairs at the end of the hall. As the trio arrived at the base of the spiraling staircase they found Osric Bellinus waiting for them as promised, curiously staring at the odd combination before him. Ordering them to follow him quickly, he turned and began leading them through several more of the golden hallways decorated with crystalline sculptures and arching framework reflecting the bright sunlight from outside the various windows. A collection of servants handed them a meager breakfast as they walked, which they hurriedly forced down. At last reaching a set of open double doors leading into an expansive yet barren chamber, Edge and the two girls on his sides caught sight of a group of large white birds perched on a wide balcony outside.

Striding toward it, Osric Bellinus motioned for the two sentries at the entrance to the balcony to leave them and turned to the three youths behind him. Motioning with a sweeping gesture of his hands for them to proceed through, he announced them to the seven white robed figures waiting behind the massive birds with the golden halos set on their heads shining in the sunlight. Though previously huddled together conversing with their voices hushed, the group spread to face the trio. First Hierarch Centrioc smiled as his eyes fell upon them.

"Good morning, young ones," he spoke warmly. "I trust you slept well?" Never a question he enjoyed being asked, Edge folded his arms impatiently and ignored it.

"We understand there are Trials we must pass before we can acquire a new Granic Crystal," he started, getting to the point and once more causing Kaylan to frown at his curtness. Centrioc merely nodded.

"That is correct," he affirmed. "If Kaylan is indeed capable of wielding a miracle gem she must prove so by completing the sacred Trials."

"In the interest of time it would be of greater help to us if you simple grant us a new crystal so we can be on our way," Edge rejoined.

"I'm afraid it is not within our power to merely bestow a crystal upon anyone, young man," Centrioc returned. "The Shrine of Gavanos was constructed by the ancient Hierarchs before the separation of Godsmark from the homeland to house the remaining miracle gems and protect them. There are three Trials that lie within, safeguarding them from those who are unworthy to wield them. If you are to obtain a new gem these Trials must be overcome."

"I have to face these Trials alone, First Hierarch?" Kaylan asked doubtfully.

"No, traditionally a reclaimer is allowed a small number of guardians to accompany him or her inside the shrine," he answered. "If you so desire your companions may aid you in the Trials."

"And what exactly do these Trials entail?" Edge continued to press. First Hierarch Centrioc folded his hands before him and looked into the morning sky as if to collect his thoughts.

"As I said, there are three Trials," he began. "Unfortunately, we do not know the exact nature of the Trials as a new miracle gem has not been gathered in many years, but we have been able to discern some knowledge of what they may be. The first is the Trial of Strength, followed by a Trial of Wisdom and completed by a third Trial we have not been able to identify."

Trial of a Maven

"Well that certainly lights our way, doesn't it?" Kaotica commented sarcastically, tapping her heel impatiently.

"Wait," Edge interjected skeptically, "I thought the Hierarchs are the ones who made the Trials. How do you not know exactly what they are?" Centrioc shifted on the high balcony and glanced to the other Hierarchs to his left and right, groping for the words to respond.

"I'm afraid only reclaimers have the power to complete the Trials, not we Hierarchs, so we cannot say for ourselves what lies before you," Centrioc answered vaguely. "Much knowledge we have of the ancient Hierarchs has been lost to time."

"But aren't the Hierarchs the people who can use the Granic Crystal's power?" Kaylan asked beating Edge to the punch. "If you can't obtain them who does? What exactly is a reclaimer?"

"That is merely a term we use for those who have the chosen bloodline to pass the Trials, young one," Centrioc answered sweeping away the significance appearing to rest behind the word. "Think nothing of it. For now you should focus on what waits ahead. The Shrine of Gavanos where the miracle gems are housed lies in the mountains at the opposite side of the island. Osric will lead you there on these Fethiotts. From there it will be up to you to obtain the miracle gem within. Are you ready to proceed?" Though looking back to Edge uncertainly, Kaylan found the same doubt in his eyes as hers and knew their only option was to move forward. Replying they were ready, the Centrioc summoned Osric Bellinus and his armored men in the chamber where he stood to come forward and help them individually mount the Fethiotts. While Edge and Kaylan climbed onto the wide saddles on their feathered backs behind a soldier handling the reins, Kaotica raised her eyebrows and stood firmly on the ground when Osric Bellinus tried to help her up.

"Thanks sweetie but this girl's got her own pair of wings," she replied tersely. Edge frowned at her.

"Kaotica, get on the Fethiott," he ordered resolutely. The dark girl squinted her eyes incredulously and threw her arms in the air.

"Edge, do you honestly expect me to ride this flying slug thing when I could be anywhere on this floating rock myself in a few minutes?" she questioned in disbelief. Though ready to remind her Dark Mages would sense her power even as far away as Godsmark, he chose to keep their Drakkaidian pursuers concealed in front of the sensitive Hierarchs and merely glared her down hard.

"What is the first rule, Kaotica?" he asked her firmly, to which the girl sighed and lifted her hand for Bellinus to help her up. Silently grateful for her cooperation, the Maven looked to Kaylan to make sure she was safe and gave her a single nod to assure her everything would be alright.

"Good luck in your quest then, young ones," Centrioc smiled with a slight bow of his head. "We will see you soon." Turning to face him one last time as Osric and his men commanded the Fethiotts to beat their massive wings, Edge warily narrowed his eyes and held them that way until the white birds launched off the balcony to soar into the sky high above the busy roads and courtyards of Godsmark below. Lifting higher into the skies much faster than they had guessed the Fethiotts could travel, Edge and the girls nervously gripped the riders before them as they pulled into a high cloud cover for the Shrine of Gavanos beyond.

Chapter 35

<u>Crystal Cavern</u>

The countryside below the three Fethiotts soaring above clouds over Godsmark Isle was beautiful but hauntingly familiar to Kaylan as she gazed down at it. It really did look as if the island had been uprooted from Grandaria itself—abundant with grassy fields spotted with meadows of tall trees along the smooth rolling terrain. Only a few small villages lying adjacent to the city of Godsmark itself interrupted the beautiful green scenery. As they drew on through the blue sky toward the small mountains in the distance appearing to jut from the other side of the island, the emerald milieu beneath them gradually hardened into rocky terrain rising to one large peak in the distance. Closing in on it over the next several minutes and climbing higher and higher in the expansive sky, the Fethiotts at last began to descend on the highest peak in a much steeper dive than Kaylan or Edge particularly felt comfortable with. Gripping the riders before them who were driving the birds downward, both the Maven and the girls looked in awe to find a deep crevice running all the way down through the mountainside to a flat stone basin opening far below. Dropping into the open expanse in the otherwise unyielding mountains, the three white Fethiotts gracefully touched down on the stone earth to close their wings around them and lay down on their talons for the riders to disembark.

Edge was quick to leap off the large bird, silently thankful to be back on steady ground and rushed to the Fethiott closest to him to help Kaotica down. Accepting his hand and practically leaping into his arms thereby forcing him to catch her, the dark girl spitefully narrowed her eyes at Kaylan. As the Grandarian spied Kaotica's arms around the boy's neck, she pretended to look away and leapt off her Fethiott by herself. She swept her distrustful gaze around the crevice in the mountains and the flat area at its bottom in which she now stood with her blue eyes going wide. Behind them was one of the most magnificent views she had ever seen, revealing the path through the mountains all the way back to the gleaming city of Godsmark far on the horizon.

Hearing her companions starting forward without her Kaylan forced herself to turn to the dense walls of the crevice before them. Inspecting them more closely she observed massive transparent crystals protruding from the rock, shimmering and casting colorful rainbows like prisms in the sun around them. The crystals seemed to be larger and more clustered the farther into the crevice they walked, over twice as tall as any of them at the end where the gaping mouth of a cave opened up surrounded by the enormous gems on all sides. Glancing at Edge to read his determined face and discern what he made of this, Kaylan heard the large form of Osric Bellinus drawing a sword from behind his back. Though tightening with fret as he turned toward the Maven, she eased to find him merely holding its hilt out to him.

"You'll need this, boy," he stated in his gruff voice. Edge narrowed his eyes but tentatively accepted the blade, slinging it behind his back where he usually kept his old broadsword. Bellinus raised his hand to extend it to the opening of the cave before them. "This is the entrance to the Shrine of Gavanos. The transparent crystals you see around you are the byproducts of the inactive miracle gems gathered inside by the ancient Hierarchs who took us from the homeland. As soon as you enter, the Trials will commence. If you succeed we will be here to take you back to Godsmark. If not, may Lord Gavanos show you mercy."

"Somebody doesn't have much confidence in us, does he?" Kaotica asked sarcastically as she folded her arms. Ignoring her, Bellinus motioned for his men to pull back from the entrance to wait by their Fethiotts.

"Good luck, young ones," was his final statement as he turned to stride after his men. Watching him walk away, Kaylan gulped uncertainly and looked at Edge.

"You still don't feel good about this, do you?" she asked quietly so as not to be heard by the Godsmark soldiers. The Maven kept his eyes on Osric Bellinus for another long moment before at last glancing away to look upon her.

"Whatever I think anymore is beside the point," he spoke candidly. "We've come this far and there's no turning back. We're running out of time." They both shot an uncertain glance at their third party member who was curiously staring into one of the large transparent crystals jutting from the rock wall with hands behind her back and a mystified smile on her lips, enticed by her reflection. Giving Kaylan a single nod to reassure her once more, Edge instructed her to stay close and drew nearer to the black entrance of the cave. The dark girl turned to face them as they came.

"So are we going to do this or what, brave Maven?" she asked, giddy with childlike excitement racing through her voice, raising her body full length and fidgeting with her skirt behind her back.

"Kaotica, this isn't one of your games," he admonished quickly. "We have no idea what's in there waiting for us—we could be walking into a trap. Do you understand how serious this is?" Kaotica smiled dramatically and reached out to tug on Edge's cheek.

"Oh don't worry mister serious, I won't let the big bad cave monster get you," she toyed with him, aware she was inviting his wrath. "If you get scared I might even let you hold my hand." Seeing him about to burst with anger the dark girl raised her hands defensively and stepped forward. "Okay, okay, I'm sorry. I promise I'll be a good girl. Besides—somebody's got to keep an eye on you two or who knows what danger you'll get us into." Letting out a deep breath as she passed him and ambled toward the mouth of the cave looking around, Edge repositioned his new blade over his back and began following, telling both the girls to stay behind him as they entered. Passing through the maw of the suddenly foreboding cave, the light from the cloudy sky outside gradually slipped away the further in they ventured. Continuing forward for several long minutes without saying anything, they found the cave gradually narrowing until they were virtually consumed by darkness. Slowing to a crawl to readjust their eyes to the dim light, they continued on down the tight path in the bottlenecked cave until it at last opened up when the entrance was almost too far back to see.

The Maven came to a slow halt on the dark cave floor, staring in awe at the open cavern now lying before them. The girls slowly stepped on either side of him, curious smiles of amazement forming from the corners of their mouths at the mysteriously beautiful sight. Ahead of them stretched a narrow winding path connecting the cave entrance to a massive column of rock above them and the elaborate stone edifice resting on top of it. It was faintly illuminated in silver light exuded by the clear crystals protruding from the enormous rock walls surrounding them. Below the rising stone path endless darkness gradually consumed the silver light as if reaching out for the Shrine of Gavanos above. Turning to each other in silence, the trio exchanged amazed glances.

"It almost looks like an Elemental Temple like the ones my parents told me about," Kaylan murmured, her mere whisper echoing inside the crystalline cavern.

"Oh fun, fun, fun!" Kaotica merrily chimed, clapping her hands on each syllable. "Look how shiny all the diamonds are! I think you should get me one, Edgy." The Maven frowned at her and gave her a look that told her to focus, but as she returned his gaze he could tell she was merely toying with him once more. Forcing her flirtatious smile out of his mind Edge quietly ordered them to follow behind him and to keep a sharp eye on their footing as they started up the long stone bridge across the extensive crevice. As they drew closer to the Shrine of Gavanos beyond the pathway for the next several minutes, they could all see the structure itself giving off a faint aura of white light from its very bricks. At last stepping off the pathway for the top of the large stone column and the flat surface leading to the shrine, the group slowed once more to take in its detailed beauty. The walls of the shrine angled in to meet at its flat roof with statues of what looked to be holy swordsmen on either side riding Fethiotts. At its base there was a large entrance to the temple standing in the center. Six suites of ancient Godsmark armor flanked it, posing at attention to hold large broadswords.

Guessing the Trials and the Granic Crystal waited inside the faintly glowing shrine, Edge motioned for the girls to follow closely, carefully scanning the entrance of the shrine for any kind of concealed trap. Appearing to be safe, the Maven slowly made his way up to it easing his guard. The moment his foot stepped onto the first brick outside the entrance two lances suddenly crossed together before him with a loud clash of metal on metal echoing through the cavern air, scaring all three youths off their feet to tumble to the ground clutching their hearts. Gaping up to the crossed lances that nearly cut his head in two, Edge saw they had been extended by the empty suits of armor on either side of

… Trial of a Maven

the entrance. His eyes going wide, the Maven watched as the faint silver light around them slowly filled the cracks in the armor and beckoned them to move. Two suits abruptly leapt forward with surprising dexterity to extend their lances out for the group sitting before them. His fighter's instinct taking control, Edge immediately rolled back onto his hands to flip up and snatch the girls from the stone surface before the lances could stab out to splinter the rock where they had been.

Casting them behind him and heaving the wide sword Osric Bellinus had granted him from behind his back, the Maven savagely swung it outward to slam into the helmet of the attacking armor as it rose, knocking its head away to slam into the other beside it. With their helmets gone both bodies abruptly froze with the segments of armor falling to the ground in a heap. As they did the faint glow from inside faded but swept through the air toward the other four suits of much more illustrious armor still motionless beside the entrance to the shrine. With the white light seeping through the cracks in the bulky armor, Edge and the girls watched in horror as all four sets came alive and drew the various weapons at their sides to leap out for them. An overwhelming disbelief encompassing his face, Edge rolled to his side as the first sword wielding suit thrust out its blade for him. Rising to meet another brandishing a spiked mace the Maven dexterously parried it away and began clashing blades with the others.

Observing her protector in trouble, Kaylan forced herself to conquer her fear and leapt past a charging suit of armor to roll on the ground and pluck one of the swords from the piles of armor where Edge had downed the first of their assailants. Taking it in both her hands the Grandarian girl spun around to meet the blade of an enchanted attacker. Remembering her long training with the sword over the years from her father, Kaylan nimbly darted her blade to match her opponents while carefully dodging its clumsy slashes. Though trying to scream out for her to flee while she could, Edge found Kaylan holding her own with the skill he tended to forget she possessed and focused on savagely slashing out for the helmet of the suit of armor he had knocked off balance.

"Go for the head, Kaylan!" he bellowed spinning around to slice through the fragile link between the helmet and the breastplate of the armored warrior whose body fell into a pile as had the others. The Grandarian girl blocked a horizontal slash at her middle with ease and shouted back that she was trying. Holding the enchanted foe back she tripped over a fallen metal gauntlet on the ground and lost her footing to tumble back defenseless. Parrying the mace sailing down for him and booted it away with his right foot, Edge kicked off from the earth to rush to Kaylan's side. Seeing a heavy slash coming down for her, he met the suit's blade alongside her and pushed it back with all his might. As the suit stumbled back the armor abruptly stopped as if caught in place and slammed into the ground with its various segments flying over the surface of the column.

Staring in amazement they found Kaotica standing over its decimated form with the helmet she had plucked out of the air still in her supernatural grasp. Looking up to find the final enchanted suit of armor turning to face them, she picked up a fallen shield beside her to heave it like a disc past Edge's head to slam into the other suit, dropping the rest of its body in a heap. Observing the last suit of armor in pieces behind him as well, the Maven let out a deep breath of relief and loosened his tense form alongside Kaylan.

"Are you alright?" he asked both of them, looking them up and down to make sure they were unharmed. Though Kaylan looked winded from rushing to battle so quickly, Kaotica stood with a look of disgust over her face and dropped the helmet from her right hand to sweep it through her long hair without having broken a sweat.

"Child's play," she commented coldly. Edge shook his head and frowned.

"Kaotica, I told you I don't want you using your power, remember? The last thing we need is Drakkaidians coming after us here." He turned back to the girl beside him and raised an eyebrow. "What about you?" Kaylan continued breathing hard but locked her gaze onto Edge's and nodded.

"I'm fine, thanks to you," she returned gratefully. "I guess that was the Trial of Strength." Edge nodded slowly, assuming she was right. He looked down to the pieces of armor around him. He then looked to the shrine to make sure there were no more suits lurking that he hadn't noticed. Though not seeing any more, a rustling at his feet caused him to stare down in dread. The faint light hovering around the armor at their feet intensifying by the second, all three stood with jaws dropped as it began to fly off the ground to collect itself into a pair of legs before the entrance of the Shrine of Gavanos, followed by a bulky torso with two arms branching off either side.

"You mean this *is* the Trial of Strength," Edge returned with dread as the head of the beastly suit of armor formed from fallen helmets scattered around the ground. Filling with the most intense white light yet, the massive suit looked down with its nonexistent eyes to spot the three figures staring up at it and charged forward. Throwing its left fist where Kaotica stood the girl was knocked off her feet and sent tumbling to her right near the edge of the column while its left hammered toward Edge and Kaylan. Seeing the attack coming the Maven took hold of Kaylan and leapt to his side, rolling over the hard ground enraged. "How are we supposed to kill this thing!?!" Struggling back to her feet beside him as the armor turned for them, Kaylan shouted out that it was exuding elemental power of light. As if in response, the suit clamped its hands together and extended them toward Edge and Kaylan allowing a bursting ball of white energy to rocket toward them. Somehow sensing what the armor was going to do before it happened, Edge grabbed Kaylan's waist and brought up his forearm to attempt to summon his power at the last moment.

Just as it slammed into them the invisible barrier of power came alive to block the attack, spreading the volatile light energy around them. So intense was the force of the blast they were blown off their feet to slide to the opposite side of the column. Though tightly holding onto Kaylan, Edge felt as if he had been hit by a boulder head on. Deflecting the water from Vorkoise was completely different than actual magic as he could now feel pain tearing through his body. Rising to her knees over him, Kaylan yelled for him to get up but he was so stunned by the armor's attack he could barely breathe. While trying to pull her protector away she flipped her head up to watch the enormous suit of armor stride forward. Though its white aura of power continued rising to illuminate the entire cavern, the light behind Kaylan seemed to suddenly diminish and fade in contrast. Wheeling around, Kaylan found Kaotica hovering behind them with her electrified wings of darkness spread behind her back, surges of dark energy building around her fists. Narrowing her eyes resolutely, Kaotica dropped in front of Kaylan and

Edge with the dark purple aura of energy around her flaring to life.

Noting the foreign challenge to its power before it, the enchanted suit of armor lifted its hands once more to form an enormous ball of light in its palms. As the moments slipped by with its power peaking beyond anything Kaylan had felt before, the suit lifted the energy over its head to cast it down on the intruders before it. Frowning as the light careened toward her, Kaotica extended her hands to accept the energy as it slammed into her. Though fragmenting the ground at her feet from the force, Kaotica stood firm and tightened her fingers around the energy in her palms, clawing her grip into it. As the seconds passed by in what felt like a lifetime for Kaylan, the light began to slowly seep black with smoking darkness overtaking it. When the entire ball was consumed by the black energy, Kaotica leapt off the ground with her wings spreading and savagely heaved it back down into her foe's head. Surging purple electricity exploded forth as the armor was blasted to pieces once more, this time flying all over the cavern to slam into the walls and fall into the endless black below.

With their mammoth attacker gone and the last remnant of the dark energy dissipating into the still cavern air, Kaotica dropped back to her feet with a blank expression on her face, her field of power disappearing. As the black wings on her back dematerialized in a sharp mist, she turned back to face Kaylan and wordlessly set her hands on her hips.

"You saved us, Kaotica," Kaylan slowly spoke, to which she merely shrugged. The tingling shock shooting up and down his stunned body beginning to disperse, Edge curiously stared into the dark girl's purple eyes as they drifted to his.

"It didn't look like you did that for fun, Kaotica," he managed through his taut voice. The dark girl remained vacant, unsure what he was trying to say. With Kaylan's help the Maven rose and shook off the last pain from having used his power. "I think you did that because you knew it was right. Didn't you?" A nervous look came over Kaotica's face as her eyes passed between his and Kaylan's, staring at her uncertainly. Her face warped with confusion and she threw her arms above her head.

"Well I wasn't going to let you guys get blown away," she stated plainly. "Then who would I follow around?" Edge merely shot Kaylan a knowing glance, to which the Grandarian girl stared at him doubtfully, aware of what he was trying to get at. Ambling back to the entrance of the Shrine of Gavanos the Maven plucked his blade from the ground and rested it behind his back once more. Kaylan and Kaotica followed after him quietly, looking at each other. "Besides that thing had it coming, the annoying hunk of metal."

"I'm glad you saved us, Kaotica, but don't use your power again unless you have to," Edge reminded her dusting himself off. "Trouble tends to follow." The Maven slowly turned to cast his gaze toward the entrance of the Shrine of Gavanos once more. "Hopefully that was the end to the Trial of Strength. Are you both ready to go in?"

"As long as you are," Kaylan returned straightening herself out. Kaotica tilted her head with a look that told them she was always ready. Nodding, Edge slowly stepped through the entrance to the shrine taking care to watch for any more booby traps that lay in wait. Passing inside, the trio found a small single chamber illuminated by more of the transparent crystals mounted on the walls. Before them was a stone doorway closed shut with a brick pedestal before it. There was a clean but ancient tablet over its top containing six holes just large enough for any of them to fit their fists inside. Shifting his puzzled gaze between the pedestal and the sealed doorway beyond it, Edge squinted in amazement to find an inscription being written over its ancient surface as if straight from a pen in a language he did not recognize. He quickly pointed toward it to get the girls' attention as the last of the message magically appeared. Shooting each other amazed glances, Edge told them to stay put while he strode forward to try to discern what language it was. As he stared at the inscription the puzzled frown on his face deepened.

"It's in gibberish," he spoke turning back to the girls still staring at the pedestal. Kaotica looked up raising an eyebrow, her right hand with a surge of electrified purple energy flashing to life.

"Who cares what it's in? If it won't open we'll make it open," she spoke vigorously. Kaylan spun her head to the dark girl with a frown and reached out to force her hand back to her side.

"Brute force won't work in here, Kaotica," she admonished quietly. "If this is a Grandarian sacred place like any other, dark power won't budge anything in here. This must be the Trial of Wisdom so let's try to figure it out before blowing everything up, okay?" Kaylan's words sinking in, Kaotica sneered and folded her arms together with the dark power fading around her hand.

"Fine, little miss killjoy," she returned rolling her purple eyes. "How are *you* going to get the door open?" Kaylan shifted her gaze back to the doorway where her Maven protector stood waiting and narrowed her eyes thinking.

"By using my head," she said stepping aside from the pedestal and making her way to the door. "This writing isn't gibberish, Edge. It's ancient Grandarian script—the language of Lord Granis before the common tongue came about."

"Can you read it, Kaylan?" Edge asked hopefully. The girl's blue eyes passed along the foreign letters on the door and slowly nodded.

"The ancient script isn't spoken anymore but my father made me learn how to read it because the prophesies left by Lord Granis are all written in this language. I should be able to…" Hearing her trail off uncertainly, Kaotica let out an impatient huff of breath and began tapping her heel on the stone floor of the small chamber.

"We're waiting," she spoke edgily. Though Kaylan shot her a quick glance of irritation, she slowly opened her mouth and pressed her finger underneath each word as she began to sound them out.

"It says, 'There are six brothers in this world that were all born together. The first runs but never wearies. The second eats but is never full. The third drinks but is always thirsty. The fourth sings a song that is never good and the last two stand before you now.'" As she finished and looked at Edge she found him already staring at her with a befuddled look on his face.

"It's a riddle," he observed out loud. "Do you know what it means?" Running the words through her head once more, Kaylan desperately groped for any clue as to what the enigma could have meant but couldn't think of anything. The part about the last two standing before them didn't make any sense—they were the only things in the chamber besides the pedestal and the door. Returning Edge's perplexed gaze, the two stood in silence for a long moment before a third voice from behind them abruptly spoke up.

"The elements," Kaotica suddenly chimed in, dropping her hands to her sides. Edge and Kaylan wheeled around, staring at her confused. Noting their confusion, Kaotica shot them knowing glances and placed her hands on her hips. "Six brothers. Water, who runs but never wearies, fire, who eats but is never full, earth, who drinks but is always thirsty, and wind, who sings a song but never good. Or so they say. It's the elements." Edge and Kaylan glanced at each other, realizing it made sense. Her brow furrowing, Kaylan looked back to her dark half.

"But what about light and darkness?" she pressed. "The riddle said the last two brothers stood before us." Kaotica gave her a knowing smile.

"Well, maybe they should have said sisters then," she said playfully. "Come on, Kay-Kay, that's the most obvious part. It's you and me." Kaylan's eyes widened in shock, recognizing what she meant. If Kaotica was the embodiment of darkness, it would mean her opposite half would embody light. Light and darkness stood before them. She turned to Edge with a mesmerized look in her eyes, astonished how Kaotica had managed to solve the riddle so quickly when they could not. Remembering how different the track on which her mind rested was compared to theirs, however, she pushed it from her thoughts.

"So now what happens?" she asked puzzled once more. "We know the answer but the door isn't moving. Is that not the right answer?"

"Of course that's the right answer," Kaotica sneered offended, angrily folding her arms once more. "Yell it at the door or something." Edge shook his head as his eyes fell back upon the pedestal beside Kaotica.

"No, wait," he spoke softly, remembering the six holes he had noticed over its top before. He strode back to the pedestal curiously, an idea sparkling in his eyes. The Maven quickly pulled out a piece of flint he kept in a pouch in his black vest and leaned over to strike against the stone edge of the upper right hole of the six around its perimeter. To Kaylan and Kaotica's surprise, the moment the sparks shooting off the flint fell into the bottom of the hole they widened and spread to ignite into a bright burning flame, hovering inside the pedestal. A smile overtaking his face, he called for the girls to come beside him. Seeing what had happed for themselves they knew what they had to do and began searching for other ways to offer the six brothers to the pedestal. Reaching into the small pack on her waist Kaylan pulled out a flask of water and poured a few drops into the second hole that instantly spread to fill it full of the clear liquid.

"Is there a rock in here we could drop in?" Edge asked looking around the empty chamber. Though hesitant, Kaotica reached up into her hair to pluck the white flower she had placed there that morning and raised it before Edge's eyes.

"Will this work?" she mused hopefully. Edge shrugged but told her to try, to which the girl gently dropped it into the third hole. The flower immediately shot up blooming anew with several more flowers opening around it. Looking back to him with a smile Kaotica tipped her head graciously.

"Now how are we going to give this thing wind?" Kaylan asked from beside them with a perplexed look on her face.

"That shouldn't be too hard," Edge spoke, leaning down to mightily inhale and blow a steady jet of air from his lips into the fourth hole on the bottom of the pedestal. Amazed such a simple idea had worked, Kaylan placed her hand around the hole as he brought his head up to feel a turbulent swirling of air rising from the bottom. Kaylan smiled and shook her head at Edge.

"It's just because you're so full of hot air," she stated playful, her smile spreading to his mouth as well. Seeing there were only two more elements left, Kaylan hesitantly shifted her gaze to Kaotica. Staring at each other uncertainly, they slowly brought their hands from their sides to set them inside the last remaining holes in the pedestal. Without having to activate her power a dark mist of shadow formed around Kaotica's hand to spread into the hole, while a soft glow of radiant golden light pulsated around Kaylan's hand that spread a warmth through her she had not felt since holding the old Granic Crystal. As the two girls withdrew their hands they couldn't help but exchange smiling glances, realizing that for however much they were opposites they were in some way still the same.

With all six holes in the pedestal's surface full of an element, the trio looked up to notice the ancient inscription on the door fading, signaling the end of the second Trial. As the last letter disappeared, a deep grinding rumble sounded through the chamber as the stone door began to lift open revealing a black expanse beyond. Slowly walking from the pedestal toward the doorway as the grinding stopped and the room beyond stood revealed, the trio wordlessly shifted their gazes to one another to confirm they were ready for the final Trial and whatever lay before them. With Edge in the lead and his hand rising to the hilt of his sword, they slowly stepped through the door into the blackness and the heart of the Shrine of Gavanos.

Chapter 36

<u>Titans</u>

 It had been several hours since the battle at the Wall of Light began, signaling to its defenders their assailants would not be simply deterred with their arrows and catapults. They were there to bring down the wall or die to the last man trying. Though Tavin was hopeful the Drakkaidian horde was merely the means for Verix to prove his point that he was finished with words and they would at least pull back to wait for full siege strength to build, over the morning several thousand more Drakkaidian reinforcements arrived on the horizon to replace the ones they had downed in the initial attack. The enemy forces building with the siege towers rising in the distance quickly put out Tavin's hopes, proving the Dark Prince was investing the entirety of his army into the siege. It had come to a Third Holy War and Tavin knew full well nothing would satisfy Verix but victory.

 As the sun rose to the center of the sky over the western border mountains it was blotted out by the heavy cloud cover that had been building for the past several days along with the constant shower of arrows and catapulted boulders flying back and forth over the wall. There had been a soft rain drizzling amid the soldiers since the battle began but as the late morning came the soft rain gradually morphed into a fiercely pouring storm reflecting the rising clamor of battle. Though the Drakkaidians had persistently fired massive spears from their iron shot cannons to lift ropes and ladders to the wall for hours, not so much as a single solider had made it up without being cut down by the constant barrage of arrows or without the ladder being knocked away as they climbed. Though Tavin had stood firm at the wall since the beginning directing his troops and using his power in emergencies to knock away the huge ladders and iron shot ropes, Verix had not yet appeared aside from riding to the wall before the battle commenced. Curious why the Dark Prince and his strongest weapons had not yet been unleashed, the Warrior of Light took his first relief before noon to clean himself up and don a new set of the regal armor he found prepared in his quarters.

Taking a quick bite of a meager meal and gulping down several flasks of water, he was interrupted by a messenger sent by General Ronus rushing to alert him of something approaching on the horizon. Rising and ordering Ronus to activate the multiple reserve battalions to the wall to allow the primary troops a break after the long morning and have fresh men to face whatever was coming, Tavin rushed back to the wall top soaking wet in the downpour of thick rain. Drawing his sword as he looked over bulwark shields lining the ramparts of the wall top to the fields beyond black with Drakkaidians, his eyes drew wide with what was lumbering toward them. The enormous siege towers he had seen being erected earlier in the day were rolling toward the wall with several hundred more enemy troops at their bases. Ordering his archers to focus at the bases of the towers to slow their approach and for the ranks of swordsmen below the wall at the ready to repel invaders, he wheeled back to the towers to more closely inspect them through the falling rain. They were unlike anything he had known the Drakkaidians to have built in the previous Holy Wars, thickly coated in armor from bottom to top and stretching wide to hold twice the men of a traditional tower. There were two rows of over ten towers that would strike the wall in waves to deliver the soldiers right to the top.

The Warrior of Light shouted down the walkway for the iron shots mounted along the ramparts protruding from the wall to load. Cannons similar to the Drakkaidians lined the Wall of Light every fifty yards. Heavy stone bricks that hung over one side a rampart were connected to butterfly spears loaded into iron shots by means of thick rope. When the spears punctured one side of a siege tower close enough to unload invaders the stones were released, pulling the tower to the ground with it. Aware Verix would take this defense into account, Tavin guessed the first wave of towers would align themselves with the protruding ramparts to nullify the threat of the iron shots that could bring them down. Ordering the catapults behind the wall to take what aim they could for the siege towers when they came within range of their flaming projectiles, the Warrior of Light rushed to the central rampart in the wall where he had spoken to Verix that morning and sheathed his sword, waiting. As the siege towers came within range of the catapults and they began firing, a row of Drakkaidian iron shots once more masked by a surge of soldiers pressing forward lifted up and began firing toward the ramparts along the Wall of Light. Observing a massive iron spear headed for his position Tavin leapt to his side as it came crashing though the bulwark shield at his feet and destroyed the iron shot behind him. Realizing what the Drakkaidians were doing Tavin bellowed for one of his captains to come to him.

"Send word to the ramparts to raise the bulwark shields and pull back our iron shots until their siege towers are aligned with the wall and in range or they'll be cut down by their iron shots!" he bellowed. "And get me more scythers up here to cut these blasted ropes away from the wall! If those towers reach us we'll be overrun! We are going to hold this wall top!" With that the captain nodded and wordlessly scurried back into the fray toward his lieutenants to relay the orders. Standing full length once more the Warrior of Light tightened with determination, aware it was time to play their trump card. Clenching his fists, a faint aura of light began to shimmer around his body, at once blasting alive with circulating golden energy flowing off of him into the air. The entire wall quickly shot a glance at the shining beacon of light and called out in cheers as their greatest warrior stood tall with his power flaring around him. Waiting with his fists clenched as the siege towers drew ever closer and their bridges began to tremble with anticipation to be set down, the charging power around Tavin's fists burst alive and he threw them forward to fire a beam of golden energy into the tower before him, blasting through its armor and blowing away rows of soldiers inside to fall to their deaths far below. So powerful was the energy that the entire tower toppled to its side, slamming into the trampled earth below to ensure death to whatever Drakkaidians were unlucky enough to be there.

Lowering his fists and concentrating his power around him once more, the Warrior of Light scanned the battlefield for any sign of the Dark Prince. Aware Verix would have anticipated that he would use his power against the war machines, Tavin expected the prince to summon his own power and charge to the Drakkaidian soldiers' defense as soon. Though Tavin stood alight through the storm of rain and arrows coming down around the wall there was no sign of the prince and he narrowed his eyes suspiciously. Guessing Verix was still at the rear of the army preparing the next wave of their attack, he ordered the lieutenant at the central rampart to get another iron shot in place for the second siege tower rolling toward them and to be ready to repel any invaders that made it over. Rushing through the ranks of golden plated soldiers for the next rampart beside him, Tavin balled up his right fist once more and began charging a burst of golden energy around it to be ready when he leapt onto the rampart and ordered the bulwark shield down.

    As he jumped over a dead Grandarian solider below him and onto the edge of the rampart, the Warrior of Light found the bridge of the tower rolling toward them coming down prematurely when it was still over ten yards away. Gritting his teeth and mustering the peak of his power he threw the potent energy around his fist forward to careen toward the top of the tower and its falling gate. As his bolt of golden power approached it, however, Tavin was shocked to find an even more powerful blast of dark crimson energy suddenly explode from behind the downed gate to soar into his and blow it off its trajectory. Leaping to his right just as the dark power collided into the wall to blow the bulwark shield at his feet to rubble, Tavin spun around to find Verix Montrox standing before the first row of Drakkaidian soldiers lined up behind the open gate of the tower with swords all drawn and screaming out battle cries. Before Tavin had time to rise the Dark Prince dashed onto the bridge and leapt over the ten yard gap between it and the wall. He landed before the Warrior of Light with an aura of electrified crimson power exploding around him as his boots touched down onto the wall. The Grandarian troops around him stumbled back in astonishment and fear, aware that he was the first Drakkaidian to have made it to the top of the wall in over a century. He stood full length encased in traditional royal armor, similar to the suit Tavin had seen his twisted father wear in their single encounter near the end of the Days of Destiny.

    Not hesitating in his attack, the Drakkaidian warrior slashed his massive broadsword for Tavin only just beginning to rise and draw his own. Denied the time to even unsheathe

the entirety of his blade he managed to block Verix's attack and roll away in his thick armor to flip to his feet and brace himself for the charging Dark Prince. Pulling the tip of his blade free from his sheath the Warrior of Light flexed his elemental power around his body with the aura of golden light swirling around him faster by the second. As he savagely swung out for Tavin again Verix's crimson field of power grew as well, blowing several Grandarian soldiers around him off their feet. As their blades locked again, Tavin and Verix stared each other down hard, blinding hatred mirrored in both their eyes. The growing fields of power rustled their wet capes and hair, forcing the dumping rain to fly away. Noticing the siege tower Verix had leapt from arriving at the wall to unleash several ranks of Drakkaidian soldiers onto the ramparts, Tavin pushed Verix's blade away in an attempt to summon another blast of power to blow it away. Recovering much faster than Tavin expected Verix leapt back to thrust his blade out for his opponent's side and keep him busy.

"You deal with *me* now, Grandarian," Verix stated with acid dripping from his words, obvious hatred boiling inside him. "Steel yourself!" Kicking back only to throw his blade out again, Tavin was forced to parry it away and keep his full attention on his attacker, watching helplessly as Drakkaidian soldiers leapt onto the ramparts of the Wall of Light. Savagely pressing his attack, Verix batted the Warrior of Light around the wall top, their powers exploding and knocking Grandarian's off their feet as they leapt over its narrow surface dexterously trading blows. Though Tavin held his ground, in trying to spare his men from being blasted off the wall by their power he was forced to stay on the defensive side of the clash for the next several minutes until a section of the wall top near the central rampart had been cleared by both Grandarian soldiers and the increasing numbers of Drakkaidians pouring onto the wall around them. Grandarian iron shots began firing as the towers came within range to drop their bridges onto the wall to send their massive butterfly spears through the sides and pull them down with the prodigious weight of the stones at their bases heaving them to their sides. The attack was rendered useless when many of the towers landed on the ramparts themselves however, allowing the Drakkaidians to penetrate onto the wall.

Trial of a Maven

Gritting his teeth in fury to see the black armored invaders covering the wall top from both siege towers and the ladders now landing along its side once more, the desperate need to help his men fueled his power and gave him the strength to swat Verix's incoming slash to the side and kick him off his feet. Realizing the fate of the wall ultimately rested on his and Verix's battle, he flared his golden power around him and prepared to give the prince his all. Summoning a wave of shimmering white energy around the edge of his blade as Verix rolled back to his feet the Warrior of Light arched it downward to strike where he had been and cleave the stone surface and rumble the entire wall top.

Nimbly leaping back to his feet Verix charged ahead once more to throw his right hand down and blast a spherical bolt of crimson energy into the wall with force enough to propel him into the air over Tavin. Not anticipating the errant move the Warrior of Light swung out to block the attack that never came and found his sword passing through the air and crimson energy alone. Flipping his blade down and plummeting toward Tavin as he had in their previous battle at the portal to the void, the Grandarian barely realized where his foe had gone but strafed to his left at the last minute to avoid the attack. Verix's sword caught the ends of Tavin's cape, catching him off balance and allowing the prince to reach out with his already rising hilt to slam it into Tavin's chest and lift him off the ground. Screaming at the top of his lungs for the entire Wall of Light to hear Verix threw his weight behind his sword and smashed Tavin's body into the stone surface to crumble the ground around him.

With the wind knocked out of him, Tavin could barely summon enough energy in his balled fist to blast Verix's chest and send him stumbling back to preclude the prince from stabbing him through the chest and ending their clash right there. Though his torso smoldered in golden light, Verix quickly regained his balance and thrust the tip of his glowing broadsword into the stone surface beneath him. Seeing the cracks in the stone bricks around him emanating Verix's crimson power, Tavin's eyes shot open and he flipped onto his legs to charge ahead as a beam of electrified energy rose from the ground where he had lain. With massive segments of stone exploding into the air and dropping around them Tavin was hit in the back of his head and stumbled forward directly toward the Dark Prince. With the Grandarian's guard down Verix was easily able to kick the sword from his hands and lift him off the ground, taking hold of the bloodied hair behind him. In the prince's grip, Tavin could only watch as one of his armored hands began radiating with surging dark power ready to be blasted forth. Feeding off his unyielding determination to keep fighting the Grandarian champion threw his knee up to slam into Verix's gut, stunning him yet again. Throwing his free fist forward, Tavin blasted it into the prince's face to send him tumbling.

Stumbling around to pluck his sword from the ground Tavin's eyes drifted to the battle raging beyond them and the chaos that was ensuing. Over half of the siege towers from the first wave had successfully landed on the wall to distribute waves of Drakkaidians swarming forward. The reserve ranks of Grandarian swordsman from below were being quickly overwhelmed and the catapults could not down the towers already at the wall. If the second wave of towers reached them they would be overwhelmed and the Drakkaidians could pour over the wall into the courtyard and the grounds beyond. Before he could shout an order to his captains Verix was back on his feet firing a crimson beam of energy over twice his size toward him. Dropping his blade once more Tavin opened his hands to accept it and summon his full elemental power to hold it at bay. Though aware Verix's energy would quickly overpower him as it had at the portal to the void, if he didn't hold it, the blast would soar into his troops and the ramparts behind him. Standing firm and throwing his weight into the beam, Tavin looked to his right to find a siege tower approaching them. Getting an idea, he reached one of his hands out for it and summoned a golden blast of energy from his palm to careen toward it. Seeing Tavin's attack at the last minute, Verix let up his beam to fire another superior blast of energy to blow it away and protect his men.

Knowing the Drakkaidian prince would protect his soldiers at all costs Tavin leapt forward with the last pocket of strength he had to throw himself into Verix and knock him to his feet in the split second of pause during which he had left himself open. Landing over his enemy Tavin cocked his golden fist to slam it down toward Verix's head. The Dark Prince barely dodged the blow sending Tavin's fist slamming through the stone surface. Verix quickly threw his elbow up to catch the left side of Tavin's head and stun him.

Fighting toward the edge of the decimated bulwark shield on the rampart to which they had rolled, Verix ended up on top and head butted his adversary back to the hard stone surface. His energy virtually gone, Tavin's golden field of light waned to a faint aura around his skin. Though exhausted himself, Verix reached out for his broadsword lying back on the walkway willing it to disappear and materialize in his right hand the next second in a cloud of crimson mist. Seeing Verix reaching up to send the blade through his chest, Tavin looked to his left to spy a short sword lying beside a dead Grandarian solider crushed by one of the segments of the wall Verix had uplifted with his power. Clenching it in his bloody grasp Tavin screamed and stabbed it over his head to wedge it through Verix's armor and puncture his shoulder. Dropping his sword and screaming out in anguish, Verix fell to his left but grit his teeth with fortitude to finish his mortal enemy.

Before he could summon a final blast of energy to do the job, Tavin seized on his position and kicked him with all his strength to force him over the destroyed bulwark shield and hang from the edge of the wall over fifty feet high. Though holding on with both hands the wound in his shoulder forced him to drop one. With only one hand holding his heavy form up his grip quickly weakened. Tavin's rage building once more, he opened his hand to build a surge of shimmering light around his palm to blast away what was left of the bulwark shield and Verix's grip. Rolling to his side to watch the Drakkaidian prince fall, the blood dripped from his head in the flowing rainwater and ran into his eyes. Forced to look away as Verix disappeared into the sea of black soldiers swarming below, Tavin wiped the blood away to look back down and see what fate had befallen the prince. Though frantically searching he could not find him anywhere nor any sign of the soldiers reacting. Though aware Verix was one of the strongest warriors ever to live, falling fifty feet onto soldiers with swords and lances pointed upward was enough to finish one even as powerful as he.

Looking to his right to observe the siege tower he had almost destroyed arrive alongside the wall and drop its gate, the Warrior of Light rose and flexed energy he no longer had around his body with his golden field of power flaring to life. Extending his hands as the bridge fell onto the wall, the Drakkaidian soldiers inside were met with a scream of fortitude and a final beam of golden energy blasting them away to their deaths. The siege tower itself was blown in half with its segments further splintering as they landed on the ground crushing any unlucky enough to be standing there. Lowering his hands to gasp for breath, the Warrior of Light stood alone on the destroyed rampart of the Wall of Light with his aura of golden energy fading into the rain still pouring around him. With Verix neutralized, the wall stood firm without any power strong enough to penetrate it. Shouting out for his captains to signal reinforcements from the courtyard to repel the Drakkaidians from the first wave of towers, he weakly fell to his knees over the wall top with the knowledge they held firm for now.

Chapter 37

The Choice

It was a massive chamber consumed by darkness that awaited Edge, Kaylan and Kaotica as they stepped through the doorway inside the Shrine of Gavanos that held the last of the three Trials. Inching his way into the blackness ahead carefully checking his footing with each step, Edge drew his blade from behind his back to grasp its hilt in both hands and raise it before him defensively. Just as Kaylan and Kaotica were about to ask if they should go back and try to find some kind of a torch they had missed along the walls of the last chamber, a faint glow from the massive walls of the chamber suddenly cast its silver light around them to illuminate their surroundings. Expecting the last Trial to commence, the trio was surprised to find that the chamber remained quiet. They all nervously shifted their eyes around their surroundings to find the source of the sudden light. The core of the Shrine of Gavanos looked more like the crystal cavern outside, composed of rock walls with the same transparent crystals alight with a silver luminosity they had seen before. It was the opposite end of the chamber that harbored an item that drew the trio's complete attention. Growing out of the rock wall facing them were several small golden crystals perfectly formed with equal size and symmetry.

Kaylan's jaw dropped as she realized the dim crystals along the wall were all dormant Granic Crystals—the miracle gems that powered the Sword of Granis and kept the isle of Godsmark afloat. After all they had overcome and survived to make it this far they had finally found the object they had set out to collect. Letting a faint smile cross her lips she glanced to Kaotica to find a melancholy frown sweeping across her face, turning her purple eyes away from the golden crystals at the opposite end of the chamber. Though happy that they had finally found the item that would save them, Kaylan felt a momentary pang of qualm realizing what it meant for the girl standing beside her. Forcing such thoughts from her mind, the Grandarian girl turned to Edge still staring at the golden crystals with his hands wrapped around his sword. Though she began to stride toward him he extended a hand behind him signaling her to wait. She froze uncertainly, wondering if he had seen something.

"What's wrong?" she asked in a whisper. The Maven remained still and silent for a long moment but eventually turned his head back to face her and lowered his blade.

"It's the lack of something being wrong that's got me worried," he returned suspiciously. "The Hierarchs said there would be three Trials but the Granic Crystals are sitting right over there in front our faces. Either there were only two or there's some kind of trap waiting for us."

"So what do we do?" she asked with hope in her voice, obviously thinking he had a plan. Edge took in a deep breath and let it out before placing his sword behind his back.

"Spring the trap," he replied softly. "I'll go over there and try to take one of the crystals from the wall. If something happens to me Kaotica can use her power to get you two out of here." Kaylan frowned at this and shook her head.

"And you get left behind?" she finished disbelievingly. "Edge, I'm the one who's supposed to bear the crystal. Maybe it will only budge for me. It's my responsibility—I should go."

"And my responsibility is to keep you safe at all costs," he returned turning to face her. "I won't risk anything happening to you so forget it. Wait here with Kaotica." Kaylan took a quick step toward him, worry in her blue eyes.

"Edge, I—"

"Trust me, Kaylan," he cut her off softly, raising a single gloved finger before her mouth. Seeing the enduring worry lingering in her eyes the Maven tried a faint smile from the corner of his mouth to assure her everything would be fine. Though she didn't like it Kaylan at last nodded and planted her feet next to the dark girl ambling next to her with her arms folded across her chest.

"Careful, Edgy," Kaotica smiled unfolding her arms and reaching out for the boy's chest to pull him close. "Don't do anything I wouldn't." With that she leaned in to bat her eye lashes and give him a quick kiss on his lips, at which Edge stiffened in surprise and Kaylan clenched her fists as her heart threatened to pound out of her chest in frenzy.

Kaotica pulled away slowly, flashing her alluring smile and keeping her bright eyes on the boy. He glanced uncertainly at Kaylan who looked away the moment she felt his eyes on her. Forcing the awkward position he found himself in from his mind and focusing on the task at hand, Edge swiftly turned from the girls to cautiously begin his trek across the large chamber for the opposite wall and the golden crystals resting there. As he began walking away Kaylan couldn't help but shoot Kaotica a burning glance, sensing her eyes on her with a mocking smile on her face and a confident air of superiority emanating from her expression.

Far more concerned with her Maven protector's safety as he continued forward into the chamber, Kaylan ignored her dark half's gaze and fixed hers upon Edge, gradually inching his way to the opposite wall across from them. The darkly clad boy arrived there a minute later, guardedly sweeping the wall and the floor for any obvious pitfalls he had missed. Seeing none, the Maven gulped and took a slow step forward to reach his gloved hand out for one of the many golden crystals mounted to the wall. His hand grazed upon them slowly, expecting a trap to spring the moment his touch fell to the crystal's surface. His fears were once more put to rest as nothing happened, allowing the boy to let out a deep breath. His confidence restored, the Maven wedged his fingers around the crystal protruding the farthest from the wall and grit his teeth as he pulled with all his might to heave it out with an audible cracking of stone behind it. Looking down at the brilliant golden gem silent and sleeping in his palm he inspected it to make sure it was free of blemishes and nodded to himself that it was the object for which they had come.

The Maven let a small smile escape from his lips as he reached down to tuck the powerful talisman into a pocket in his black vest, securely fastening it within. As he turned and patted his chest where the inactive Granic Crystal now lay, Edge slowed to a halt and narrowed his eyes to find the silver light emanating from the transparent crystals around the room slowly waning to let the darkness slip back once more. His body going taut with anxiety, he spun to the girls who were nervously looking around the room as well. Before he could so much as call for them to make for the doorway and get out, a violent shockwave slammed through the chamber as if in the grip of an earthquake. Knocked to his feet on the hard ground Edge watched in horror as the cavern floor suddenly split with a massive rift tearing down the center to fragment the ground around Kaylan and Kaotica's feet. With the surface holding them up quickly disintegrating, a massive crevice that stretched into the same endless black as outside the shrine opened beneath their feet. Edge's face tensed with the utmost determination and he forced himself up through the earthquake to careen toward the two girls.

As the Maven leapt forward with all speed, the clamor of the rumbling shrine around him gradually began to fade and the urgency of the situation slowed to a halt. Curiously scanning the chamber as the world seemed to freeze before him, Edge found even he had come to a complete standstill in the middle of his sprint across the failing cavern floor. His mind reeling, his terrified eyes spotted Kaylan and Kaotica hovering motionless over the disintegrating earth beneath their feet about to give way and drop them to their deaths. The silver light from the crystals in the wall steadily washed away to be replaced by a heavy grey hue encompassing all that lay before him. Desperate to know what was happening, the boy's sharp ears detected a faint voice from all around him through the silence.

"What will you do now, Lightning's Edge?" the voice asked echoing throughout his mind. "How will the famous Blue Maven escape this quandary he has worked himself into?" Though Edge could not move his mouth to speak he found himself mentally asking himself to whom the voice belonged. "Who am I, you're asking yourself? You know me better than anyone, Edge. In fact you're the only person left alive who knows—who has any memory of me at all. Don't you recognize my voice?" Edge was struck by this, realizing how familiar the voice was sounding through his mind. Hoping the voice could indeed read his thoughts he spoke inside his mind.

"What is this?" the boy silently questioned. "What's happening?"

"This is the final Trial, Edge," the voice returned, answering his question. "The Trial of Self. If you are to claim a Granic Crystal from this shrine you must be strong, wise and true to your heart. You have proven your strength and wisdom but now you and you alone must prove your purity. For you, Blue Maven, this may prove to be a difficult task. You have woven so many stories and false justifications around your life to convince yourself you are something other than who you were when born that over the years I doubt you even remember the look of your own face. The look of my face." Edge's mind reeled at this, suddenly hearing the sound of footsteps behind him. Amazed at how the unknown other was somehow moving closer to him amidst the frozen world, Edge waited in fear for whatever was to appear. After a seemingly eternal wait Edge's mesmerized eyes at last fell upon a figure dressed in simple brown trousers and boots with a common forest tunic walking from his right to stand in front of him and look down. As his eyes drifted up to meet with the mysterious figure before him, Edge felt his heart skip a beat in astonishment.

The face that stared back at him with blue eyes and black hair sweeping off his head was his own, a familiar expression of aloof emotion on his face. Staring at himself with incredulity pounding through him, Edge found himself too stunned to formulate any words to speak.

"What's the matter, Revond?" the replica asked folding his arms. "Don't recognize your own face? Well I can't say I'm surprised—you haven't acknowledged for years the fact that I'm still alive within you."

"What is this? What are you?" Edge asked with frustrated bewilderment tearing through him.

"I already told you, Revond," the doppelganger replied. "This is the Trial of Self. It is individually tailored to fit each and every soul who makes it this far, however few there have been. To pass, you must face your true self without the illusions with which you have masked me over the years to paint me as something else. Some who are faced with this Trial can accept what they see but others go insane when they are forced to look upon their true face. I am who you really are in the deepest part of your soul; the person you were born to be and have continued to be beneath this veneer of a Maven you have made yourself out to be." Though still frozen in place, Edge could feel a deep fear overcoming him.

"You died that night along with everyone else in the village you destroyed," Edge suddenly returned, hatred seeping from his words. The other form standing before him shook his head and leaned down to crouch to his knees.

"No Edge, you just buried me so deep within you that you forgot I was there," the figure stated. "But I have been there, growing with you in the truest part of your heart driving you forward and giving this Maven you have created the strength and the will to live. You still wear my face in the deepest pocket of your being; you are still Revond at heart."

"Don't say that name!" Edge shouted with rage in his mind. "Revond is a monster!"

"A monster is a being that destroys out of desire, Revond," the doppelganger returned. "I destroyed because of the power I was born with that Edge has used when convenient and then ran from over the years. But you can't run from it anymore, Revond. You faced it at the Mystic Tower and you face me now. And just like the power would have destroyed you if you hadn't accepted it then, you will be destroyed here if you can't accept me. You are staring into the mirror of your soul, Revond. You can either admit to the power and clarity of your heart or be consumed by it, but you must face it now." With that, the reflection of Edge's soul locked his gaze onto the Maven's face forcing him to stare into his endless blue eyes as a wave of memories and emotions sucked him inside them. All the images of his life unfolding before him, Edge was forced to remember the boy he was born as behind each and every one, subconsciously giving him the power and spirit to endure.

The boy quickly felt himself beginning to break realizing that the past he had tried to abandon all those years ago had been with him all along, driving his every decision and belief. Even if he had come to terms with the power that had destroyed the small forest village in the east, he had given up the boy named Revond years ago. The Maven, Edge, was all he knew anymore and abandoning that comfort now for what he had abandoned before was too great a trial to endure. Desperately trying to reject Revond and fall back to Edge, the boy remembered back to the night his power had awakened at the Mystic Tower and what Kaylan had said to him to save him. She was screaming that he had to accept who he was or he would die and that meant she would too because he was the only one who could save her by getting her to the new Granic Crystal. The boy forced his eyes past all the memories of his life blurring his mind and focused on the frozen image of her and Kaotica about to fall into the endless abyss in front of him. He was still the only one who could save her from the fate about to befall her. He had promised her he wouldn't let any harm come to her. Time and again he had promised. As this one truth pounded through his mind all the fear of Revond and his true self gradually began to fade into insignificance. The only thing that mattered then was saving Kaylan and finishing what he had started on this quest, whether it be Edge or Revond there at the end.

All at once the images of his life disappeared and Edge found himself staring back into the eyes of Revond, standing before him once more with a soft smile on his face.

"You can look your life in the mirror and see yourself as you are, Revond," the voice returned. "But now your real Trial awaits. You can see what's happening to them, can't you? There's only enough time to save one of them. Which will it be? Can you make that choice?" As the question soaked through him Edge didn't know how to respond. In looking into the truth of his soul he knew Revond was right. He did care for both of them; even love them, but there was no way he could get to both of them before they were consumed by the endless black below. Despite all his feelings for Kaylan that had been mounting over their long quest together he knew Kaotica was more than the demonic vessel of Drakkan that they had set out to destroy. She was a real person with a heart and soul the same as any. Could he let her fall as if she were somehow undeserving of being saved compared to her twin? Seeing Revond's frame begin to soften and become transparent, he felt the boy dissolve and sweep into his body to fill the core of his being once more.

As soon as he was gone the frozen world of grey steadily began to budge again, slowly filling with the faint silver light of the transparent crystals on the quaking rock walls around them. Realizing he was out of time and the moment to act was upon him as his foot gradually dropped onto the ground in mid-stride, his mind locked up with panic. He had to make a choice because in a second the world would be moving at full speed once more. Sweeping his eyes between the two girls both of their smiles passed through his mind. It was an impossible dilemma with no adequate or ethical solution. It would come down to his own heart. Seemingly all at once, a wave of color flushed back into the world and the violent quaking resumed, further slitting the earth beneath the girls' feet to give way and send them in free fall for the black below. Screaming in fright, Kaylan watched Kaotica's confused and disbelieving eyes sweep to her as the sudden jolt of something colliding into her and clamping its limbs around her sides snatched her from midair and pulled her away from the failing ground to land uncomfortably on the solid surface behind them close to the doorway of the shrine.

Kaylan rolled painfully onto her side with the her savior desperately holding onto her with all his strength taking the brunt of the sting for her, stopping as they collided with the rock wall of the chamber. Opening her eyes Kaylan witnessed Kaotica's dark form disappear into the chasm that had opened at her feet where she had been standing a moment before. The girl did not scream out in fright or call to anyone for help as she fell, but merely stared at Kaylan with a look of excruciating confusion encompassing her eyes. The quaking shockwaves ripping through the chamber and the cavern outside continued for another long minute in which Kaylan looked down to find the black gloved hands tightly holding onto her the entire time. As the freak earthquake at last faded back into the bowls of the floating island below them and the fissure in the center of the room somehow grinded shut as quickly as it had opened, the two figures sat in the still chamber for several long minutes just breathing hard.

At last, Kaylan slowly turned back to find Edge's head buried in her back, his eyes tightly sealed shut. As they at last opened, she was shocked to find tears welled up inside and slowly streaming onto his cheeks. Confused at what had evoked such emotion from him, the image of Kaotica disappearing into the crevice in the floor bounded back into her mind and she realized what he had just been forced to do. He had saved her over her dark twin.

"...You saved me," Kaylan whispered almost inaudibly, watching Edge's eyes slowly sweep up to her. He held her gaze for a long moment but at last eased his grip on her and nodded, pulling back to rest his head on the wall behind them.

"Yes," he replied with his voice choking with emotion. "I saved you." Realizing he meant that he hadn't saved Kaotica, Kaylan fell silent once more. As she watched the boy struggle to fight his emotions over what he had just done she slowly leaned against his chest, pressing her head against it. The two sat there unmoving and wordless for several long moments before Edge's eyes at last squinted, noticing a change in the silver lighting in the room. This faint aura of light was suddenly shining from the cracks in the floor where the crevice had opened and shut, rising to spread along the

Trial of a Maven

entire floor as the moments passed by. Thrusting his back off the wall uncertainly, Edge took hold of Kaylan as a faint rumbling from below shook the chamber once more. They still had to get out of the Shrine of Gavanos alive. Wondering if the there was more to the Trial of Self than he had thought, Edge forced himself to rise and shouted for Kaylan to do so as well. As they were about to turn and make for the door, a surge of purple electricity danced across the cracks in the floor and a flood of dark light blasted alive in the room. The next moment half the floor in the chamber exploded up with massive segments of stone flying everywhere. Protectively seizing Kaylan in his arms and wheeling around to guard her from the heavy debris as it fell, the quaking at last stopped and the room was illuminated by the fierce field of dark purple energy blasting in the air above the destroyed floor.

Turning around in incredulity, Edge and Kaylan found Kaotica hovering before them with her jagged wings spread on her back, an aura of dark power crackling around her bruised and bloodied body. Edge narrowed his eyes in dismay, never having seen the supernaturally empowered girl wounded before. There were several cuts on her exposed skin all trailing blood onto her torn and frayed clothing. The most dreadful thing Edge found on her decimated form was the sickening look of bewildered anguish on her face—betrayed. Her purple eyes were fixed on Edge's arms wrapped around the Grandarian girl, tears streaming down her dirtied cheeks. Both Edge and Kaylan felt their hearts sink as the shattered expression of suffering in her eyes swept over her entire body, levitating before them as if having lost everything that mattered in the world.

Though almost too ashamed to act, Edge at last released Kaylan to face her and open his mouth to speak. Before he could utter so much as a single syllable Kaotica's entire form tightened and her dark power exploded around her, pushing him back with the massive slabs of rubble grinding away from her as if in fear. With the tears still dripping from her cheeks and her voice taut with emotion she thrust her head forward to scream down at him with pain he had never heard before pouring from her voice.

"I just wanted you to love me too!" she screamed in torment, her every word stabbing into the boy before her. Before he could say a thing in response she balled up and furiously beat her wings of darkness down to blast through the ceiling of the Shrine of Gavanos and the crystal cavern beyond with the last remnant of her aura of power fading from the room as she crashed out of the mountain altogether. Raising a hand above his eyes to protect them from the stones and dust falling into the shrine after her, Edge rushed to the border of the fissure in the ground she had just made to stare up after her and the hole in the ceiling. Though screaming her name and for her to come back, the Maven realized the futility of his efforts as the seconds turned into long moments and he let his arms drop to his sides in defeat. Though standing still for a long moment he at last rotated back to amble toward the blond haired girl waiting for him at the door to the chamber. He stopped before her planting both feet in front of hers and slowly looked into her eyes with the last remaining tears falling down his soiled face.

"No matter what good I do it always ends bad," he said bleakly. "Now she's gone and we may never find her. What are we supposed to do now?" Kaylan swallowed hard but kept her strong blue eyes on his as she replied.

"We keep going," she answered taking his hand in hers. "Thanks to you we have the Granic Crystal and I'm still alive to use it. You saved me, Edge."

"I had to make a choice," he told her blankly, aware she already knew. Kaylan nodded and took a step closer, her eyes softening.

"And you chose me?" she spoke in more of a question that a statement. Edge held her gaze intently, searching the beautiful face burning in his mind in the split second he had to decide which girl he would save.

"Yes," he replied softly, aware he was answering another question hidden inside the first. Kaylan kept her eyes on his longingly, realizing the single word meant something much more as well. Though she wanted to say a thousand different things to the boy before her, she wanted to do one thing more and slowly leaned in to close her soft blue eyes and press her lips against his, gently kissing him for the long moment of still beauty that she had been yearning for. Though he had always been surprised by Kaotica's admittedly pleasant kisses, Kaylan's lips felt natural as if they had been destined to fall on his all along. Gradually kissing her back Edge felt his worries and doubts about all the strife around him temporarily disappear, granting him renewed life. As they at last slowed and pulled apart with their moist lips tenderly

Trial of a Maven

sticking to each other before separating in the fraction of space between them, Kaylan's eyes slowly opened to reveal a deep peace and bliss that had not been there since first learning of her quest weeks ago in Eirinor.

Wordlessly lowering her head to pass her forehead along Edge's face, Kaylan buried her head in his shoulder and slowly wrapped her arms around his comforting frame. Despite all the forces working against them still, somehow this assured her everything was alright and she would be safe. Letting out a deep breath Edge returned her embrace, just holding in his arms the only thing that mattered beyond the world and its troubles. As Kaylan at last pulled away she opened her eyes to quietly stare into his as he reached down into his black vest to pull out a small object in his gloved hand. Shifting her gaze down to it her eyes lit up to find a small golden crystal lying in his palm, silently waiting to be awakened.

"I think you should hold onto this," Edge told her softly. Kaylan slowly nodded, accepting the gem in her cupped hands. Though nothing happened she could instantly feel a familiar surge of a friendly presence course through her as it touched her bare skin, pledging its strength to her once she activated it. A beaming smile of hope spread across her mouth and she leaned in to kiss him once more. Slowly taking her hands to tuck the crystal into a pouch along her waist, Edge nudged her out the door for the chamber beyond and began leading her back out of the Shrine of Gavanos.

Chapter 38

<u>Betrayal</u>

The minimal cloud cover from earlier in the morning had strengthened to a building storm of dark gray billows above them as Edge and Kaylan finally stepped out of the darkness of the crystal cavern harboring the Shrine of Gavanos, squinting and raising their forearms before their eyes to shield them from the intense daylight. Stepping through the massive jaws of the cave into the flat basin of rock outside, Edge blinked rapidly to acclimatize his eyes to the normal light and scanned around them to spy the men from Godsmark who they had left behind. Squinting carefully, the Maven found Osric Bellinus and the golden armored soldiers under his command all standing motionless beside the Fethiotts they had ridden on, staring at them. Repositioning his sword over his back and glancing at Kaylan with a look of relief in his blue eyes, he nodded for her to continue following him and they began to press forward with the girl reaching out to nervously take hold of his right gloved hand.

As the pair strode forward to the large Fethiotts, Edge noticed Osric Bellinus turn to the soldier standing beside him and give him a single nod. The next moment, the soldier raised a crossbow previously hidden behind his body to point it at the pair and let a bolt fly, slamming into Edge below his left shoulder. His eyes going wide with shock, the Maven instantly froze in place and looked down to find the steel tipped bolt protruding from high on his chest. Kaylan instantly screamed out in disbelief, releasing his hand to cover her mouth in terror. Keeping his confused and stunned eyes forward, the Maven gradually fell to his knees with a weakened sensation flowing through him. Dropping to his side with tears in her eyes, Kaylan's trembling form reached down to hold his upper body upright and stare down in horror at the bolt jutting from his chest and the blood beginning to seep forth. Before she could say anything two of the Godsmark soldiers appeared behind her to take hold of her arms and heave her off the ground. The petrified Grandarian cried out Edge's name, struggling to be free. His men holding her tightly, Osric Bellinus strode closer and looked her over, folding his arms as if to wait.

"Where is the third member of your group?" he asked impassively. Though Kaylan screamed and cursed out at him to ask him what he thought he was doing, another two Fethiotts suddenly appeared from the skies to plummet down to the rocky basin inside the mountain crevice and touch down before them over the next several moments. Though curiously struggling for breath as he sat incapacitated on the hard ground with blood trickling from his wound, Edge watched as several more soldiers and a familiar white robed figure dismounted their winged steeds to stride toward them. Kaylan's face tightened with confusion and her body loosened as First Hierarch Centrioc approached and halted in front of her, a hopeful look in his eyes.

"Where is the miracle gem, young one?" he asked coolly, folding his fingers together before him. Kaylan shook her head incredulously, still unable to believe this was happening.

"...We trusted you!" she cried with her voice choking with emotion, fighting to kick her way free. Centrioc rolled his eyes impatiently and motioned for Bellinus to find it himself. The massive man quickly reached around Kaylan's side to open the few pouches around her waist, quickly finding the dormant Granic Crystal resting there. Bellinus turned to present it to Centrioc, who opened his hand for it.

"Dignified Hierarch," Bellinus stated as he dropped it into Centrioc's outstretched grasp. The Hierarch's eyes grew wide as he stared at the gem in his flat palm, slowly passing his fingers over its perfectly cut surface. As he stared at it mesmerized, Kaylan shook her head with fresh tears streaming down her cheeks again.

"I don't understand! Why are you doing this?" she cried helplessly. Centrioc at last broke his gaze from the crystal in his hands and raised his eyes to hers with his brow furrowing.

"I'm afraid we were not completely honest with you, young Kaylan," he informed her plainly. "You see, while we Hierarchs can indeed use the power of the miracle gems to keep Godsmark afloat, the power of each gem is not eternal. Like on your enchanted sword in the homeland, once every few millennia it must be replaced with a new one from the Shrine of Gavanos. But only a reclaimer with a chosen bloodline and inherent command over the element of light is capable of activating a gem's energies. As the gem on your sword failed, soon will the one keeping this island afloat. We would have likely had to return to the homeland to abduct a reclaimer to activate a new gem but as fate played out one came to us."

"So you were just using me the whole time?" Kaylan pressed in disbelief. Centrioc tilted his head to the side and let a dramatic smile spread across his lips.

"Don't think of it like that, young one," he told her. "You and your power will activate this crystal to save our world. Your purpose is still justified."

"If we don't put this crystal back on the Sword of Granis there won't be a world left to save, Centrioc!" Kaylan yelled in fury. "You have to let us go!" Smiling once more and placing the dormant crystal into a satchel at his side, Centrioc shook his head and motioned for his guards to take Kaylan back to the Fethiotts. As she was lifted off her feet screaming for Edge, Centrioc let out a deep breath and turned to Bellinus.

"Stay here and find the other girl," he ordered. "Kill her quickly. I will return to the palace with the reclaimer to prepare her for the Sacrificial Ceremony tonight." Bellinus raised an eyebrow at this.

"You'll activate the new gem so soon, Dignified Hierarch?" he asked respectfully.

"There is no point in keeping the reclaimer any longer than necessary when the current crystal is only weakening by the day," he said callously, looking down at the wounded Maven sitting in a heap before them with burning hatred scorching his eyes. "But I am not without a heart. Wait to kill this one until after the reclaimer is out of sight." With that, Centrioc wheeled around with his white robes twirling with him and he mounted his Fethiott to leave. As the soldiers bound Kaylan's hands to the saddle over the massive white bird's back and forced her to sit still as it began flapping its wings to thrust off the earth into the skies, Edge felt his heart sink to hear her screaming for him until she was too far away to hear. Though he wished with burning desire that his once hidden power would explode with his emotions as it once had in response to his desperate need to leap up and save her, the magic was no longer spontaneous and he didn't know how to focus it to heal himself as it once had on its own.

As the multiple Fethiotts faded into the clouds for the shining city of Godsmark far in the distance, Osric Bellinus slowly unfolded his arms before his golden plated chest and scratched his thick brown beard, staring down at the bleeding Maven at his feet. Unsheathing the large blade at his side, Bellinus took hold of its leather wrapped hilt with both hands and prepared to lift it to the boy's neck. As he was about to reach back to swing it he was surprised to find the Maven roll to his side and attempt to lift his sword off his back, screaming as his arm reached too high and tightened his muscles around the sharp steel in his chest. Dropping the blade in excruciating pain, Edge rose to his knees desperately trying to stand. Bellinus slowly strode forward lifting a leg to stomp the right side of his chest down and send him toppling over his back into the hard ground. Standing over him, Bellinus lifted the tip of his blade above the boy's chest preparing to shove it down. Trapped with no way to escape, Edge could only watch in defeat as an overwhelming sense of failure washed through him. After all he had accomplished and as far as he had come, he had lost the Granic Crystal, Kaylan was going to be sacrificed by the Hierarchs, and he was about to be run through.

Just as he could see Osric Bellinus thrusting his blade downward, a flash of exploding sound from behind him suddenly echoed through the crevice causing the large man to look up in confusion. His eyes going wide, Edge watched in shock as a blast of electrified purple light slammed into Bellinus to send him flying away and off the mountainside to fall to his death beyond. His mind reeling at what had happened, Edge forced himself to rise through the pain back to his knees and turned his head back. Finding nothing but feeling a jet of wind rushing past his face, he turned back in bewilderment to find Kaotica suddenly levitating before him inches above the ground with her dark wings spread and a passionate black energy dancing over her body like flame. The last Fethiott lifted off into the sky in sudden alarm as the girl lowered to the earth. All the cuts and bloodstains on her body were gone and a look of hard determination had replaced the sorrow that had been there before. Never having been so glad to see her, Edge extended a hand up for her to help him to his feet.

"Thanks, Kaotica," he managed through his pain. "Hurry, we have to go save Kaylan." Though motionless for a long moment, Kaotica slowly extended her hand to his to lift him to his feet before her with the cold expression in her purple eyes remaining. She remained silent and still as she released him, holding his nervous gaze. At last her eyes swept to the bolt protruding from his chest and she lifted her hand to it.

"You're hurt, Edge," she spoke calmly, rubbing her fingers against he shaft of the arrow. "Let me help." With that, the girl tightened her grip on the bolt and fiercely snapped away the shaft, causing Edge to scream out in anguish and fall back. Kaotica shot forward to catch his shirt in a single fist and lift the boy off his feet. "So you think I'll just forget everything and forgive you so we can rush off and save *Kaylan* again? Oh, whenever she needs to be saved you rush to help but when I need you what do you do!?! You leave me to die!" Kaotica's was screaming now and she turned to throw the boy into the cliff wall to her right, his body helpless as a rag doll in her clutches. He fell to his side in pain once more, blood rushing from his chest wound to soak his tunic and his black vest. A surge of electric energy swept over him and he was lifted back in the air, his body constricted by her grip the same as when they had first met in the Battlemount.

"Kaotica, I had to save her—"

"That's right, save miss goodie-goodie but not me!" she cut him off, flying over to him to scream in front of his face once more. "Does her life really mean that much more to you than mine!?!" Kaotica furiously beat her wings of dark light and shot into the sky with Edge following next to her, still enveloped in her dark grip. The two blasted through the clouds in the blink of an eye, Kaotica's aura of energy exploding with violent waves of power unlike anything Edge had ever seen. As they came to a jarring halt inside the clouds Kaotica's hand shot forward to grip the boy's neck and hold him away from her. "You don't even give a damn about me, do you?" Edge could see tears welling in her eyes once more as her emotions took control of her again. "No matter how much I wanted you to love me too you never even gave me a chance!"

Trial of a Maven

The girl savagely threw him back down through the clouds away from her. Plummeting through the sky at terminal velocity the boy realized he was dead now no matter what. One way or another Kaotica was going to kill him. As he continued falling past the mountain toward the rocky basin once more, Edge spied Kaotica blasting through the clouds to soar past him and catch him with her electrified grip the moment before his body would have slammed into the ground. Pulling him close, she swallowed her tears and tightened her face.

"Well that's fine with me. Since you don't care I'll go find someone who does. I'll go find this Zalnaught who wants me so bad and we'll show both of you. You'll wish you had never met me when I'm done! I hate you, Edge, I..." She trailed off then, her voice succumbing to the emotion within. Her body quaking, Edge could tell she was debating whether or not to tear him in half, something well within her power to do. Though shaking as she held him over the ground, he was surprised to find her at last simply drop him to his feet to fall onto his back in the grip of gravity. Hovering before him for a long minute staring down at his besieged eyes, she continued crying and spun around to blast off into the skies with power and speed he had never thought possible. Once she disappeared into the clouds for good and the last remnants of her electrified dark energy faded into the tense air, Edge was left alone on the rocky terrain in the peaks of Godsmark Isle struggling to hold onto life. His mind racing for any semblance of an idea, it was all he could think of to pray to Granis for a miracle.

Chapter 39

Transfusion

The clamoring of the thousands of troops mobilized around the Cathedral of Dalorosk over the past few days was a mere whisper of a distant uproar from the balcony of the Drakkaidian edifice at its highest point. The High Priest Zalnaught stood there carefully overlooked the swarm of his soldiers and the various red flags bearing the crest of the New Fellowship of Drakkan flying amid their ranks. Since receiving word from a scout two days ago that the leader of his horde in the war zone, General Nedross, had been killed in rebellion upon the arrival of Verix Montrox, he had known it was only a matter of time until the Third Holy War would begin. His belief had been proven correct earlier in the day when he sensed Verix's power erupt once more, obviously in response to the Warrior of Light at the wall. It could only mean the war had begun without him.

Zalnaught silently grit his teeth in frustration and writhed the dormant talisman of power at his side tighter in his grip. The Staff of the Ancient was still useless to him as it was; he needed the vessel of Drakkan still at large somewhere beyond the Eastern Sea. If she wasn't captured soon the war would be over before he could use its power to shift it in his favor. Even if Verix and his battalions succeeded in bringing down the Wall of Light, Zalnaught could not risk Verix uniting the two factions under one banner and robbing his rule from him until he had the power to defeat the prince. The Loyalists were already on their way to the wall—if they were victorious alongside the New Fellowship everything could be undone. The High Priest shook his head and leaned down on the wooden staff in his hands. Everything hinged on the Dark Mages recovering the vessel for him to absorb into the Staff of the Ancients before he ran out of time. Until then he had to proceed as planned. After learning of Verix's commandeering of his troops in the war zone Zalnaught had ordered the bulk of his army around the Cathedral of Dalorosk at the ready to march on Dalastrak and wipe out the Loyalists with Verix away. If he could not yet destroy the Grandarians he would at least be able to remove the thorn in his side within his own borders without the Dark Prince to interfere.

As Zalnaught continued sweeping his biting gaze over the teeming battalions of troops below, the sound of footsteps from behind him prompted him to turn and face a black robed figure and a warrior adorned in heavy black armor with crimson engravings over its surface as it came striding out onto the balcony. The High Priest let out a sigh of relief at their coming, praying for favorable news. Before either the Dark Mage or the general could bow to him Zalnaught started forward hopefully.

"What news of the mages in the east?" he pressed immediately, the tails of his robes drifting in the gusts of wind passing through them from the tempestuous skies above. The mage took a deep breath and swallowed hard, obviously tentative to relate his report.

"I have just learned that they were able to commandeer a Red Maven ship out of Listra Port, Your Excellency," he began sheepishly. "They have sensed the vessel's power which became active just this morning and are headed out for the sea to search for her." Zalnaught was still for a moment but at last let out a long breath and gave him a single nod, looking down to inspect the staff in his hands.

"Do you remember how I told you this staff would mutate and alter its physical form the more power I poured into it?" he asked suddenly, catching him off guard. "Then why is it, mage, that my staff still only looks like this!?!" As he shouted these final words Zalnaught threw the tip of the Staff of the Ancients forward toward the Dark Mage to lift him off his feet and catapult him back into the dark chamber behind him. The guards and advisors lining the chamber spun to see the Dark Mage land with an audible thud on his back, cowering away from the balcony. His face twisting in rage, Zalnaught followed after him in a steady stride with the staff outstretched before him. "Because you promised me that by now I would have enough power from the vessel to transform this pathetic piece of wood into a talisman of darkness worthy of Drakkan himself! Now, the Holy War has begun and I am still confined to this blasted church while

Verix Montrox unifies what I have strove to divide for years!" Zalnaught towered over the mage at his feet, feebly curled up into a ball in fear of the High Priest's rage. "I should have enough power to blast all of Grandaria to oblivion, but I only have the strength to do so to you." His eyes widening with terror, the mage opened his mouth to scream for mercy as Zalnaught drove the end of his staff downward to slam into the man's chest and spread a wave of invisible force around his body to tear it apart in mere moments, his very flesh dissolving into the air in a single flash.

As the last remnant of the Dark Mage's form dissipated into the atmosphere, Zalnaught wheeled around to the speechless general that had walked in with him.

"For your sake I hope you have better news to report," the High Priest breathed icily. The general instantly bowed and nodded yes, stepping forward to speak.

"The battalions you ordered mobilized are ready to march at once, Your Excellency," he stated quickly, his voice cracking with fear. "They are prepared to fight and die at the Wall of Light for the New Fellowship." Zalnaught slowly shifted his gaze back to the Staff of the Ancients in his hands and shifted in his robes.

"These troops do not march for Holy War, general," he informed plainly. "If we are to wage war and defend our nation from foes abroad we must first eliminate all our foes within our borders. You will lead this battalion to Dalastrak and raze to the ground what's left of that accursed pit. Take no prisoners, grant no clemency. Kill everything." The general's eyes blinked uncertainly at this, sweeping to the other advisors around the room mirroring his shock.

"Your Excellency, we're really going to kill our own countrymen in the midst of a Holy War?" he asked incredulously. Zalnaught twisted his head to him in rage, enmity emanating from his dark eyes.

"Either you will or I'll find someone alive who can," he barked heatedly. "Or do you prefer to join the Dark Mage in the Netherworld so quickly?" The general swiftly shook his head no and bowed, ordering the commanders under him to follow him out of the chamber to make their way back down to the base of the cathedral. As they were stepping out of the room, however, Zalnaught suddenly loosened and froze, the furious expression on his face subsiding. He slowly lifted his eyes to the balcony to stare out into the angry skies above

Trial of a Maven

the city, rolling black clouds crashing together. Noticing the High Priest's unusual stillness after such a heated display, the room fell quiet, staring at him as he remained fixated on the sky above the cathedral.

Zalnaught took an uncertain step forward, squinting hesitantly at the strange sensation suddenly present in the back of his mind. He could sense a massive power far on the horizon, somehow rocketing toward him as if soaring through the skies like lightning toward his exact position. Focusing harder on it, his jaws slipped open realizing it was rising with each passing second as it drew nearer.

Standing in confused and frightened awe as the coming power grew over the next long moments, the High Priest caught a glimpse of a flash of light within the rolling black billows on the outskirts of the city followed by the darkening of the sky over the city as if falling into night itself. Drawn to the amazing display of power like nothing he had ever sensed before, Zalnaught cautiously drifted to the entrance of his balcony, staring up at the shadowy storm clouds as flashes of purple lightning began surging forward growing more intense with each passing second. Watching the supernatural display for another moment, Zalnaught felt his heart rise into his chest at the coming of the epicenter of the dark power through the sea of clouds, abruptly stopping when right overhead at the Cathedral of Dalorosk. Gaping up in bewilderment, the High Priest and his advisors watched as the electric power surging through the dark billows focused on one point where a field of radiating purple light emerged from the sky to descend on them.

As the frightening power dropped out of the sky and plummeted downward, Zalnaught was shocked to find a darkly radiant form suddenly emerging from it, stopping to silently hover over the balcony of the cathedral with its fierce aura of darkness gently subsiding to reveal the figure hidden inside. His eyes going wide, Zalnaught saw the outline of a girl appear from behind the veil of dark power and gently drop down to the surface of the balcony to land on her feet. The girl was still electrified with dark purple surges of energy leaping off her slender body and long dark hair, falling between the pair of bat-like wings of light mounted near her shoulder blades. Examining the girl's face, Zalnaught could see tearstains covering her soft cheeks from where her bright purple eyes had been crying moments before. As her power peaked at a level he had not thought possible to originate from a single being, the High Priest shook his head in disbelief, realizing who the girl was. Somehow the vessel of Drakkan had come to him. A small smile crept insidiously from the corner of Zalnaught's mouth as he took a step toward her. The girl's suddenly biting eyes instantly swept to him and she looked him up and down.

"You're Zalnaught?" she asked quickly with hostility in her voice. The High Priest narrowed his gaze in confusion of how she knew of him but slowly nodded.

"I am," he replied gently. "And what is your name, young one?" The girl kept her eyes on him uncertainly but at last lost the biting hate mirrored within and softened in defeat.

"I'll do whatever you want," she spoke with fresh tears welling in her eyes. Zalnaught's heart began beating rapidly, his smile growing to spread across his face.

"Good..." he returned slowly, savoring this moment he had been waiting for as long as he could remember. Seeing her tears as he walked forward a look of feigned empathy enveloped his face. "Why do you cry?" The girl continued staring at the ground for a long moment but finally opened her trembling mouth.

"What do you do when the only one that can make you stop crying is the person who made you cry?" she asked suddenly, catching the High Priest off guard.

"I wish to know your story, young one, but first I need you to do something of great importance," he returned slowly ambling forward with his robes swaying around him at each step. Standing before her, the High Priest outstretched the wooden staff in his hands before her with both hands wrapped around it. Kaotica glanced at it but seemed to shrink back uncertainly, to which Zalnaught smiled. "Don't be afraid, child. The staff cannot harm you if it is your power fueling it. Touch it. Kaotica's nervous eyes swept to his at first, aware of what he held in his grasp. Her sorrow consuming her once more, however, she hesitantly reached up to place the tips of her fingers around the talisman until her hands were firmly wrapped around it alongside Zalnaught's. Letting his eyes slip shut with a beaming smile on his face, Zalnaught focused his will to the object in his hands to open the recesses of its vast power. Responding, the Staff of the Ancients slowly pulsated with a deep energy seeming to reach out and gravitate toward the immense power connected to it in the form of the dark girl. The next moment Kaotica's field of electrified power exploded around her once more, slowly passing over the surface of the staff to consume it in the dark purple aura. As the minutes passed its simple wooden surface began to change, darkening to a heavy black and twisting with sharp designs and jagged edges protruding from its tips.

After several long moments of holding still absorbing the energies of the dark girl grasping onto it, the Staff of the Ancients flashed with dark power equal to that of Kaotica's and forced both her and Zalnaught to let go. Taking a frightened step back, Zalnaught opened his mouth to observe the transformed staff levitating in the air with dark electric surges sweeping over its black surface. A twisted smile encompassing his visage, he reached out to carefully grasp it once more. Feeling the vast energy now radiating from its core, Zalnaught lifted his joyous eyes to the girl standing before him with a mixed look of shame and sorrow mirrored in her eyes as she withdrew the dark wings behind her back to stare down at the balcony floor. Slowly rotating his head back to the chamber where his advisors stood motionless with jaws dropped, he spied his general still waiting by the doorway with a look of disbelief strapped to his hard face.

"General, disregard that last order," Zalnaught spoke just loud enough to be heard. "We're going to the Wall of Light."

Part Four
Trial of a Scion

Chapter 40

<u>Desperation</u>

Edge swallowed hard in disbelief that he was somehow still alive. He was alone on the rocky expanse outside the crevice leading to the crystal caverns around the Shrine of Gavanos physically and mentally exhausted while bleeding to death. The Maven had been lying motionless for hours through the afternoon desperately fighting to hold onto what life was left in him. The sky had turned dark and foreboding as he stared up at it through the afternoon, the golden rainbow from the miracle gem holding the island aloft beginning to disappear in the veil of clouds. The wound in Edge's chest had drained much of his blood and Kaotica's furious assault on his body had weakened him to the point where he could barely draw breath. As his thoughts drifted back to both girls now gone and in danger because of his failure to keep them safe, he silently cursed himself and coughed up fresh blood. Now Zalnaught would be able to absorb Drakkan from Kaotica and Kaylan was powerless to stop him because she was about to be killed. It was over. The world would end because of his failure to protect them. He had failed as both a Maven and as the Scion of the Order of Alberic. Edge and Revond were about to die.

As this thought entered his mind, flashes of remembrance from his visions in the Sage's Draught returned to him, faintly revealing one of the many images he had seen leading him there and of the future beyond. His feelings dictating his thoughts, Edge glimpsed a vision of Kaylan in pain, levitating over a circular dais alight with a golden glow. Aware it must have been the fate that awaited her that night at the Sacrificial Ceremony Centrioc had mentioned before fleeing back to his palace, fresh tears welled in the boy's eyes once more. Through all the failures and consequences the world would have to endure because of what had transpired that morning, the thought of Kaylan suffering was the one that Edge could not bear. The beautiful Grandarian girl had been his reason for living for weeks now. If not for her he would have been dead long ago or worse—still alive but unable to bear the thought of his existence. Next to her nothing else of their quest mattered.

Edge grit his teeth and struggled to draw deeper breaths, desperately trying to summon any strength left in his broken body to rise. When none came and the images of Kaylan fading away in his vision only intensified, the boy screamed out in maddened rage. Falling limply back to the earth and the small pool of his own blood soaking his back, the boy let his eyes slip shut in defeat. He didn't have anything left to give. Edge's broken body gradually went limp as this truth echoed through his mind, the very beats of his heart slowing. As the world around him began to wane and darken, a low hum from behind the images slowly seeping through his mind began to echo throughout, blocking out all other sound around him. As it lingered the hum slowly morphed into a familiar voice sounding from all directions.

"I foretold this moment to you from the first time I revealed your heritage, young Revond," the voice spoke inside his mind. Edge's eyes remained closed but he opened his mouth to inaudibly mouth a word.

"Zeroan?" he tried to utter faintly. "Help me..."

"The doom of the world is upon you and you alone, young one," the voice continued. "This is your time and your trial in it. I cannot interfere. You are the only one with the power to save the Granic Crystal and defeat the Staff of the Ancients now that it is activated. You must endure." Letting the words seep through him Edge weakly shook his head and mentally responded in his head.

"...I'm going to die, Zeroan," he responded. "What can I do?"

"You have already accepted both your power as the scion and yourself as you truly are at heart, Revond," the voice answered. "With a pure soul you are capable of taking hold of the power dormant within that has so long besieged you. Call it forth and let it flow as it did before when needed. Become who you were born to be, scion." As the gently resonating voice began to fade from his mind the darkness blurring the images in his mind gradually dispelled, revealing a light within himself Edge could see as clearly as daylight. It was as if he was staring into his own soul. As the light grew brighter he could see both Kaylan and Kaotica illuminated within, unhurriedly looking toward him to softly smile. Realizing they were his power buried within he reached out with his spirit and took hold of them both, wrapping them together and holding them tightly in his embrace.

Still staring at the glowing power flooding his being as it dispersed, the faces of the girls came together to create that of his own staring back at him. Feeling the spirit of Revond encompassing him, the boy pulled out of himself and relaxed as the darkness that had threatened to close in on him forever was driven away and the world before him entered his eyes once more. Staring down at his chest, the bolt that had been lodged there lay beside him on the ground and the bloody hole it had caused was sealed shut without so much as a scar present on his revitalized form. There was a familiar semitransparent energy hovering around his body with a tranquil blue mist around it, moving with him and reflecting not his emotion but his resolve. Edge faintly smiled as he felt the power hovering around him bending to his will, at one with his heart and mind for the first time. As the boy's energy at last began to fill his body the voice resounding around him spoke once more, growing more centralized before him with each word.

"Edge, you did it," it spoke cheerfully. "You're controlling it!" Realizing the sound of the voice did not belong to Zeroan, Edge's eyes carefully opened to scan around him for its source. He found it at once, focusing to see a small purple frame hovering at his side with a wide smile on his wide yellow beak. Edge thrust his torso off the ground immediately, realizing who the voice belonged to. "Whoa, easy partner! You were nearly dead a few minutes ago—give yourself a second to rest or you're liable to give *me* a heart attack!" The boy shook his head incredulously as he watched Zephyr lift into the air before him with his wings spread.

"Zeph," he began groping for the words to start, "how did you get here? Are you alright? I thought you were dead..."

"I'm fine, Edge," the little sprite assured him motioning for him to lie back down and take it easy. "I told you before you can't get rid of me that easily. I was knocked away by that blast in the ocean but I've been looking for you and Kaylan ever since. I saw Kaotica's power over here this morning and

I've been scanning these hills for you ever since. When I found you a minute ago I thought you were dead but your power came out and healed you. I pulled that bolt in your chest out but you took care of the rest. You did it, didn't you? You have it under control!" Letting all his partner's words digest, the boy at last nodded yes and sat up straight on the hard earth. He slowly stared down at his gloved hands and the faint blue mist dissipating around them at his mental command.

"Yes, for the first time I think so, Zeph," he returned softly.

"But how did this happen?" Zephyr pressed frantically flying up and down. "How did you get shot in the first place? And where is Kaylan? Or has Kaotica ditched us again? What's going on here with this floating island?" Motioning for the frenzied sprite to calm down, Edge proceeded to briefly relate to him all that had transpired on the island of Godsmark since they arrived and were betrayed by the Hierarchs that morning. Finishing telling him how Kaotica had flown off to take her revenge on him by finding Zalnaught, Zephyr's face turned grave. "I knew that girl would be the end of us. What are we going to do now?" Edge held his partner's concerned gaze for a long moment before inhaling and slowly rising to his feet, his remaining energy flooding back into him. He stood tightening his body, overlooking the shining city far on the horizon of the island. The gentle breeze swayed his torn blue scarf back and forth behind him. A passionate expression of determination like nothing Zephyr had ever seen from his partner swept across his eyes and his fists tightened at his sides. As the boy stared at the city on the horizon the image of Kaylan suffering over the dais flashed into his mind once more.

"We're going to save Kaylan and get back what's ours," he declared as if already an absolute truth.

"And just how do you plan on doing that, partner?" Zephyr asked carefully. "You said this Sacrificial Ceremony is tonight and the sun is already starting to sink. How are you going to get to her in time?" Edge kept his gaze fixed on Godsmark as he responded.

"You're going to get me there and I'll take care of the rest," he returned confidently. Zephyr rose to the boy's face and raised an eyebrow.

"What does that mean?" he spoke uncertainly. "I know you're going to do what you have to but you can't just storm that entire city and fight your way through a legion of guards to get to her, Edge." The boy didn't respond but placed his gaze on the sprite with a resolute fervor within. Zephyr let out a large huff of breath and shook his head. "Edge, I want her back as badly as you do but you're talking about fighting through an entire civilization from their commoners to these Hierarchs. Even a Maven as skilled as you can't take on that many people with Granis knows what kind of magic and power they have to stop you."

"I'm not just a Maven anymore, Zephyr," the boy responded self-assuredly. "You said it yourself—the power is mine to control now. I'm going to use it." Though Zephyr was about to state his reservations once more Edge shook his head to cut him off. "I know you're concerned about me, partner but this is the only way. I have to put this right. The world's only hope is Kaylan and I'm the only one who can save her now. I know this won't be easy but you're going to have to trust me. I can do this." Zephyr held his partner's gaze tentatively, having never seen him so firm and indomitable in his life. "Are you with me, partner?" The purple sprite took a deep breath and let it out, running his miniature fingers through the long feathers stretching out of his head.

"When have I ever not been?" he replied, slowly nodding.

Chapter 41

The Ceremony

The auburn skies to the west had gradually been replaced by the fall of a moonless night by the time the gates of the Hierarch's Palace in the central city of Godsmark Isle abruptly lurched to unhurriedly spread open, allowing in the massive crowd that had been gathering outside in the city for the past several hours. As the populace of the city began pouring through the relatively small bottleneck for the gate yard beyond, a figure streaking above ramparts and rooftops quietly dropped from the eastern sky into a dark alley between two buildings in the city pathway leading toward the massive palace. The semitransparent sphere of Lift Power dissipating around his body, the darkly clad form of Edge carefully peered out from the corner of the alley to observe the crowds of citizens trudging toward the palace gates at the end of the rising stone road. Narrowing his determined blue eyes he withdrew his head back into the shadows to quickly exhale and shift his gaze to the purple Sky Sprite resting on a barrel beside him.

"My guess is this Sacrificial Ceremony is public and the Hierarchs announced it as soon as they returned from the shrine this morning," he stated in a whisper. "I have to get in there."

"So what does that mean you want me doing?" the sprite returned questioningly.

"You're our lifeline, Zeph," the boy returned pulling his gloves tight against his fingers and refastening the belt around his waist. "You keep to the shadows on rooftops and ramparts along the walls keeping an eye on me. By the time I get to Kaylan I'm sure they're going to know I'm here so we're probably going to need instant extraction. And if anything happens to me it'll be up to you to get her out of here, so don't show yourself until I've got her or I go down." Zephyr sighed deeply as his partner turned to look back out at the masses pouring down the street into the palace.

"Do you think they're going to just let you waltz in there, Edge?" he asked flustered. "The Hierarchs are going to know this Bellinus guy you told me about never came back so they have to assume you're still alive. They're going to be looking for you and if they find you they aren't going to give you a chance to get to Kaylan. You can't fight back an entire castle full of guards—plus who knows what kind of power the Hierarchs have—by yourself." Though quiet for a moment, Edge turned back into the alley to reposition the sword over his back unaffected by his partner's concern.

"I'm not sure what kind of power Centrioc and his little minions have but they're going to need every trick up their sleeve to deal with me tonight," he replied resolutely. Looking up into his partner's concerned purple eyes, Edge let out a deep breath and kneeled to his level. "I know these aren't good odds but everything depends on this, Zeph. I won't fail her again." Zephyr held the boy's gaze for a long moment, noting the unyielding sincerity within.

"Just listen for whistle cover, all right?" he at last gave in, spreading his wings to lift off the barrel. Edge gave him a single nod and watched him lift into the night sky for the palace beyond. Turning back to the last of the populace making their way up the wide city street for the palace ahead, the boy let out a deep breath of determination and forced all the doubts and insecurities from his mind to focus on the task ahead and the girl that awaited him at its end. Fusing his trained Maven instinct with the power of the scion waiting to be unleashed beneath his skin, Edge lifted his right foot and stepped into the light of the busy street to begin marching toward the Hierarch's Palace. He melted into the crowd at once, maneuvering through the horde to weave his way down their middle at a much quicker pace than the rest. Remembering his partner's words that the Hierarchs and guards would be keeping an eye out for the black clad Maven, he swept his eyes through the crowd to spy ahead a slow moving old man to his right carrying a large backpack with blankets and robes overflowing from the sides. Darting through a group of women as they neared the massive gates, Edge silently lifted one of the hanging cloaks from the man's pack without being noticed and drifted back to the center of the crowd to slowly drape it around his shoulders and lift the hood over his face.

    Disguised as best he could be in the moments he had before arriving at the towering gates to the palace, Edge kept his head down as he passed by rows of golden plated soldiers on either side of the gates sweeping the crowd with searching eyes behind their metal helms. Penetrating inside the walls undetected, the dark boy let out a sharp breath of relief and swept his eyes around to find himself in the same courtyard where Osric Bellinus had first brought Kaylan and himself to unload them from the wagon. Though the path from which they had entered the palace itself lay closed to his right, the crowds were slowly drifting to the left toward an even more massive doorway leading to an expansive area beyond which he had not noticed last time. Guessing the ceremony would take place there, the boy darted into the crowds once more to quietly drive his way through the courtyard toward the next gate.

    The Maven stopped short as he grew near a group of soldiers at the gate checking all the citizens for weapons. Listening carefully over the roar of the crowd around him he could hear a man yelling to leave any blades or bows at the entrance to the open arena beyond, simultaneously throwing confiscated weapons in a pile to his right. Realizing he would not be able to penetrate further into the palace without confronting the guards and not willing to give up his only weapon without having even found Kaylan yet, the cloaked boy turned away to shuffle out of the crowd at his left and find an alternate route into the expansive section of the palace. Scanning the walls around the gate Edge quickly found several staircases leading to a pathway atop the wall that curved into the arena beyond. He frowned, realizing the dozens of sentries at the base of the stairs coupled with the soldiers patrolling the pathway above would never let him through. Searching the courtyard for a possible distraction, the Maven spotted a large stack of wooden boxes beside a haystack in the corner of the courtyard beside him. Focusing his mind and faintly reaching out with his hand Edge made a sweeping gesture with his eyes softly pulsating blue at the same moment. The next instant the entire stack of wooden boxes slowly budged and began leaning over until the entire pile fell over into the empty portion of the courtyard behind them, scattering splintered wood in all directions.

The crowd collectively surged with fright at the loud crash, forcing the surprised soldiers along the wall to rush in confusion to try to manage the dispersing citizens. As the sentries previously holding the staircase closest to him rushed by along with three of the guards from atop the wall, Edge turned with his robes drifting behind him to quickly rush up the stone stairs for the top of the torch lit wall praying he would not be detected as he climbed. Though sure he had been noticed by someone, no shouts of alarmed soldiers sounded through the night air and the boy was able to penetrate the wall moving through a stone hallway to emerge on the other side and face the amazing sight that lay before him.

Edge was forced to slow to a halt as his eyes fell upon the expansive arena sprawling before him in the center of the Hierarch's Palace. He had never before seen anything so amazing in all of Iairia. The arena was a massive circular expanse surrounded by tall walls, holding hundreds of civilians all staring at the opposite side of the arena and the edifice that rested there. A circular column of stone rose from the surface of the arena joined together with stairs at all sides and several golden suited guards around its perimeter. Behind the massive column meticulously decorated with flowing emblems throughout was another enormous doorway leading into the heart of the Hierarch's Palace. Hovering over the castle directly above the column and lighting the night sky was the shining form of the miracle gem keeping the island aloft. Guessing the ceremony where Kaylan would be sacrificed would take place on the stone structure, Edge tightened with renewed determination and began striding along the circular pathway of the rising stone wall to the opposite end of the arena. The Maven didn't get far before another of the many guards on the wall top spied his cloaked form treading toward him, suspiciously narrowing his eyes and starting forward to halt him.

Seeing the guard coming and realizing there was no way he could hide on the wall, Edge slowed and pretended to start coughing as he continued. The guard frowned and pointed his lance toward the figure as he approached.

"What do you think you're doing up here?" he asked forcefully, though getting no response other than coughs. As the figure's coughing grew worse the soldier let his guard down uncertainly and stood beside him waiting as Edge extended a hand, signaling for him to wait. At last seeing the guard's lance drop to his side in confusion, Edge finished coughing and cleared his throat to rise full length. Before the soldier had a moment to bring up his guard Edge flew to take hold of the back of his head and heave him to the side of the ramparts of the wall and flip him over with all his strength. He fell outside the palace over thirty feet down to his death. Spinning around to see if any of the other soldiers had noticed, the Maven spied a rope coiled to his left and quickly unfurled it and cast it down the length of the inner wall. As he started his descent the sound of several regal trumpets called through the night air signaling the crowds to begin cheering wildly. Though momentarily afraid he had been caught, he immediately turned to find several armed guards passing through the doorway at the end of the arena followed by seven white robed figures one by one emerging from the hallway of the palace. Edge felt his body tense at once as another soldier emerged carrying the form of a bound girl on his back. Though he could tell she was struggling to be free, Kaylan's hands and feet were bound together by thick rope and it looked like she was drained of energy. Her clothes from that morning had been replaced by a simple white dress stretching from her shoulders to her exposed feet and her long hair fell wildly over her shoulders.

Noticing the crash of the soldier from the wall and the dropping of the large rope several more soldiers found Edge crouched on the wall and shouted out to alert each other of an intruder. Coming back to his senses, Edge forced his view from Kaylan and dropped down from the wall to land on the stone surface beyond. Though groups of soldiers rushed for the stairs to chase after him, Edge ran to meld back into the crowd and quickly discarded his robe to cast it into the crowd and disappear once more. With his blade dangerously exposed, Edge quickly unstrapped it from his back and lowered it to his side, weaving through the crowd toward the large column at the end of the expansive arena. Sweeping his eyes from the soldiers descending from the wall looking for him to his objective atop the column, Edge watched in dread as a much smaller dais rose from its center and a pair of elaborately armored soldiers laid Kaylan over it, clamping her wrists and ankles in iron shackles as she struggled to be free.

As Edge continued jostling through the crowd with revitalized desire to get to its end still far away, First Hierarch

Trial of a Maven

Centrioc moved to the front of the column to raise his hands for silence amid the cheering crowd. As they fell silent he lowered his hands with a soft smile on his face and began to speak.

"My children of Godsmark, welcome to the palace," he greeted warmly, his voice somehow carrying far louder than it should have been able to. "You have been summoned here this night to witness what has not transpired in thousands of years since the ancient days when our world first ascended into the heavens from the homeland. The miracle gem that keeps our home safely soaring through the clouds is approaching its time of renewal, and for this renewal we look to a new miracle gem that has been gathered for us by a reclaimer. Tonight this reclaimer will offer herself to the miracle gem so that its glorious shine may emerge and keep our world floating in the realm nearest to Lord Gavanos. Show your love and faith to him by applauding the reclaimer he has offered us who will give herself to confirm our hope tonight!" With that the crowd of thousands burst alive again, raising their voices in praise for Gavanos and savagely chanting "sacrifice" while pumping their fists toward the girl chained down to the column behind the Hierarchs. Gritting his teeth at the ignorance of the barbarous crowd screaming for the ritualistic sacrifice of an innocent girl at the hands of their corrupt leaders, Edge realized that while these people looked like the proud and honorable Grandarians they came from, they had fallen into a state of moral decay that rivaled Drakkaidia itself. Whatever fate that befell them this night would be deserved.

As Centrioc withdrew and made his way back to converse with the other Hierarchs, Edge at last reached the border of the cheering crowds to find a row of guards holding them back from getting too close to the stairs leading up to the top of the column. Realizing he could easily be cut down by the vast number of soldiers between himself and Kaylan before he could reach her if he merely leapt through and attempted to run for her, he urgently swept his gaze around the arena for any semblance of an idea. Aware that the top of the wall was not an option and there was no way to the open column without being seen, the Maven shot a glance at the open doorway where the Hierarchs had emerged and the soldiers were walking in and out on patrol. Getting an idea, Edge turned to find the nearest dark doorway leading to another passage away from the arena and nodded to himself with assurance.

Quickly withdrawing back into the crowd the boy darted through the masses to emerge to their right and sneak up on a soldier holding the far side of the arena. Waiting for him to look to his right toward the column, Edge raised the flat of his sheathed sword to swing it into the soldier's helmet. Several dozen people in the crowd shot shocked glances at the boy as the soldier spun around with fury in his face, chasing after him as the boy took off into the dark passageway he had spied earlier. Disappearing within, Edge pressed his back against a dark passageway and quickly unfastened his decimated blue scarf to wrap its ends around his fists. The moment he pulled it taut in his grip the soldier came running up to him to be caught by surprise with the scarf catching him around his helmet to slam into the stone wall beside him and knock him out cold.

Though the nervous people to the right of the arena who had seen the soldier disappear after the boy vigilantly waited for him to reappear over the several long moments that followed, he eventually walked out from the shadows with a dent in the back of his helmet. Though shooting each other confused glances, they let it pass from thought as the soldier stepped past his previous position to start making his way toward the large column in front of him and the other golden armed guards around it. Amazed none of the civilians had noticed how much shorter the soldier suddenly was, encased in his suit of armor, Edge felt his heart rapidly beating as he gradually approached the column in a normal walk so as not to attract any unnecessary attention. Looking up to its top he found the Hierarchs had circled around the small platform in its center, the girl lying on top of it with her golden hair draping over the sides.

Stepping toward her, Centrioc slowly pulled a small object from his robes and raised his hand to open it over her upper body. Kaylan's blue eyes were enveloped in fear as he set the dormant Granic Crystal she had found that morning on her chest, slowly withdrawing to stand back in the circle with the other Hierarchs. Each of them stood on a unique curving design engraved into the column, extending toward the pedestal in the center. In formation once more, the seven white robed figures simultaneously raised their hands toward each other and closed their eyes. Though the six Hierarchs around Centrioc began humming a faint mantra, the First Hierarch loudly threw his voice over the rest.

"Lord Gavanos, we offer this reclaimer to you to activate the miracle gem with her chosen blood," he began in prayer. "With our power from the gem of old we awake this girl's dormant light. We pray her soul is acceptable in your vast sight." With that, the Hierarchs ceased their mantra and raised their arms toward the shining miracle gem aloft in the sky above them, reaching out for its power. Soon after, the majestic engravings similar to those found in the Temple of Light began to softly palpitate with a heavy golden glow, steadily spreading through the column to the pedestal where Kaylan lay. As the light swept through the cylindrical sides of the platform to reach the top where the crying girl lay, Edge finally reached the top of the stairs near the doorway to the palace where the Hierarchs had emerged. Keeping his gaze fixed on Kaylan he found her suddenly froze as a foreign sensation took hold of her. Preparing to begin his advance toward her and the treacherous Hierarchs, Edge stopped short when a captain of the golden soldiers approached him from behind asking him what he was doing.

Trying to appease him and the rest of the soldiers gathering around him wondering what the problem was, Edge saw Kaylan's eyes squint in pain as the golden glow on the pedestal below her began to spread over her body accessing the power within her soul and unnaturally trigger it out. Though constricted the moment before, Kaylan suddenly fell limply over the surface of the platform with eyes wide open, a wave of awe spreading through her body. The moment her entire form was softly glowing in the golden aura, the soldiers around Edge let him pass so they could turn to watch the column at the top of the stairs suddenly quake and grind as it began slowly ascending into the air away from him. Seeing Kaylan disappear as her head fell flaccid to her right, he took a nervous step forward gritting his teeth. This was it. He wasn't going to get any closer and if he didn't act now she would be lost to him. His eyes slowly burning crimson red reflecting his determination and the boiling power rising around his body, Edge tucked the sheathed sword in his hands behind his back and flexed his muscles, preparing to release the formulating wave of red mist around his body.

Clenching his fists, Edge ripped off his helmet and let his power explode around his body to send all the soldiers

Tales of Iairia

crowding around him blasting off their feet. The crowd instantly caught sight of the bizarre display from behind the rising column of stone, curiously peering around it to find a single soldier raising his arms up to the column and closing his eyes. His reaching fingers suddenly clenched as if grasping onto something before him, the entire massive column of stone abruptly froze where it was, the grinding noise of its ascension halting. Opening his eyes in confusion and shock, First Hierarch Centrioc broke from his position and wheeled around toward the active foreign power he sensed burning behind him. He locked his eyes onto the dark haired boy reaching up to begin lowering the entire column back down with his mind. Centrioc's face twisting with rage realizing who it was, he pointed down to the figure and bellowed out to his troops.

"That boy is an instigator trying to abduct the reclaimer!" he boomed for the entire arena to hear. "*Kill him!*" As soon as these two words resounded through the palace Edge heard the sound of rushing boots racing toward him in all directions. Spinning his head around in surprise toward the open doorway behind him, he found a brigade of Godsmark soldiers pouring forth with lances and sword points extended in his direction. Realizing he would be overrun if he didn't do something immediately, the boy swung his arms around to seize the massive double doors outside and push them shut just as the troops began pouring out, temporarily barring them inside. Unsheathing his sword as the few guards who had made it out of the doorway leapt forth at him, Edge rolled to his side to thrust his blade out and catch two of them at their feet and send them tumbling down the stairs. Looking past them Edge found scores of additional soldiers from the perimeter of the crowd racing toward him.

Pointing his blade downward, the Maven threw it skyward to uplift the stone steps they ran on sending half of their number toppling over each other and falling back to the surface of the arena. Leaping to his side to avoid a slashing blade crashing into the ground where he had been, Edge flipped onto his back and extended his hands to throw the attacking soldier off his feet into another two behind him. On the defensive once more, Edge ducked as another sword swung out for him threatening to horizontally careen through his neck. Rising with the hilt of his sword to slam it into the soldier above him while kicking out for another charging from the opposite side of the stairs, Edge looked around to find himself completely outnumbered and outmatched with the doors to the palace opening once more. Losing his footing as the rumbling of the mammoth column of stone began to rise again, Edge realized he couldn't fight off the Godsmark soldiers and stop the Hierarchs at the same time.

His eyes burning crimson, Edge let the red mist boiling around his body explode again to more violently throw the men around him off their feet far back from him while cleaving the stone surface under his feet with his power. As ranks of more soldiers charged over the ones he had downed Edge saw several Fethiotts taking flight with riders on their backs from behind the wall in the courtyard. Seeing waves of light beginning to twist around the gradually rising column now towering over him and the rest of the palace, Edge was struck with a desperate idea as several volleys of arrows began landing around him. Kicking forward to rush onto the stairs around which the column was rising, the Maven parried blades outstretched for him and swatted them away, dexterously leaping over and through ranks of soldiers screaming out to cut the boy down.

As he ran to the edge of the stairs one of the Fethiotts carrying a rider and a bowman on its back began a dive for him with its wings folded. Seeing it come and the dozens of soldiers behind him building to charge, Edge threw a hand up to knock away the two riders with his power on the Fethiott's back as it swept within twenty feet of him. As the two riders fell Edge focused his power around himself to leap from the ground as several soldiers' blades slashed out for him. Flipping in midair to land on the vertical wall of the rising column behind him, he kicked off to lunge toward the diving Fethiott sporadically pulling up without its riders. Soaring through the air with his power to lend him supernatural speed and distance he landed on the saddle over the Fethiott's back, clawing his grip onto its reins to hold on as it frantically rose back into the sky. Lifting himself onto the massive white bird as it rose, Edge focused his power once more to emanate a soft blue mist around his body that reached out the next instant and spread around the back of the Fethiott. Feeling the bird calm down and respond to him, Edge directed it to beat its wings hard and ascend toward the top of the rising column through the barrage of arrows flying around them.

Soaring up around the steadily rising stone column with the waves of light stretching over its surface, Edge and the Fethiott quickly rose above the highest peak of the Hierarch's palace. As he neared the top of the column and the white robed figures around its perimeter came into view, Edge grit his teeth with determination and swung his winged steed around to pass over its surface. Mustering his courage the Maven leapt off the Fethiott with the Hierarch's staring in horror as he dropped along the edge of the column right behind them. Seeing his figure drop from the sky Kaylan swung her head to face him with her face lighting up with shock and hope. The Granic Crystal, though still dormant and lifeless, levitated above Kaylan's chest surrounded in the same faint aura of light was she. Though she screamed Edge's name in desperation, Centrioc instantly extended a hand toward the base of the platform to summon a flash of light around the base of the Hierarchs that spread to form a dome of light around them and the girl on the platform, blocking him out.

Though unsure what the bubble of light's purpose, as he pounded against its surface solid as stone wall, the boy quickly realized he could not penetrate it. Though savagely swinging his sword against it and trying to focus his power to will it to lift, Centrioc merely smirked and shook his head.

"Whatever power you possess will do you no good here, boy," he barked spitefully. "I'm not sure how you survived but the light you see stems from the power of the miracle gem of Lord Gavanos; you cannot break it."

"I swear to Granis if any harm comes to her, the moment this shield comes down I will snatch the life right out of you, Centrioc!" Edge declared with hate dripping from his words.

"I'm afraid your threats will have no affect on Hierarchs of Godsmark, instigator," Centrioc returned. "This reclaimer must be sacrificed to activate the new miracle gem and you can do nothing to stop it." Turning from the boy to face Kaylan who was desperately crying out for her protector, Centrioc took a step toward her and extended his hands for the crystal hovering above her. Watching helplessly as the Granic Crystal lowered to her body and a flash of light burst forth from its core, Kaylan's frantic expression abruptly froze, a look of astonished awakening overcoming her glowing form. Pounding his fists against the impenetrable dome of light barring him from her, Edge felt his heart threatening to beat out of his chest as Centrioc continued inching his way toward her. His mind reeling for a plan as he spun his head around for a weakness in the bubble, he caught sight of the shimmering Granic Crystal above Kaylan was struck with an idea he couldn't believe he hadn't thought of in the first place. Staring up into the sky, he found the old Granic Crystal keeping Godsmark aloft hovering not more than sixty feet above him with the golden rainbow on each side arching down on either side. Tightening his face with fortitude, the Maven flipped the blade of his sword down and shouted out for the Hierarchs.

"Centrioc!" he blasted. "I may not be able to get to you in there, but that means you can't get to me out here!" Narrowing his eyes suspiciously and turning to face the boy in confusion, Centrioc watched as he cocked his arm and threw his sword into the sky with his power propelling it forward toward the miracle gem above them. His jaw dropping in horror, Centrioc screamed out as Edge's blade slammed into the crystal to shatter it and spread its golden power exploding forth to light the entire sky as if in the middle of the day, forcing them all to shield their eyes and look away. The intense light bright as the sun itself quickly dissipated as if it had never been, the golden aura of light circling the column quickly fading along with the Hierarch's power and the palpitating glow at their feet. With the shining dome of power between him and the boy gone, Centrioc reeled back in shock as if in the grip of a seizure.

"*What have you done*!?!" Centrioc bellowed with all his strength, collapsing to the floor on his knees. Feeling the entire island suddenly begin to shake they all looked to the sky to find the golden rainbow slowly deteriorating, falling into the darkness of the night. Not needing to see anymore to realize he had to move, Edge leapt over the downed form of Centrioc and outstretched a hand to will the shackles around Kaylan's wrists and ankles apart. Plucking the lustrous Granic Crystal from her chest to shove it into one of the pockets in his tunic, the Maven collected the frail glowing girl in his arms and stared into her eyes. Feeling the gravity beneath their feet slowly beginning to lessen, Edge realized what was happening and wheeled around to lunge off the column and plummet back down to the arena below them. Seeing the column beside them suddenly begin to fall as well,

Edge realized the entire island was in freefall alongside them. His gambit to destroy the miracle gem had doomed them all. Gritting his teeth in desperation, the Maven saw the Fethiott he had leapt from soaring to their right away from them.

Though Edge knew they could never reach it and they were going to fall to their deaths as soon as the island slammed into the ocean below them, the boy suddenly saw what he had been praying for forming around them. A semitransparent sphere of energy wrapping around his body, Edge looked up to find Zephyr taking hold of them to lift them away from the falling column and the screaming Hierarchs as they fell beside it. Pointing with his right hand for the Fethiott now circling above them, Zephyr heaved the two humans up to fly them beside the enormous bird and try to position them above it to gently set them on the saddle over its back. Summoning the blue mist of soothing energy once more to calm the Fethiott and allow him to place Kaylan in front of him as he mounted it, he rapidly commanded it higher into the sky.

Desperate to regain the altitude they had lost before Godsmark fell to meet its fate, Edge and Kaylan looked down to find the forgotten world descend into the darkness of night with the screams of thousands fading to nothing. They both flinched in horror as the sound of the island plunging into the ocean echoed up to them with the faint silhouette of tidal waves leaping up around it. Though aware Kaylan's rescue had cost an entire civilization of people their lives, Edge tightened his grip on the girl sitting before him with the knowledge the greater good depended on her safety at all costs and the morally decadent world had its fate coming. As the landmass began to drop into the depths of the ocean he held onto the Grandarian girl in his arms thanking Granis she was still alive.

The aura of light around her body at last completely fading, Kaylan forced herself to weakly turn back to her savior and stare into his exhausted eyes as he sat struggling for breath with several cuts and bruises littering his body. Though a thousand thoughts and feelings of shock and euphoria pounded through her, she could not find the words to speak—too amazed at what he had just done for her.

"I don't know what do say right now," she at last breathed almost too choked up to speak. Still breathing heavily, the boy holding her remained quiet, just blissful to have her

Trial of a Maven

safely in his arms again. With tears of joy forming over her longing eyes, Kaylan leaned back into him. "Except that I love you." Closing her eyes she lifted her head to kiss him, harder and more passionate than before. Touching down on the back of the Fethiott to draw his exhausted wings behind his back after having saved his two companions, Zephyr was surprised to find the loving exchange but silently turned to lie down and rest his drained body. Holding together for another long moment, the pair at last pulled apart and wordlessly fixed their gazes onto each other. Though dying to ask Edge how he had done anything and everything he had to get to her, Kaylan's energy was virtually gone from the experience and Edge shook his head for her to remain quiet. Pushing his shoulder behind her head for her to rest on, the girl let her body completely fall into his as they looked down to watch the last remnant of Godsmark disappear into the abyss of the ocean depths.

Chapter 42

Penetration

"Commander, bring down that ladder!" was Tavin Tieloc's barking order from a rampart on the Wall of Light as he shouted through the chaotic noise of battle to the central rampart where several ladders granting Drakkaidian soldiers access to the wall top had managed to concentrate. Though about to rush over and use his elemental power to blast the ladders away another surge of Drakkaidians appeared behind him along the wall, savagely throwing themselves at the overwhelmed Grandarians trying to hold their ground. Gritting his teeth and rolling to his left as a flaming projectile from an enemy catapult descended onto the rampart where he stood, Tavin leapt to his feet to pick up another bloodstained sword chilling in the cool night air and rushed to the aid of his men as the projectile slammed into the wall, loosening stone and shaking the ground once more. Fiercely swinging his blade for a Drakkaidian he spun around an incoming thrust only to parry another away the next moment. Overwhelmed, the warrior dipped into his golden power to summon a wave of energy flashing to life on the blade in his hands. With a single horizontal slash he cut clean through three Drakkaidian soldiers before they could so much as raise their blades in defense. His power active, Tavin wheeled around and extended an open hand toward the group of ladders where Drakkaidian troops were pouring onto the wall top and discharged a shimmering blast of volatile light to careen out and splinter them to shreds.

With the Drakkaidians temporarily contained, the exhausted Warrior of Light turned back to the torch lit courtyard behind the wall. His taut form covered in the scratched and slashed armor loosened as he moved, nearly ready to fall off. Scanning the wall top for one of his captains he at last stopped one rushing to a besieged rampart with sword in hand. Calling out for him, Tavin dodged an arrow from the fields and stepped over a dead Drakkaidian body to shout his order.

"Relay to the catapults to cease fire!" he bellowed as loud as his lungs would allow. "Conserve ammunition until the next surge begins. They're rebuilding siege towers on the horizon." Nodding his head, the captain drew closer to put a hand on the Warrior of Light's armored shoulder.

"Sir Tieloc, you've been atop the wall for almost a day straight," he shouted. "Please retire to your quarters to refresh your armor at least until the next surge begins." Tavin shook his head as he threw his torn cape back behind him and wiped away the sweat on his forehead.

"Send for Ronus to switch out the archers for reserves first," he stated breathing hard. "And I want those provisional bulwarks repaired as soon as possible. The central rampart is almost too torn up to walk across." The captain nodded once more, taking a slight bow and ducking to run off the wall down the stairs. Though preparing to rush back to the northern side of the wall to help his men drive back the last of the Drakkaidians ferociously fighting to maintain their foothold on the wall, Tavin turned his attention to the fields of Drakkaidians beyond him as the sound of several horns sounded through the air from the rear of the first battalion. Narrowing his eyes in suspicion as the constant barrage of arrows from the Drakkaidians ceased, Tavin watched in surprise as the troops below the wall began to pull back out of range of their archers leaving the iron shots and other large weapons behind. Though the Wall of Light erupted with cheers at the sight of the Drakkaidians fleeing for the first time in the day the battle had raged, Tavin realized the Drakkaidians were far from defeated and Verix would never abandon his goal to take the wall. Though the Drakkaidian prince had not shown his face since falling from the wall two days prior, Tavin could feel he was still alive somewhere in the rear of the Drakkaidian ranks. The one thing Tavin had feared more than anything was the thought of Verix summoning his full power and merely trying to blow a hole through the wall himself. Though the Dark Prince had been weakened after their last battle, his power was still superior to Tavin's and the Warrior of Light would not be able to hold him forever.

Staring out at the battalions of Drakkaidians with his sword still firmly in his grasp, Tavin trudged to the destroyed central rampart of the still intact wall waiting for something to happen. Over the next several long minutes, the Grandarian cheers gradually fell silent seeing a bizarre scene on the field unfold. The unusually disciplined and closely controlled troops had begun shouting and swinging swords into their own ranks, breaking formations and falling into a loose mob screaming out at whatever was happening behind them. Watching in bewilderment several of the Grandarian soldiers beside Tavin stepped forward shaking their heads.

"What are they doing out there, Sir Tieloc? Is this some kind of trick?" one of them asked for the group. The Warrior of Light kept his gaze focused on the volatile scene taking place before him, a dark feeling of dread silently filling the back of his mind.

"I don't think so," he replied turning to glance at the damaged ramparts along the wall. "Something's happening back there we can't see." Tavin turned from them and began swiftly striding toward the northern end of the wall where the last pocket of Drakkaidian resistance lingered. As he walked he called loudly to reach his voice out to as many ears as he could. "Stand by for anything, men! Have the catapults at the ready and get me that new wave of archers!" With that the Warrior of Light quickened his step to a steady jog as he commanded a few soldiers standing in his path to get behind him and follow him to the northern wall to clean up the last resistance. As they made their way to the north end, however, several of Tavin's men stopped short calling out for him to look to the fields. Halting and spinning his head back to the war zone, the Warrior of Light froze to find the Drakkaidians quiet once more but parting down the middle from the rear of their number. Narrowing his eyes with suspicion again, Tavin gradually strode to the nearest rampart of the wall to observe the torches in the night slowly separate to clear a path all the way to the front line where three figures appeared on foot, unhurriedly walking out through the empty fields within range of the Grandarian longbows.

Fixing his gaze on the three figures surrounded by men with torches in hand, Tavin swept over them without recognizing any. The men on the left and in the center were draped in black and crimson robes, suggesting they were Dark Mages. The figure on the right was what caught the

Trial of a Maven

Warrior of Light's eye, however: a young girl with long dark hair. Remembering what General Ronus had told him of a dark girl destroying the Battlemount, Tavin's eyes immediately grew wide with panic and he spun his head around to scream for Ronus at once. Wheeling back to gaze out at the fields in apprehension, Tavin found the cloaked figure in the center of the three slowly pull forth a long black object from inside his robes, setting it on the ground before him. The very earth around his feet withered as it touched down and the few clouds in the night sky above the Wall of Light seemed to suddenly expand and darken by the second. Realizing something was horribly wrong, Tavin could only watch as the figure holding the dark staff in his hands slowly raised it before him with a black aura of electrified light appearing around it. Slowly lowering it to point at the center of the wall where he had just been, Tavin felt an immense familiar power radiate from the talisman. It was the same energy signature that he had sensed at both the portal to the void and the Battlemount. Turning his head to the center of the wall, Tavin dropped his sword to cup his hands around his mouth and lean forward to scream as loud as he could for his men to abandon their posts and retreat into the courtyard.

Before his voice could carry down to reach most of them, an enormous surge of dark light enveloped the space around the central figure in the field that darkened the very air around the defenders on the wall top. Looking down in bewildered horror, Tavin saw the earth at the wall's base begin radiating ominous dark energy that seeped into the very cracks between the bricks of the central wall. As the threatening light continued to expand and flare out with electric, purple flashes, the earth began to quake as the threatening glow exploded forth to heave over half of the Wall of Light out of the ground and blast its once unyielding stones into the air. Knocked off his feet and onto his back with the rest of the soldiers on the northern side of the shaking wall, Tavin stared in horror as the mammoth detonation of dark power threw hundreds of Grandarian troops into the air by the to be incinerated before they ever came down.

When the explosion of dark energy at last subsided and the ground stopped rumbling, over half of the Wall of Light was gone, massive segments of rubble still soaring through the turbulent atmosphere to drop miles away every direction, heaved up as if they were a child's play blocks.

When the air was finally quiet once more, Tavin's ears were still ringing and the world remained a blur of dark colors swirling together. Blinking rapidly and focusing his shell-shocked senses he looked ahead with wide eyes to observe a massive crater smoldering with dark waves of jagged light sunken into the earth where the center wall had been. Slowly overcoming his astonishment as the sound of thousands of cheering Drakkaidians began rushing forward in full charge from the fields of the war zone, Tavin forced himself to roll over and fumble to his feet, groping for something to help him stand. The ringing in his ears fading, he brought his gaze up to find the entire Drakkaidian army in a full charge for the decimated wall. Casting his eyes around the smoldering corpses and shocked soldiers around him, the Warrior of Light realized that even with the thousands of reserves behind the devastated wall they would not be able to hold for more than a few minutes before being completely overrun. Turning to help a soldier on his hands and knees to his feet, Tavin swallowed hard and tired to summon his beleaguered voice.

"Can you hear me?" he spoke staring into the soldier's confused eyes, to which he slowly nodded yes. "Go find General Ronus and any of his staff in the courtyard. Tell him to order a full retreat to the Battlemount at once. Spread word to all that you are able to along the way. Do you understand?" The solider was quiet at first, staring into Tavin's eyes with disbelief. Tavin's face tightened and he shouted. "I said do you understand?"

"Yes sir!" the man at last answered, coming to his senses.

"Then hurry!" Tavin told him pushing him in the right direction. Turning back to find the Drakkaidians coming within range of the archers, Tavin bellowed his voice as loud as he was able once more. "The wall is lost! All forces fall back to the Battlemount! Full retreat! Full retreat!" Though many of the soldiers rising around him stared at him with the same incredulity the man he had sent to find Ronus had, as their eyes fell upon the charging Drakkaidian horde they slowly nodded in agreement and began running for the staircases along the wall, holding their weapons tightly. Leaning down to pick up a sword at his side, Tavin shook off the last of his shock from the explosion and ran to the staircase beside him to get down to the penetrated wall and hold back the Drakkaidians for as long as he could.

As the swell of Drakkaidian troops continued to pass by him in their mad rush to the breach in the Wall of the Light, the High Priest Zalnaught stood with a deep frown over his confused face. He held the softly radiating Staff of the Ancients in his hands, palpitating with energy after expending its full power for the first time in eons. As he glanced up to the ravaged Wall of Light, however, he knew something was wrong. Shouting for his voice to be heard over the charging troops around them, the Dark Mage Zalnaught had brought with him from the Cathedral of Dalorosk stepped forward to bow and smile.

"You have done it, Your Excellence," he stated. "You have destroyed the Wall of Light!" Gritting his teeth in fury, Zalnaught spun around to forcefully slap the end of the Staff of the Ancients against the mage's face and knock him off his feet in surprise. Landing painfully on his back and reaching to his face to feel blood trailing from a cut along his cheek, he was shocked to find Zalnaught towering over him with rage in his eyes.

"Destroyed the Wall of Light you say?" he shouted. "This infernal staff should have been able to level the entire wall and the mountain range on either side! All that happened was a mere puncture in the center!"

"I don't understand, Your Excellency," the Dark Mage returned sheepishly. "You may not have brought down the entire wall but it is still destroyed—"

"I should have the power to level mountains, you imbecile!" Zalnaught returned spinning away. "Something must have gone wrong during the transfusion of power. If I had the full strength of Drakkan at my fingertips the staff would have cut a path clear through the mountains to Galantia itself. Why didn't it work?" As he ran this last thought through his head, the anger in his face slowly dissipated. The High Priest gradually turned to the dark haired girl standing beside him, staring out at the destruction before her.

"Kaotica," he called, getting her attention. "You gave me your full power before you flew us here, didn't you?" The girl stared at him uncertainly for a long moment but silently nodded.

"That's what I said," she replied passively. Zalnaught took a step closer to her with frustration filling his dangerous eyes again.

"Then why..." he stopped short, realizing for himself the answer to his question. It was obvious. The girl standing before him was the vessel of Drakkan, not Drakkan himself. It was how her power had recuperated and replenished itself after he absorbed it from her. If he wanted to soak up the dark god's full power he would need Drakkan to emerge through her completely. Gritting his teeth and closing his hands around the staff between them he silently cursed the minute detail for which he had failed to account. Staring at Kaotica he quickly came up with a solution.

"All right, Kaotica, it's time for you to take your revenge on the boy and girl you told me about," he started moving closer to her to speak into her ear. "Now is your chance to exact your vengeance. Go and destroy the Grandarian soldiers and the Warrior of Light running away into the mountains. Use as much of your power as possible. Summon it all out." Though Kaotica turned back to face him hesitantly, she slowly nodded and prepared to call forth the dark wings on her back. Before she had a chance the sound of hoof beats from the mass of soldiers still charging around them drew close and Zalnaught wheeled around to find Verix Montrox riding toward him on his black steed with an awestruck expression on his face. The Dark Prince was still severely wounded from his battle with Tavin days before but he stood firm with his long broadsword in his right hand as his jaw dropped at the devastation before him. At last turning his attention to Zalnaught and the dark girl behind him, the prince spoke.

"How?" was all he could manage to say. Zalnaught merely kept his gaze on the prince as he responded and tried his best to hide Kaotica from him.

"I have not been sitting idly in my cathedral to the north over the years, young prince," he returned cryptically. "I built power for myself that I have waited to unleash today." Though Verix narrowed his eyes in suspicion, he slowly nodded and let it pass for the moment.

"Your horses are at the rear with my personal vanguard, High Priest," he returned. "I will take over from here. Follow

Trial of a Maven

with this power of yours but do not use it again without my permission. If the Battlemount is in the disrepair you claim then Tavin will ultimately have no choice but to fall back to Galantia to make his last stand there. He will stand to fight himself but in the end he will submit to my terms to save his people." Verix fell silent then, his eyes shifting to the girl standing behind the High Priest. "Who is that?" The High Priest swallowed hard but tried his best to seem unaffected.

"The girl?" he answered. "Merely an apprentice under my wing."

"I've never known the Black Church, much less you, to take a female to become a mage, Zalnaught," Verix returned skeptically.

"You had never known me to possess power greater than your own either, yet I believe you now know the truth of the matter," the High Priest returned challengingly, to which Verix tightened but remained in control.

"Follow after the rear battalion, Zalnaught," Verix ordered kicking his steed forward toward the crater in the center of the Wall of Light. "We'll continue this later." With that the Dark Prince shot into the advancing ranks of troops pouring toward the wall, disappearing from sight quickly after. Spinning around in frustration, Zalnaught met his Dark Mage's perturbed gaze.

"Now I cannot unleash the vessel on the Grandarians," the High Priest sighed.

"Because of the prince, Your Excellency?" the mage asked puzzled. "Both you and she are strong enough to destroy him now. Why not remove him as we have been planning for years?" Zalnaught shook his head as he set his staff back on the ground.

"No, I'll need him to keep our forces united and mobilized until this is over," he answered staring back at Kaotica, searching for an idea. As the High Priest withdrew into his thoughts for another way to muster her full power and unleash the trapped God of Darkness within her, he noticed something in the back of his mind he had not acknowledged in his excitement and rage about using the Staff of the Ancients. There was a faint light power far to the south near the coast of the eastern Southland that he had not sensed in weeks. Remembering Kaotica's story of how her dormant half and the meddling Maven traveling with her had found a new Granic Crystal to restore the Sword of

Granis, he was suddenly struck with an idea to solve both his problems at once. "Kaotica, I have changed my mind." The girl beside him shifted her gaze back to him waiting for him to elaborate. "Instead of wasting your power on weakling soldiers who cannot challenge you in the least, wouldn't you rather take your vengeance on the girl who robbed Edge from you in the first place?" Kaotica's eyes fluttered doubtfully at this, unsure what he was talking about. Smiling, Zalnaught wrapped the Staff of the Ancients back in his robes and put and hand on her shoulder. "Take me to the portal to the void."

Chapter 43

Convalescence

    After escaping from the fallen isle of Godsmark earlier that night, Edge, Kaylan and Zephyr had ridden the lone Fethiott high above the clouds over the Eastern Sea for several hours until at last reaching mainland Iairia once again. Though aware every second that passed was one that Zalnaught could have been using to destroy Grandaria, the Maven also knew Kaylan was in no condition to do anything to stop him in her weakened state and the Fethiott that would transport them to the Sword of Granis was already too fatigued to keep going. Deciding to concede the night to Zalnaught so they could face him at their strongest the next day, he directed the massive white bird down to the first patch of land he saw on the coast of the eastland. It came in the form of a modest beach within a small bay cut off from the rest of the world by towering cliffs behind it. Though concerned with the large waves from the fall of Godsmark reaching the coast, Edge saw that the bay was protected by large rocks that broke waves in the crescent sides of the gulf far away from shore.

    Descending through the clouds to stretch its wings and slowly loft down onto a boulder lying in a sandy beach below them, Edge gingerly gathered the girl before him in his arms and lifted her off the Fethiott, instructing Zephyr to keep watch on their transportation while he tended to Kaylan. Softly replying he would, the miniature Sky Sprite gave him a reassuring smile that told him he was doing a good job and he was proud of him. Reading all this from his partner's eyes and smile alone, Edge gave him a single nod and reaffirmed his grip on Kaylan to carry her off the beach and lay her in a soft collection of tropical foliage where the sandy beach disappeared into the trees behind them. Remembering the packs of supplies he had seen Osric Bellinus and his men use in the saddles on their winged steeds, Edge ran back to the Fethiott on the beach to search it for anything they could use. Though hoping to find a blanket, the Maven discovered only a crossbow like the one that had shot him earlier in the day, a pack of rations and a fresh set of clothing meant for a rider. Wrapping up the golden tunic for Kaylan who was still dressed only in the thin white stitched dress the Hierarchs had put her in for the ceremony, he hurried back to her in the trees to gently lift her head and set the tunic under it as a pillow.

Immediately setting to work making a makeshift bed for the exhausted girl, Edge tore down several large palm leaves from the trees around them and neatly placed them over a patch of soft grass he found underneath the protective cover of the trees. As he worked he removed the golden Godsmark armor still adorning his body and ripped off the bloody black vest to permanently abandon it along with the uncomfortable armor, too frayed and dilapidated to stay securely on his frame. Pulling off his torn black gloves and using them to wipe the sweat from his face, he set back to work padding the makeshift bedding with more leaves from the trees around him.

When he was finishing clearing the rest of the uncomfortable undergrowth from the area, a warm sea breeze sweeping into the shore rustled the tree tops back and forth. Looking up into the trees to make sure they wouldn't have to worry about rain during their sleep, the Maven found a crystal clear night sky with the stars brilliantly shining to illuminate the world even without the moon. As he sat staring up into the sea of stars for a long moment he heard the faint sound of footsteps over the grassy earth behind him and turned to find Kaylan standing there, her golden hair and the ends of the sleeveless white dress gently wafting in the breeze revealing her curving form underneath. There was a serene expression over her searching face, her blue eyes staring into his. Before he could tell her he was almost done and she should be lying down to get her rest, she spoke just louder than a whisper.

"Do you think she's alright?" she asked. Though caught off guard by the question at first, Edge quickly guessed who she was talking about. Breaking eye contact with her he let out a soft sigh and shook his head.

Trial of a Maven

"It won't matter if she is or not after tomorrow, will it?" he returned bleakly, to which Kaylan unhurriedly ambled toward him.

"You say that like we have a choice," she spoke quickly. "If we don't destroy her she'll let Drakkan destroy the world."

"I know she has to be contained but taking an innocent life to save any amount of others is still taking an innocent life, Kaylan," he told her. "Past all her dark power and selfish recklessness she's a girl just like any other who only wanted to be loved. If there's one thing I've learned on this quest it's that just because something is light or dark doesn't mean it's necessarily good or evil. I just wish there was another way." Kaylan slowly nodded in silent agreement, continuing to come near him until her bare feet stepped beside his dark boots and she stared up into his eyes. Though he could see her groping for something she was yearning to say, her minimal strength gave out and she fell against him exhausted. The Maven carefully caught her before she could fall, gently picking her up once more to lay her down on the crude bed he had constructed. When she merely stared up at him wordlessly for the next long moments, the Maven tilted his head and swept a rarely exposed hand across her forehead to wipe a lock of her beautiful hair behind her ear. "Are you alright? They didn't... hurt you today, did they?" Kaylan shook her head.

"Only when I thought they had killed you," she said tenderly. "I couldn't bear the thought of living without you anymore." She stopped there, slowly blinking back tears and staring at him longingly. "I don't want to lose you, Edge."

"You won't, Kaylan," he promised. Holding her gaze for another long minute, Edge swallowed hard and lifted his upper body up with his free hand preparing to rise and leave her to her sleep. Before he could lift himself upright he felt Kaylan's hand gently pressing against his back, holding him down.

"Don't go," she said swiftly, catching him by surprise. Though hesitant, he knelt over her for a long moment, watching her formulate her next words. "Have you ever told anyone you loved them before, Edge?" The boy remained silent for a long moment, his desire to tell her she meant everything to him burning the back of his mind.

"No," he answered simply, almost afraid to commit to his feelings and speak the words he knew she wanted to hear. "I've never had a reason to before." Kaylan's breath grew louder as her mouth slightly opened and her hand slipped around his shoulder onto his chest, gingerly swaying back and forth over the muscle underneath his silver tunic.

"Can I give you a reason to?" she asked in a whisper, her eyes sincere. Edge remained motionless above her but at last felt his desires threatening to overflow from his body and spill on to her if he didn't move. Unsure how to respond, he merely nodded and allowed his body to slowly lower closer to hers. Feeling the heat emanate from his warm figure as he drew closer, Kaylan raised her other hand to reach down to the end of his frayed silver shirt and pulled it up revealing his hard chest. Kaylan's eyes widened in pain as she found the various scars covering his exposed skin but unhurriedly swept her fingertips along them as if to erase them from existence for that moment alone. Feeling her soft touch over his body, Edge felt the emotions that had been building inside him since their lips first came together that morning rising past his inhibitions and taking control of his heart, saturated by passion. As Kaylan pulled his tunic free of his head and laid it behind her with her arms falling above her head beside it, Edge's eyes fell upon hers to see the desire inside. Losing himself to the shared feeling between them the boy thrust his head down to her to passionately kiss her. Closing her eyes as a wave of elation flowed through her washing her worries and doubts about the coming day away, Kaylan returned his kiss and let her mind succumb to the fervent need to stay in the boy's embrace as long as she could. As they continued kissing Edge swept his right hand into her soft golden hair to pull her head into him while his left gently caressed the curves of her body down to the glossy skin exposed on her leg.

Pulling up the thin fabric along her frame as his free fingers passed along her silky skin to her waist and finally above her neck to smoothly push the dress above her raised arms, the boy found himself on his back with Kaylan revolving to lie herself on top of him, her golden tresses spilling around his head as her lips continued ardently kissing his. As the bright starlight shone white against her revealed skin and the warm breeze sweeping in from the sea stroked her with its gentle touch, the two lovers let their concerns of the world lift if only for the night and folded deeper into each other's arms thinking only of each other.

Edge awoke later that night as a chill swept down his body, slowly letting his eyes slip open to look for the warm girl that had been in his embrace as he slept. Realizing she was not beside him, the Maven forced himself to raise his head and sweep the makeshift bed for where she had gone. Looking past the trees to the shore beyond, he found a lone figure standing on the sandy beach unmoving except for her golden hair and the ends of the white dress covering her body, sweeping around her in the warm breeze. Rising from the bed to cover himself with his black pants lying beside him, the boy stepped out from the trees to wade his feet through the chilled sand and make his way toward her. Slowly walking across the beach to stand behind the Grandarian girl he stopped, expecting her to turn around. She didn't move at first, just wordlessly staring out into the sea with something in her hands. Seeing her so still the boy softly cleared his throat.

"You need to get your rest while you can, Kay," he said softly. Kaylan remained still for another long moment but at last turned her head around to stare down at his feet, her blue eyes moist.

"I'm afraid," the girl almost whispered as she stared into space, a single tear dropping down to fall from her soft cheek. Guessing she was still emotional about all that had happened earlier in the day, Edge continued forward to softly run his hands along her bare arms, gently taking hold of her.

"You don't have to be, Kaylan," he told her assuredly. "Yesterday is over and we're safe."

"But what about tomorrow?" she asked still staring at nothing. "Do you know what's going to happen, Edge?" The Maven was silent for a moment but shook his head, touching her soft hair with his face to fill his nostrils with its sweet scent.

"No," he answered softly, unable to lie to her even to make her feel better. "But I do know we're going to put this right and no matter what happens I'll keep you safe the same as yesterday." Kaylan finally raised her eyes to set them on his, searching past them into his very soul.

"What if you can't, Edge?" she asked suddenly. "What if something is supposed to happen tomorrow that you can't save me from?" Edge narrowed his eyes uncertainly at this, unaware of what she meant.

"What do you mean?" he replied worriedly. "What are you talking about?" Kaylan was forced to break her gaze from him at this, setting it on the sandy earth before her.

"I can still see the look in Kaotica's eyes from this morning when she knew she had lost you, Edge," she said at last. "It was the look of someone who had lost everything. I couldn't imagine how it must have felt but now the same feeling is in front of me, waiting." Completely lost at what she was getting at, Edge didn't know what to say.

"What's bothering you, Kaylan?" he asked worried. Slowly turning to face him with tears falling from her eyes, Edge saw the object she held in her hands. It was the Granic Crystal, faintly glowing from its core.

"You may not know what's going to happen tomorrow, Edge, but I do," she said frightened. "I... I know what I have to do but I don't want to."

"I don't understand," Edge told her baffled. "What are you trying to tell me?" The girl shifted her gaze from him to stare down at the golden gem in her palms, its steady light reaching out to her. Slowly shaking her head, she directed her eyes back to his.

"Not tonight," she told him trying to suppress the emotion rising behind her voice. "I just want to be with you without worrying about it for one more night. I'll tell you tomorrow, all right? I promise I'll tell you." Though painfully confused at what could have been troubling her, as she pressed her body against his once more he exhaled deeply trusting she would tell him when she was ready. Leaning up to wrap her arms around his neck, the Grandarian girl tilted her head to kiss him with only the sound of the waves gently lapping against the shoreline filling the night air.

Chapter 44

The Granic Crystal

Edge and Kaylan woke early the next morning as the warming rays of the eastern sun fell upon their bodies intertwined on the tropical bed Edge had constructed for them, rising to prepare for the final chapter of their quest. Rinsing themselves in the brisk ocean water off the shore, Edge pulled his torn silver tunic back over his head along with his sturdy black boots and gloves to cover his hands and feet while Kaylan dressed herself in the warm attire Edge had found in the saddle of the Fethiott, aware she would need to be warm at the frigid portal to the void when they arrived. Though the brown pants and boots were slightly too large for her delicate form, the golden tunic fit perfectly over her top with its ends stretching below her waist and the belt tightly wrapped around it. Carefully placing the awakened but still inactive Granic Crystal in a pocket over her chest, she rose from their bedding to make her way back onto the beach to find Edge warming their rations over a small fire he had started. The Maven remained sitting on a rock near the rested Fethiott as she approached, wordlessly meeting her gaze as she sat on the rock between his legs and pressed her body against his to stare at the fire with an emotionless expression on her soft face.

The comfortable silence hung as they quickly consumed the entire pack of rations over the fire, getting their fill for the day that lay ahead of them. As they finished, Zephyr dropped down from above the trees behind them to hover next to them with a smile on his wide beak.

"Morning, Kaylan," he told her amiably, sensitive to her obvious emotional state after all that had befallen her the day before. She forced a smile back to the warm sprite, slightly blushing as he smiled at her sitting in Edge's lap. "All's clear, partner." Upon hearing the report Edge silently nodded, shifting his gaze to the girl in his lap. Feeling his eyes on her Kaylan slowly turned her head to see the serious expression restored to his determined face.

"Are you ready, Kaylan?" he asked her softly, to which she gulped but nodded. Remembering that she had something to tell him but guessing she still wasn't quite ready, the Maven softly exhaled and rose with her to put out their fire and help her mount the Fethiott. Climbing up behind her with Zephyr perched on the end of the saddle behind them both, the Maven took hold of the reins and focused his mind. Summoning the serene blue mist around his frame that spread to calm the white bird, it slowly spread it massive wings and thrust itself up into the sky once more, leaving the small beach behind. Ascending above the clouds in the blue morning sky, the trio sped off for the northern Border Mountains and the ancient Grandarian talisman that rested in disrepair at their summit. Though she did not have an active Granic Crystal to point her in the right direction as the last time they had traveled for the portal to the void weeks ago, Kaylan could somehow feel their destination far beyond and pointed Edge in the right direction. Pushing the Fethiott as hard as it would fly, within two hours the warm morning air of the south had been replaced by the chill of the northern mountains along with a heavy cloud cover gently releasing faint flurries of snow the farther they penetrated into the frozen peaks. Though they would have frozen to death so high in the clothes they were wearing, Edge had retained the Lavlas Rock they had collected before the first visit to the portal and the cold barely affected them at all.

As they traveled the two had conversed little but when the snowcapped mountains of the Border Mountains came into view Edge was quick to tighten with resolve and inform Kaylan that no matter what happened she had to be careful and let him do what he had to do to protect her. The last thing he wanted was another freak explosion of power as had happened the last time they had been at the portal. Kaylan wordlessly nodded in compliance, still unwilling to divulge whatever had been on her mind since the previous night. As the pair looked down into the sprawling mountains with the cold air biting at their skin, Kaylan at last pointed to their right toward a steep glacier in the distance on the side of a rising summit. Spying it himself, Edge pulled on the reins of the Fethiott to direct it where she was pointing. Dropping

Trial of a Maven

out of the skies through the snow flurries for the top of the summit, Kaylan and Edge spotted a familiar expanse of stone stretching for hundreds of yards before them. Sweeping his meticulous gaze over the portal for anything out of the ordinary, he turned back to his Sky Sprite partner behind him.

"See anything?" he asked quickly, to which Zephyr slowly shook his head.

"The surface has been torn up since we were last here but I can't see anything down there waiting for us," he replied. "I'll go take a closer look." A sphere of Lift Power encasing him, the purple sprite shot off from the Fethiott to soar toward the opposite side of the platform. Swallowing hard and nodding to himself to confirm everything was safe, the Maven directed the Fethiott toward the earth to touch down with a soft landing on the outskirts of the mammoth stone portal. Leaping off the saddle onto the hard surface he repositioned the sword strapped to his back. Extending his arms up to her to help her down, Kaylan hopped off the Fethiott after him, careful to avoid his gaze as she came. Merely staring at her in the silence of the falling snow that somehow never touched the stone platform they stood on, Edge watched as her eyes swept in dread across the surface of the portal.

"What do you think happened here?" he asked her quietly, her eyes glancing up to his. She shook her head uncertainly, drawing closer to him and the warmth of the Lavlas Rock in his pants pocket.

"I don't know," she answered vaguely. Another long silence hanging between them, Edge shifted his gaze toward the object at rest in the center of the platform.

"Are you sure you're ready to do this?" he asked again. Kaylan swallowed hard but nodded, grasping his hand in hers to reply yes. Gripping her hand back, the Maven began slowly walking beside her for the Sword of Granis waiting for them beyond. As they strode toward it, Edge could barely believe they had finally returned with the Granic Crystal they set out to find after surviving so many times when he thought they were doomed beyond a shadow of a doubt. Reflecting over all they had fought through and accomplished to get here and the changed person he now was as a result, he felt Kaylan begin to faintly tremble beside him. Turning to face her, he found her eyes on him once more with tears welling inside.

"Edge," she spoke softly, obviously choked up by something. Slowing his steps beside her he narrowed his eyes with concern.

"What is it, Kaylan?" he asked her, confused at why she could be so upset when their quest was almost complete. She held his gaze steadily, fighting to articulate the words she knew she had to speak.

"Edge, I have to tell you something," she managed with the tears falling onto her cheeks. "I don't want to, but I have to tell you."

"You can tell me anything," he returned assuredly.

"I know..." she trailed off struggling to fight back her emotions. "But if I tell you, you have to promise me that you won't try to stop me. You have to promise." Edge tilted his head in sudden nervous bewilderment.

"I don't understand, Kaylan," he returned. "Stop you from doing what?" Swallowing her fears, the Grandarian girl finally summoned her full courage to stare into the boy's eyes and open her mouth to speak.

"Edge, I'm the only one who can activate the Granic Crystal," she said softly. "But the moment the Hierarchs awakened my power I knew it wasn't so simple. I knew I would have to make a choice today..." Before she could finish, Edge suddenly went rigid noticing from the corner of his eye a familiar dark light flashing to his left. Instinctively wrapping Kaylan in his arms he spun to his left to find an electrified blast of dark energy sailing toward them faster than he could move. Realizing they would be obliterated in an instant, the boy raised his forearm to summon what power he could into an invisible shield before him, protecting them as the dark matter slammed around them exploding with volatile energy. So powerful was the force of the blast both Edge and Kaylan were lifted off their feet to fly back and painfully land on their backs over a fissure in the stone portal. Though stunned by the sheer force of the attack, Edge instantly forced himself up and rolled to Kaylan lying beside him. Pulling her upper body off the ground as their senses slowly sharpened again, the pair wheeled around to find a familiar figure hovering beyond the edge of the portal with a dark aura of dark purple power around her slender frame and the arm extended that had just blasted them away.

Kaotica hovered there with a hateful look of pain in her purple eyes, her wings of dark light dematerializing to reveal another figure draped in flowing black and crimson robes behind her. He stepped into their view with a dark smile across his lips, holding in his hands a black staff radiating with the same field of power around Kaotica. His eyes narrowing with abhorrence, Edge realized what the object in his grip was. Kaotica had found the High Priest Zalnaught and given him her power to be absorbed into the Staff of the Ancients. They had arrived too late. The High Priest casually reached behind his back to cast the miniature frame of Zephyr onto the ground next to him, his feathers burned by dark magic that had ensnared him. As Zalnaught's eyes fell upon the darkly clad boy knelt over the portal before him, the smile on his face disappeared.

"So this is the meddlesome Maven that has been interfering with my plans," he spoke just loud enough to be heard over the large gap between them. "I expected you to be older..." Edge grit his teeth but remained silent, slowly helping Kaylan to her feet and staring at his defeated partner on the portal. Seeing the pair moving, Zalnaught turned to the dark girl hovering beside him narrowing his eyes with a dramatic expression encompassing his visage. "This is the moment you have waited for, Kaotica. The moment for which you are destined. The girl who stole your love away from you stands before you. Her very existence defies yours. Take your vengeance and destroy her now." Hearing this, Edge clenched his fists at his sides and violently shook his head.

"Kaotica, don't listen to him!" he shouted desperately. "Zalnaught is only using you! He doesn't care about you—he just wants your power! You were right about me, Kaotica! I do care about you—both of us do! Don't listen to him!" Kaotica fidgeted uncertainly at this, her wings drooping to hang behind her. His face tightening, Zalnaught neared Kaotica and whispered into her ear.

"This comes from the boy that would have let you die while he rescued his precious Grandarian instead of you. And then when you returned to him what did he want? Just to use you to save her again as if you were his tool," he snarled. "I do care about you—I want you to become what you were created to be. Summon your full power and unleash yourself on the girl."

"Kaotica please!" Edge shouted, seeing her expression turn cold once more. "I know you have a good heart inside you—you proved that to me! Don't let him tell you you're less than you know you are!"

"I am the only one who knows what you are, and you will only become that once you have destroyed the girl!" Zalnaught bellowed, pouring poison into her ear. "If he cared a thing for you why is he here to destroy you?" Kaotica tightened at this, slowly grinding her teeth together in her closed mouth as her frown deepened again. Seeing her anger rise, Zalnaught extended the Staff of the Ancients toward the two figures standing before them. "Give in to your hate, Kaotica. Finish this once and for all!" Her eyes locking onto the blond haired girl in front of her, a surge of purple electricity swept around her body and Kaotica's jagged wings spread open as she shot into the sky. Seeing her blasting toward them, Edge cursed out loud and heaved his sword from behind his back. Frantically turning he shouted to the girl behind him.

"Get to the Sword of Granis and activate the crystal, Kaylan!" he bellowed bringing his blade before him. Kaylan shook her head and stood beside him, shouting she wouldn't leave him. With Kaotica blasting toward them, he didn't have time to repeat himself as she dove on them to fire a blast of dark energy careening toward the Grandarian girl. Summoning his power and raising the flat of his sword to parry it away, the blast spiraled behind them to explode amid the rubble lying over the platform. Kaotica grit her teeth and flexed the field of dark energy around her, growing larger and more volatile by the second. Forming a wave of power around her forearm she flipped over to land beside Edge so quickly he didn't see her move and swatted him away with constricting electricity crackling around his body. As he flew to land on his back beyond them Kaylan knew she had to do something or Kaotica would blast her to ashes.

Shaking off her hesitancy she quickly reached inside her tunic pocket to pull forth the dormant Granic Crystal within. Remembering how it had felt to have her elemental power awakened around her by the Hierarchs, she concentrated as Kaotica turned for her with electrified energy blaring like a thunderstorm. Reaching out to take hold of the blond haired girl and lift her into the air with her dark power, she was

Trial of a Maven

surprised to find a bright aura of light leap up around the golden crystal in Kaylan's hands and withdrew her arm.

"I don't want to fight you, Kaotica!" Kaylan shouted, stepping back with each word. Kaotica lifted into the air once more and shook her head, fury in her eyes.

"That might mean more if you weren't here to kill me, miss goody-good," she bit heatedly. Her fury rising, the field of dark energy around her expanded to envelope the entire portal in the ominous purple light crackling with indiscriminate power. Noting the flashes of deep black streaks pulsating over her very skin, Kaylan knew Kaotica's power had peaked and Drakkan would be able to emerge from her any time he chose if she couldn't be contained. Seeing her open hands charging with twin balls of crackling dark energy, Kaylan desperately focused on the golden crystal in her grasp and extended it in front of her defensively as her dark twin savagely screamed and threw the massive bursts of energy at her. Though Kaylan's faint aura of golden light and the untapped stamina of the awakening Granic Crystal pierced the dark matter to shield her body, the stone at her feet easily gave way and exploded away as the attack careened into it. Kaylan flew back being pelted by loosened stones flying through the air in the spiraling remnants of dark energy around her.

Watching from the edge of the rumbling platform as his charge flew through the air with her very skin burned by Kaotica's potent power, Edge grit his teeth and forced himself to rise from the cold stone surface. As he lifted himself the Maven was surprised to be thrown off his feet by a painful surge of energy from his left. Spinning through the air to land on his back once more, Edge spun around to find Zalnaught leaping at him with the sharp end of the Staff of the Ancients thrusting down for him. Clasping his hands together as it plummeted down to his chest he caught the talisman in his grip and summoned all his energy to hold it back. With the full power of the staff exerted onto him, even with his awakened power the task of matching Zalnaught quickly proved to be the greatest challenge for his new strength yet. Towering over the boy with a fierce expression of hatred in his taut face, Zalnaught grit his teeth and heaved the staff downward with his full strength.

"You have hindered my plans for the last time, boy," he breathed acidly. "I don't know what power you possess but whatever it is it cannot hold the Staff of the Ancients!" Feeling the staff pressing downward beyond what strength he could match with it, Edge's eyes slowly morphed from placid blue to a heated crimson that burned like wildfire into the High Priest before him.

"This staff isn't yours to wield, Drakkaidian," he managed to return before forcing his leg up to kick into Zalnaught's backside, knocking him forward. As he stumbled to regain his balance, Edge flipped to his feet and spun around to charge the High Priest as he found his balance once more. Edge's power burning around him, he clasped his hands around the middle of the staff to hold it at bay, their powers locking. While the High Priest and the Scion of the Order of Alberic grappled over the staff lodged between their hands, Kaylan had painfully landed over the debris of the platform caused by Kaotica's furious explosion of power. Shaking her head and wincing at the burns from the dark girl's potent energy searing into her arms and chest, the Grandarian girl saw the intense field of darkness shoot forward once more. Tightly gripping the Granic Crystal in her left hand she instinctively rolled to her right to avoid whatever was sailing toward her. As she spun over the rubble strewn platform through the darkness, Kaylan was shocked to find Kaotica plummet out of the sky to slam her electrified fist into the stone where her head had been seconds before, cleaving it into several large fragments. Wheeling her head to her left where Kaylan lay struggling to rise, Kaotica leapt on her. Forced to drop the Granic Crystal in her left hand to hold Kaotica back as she heaved her self on top of her, the girls rolled with their auras of power leaping up to counter and shield them from each other.

When the girls at last skid to a halt on the portal Kaotica remained above her twin with fury emanating from her every movement. Kaylan lay beneath with all her strength mustered to hold the girl's arms back, afraid if she let go to reach for the Granic Crystal lying beside her in the debris, her adversary would slam her fist down with the same force she had exerted on the portal moments before. Feeling her inexperienced and untamed elemental power waning without the Granic Crystal in her grasp, Kaylan desperately cried out to the girl above her.

"Kaotica, you don't have to do this!" she shouted locking her blue eyes onto the hateful purple ones staring back down at her. "Edge was telling you the truth! I know it seems like we betrayed you but we care about you!"

"You care about me?" Kaotica blasted back in disgust. "You!?! What happened to all your hate when we were talking in the mirror? Since when have you cared a thing for me?"

"I shouldn't have said that, Kaotica," the Grandarian girl returned as loud as she could, her strength failing. "I know better now! There's more to dark than the opposite of light; just because you were created from my dark side it doesn't mean you're evil. You can thank Edge for convincing me of that. We know you aren't this wicked force of destruction Zalnaught is telling you that you are, and so do you. Underneath all your power and all that darkness inside you you're just a normal girl like me. You're scared the same as I am right now—you're in pain the same as I am because you know you have to make a choice between yourself and the greater good. You may not be in my mind anymore but I can see that. I feel the same way you do. I'm sorry for not seeing it before, Kaotica. I'm sorry..." Hearing all this, the raging storm of electrified energy around Kaotica's body gradually began to soften and sway, the once indomitable hatred burning in her eyes losing its biting edge. As tears began to formulate behind her eyes, she shook her head and let her body tighten yet again.

"You still took him from me!" she cried with her power flaring once more. "He's gone! What reason do I have to choose your greater good now?" Seeing surges of dark power building around the dark girl's clenched fists, Kaylan realized that she had made a dent in the girl's heart but she was still too overcome with emotion to listen. Aware she would be destroyed if she didn't act, Kaylan released her left hand from Kaotica's arm and flung it to grasp the Granic Crystal lying beside her. Just as Kaotica's fist was about to careen down on her, Kaylan's fingers wrapped around the enchanted golden gem and released a shining field of light from its core brighter than ever before that forced Kaotica to shield her eyes and look away. Seizing on her hesitation Kaylan rolled over pinning the dark girl to the ground and pushed herself up with her last bit of strength to make a final run for the Sword of Granis, lying in wait for her no more than twenty feet away.

Seeing the display of light beyond, Edge cast his gaze to the girls to find Kaylan sprinting for the center of the portal. At first hopeful she could make it, he was horrified to find Kaotica screaming with rage and her power detonating around her larger than ever, casting shockwaves of dark purple energy flying away from her body to slam into Kaylan and the two figures wrangling over the Staff of the Ancients locked in their hands. Caught off balance by the dark girl's potent power and concern for Kaylan breaking his concentration on the battle at hand, Zalnaught swept the end of the staff closest to him to his side to wrench it out of Edge's grip. Summoning its full power the High Priest swung it into the boy's face with its infused dark power heaving the Maven off his feet to fly across the platform and sail closer to the erupting dark power near its center.

As Kaotica's dark wings appeared on her back a final time, she lifted off the ground and spun around for Kaylan now crawling toward the sword in front of her with the luminous Granic Crystal in hand. Rocketing toward her with her field of energy expanding with such power it blew Zalnaught himself back and threatened to crush Edge and Kaylan into the stone platform they lay on. Feeling Kaotica charging a final time, Kaylan forced herself up with the shield of the Granic Crystal in her grasp and prepared for the full force of her dark twin to slam into her. It came as soon as Kaotica was mere feet above her and her full power had been charged into her open hands held behind her head to be thrown down at the golden girl in front of her. The power was so immense that the very platform around them was lifted up and incinerated in midair, cracking flashes of purple lightning shooting down around the girls from the black clouds above them. Though feeling like a mountain was crushing down on her, Kaylan held the Granic Crystal firm in her hands until its edge's cut into her palms. Its righteous power had been connected to her very soul ever since she had awakened her dormant power in Godsmark, but Kaylan was aware that even the active Granic Crystal could not hold back the dark onslaught for long. About to be lifted off her feet once more, Kaylan was surprised to find Kaotica lunging toward her to plant her slender black boots on the fragmenting platform beneath her and extend her hand to take hold of Kaylan by the neck, lifting her off the ground. Struggling for air in the grip of her twin, Kaylan knew this would be their last standoff and only one would walk away after this.

"Kaotica, please," she managed using her free hand to try to pry Kaotica's iron grip away from her. "You can't..."

"Why can't I?" she returned cutting her off and lifting Kaylan higher, emotion choking her voice. "Give me one reason why I shouldn't!" Fixing her sincere blue eyes on the girl, Kaylan struggled to keep breathing.

"Because somehow someway you've turned into a good person and you know this is all wrong," she answered with honest confidence. Kaotica softened her grip at this, letting the words sink into her suddenly vulnerable frame. Seeing her fix her full attention on her, Kaylan continued. "I know you feel like you lost everything, Kaotica. I feel the same way right now because I have to make the same choice you do and it means I'll lose him too. But there is more at stake than you or me. We're each still the same person and that person has a purpose and a destiny. It isn't to let Zalnaught and Drakkan destroy the world—it's to stop them and save it. Only we have to the power to do it, Kaotica. Only us." Kaotica paused once more, slightly lowering Kaylan back through the air until the tips of her feet touched down on the portal. By the time she could breathe once more there were tears just as large as Kaotica's in Kaylan's eyes. "Please, Kaotica. Look into your heart. Remember what it told you when you saved that little boy in the harbor? What does your heart tell you now?" The dark twin held her gaze for a long moment, her field of power still flaring around her. After staring at each other for what seemed like an eternity, she slowly turned her head around to face the boy laying flat on the ground far behind staring back up at her. The last remnant of hatred in her eyes dissipating, Kaotica lost herself to her emotions and began crying freely.

"I love him," she managed to speak almost inaudibly, slowly blinking her tear-filled eyes.

"Then save him, Kaotica," Kaylan told her softly. "Let me save him." Feeling the salty tears slip down her cheek to slip into her open mouth, Kaotica tilted her head to the side as she set her gaze back to Kaylan. Her fierce field of power slowly fading and electric bursts flashing over her body subsiding to a dull aura of purple light swaying to and fro over her skin, Kaotica eased her grip around Kaylan's neck and released her, falling to her knees to cry softly. Free at last, Kaylan let the oxygen she had been deprived of the past few minutes flood back into her lungs. Casting her gaze down onto the darkly radiating figure at her feet, the

Grandarian girl slowly knelt beside her to gently open her arms and embrace her.

With the crushing might of Kaotica's power at last gone, Edge slowly rose from where he had lain immobile and stared ahead at the two girls folded together over the surface of the portal beside the Sword of Granis over a hundred feet away from him. Seeing Kaylan rise with the Granic Crystal nestled loosely in both of her hands, all other thoughts and worries drained from significance and he abandoned the High Priest somewhere behind him to begin running toward her and the sword at the center of the platform. Accelerating as fast as he could run as she made her way beside the weapon rising from the stone behind her, the Maven leapt over a large segment of the destroyed stone portal with the sudden voice of Zalnaught exploding with rage far behind him where he had landed in the snow.

"Kaotica, what are you doing!?!" he blasted furiously. *"Finish the girl now!"* Though he was too far behind the center of the massive portal to use the staff against her, it would have made no difference to the dark girl. Kaotica heard the words but let them slip through her mind without so much as a thought, staring up to her opposite half above her. Giving in to the golden light that had been calling to her since the Hierarchs had awakened her power in Godsmark, Kaylan tucked the Granic Crystal against her chest with a vibrant light spreading between it and her body. Hearing Edge rushing toward her across the gaping fissure between them caused by Kaotica's power, she slowly turned to face him with her cascading hair draping over one shoulder. Though tears were still streaming from her soft blue eyes, the Grandarian girl smiled at him as he slid to a halt at the edge of the crevice in the portal. Though they were over fifty feet away from each other Kaylan's soft words sounded into his ears louder than anything he had ever heard before.

"I told you I had to make a choice, Edge," she started, lowering the Granic Crystal from her chest. "At first I couldn't bear the thought of it because I knew I would lose you, but now... I know I have to do this for you." Edge stared at her uncertainly, groping for the words to respond.

"What are you talking about, Kaylan?" the boy returned in a whisper, the confusion over what was really going on threatening to drive him mad. Kaylan's shining blue eyes slowly looked down to the crystal in her hands, passing over its brilliant symmetrical edges.

"The Hierarchs weren't going to sacrifice me to activate the Granic Crystal, Edge, only my body," she told him, shifting her gaze back up to him. "The Granic Crystal is a live being. It's always awake and pointing its bearer in the right direction. The reason it can do that is because it has a soul of its own—the soul of the person who activates it. This time that person is me." She paused then, seeing the sudden realization of what she was saying sweeping over Edge's distraught face. The boy slowly shook his head, tears welling in his eyes as he opened his mouth to speak.

"No..." he breathed softly, emotion and disbelief choking his words inside. Kaylan merely smiled as another tear fell down her cheek. "This isn't right... It isn't fair..."

"But it's my responsibility, Edge," she told him tenderly, lowering the crystal beside the sword where blade met the illustrious hilt. "I'm the only one who can do this. I wish more than anything I didn't have to leave you, but after all the times you've saved me its time for me to save you."

"Kay..." the boy trailed off again, reaching out for her across the gaping divide in the portal. "I can't lose you... you're the only reason I'm still alive..."

"You have a new reason to live now, scion," she said. "There's nothing to hold you back anymore. Become the person you were born to be." The girl stared at him for a long moment then, the warm golden power radiating onto her from the Granic Crystal gently pushing her beautiful hair behind her shoulders. "Thank you for everything you did for me, Edge. No matter where my soul goes, you'll always have my heart." Though Edge screamed out for her to wait, the girl turned to take the Granic Crystal in her hands and push it up against the Sword of Granis where the last one had been, immediately sticking to it as if it had been destined for her touch. The moment the crystal fell upon its surface the entire gem blasted awake with intense light, spreading to engulf Kaylan's frame. As it swept over her body to transform her into a being of pure light, she turned one last time to Edge with a smile on her lips. "Goodbye, Edge." With that, her entire being softened and began sweeping into the edges of the gem on the sword, fusing with it in the most brilliant display of shimmering gold light Edge had ever seen.

As soon as Kaylan's entire form had drifted inside the crystal, the entire Sword of Granis lit up with exploding golden power brighter than the sun itself to dispel the dark clouds hovering above. The entire devastated portal slowly pulsated with light, massive chunks of stone strewn over its ravaged surface fading and the crevices torn throughout filling with light to disappear and reveal fresh stone as if it had never been harmed in the first place. Staring down around his feet to shield his eyes from the intensity of the display before him, Edge saw the beautifully sweeping designs and emblems engraved into the portal shine with golden light spreading to the perimeter to light up the entire summit of the mountain. With the entire portal restored and shimmering with golden light again, Edge heard a frightened scream from before him and forced himself to look back up to find Kaotica's dark form rising to hover before the Sword of Granis. Her arms and legs were spread as if held in place by the penetrating strength of the light blasting through her body.

As she hung before the burning Grandarian talisman in front of her, the electrified field of darkness emanating from her body began to smolder into the air in ashes, her wings of dark light incinerating on her back. As the girl screamed out in terror, a dark mist of familiar black energy came soaring out of her mouth in a wild jet of wind, sweeping and building around the Sword of Granis, larger than Kaotica herself. When the last wave of dark matter had escaped her mouth, it began viciously circling the sword with erratic pulses trying to escape back into its host away from the talisman. As Kaotica landed on her knees to fall unconscious over the smooth stone platform, Edge watched the swell of dark power violently flow back into the beautiful curving emblems of the portal. Though wildly fighting with no avail to resist the restored power of the sword and the seal it held in place, every last particle of the dark mist was quickly sucked back into the void within. As it faded, Edge squinted in confusion to find a face from the last pocket of the dark matter screaming out in anguish as it was pulled into the portal. Guessing Drakkan knew he was trapped again, Edge swallowed hard and watched with satisfaction as the last of the dark god's power slipped away into the shimmering light. When it was gone only the light from the portal and the active brilliantly shining Granic Crystal remained to illuminate the endless world of white around them. They had done it. Kaylan had done it.

Chapter 45

Fallback

As the light from the portal to the void at last began to wane and slip back into the beautiful illustrious emblems engraved in its wide surface, Edge slowly lowered the arm that had been shielding his face from the powerful spectacle to gaze on what remained fifty feet ahead of him. The Sword of Granis stood erect and shimmering in all its glory once more with the new Granic Crystal mounted to its side brilliantly shining a comforting warmth over the entire summit of the mountain. As his distraught blue eyes stared into the core of its luminous glow, the boy slowly staggered toward it but found no comfort nor warmth. Shaking his head in distraught disbelief, his face tightened with emotion and he fell to his knees over the portal. His eyes forcefully sealing shut, he propped his upper body up with his spread hands and let his head hang in sorrow. They had accomplished their mission; he had done what he was hired to do, but there was no victory or glory left for him at the end. The only thing that mattered had been sacrificed and his heart was bereft of any joy. Kaylan was gone.

The words pounding through his beleaguered mind while his tears flowed freely, the Maven slowly raised his head to stare at the soul of his lost love shining out to him. As his eyes drifted to the legendary Sword of Granis, however, something else lying next to it caught his attention. The boy froze, a painful wave of confusion sweeping over him. Somehow, Kaotica was still lying alive and intact beside the mighty sword. Narrowing his eyes in bewilderment, the Maven forced himself to rise and stumble forward to rush to her side. Running across the small gap between them, Edge slid to her side to turn her body around to face him. Slipping a hand through her dark hair to gently lift her head, he swept his confused eyes up and down her seemingly unharmed form, amazed she still lingered to rest in his arms. He thought the moment Kaylan had activated the Granic Crystal she would have been destroyed. Remembering what had happened to her, he guessed the restored Sword of Granis had merely purged the taint of Drakkan from her body and left her physical form behind.

Reflecting over how it was possible that she yet drew breath, Edge's frame tensed with hope as the girl's peaceful eyelids slowly slipped open, revealing her deep purple irises once more. She stared blankly into the sky above them for a long moment but feeling the boy's hand behind her head she at last shifted her gaze to him locking onto his tearstained face.

"I'm..." she whispered almost inaudibly, looking around at the world shining before her once more, "alive..." Edge swallowed hard again, slowly nodding and fighting to hold back his tears.

"Kaotica..." he replied softly, a salty tear falling from his cheek onto hers. Feeling the small moisture touch her soft skin, Kaotica remembered all that had just befallen her opposite half and what it surely meant for the Maven. Staring wordlessly at each other for a long moment, the girl at last groped for the words to speak only to be cut short by the sudden bloodcurdling cry from beyond them at the edge of the portal. Wheeling around defensively, Edge locked onto the form of the High Priest Zalnaught rising full length from the snow bank he had fallen into from the force of Kaotica's power. The Staff of the Ancients was still locked in his grasp, radiating a dark aura of electrified energy buried within. Edge immediately set Kaotica down on the portal to leap in front of her and heave his sword from his back, rage reflecting that of Zalnaught's visage.

"You stupid, foolish girl!" Zalnaught bellowed with dark power flaring around the staff and his very body to detonate the bank of snow behind him. "My plans are ruined! Now the power of Drakkan is gone and I will never be able to absorb it!"

"Suddenly you don't sound so confident, Drak," Edge returned heatedly, tightening his grip around the hilt of his sword. Zalnaught's furious eyes swept from Kaotica to the boy standing before him.

"You..." he breathed icily. "This is all your fault. Your meddling has unwound my plans since this began. I swear

Trial of a Maven

to Drakkan I will make you pay for this. You will fall forever before my might!" His full fury awakening the staff in his hands, the High Priest thrust it forward with a surging blast of dark matter rocketing toward them larger than anything Edge had seen from him before. Preparing to summon his power to hold it back, he was surprised to find the steady light radiating from the Granic Crystal suddenly focus into a concentrated beam that extended out for the incoming attack that burned it away before it ever reached them. Spinning around in amazement, Edge watched the golden crystal brighten further and burn its golden rays out for the High Priest standing far beyond. The moment they touched him Zalnaught screamed and wheeled away to jump off the portal to escape the burning light. Seeing him fall back in fear, Edge couldn't help but let a spiteful smile spread across his lips.

"You're the only one finished today, Zalnaught," he shouted. "Your power is gone and your plans are falling through the cracks." His distraught eyes dripping with hatred, Zalnaught swept them back to the boy standing in the center of the massive portal. Aware that challenging the restored Sword of Granis was not an option, he spied the large white bird on which Edge and Kaylan had arrived circling overhead. Reaching the staff out for it, the Fethiott turned its head to spot him and sweep down at his dark command.

"You may have won this battle, Maven, but the Third Holy War still belongs to me," he barked vehemently. "Your precious Granic Crystal may have robbed me of the power of Drakkan but I still have enough strength from the vessel in this staff to obliterate Grandaria myself. My army marches on the capital as we speak. In a matter of days we'll be at its doorstep." Edge grit his teeth and shook his head.

"In a matter of seconds you'll be dead. So long as there is breath in my body you will never get the chance to use that staff again!" Edge decreed passionately, preparing to charge forward after him.

"You are powerless to stop me, boy!" Zalnaught replied in fury. "By the time you make it down from these mountains I will have already leveled Galantia and the rest of Grandaria with it. Keep your powerless girl and pray we don't meet again." With that, Edge suddenly saw the Fethiott swooping in from the skies to land next to the High Priest and allow him to leap onto it. Before the Maven could do anything to stop him, Zalnaught lifted the winged steed into the sky and shot off for the east and Grandaria with the Staff of the Ancients tightly gripped in his arms. Watching helplessly as he disappeared into the horizon, Edge cursed out loud and threw his sword down to the portal to clash its steel against the unyielding stone. Falling back to his knees in defeat, an overwhelming sense of failure swept through him once more. After all Kaylan had sacrificed to stop Zalnaught and save the world he was still primed to destroy it starting with her home. He had let her down.

As the Maven knelt wondering how he had let this happen he felt a hand on his shoulder and turned his head to find Kaotica kneeling beside him.

"What are we going to do?" she asked abruptly, as if he had to have had some plan already prepared. He stared into her penetrating purple eyes for a long moment before shaking his head and breaking his gaze from her.

"What can we do, Kaotica?" he replied hopelessly. "Even if we had the power to stop him he'll be at the gates of Galantia before we can get off this damn mountain. There's no way to get there in time."

"Don't forget about me, partner," came a small third voice from beside him. Edge turned around to find Zephyr hovering beside him in a sphere of Lift Power, holding his limp right arm and his feathered chest smoldering from the damage Zalnaught had done to him. Edge shook his head incredulous that he was still alive.

"Zeph you're lucky to be breathing right now," he told him. "There's no way you could get us all the way to Galantia even at your healthiest." The sprite swallowed and repositioned his limp right arm in his left.

"No, but I can at least get you down this mountain to some horses," he returned. "Zalnaught said himself his army won't arrive in Galantia for days. It's a long shot but we might be able to get there before him." Though not wanting to give up, Edge still reserved his doubts.

"But then what?" he asked them both. "Zalnaught still has a copy of Kaotica's power in the staff. There's no way I'd be able to hold it back—I could barely keep him at bay when we were scraping at the edge of the portal." Falling silent at this, Zephyr shrugged and stared at him. In the silence, Kaotica suddenly let her mouth slip open and her eyes widen as a thought struck her. She quickly moved in front of Edge, her face full of hope.

"You won't be alone," she stated suddenly. "You'll have me." Edge stared at her but let out a deep breath of doubt.

"Kaotica, you don't have any power left, remember?" he told her softly. The dark girl violently shook her head at this, passionately staring into his eyes with maturity he had never seen before.

"It doesn't matter if we're strong enough to beat him or not," she declared ardently. "We can. I know what my purpose is now. I know I have a destiny and it isn't to let Zalnaught destroy the world." She paused then as tears slowly welled in her eyes. "Thanks to Kaylan... I know that now. She made her choice and I've made mine. We have to do this." Edge stared at her hard, having never seen this sincere concerned side of the dark girl before. He nodded and took her hand resting on the stone platform in his.

"I know, Kaotica," he told her. "I just wish we had a way to stop him." She let her eyes pass the brilliantly shining Granic Crystal beside her, its warmth and light reassuring her.

"I have an idea," she stated with a faint smile on her lips.

Over the next four days Tavin Tieloc and the retreating Grandarian Army had fallen back through the Border Mountains all the way into Grandaria. After the destruction of the legendary Wall of Light, the Grandarian troops had fallen into such disarray and panic that their longtime defense was gone that the advancing Drakkaidians constantly on their heals were able to continually push them back through the Border Mountains largely unchallenged. The Grandarians' numbers were dwindling by the hour. Though Tavin had been at the rear of the army trying to reorganize them and make any kind of stand in the paths of the mountains, he knew the Drakkaidians had them on the run and facing their superior numbers in such a weakened state was suicide. Without a fortified position with which the men were familiar to hold them back they would not last long. Though they arrived at the Battlemount in less than two days it was still in no condition to withstand a siege. Advance Drakkaidian troops had skirted around the Grandarian Army through the smaller mountain paths and had already arrived to destroy what was left of the base and set it ablaze. Seeing his troops further disheartened and his reinforcements already dead, Tavin ordered the army to pull back to Grandaria with the hope they could organize in the fields outside the mountains and push the enemy back.

As they continued their retreat through the mountains the massive power that had destroyed the Wall of Light reemerged to blow a craggy path which they were fortifying to shreds, further trapping another entire battalion of Tavin's men. As they escaped into Grandaria the Warrior of Light found that over half of his army had been decimated in the mountain retreat and the battalions he had called for to meet him in the fields had been pulled back in fear to Galantia by General Tycond when word of the destruction reached his terrified ears. With no choice but to fall back to their reinforcements, Tavin ordered a full scale retreat to their final stronghold of Galantia itself. Aware that treading Grandarian soil for the first time in centuries would only embolden their enemy, Tavin dispatched scouts and emissaries to the villages along the road to the capital to warn them to withdraw to Galantia or the coast for their own safety.

During the first day of the retreat Tavin was further amazed when he sensed another disturbance of dark power near the portal to the void even stronger than before. Though he wasn't sure what the same incredible dark power that had destroyed the Wall of Light was doing at the portal or how it had gotten there, when he sensed the familiar power of the Sword of Granis returned over the portal he knew beyond a shadow of a doubt something was going on behind the war and the battle at hand. Unsure of its cause or meaning, the Warrior of Light was left with no choice but to continue on to Galantia with the hope that the restoration of the Sword of Granis would furnish him with the miracle for which he found himself praying.

It was four days after the destruction of the Wall of Light that the first regiments of Grandarian troops appeared in the cloudy Valley of Galantia heading for the shining capital in the distance. Tavin had worked his way to the distressed rear line, riding hard to reach the Supreme Granisian and inform her of the coming threat himself. Galloping across the downed drawbridge through the masses of retreating villagers that had fallen back to the walled city and the protection offered by the Gate Yard, the exhausted Warrior of Light slowed to a halt and dismounted. His troops were loosely pouring inside around him, as desperate as Tavin for rest. The Supreme Granisian's Chief Advisor Miless Cerbru had been waiting for him with a convoy of elite guardsman from the Golden Castle. Taking hold of a flask of water a servant offered him to chug its contents in one ravenous gulp, Tavin looked over to find Miless striding toward him with the gravest of expressions on his face.

"When we received word from scouts that Drakkaidian soldiers had somehow penetrated the Wall of Light I was skeptical, but now I am torn by my disbelief and horror," he stated shaking his bearded face. "What has happened, Tavinious?" The bruised and bleeding Warrior of Light continued breathing heavily as he waved in General Ronus and his captain and ordered them to begin assembling the troops atop the wall around the Gate Yard and for the battalions of soldiers already there to begin assembling their catapults at once. "Sir Tieloc! Tell me what is happening?" Hearing the Chief Advisor's outburst, Tavin motioned for the captain he was addressing to wait and slowly turned around to face the old man.

"I need to speak to Mary at once," he stated softly, obvious fear intertwined in his voice. Aware that it was Tavin's way of confirming his darkest fears, Miless swallowed hard and motioned for the Warrior of Light to follow him to the carriages behind. Ordering Ronus to take command of the Gate Yard and to reorganize the troops until he returned, Tavin plucked his sword off his horse and quickly followed Miless to the carriages to enter and speed into the city toward the Golden Castle in the distance. Racing down the streets so fast passing civilians had to leap out of the way to avoid being mowed down, the convoy passed through the four tiers of the city to quickly pull into the massive courtyard of the Golden Castle. Leaping out of his carriage Tavin followed Miless and his guard into the Grand Vestibule leading into the castle with his frayed cape loosely blowing behind him. As they penetrated all the way up to the Supreme Granisian's throne room, Tavin found the doors open with elite guards pouring in to line the very walls of the chamber responding to the state of emergency Miless had ordered. There was a frantic and frightened air within the illustrious golden chamber unlike anything it had felt in centuries.

Stepping inside he found the Senior Council assembled around the arching windows of the room looking out on the fields beyond the city walls. The Supreme Granisian was among them, slowly spinning around with hesitant alarm in her eyes as she saw Tavin approaching. Casting herself away from the window and lifting her heavy crown off her head, Mary stopped the Warrior of Light from bowing and stared hard into his eyes with incredulity that burned into him.

"What's going on, Tavin?" she asked in a distressed voice, far too shaken to maintain her regal composure. The entire room turning to stare at him, Tavin knew his duty was to accept responsibility for what had happened and report to her the painful truth.

"I assume my messengers didn't make it after we began the retreat," he stated somberly. Staring hard into the trembling eyes of the woman he had known since his adolescence, the Grandarian champion braced himself and spoke clearly. "In short, the Drakkaidians have attacked and destroyed the Wall of Light and the Battlemount." His forthright statement falling upon the ears of the council, gasps of dread filled the illustrious chamber. Even the disciplined sentries took an uncertain step forward with the ultimate disbelief the words he was uttering were real. "It was as the generals feared, Your Eminence. Drakkaidia was behind the disturbances we felt after all and Verix Montrox is now leading a force of over thirty thousand New Fellowship troops against us." Before he could continue Mary began shaking her head in painful confusion, unable to believe what she was hearing.

"Tavin, I don't understand what you're saying," she interrupted softly. "What do you mean the Wall of Light is destroyed?" Tavin took in a deep breath before continuing.

"The enemy has somehow acquired a new power beyond my ability to contend with, Your Eminence," he informed her. "It literally blew the Wall of Light in half and cut half our army apart in the retreat back to Grandaria. The Battlemount had been damaged earlier in one of the disturbances we sensed but in the chaos of the retreat the Drakkaidians set fire to it and burned it to the ground. I had planned on making a stand in the mountain paths or the fields west of the Hills of Eirinor but with no reinforcements and Montrox driving his

Trial of a Maven

troops forward in a constant charge to keep us on the run I was forced to withdraw to our only chance of holding them back."

"You're telling me Drakkaidians are in Grandaria?" Mary spoke aghast. Tavin shook his head realizing she wasn't appreciating what he was saying.

"Your Eminence, Verix is right on our heals," Tavin returned shaking his head in defeat. "His army will be on the horizon in a matter of minutes." The breath in Mary's lungs escaped at this, the ultimate fear ripping down her spine. Looking around into space uncertainly, the Supreme Granisian fumbled where she stood prompting several servants to help her back to her throne atop the stairs. As she climbed the stairs she ordered them to unhand her while she took a seat on the steps, breathing hard. Seeing her grope for the words to speak, General Tycond stepped forward at Tavin with anger seeping into his face.

"Are you still ambivalent about Drakkaidia now, Tieloc?" he whispered with acid dripping from his words. "I told you this doom was coming! How could you let the Wall of Light fall? Where was your legendary power then?" Tavin remained still and controlled at the harsh attack, aware his frustration was justified. Though about to respond, Mary held up her gloved hand for silence. Raising her besieged face, she locked her eyes onto the Warrior of Light before her.

"Be honest with me Tavin," she spoke quietly, her voice trembling. "Can you hold the city?" Feeling all eyes in the chamber falling to him again, Tavin steeled himself and inhaled deeply, shifting his footing where he stood.

"With the troops of the main army that made it back through the Border Mountains and the battalions in the Gate Yard to bolster them, we almost match the Drakkaidians—"

"No Tavin," Mary interjected, shaking her head. "I don't want misleading comparisons of strength from Tycond. I'm asking my Warrior of Light a question. Can you hold the walls of Galantia?" Realizing she knew as well as he that their only defense now was his elemental power to match both Verix and whatever else the Drakkaidians had unleashed upon the Wall of Light, he let his official facade fade and his heart sink.

"I give you my word that I will throw myself on the blades of the Drakkaidians before I give up this city, Your Eminence," be declared resolutely, "but my power is not great enough to hold both Verix and this mysterious Dark Mage who destroyed the wall." Mary sank as well, an empty stare of sorrow filling her gaze. Before he could break the dead silence that had swept into the chamber after his last statement and advise the council to prepare to evacuate the populace through the mountain path at the rear of the city, the First Granisian of the Temple of Light spun back to the window pointing out to the horizon.

"They're coming!" he shouted with trepidation spreading throughout the room. Remaining where they stood and sat, Tavin and Mary shifted their gazes to the arching windows of the castle to observe the black mass of Drakkaidian soldiers approaching and widening to spread the full length of the Valley of Galantia. Remembering the unique sensation of the impossible odds of impending doom like the ones he faced in the Days of Destiny and finding them the same as the ones now marching toward him in the distance, Tavin straightened himself and shifted his gaze back to Mary. Walking toward her up the sacred steps to her throne, the Supreme Granisian turned to face him with tears welling in her eyes. Staring at him for a long moment, the Warrior of Light at last reached down to take one of her small hands in his coarse, bloodstained gauntlets with the unflinching determination for which he was renowned mirrored in his eyes.

"There is *always* hope, Mary," he declared in a fiercely passionate whisper. The next moment he lifted himself up and wheeled around to stride out of the room with the eyes of the council on him as he disappeared for the Gate Yard.

Chapter 46

<u>Last Stand</u>

Over the next few hours the green fields around the shining municipality of Galantia usually brimming with passing travelers and merchants were overrun by the black hordes of over thirty thousand Drakkaidian soldiers, lining the long walls from the primary gate to the mountainous terrain behind the city to completely surround it. Though Verix had ordered his men to leave the villages and citizens of Grandaria unharmed until the siege began, thousands of frightened Grandarians were quickly trapped between the advancing Drakkaidian Army and the closing gates of Galantia as they fled their homes during the Drakkaidians' march north. Aware they would be boxed in with no escape as soon as Verix's full strength was gathered into ranks once more, Tavin quickly rushed back down from the Golden Castle to the Gate Yard to prepare his troops as best he could in the short time before the Drakkaidians were ready to attack.

Having left Ronus to command the Gate Yard and the wall tops within the city, Tavin opted to lead the first line of defense outside the walls, aware that one way or another the outcome of the war would be decided there. If he could not make terms with Verix short of surrendering Grandaria, he would fulfill his promise to Mary and throw himself on the blades of the Drakkaidians with his last breath with the hope his bravery and that of the soldiers outside the walls might inspire the full army behind them to fight with all their courage for this most desperate last stand. When the last of the people had fled into the Gate Yard of the city, Tavin and a fresh battalion of his troops as well as all remaining soldiers in the field outside the walls mobilized to form ranks on either side of the gates. Ordering them equipped with thick shields to push back the invaders in a charge that had not been called for in centuries, this advance regiment of his finest troops would be all that stood between Verix and the golden walls that could easily be obliterated by the Drakkaidian's new weapon. Ordering the primary drawbridge closed, Tavin quickly swapped his armor and mounted a new horse, riding to the front of his troops with the path closing behind him as he stopped to face the massive black horde marching forward.

As the dark soldiers encircling them shifted back into ranks, they at last began to steadily march closer. Scanning into their vast numbers, Tavin quickly spotted the head of the enemy trotting toward him on a black horse with a regiment of crimson armored soldiers behind him. Narrowing his eyes as his horse shifted position uncomfortably amidst the deep rumbling of the coming soldiers, Tavin met Verix's gaze and held it steadily. Though the soldiers behind the Warrior of Light expected him to utter some grand speech as their enemy drew closer, he remained silent with his eyes fixed on the fiery haired warrior gradually pressing closer. Though the hundreds of archers along the walls of the city drew their bows tight as the Drakkaidians came within range, Verix knew Tavin would not provoke hostility and abandon any chance to save his last citadel at the heart of his nation.

Shortly after coming within range of the Grandarian archers, Verix raised a hand signaling his entire army to halt. Coming to a gradual standstill over the green fields, the Drakkaidians collectively dropped the ends of their spears and lances into the ground with one massive quake that sounded into the Golden Castle itself. Holding his fiercely determined gaze for several long moments on the Drakkaidian prince sitting before him, Tavin took in a deep breath, aware of what he had to do. Slowly dismounting, the Warrior of Light pulled off his blue and gold cape from his back and threw it over the saddle of his horse. Pulling his sword off his belt to strap it around his armored back, Tavin pulled his gloves tight and began steadily walking away from his troops into the open field before him. Seeing the Warrior of Light's bold move, Verix Montrox narrowed his heated red eyes and slowly nodded to himself. Dismounting from his horse, the Dark Prince instructed his generals and elite guard assembled behind him to wait for his command as he turned to tread onto the open field as well. As the two veteran warriors strode toward each other in the middle of the field, both the Drakkaidian and Grandarian armies fell

Trial of a Maven

dead silent, watching with overwrought suspense of what would unfold.

At last standing before each other, the two warriors slowly came to a halt and stared each other down, neither saying anything as a chilled breeze from the north swept down to rustle their hair back and forth. Shifting the weight on his feet with his gray cape sweeping behind him, Verix at last opened his mouth.

"I trust this time you'll be more inclined to pay heed to my terms," he spoke in a low but driven voice. The Warrior of Light remained hard and shook his head.

"You know full well every Grandarian in this city would see it erased from the face of Iairia before they see it in Drakkaidian hands," Tavin reminded him with undying resoluteness in his voice.

"You say that like your people are the victims here, Tieloc," Verix returned folding his arms. "Drakkaidia was not the one to start this war. I did not want this fate for either of us."

"Then how do you explain the dark power I keep sensing in the Border Mountains, Montrox?" Tavin pressed taking a step closer. "I've sensed this darkness your mages are wielding before—it's Drakkan's. If you're trying to tell me Drakkaidia wasn't responsible for those disturbances when I saw the same power destroy the Wall of Light with my own eyes you must take me for a fool."

"I will get to the bottom of that soon but—"

"Don't listen to him, prince!" came a voice from behind the crimson armored guards around Verix's horse. Narrowing his worried eyes as the soldiers in the front line parted to make way for a single horseman draped in black and crimson robes, Tavin spotted the same staff in his hands radiating darkness as he had seen at the Wall of Light. Verix spun around with rage in his eyes as the horseman neared.

"I ordered you to remain at the back of the army, Zalnaught," the prince shouted struggling to maintain his rage. Hearing Verix call the man's name Tavin realized he was not a Dark Mage as he had guessed but the High Priest of the Black Church, Zalnaught himself.

"The Grandarian is trying to fool you once again, Verix," Zalnaught told him reining back his horse as it arrived behind him. "Do not forget what you found at the portal."

Tales of Iairia

Verix strenuously raised a hand for silence, staring the High Priest down hard before turning back to Tavin.

"All I know is that I found you toying with the sword yourself, Tavin," Verix stated with his voice rising. "Only you have the power to manipulate the Sword of Granis and the seal. What am I supposed to believe?"

"You can believe what you sensed a few days ago, Verix," Tavin stated with fervor. "The same power that destroyed the wall was back at the portal clashing with another light power. Surely you could feel it for yourself—the seal is restored. How could I be responsible when I was retreating with my men across the mountains?" Verix froze at this, Tavin's words pounding through him to reveal the truth in what he was saying. Seeing the mistrust linger in Verix's eyes, Tavin continued. "If you didn't have anything to do with these disturbances what is really going on here? And where is my daughter, Verix? How is she caught up in this?"

"Do not waste our time with your false accusations, Tieloc!" Zalnaught shouted once more, raising the staff in his hands. "Give the order to attack, Montrox! Let us finish his treachery!" The Drakkaidian prince wheeled around, rage in his expression that instantly silenced the High Priest. Turning back he raised an eyebrow at Tavin and shook his head.

"You keep claiming I've abducted your daughter—my niece—from you, but what would I have to gain from..." Verix trailed off then, slowly unfolding his arms as a wave of realization swept over his face. "Tavin, what does this girl look like?" The Warrior of Light went rigid at this.

"She's seventeen and looks almost exactly like Ril when she was her age," he replied quickly. "Why? Where did you see her?" The Dark Prince was quiet at first, slowly shifting his gaze away from Tavin and setting into the empty space before him. Verix's mouth slipped open and his eyes widened as remembrance of the girl who stood beside Zalnaught in front of the destroyed Wall of Light ripped through his mind. Letting his eyes slip back up to Tavin, Verix clamped his jaws together and clenched his fists with a maddening rage he had never felt the likes of before boiling the blood in his veins. So great was the hate and anger brimming inside him a faint aura of Verix's dark power shone around his muscular armored frame, electrifying the grass at his feet with crimson energy.

"How was I so foolish?" he breathed with loathing dripping from his words. The Dark Prince slowly grinded his head back to meet Zalnaught's eyes and locked on.

"Where is your new apprentice, High Priest?" Verix asked menacingly quiet. "The one I met at the Wall of Light?" Zalnaught narrowed his eyes at the Dark Prince, aware he had realized what was really going on. Seeing Verix's hand slowly move to the broadsword at his side, the High Priest tightened his body and threw the staff in his hands down to thrust it out toward the crimson haired warrior. Tavin froze with confusion as he found Verix suddenly enveloped in a sphere of constricting purple electricity that lifted him off the ground and spun him around. Screaming and focusing his full power into the staff in his hands the High Priest threw it backward sending Verix flying through the air to disappear into the ranks of the troops beyond. The clamor of confusion and anger quickly swept through both armies on the field, awestruck at what they were seeing. Immediately turning his attention to the Warrior of Light drawing his sword and leaping toward him, Zalnaught slammed the tip of his powerful weapon into Tavin's chest to send him careening into the earth with impossible force that pressed the air out of his lungs. Leaping off his horse to tower over the Grandarian champion with his taut face laced with hatred, Zalnaught raised the sharp tip of his staff over his chest.

"Your meddling daughter is dead, as you, the prince and his Loyalists, and all who stand against the New Fellowship of Drakkan are doomed to be!" he bellowed as loud as his lungs would allow. As the words sounded into Tavin's ears and he saw the High Priest prepare to plunge the powerful talisman in his hands down through his chest, a faint movement from above him caught his attention out of the corner of his eye. Glancing up past the High Priest, Tavin's eyes widened as a boy clad in black dropped out of the sky with a faint sphere of semitransparent energy around him to savagely swing a broadsword gripped in both of his hands down for the staff in Zalnaught's. Though swung far too early to strike him directly, Tavin was amazed to see a wave of throbbing force leap from the edge of the blade to slam into Zalnaught and blow him off his feet just before he could run Tavin's vulnerable form through. Watching awestruck as Zalnaught landed on his back several yards away, the black boots of the mysterious boy forcefully landed in front of Tavin as he crouched in a balanced landing from wherever he had descended from. Rising at once, the boy took a broad stance and defensively brought the edge of his blade before his chest. Forcing himself to turn over and rise in confusion, Tavin shook his head and stared at the boy.

"Who in the name of Granis are you?" he asked with his mind reeling as he struggled for breath. Though the boy quickly glanced back to him he didn't have a chance to answer as the dark robed figure sprawled out before him lunged back to his feet quaking with rage.

"Right in time, weren't you," Zalnaught spitefully bellowed with rage. "You just don't know when to quit, do you boy!" The High Priest quickly flexed with new vitality the electrified dark aura around the Staff of the Ancients in his hands.

"I told you that so long as there is breath in my body you wouldn't get the chance to use that staff again," the boy stated with fortitude coursing through his every word. "I meant it."

"And you are just as powerless to stop me now as before, you infernal brat!" Zalnaught barked back lowering the staff perpendicular to the ground to point its sharp end out for the darkly clad boy and the towering city behind him. "I'm through playing these endless games! All the years of tiptoeing around my enemies waiting for this moment. Today you will all feel the full power of my might and you will be the first to fall, boy. If you're so desperate to die then so be it!" With that, the radiating aura of dark energy surrounding the staff in Zalnaught's grip expanded and intensified into a storm of circulating black light that stole the very sunlight from above from the atmosphere. Flashes of dark purple lightning striking to scorch the earth around the High Priest's feet, Tavin watched in horror as he felt the mysterious dark power that he had sensed at the portal to the void and before the Wall of Light peak once more in preparation to be let loose. Turning to stare at the boy beside him with a heated red glow suddenly emanating from his eyes, Tavin felt a touch of destiny that had faced him before descend on this moment and the ones to come. Just as Tavin could feel the full force of the dark energy about to be unleashed upon them, the boy beside him spread his jaws to shout out a single word into the chaotic air.

"*Now!*" was his strident call.

Trial of a Maven

Then it came. With power unlike anything he had unleashed before, Zalnaught screamed as a colossal beam of spiraling dark energy exploded from the tip of the tainted Staff of the Ancients to careen forward toward them. His eyes going wide, Tavin realized the beam would easily blast clear through the gates of Galantia all the way through the first tier of the city if not beyond. There was nothing he could do to stop it. Staring on in horror, a movement from above once again caught his attention and he forced himself to thrust his gaze upward as the silhouette of a figure encased in another sphere of semitransparent light dropped from the sky with a small humanoid creature flying just above her and landed right in front of the boy. Staring incredulously, Tavin realized it was a girl no older than his own daughter rising to spread her arms and brace herself for the coming dark beam. Before Tavin could guess what was happening the boy behind her wheeled around to leap from the ground and snatch him off his feet as they leapt as far away from her as they could. Landing on their backs, the boy and the Warrior of Light watched in amazement as the gargantuan shaft of energy collided into her, leaving an imprint as it swept past her where her body had been.

Though Tavin feared the girl would be incinerated or worse the moment Zalnaught's onslaught touched her slender form, she merely threw back her head with her long dark hair sweeping back over her shoulders as the energy passed around and through her harmlessly. Just before the remnants of the dark energy that sped past her were about to slam into the first rows of terrified Grandarian soldiers before the gates of Galantia, the girl's previously closed eyes shot open to reveal her deep purple irises glowing with the same ominous light as the energy flowing around her. Clenching her fists as the power from the staff flowed around her, the girl leapt into the middle of the beam of energy with a pair of jagged bat like wings materializing from an electrified field of energy ripping over her body. Savagely beating them down, the girl shot forward through the incoming energy to fly through it all the way to the High Priest at the end. Slamming down to fragment the earth beneath her the girl threw her arms forward to wrap her fingers around the end of the staff he held, leaving Zalnaught in disbelief. With a darkly painted frown the girl narrowed her glowing purple eyes and pulled him closer to her.

"Did you forget what you told me, Zalnaught?" she asked icily, tightening her grip on the staff. "The staff can't harm me if it is my power fueling it." His eyes widening in shock as he realized what she was planning, the High Priest shook his head in disbelief. "You have something that belongs to me." As the dark power continued pouring out of the powerful talisman, it ceased charging forward as a beam and began flowing freely into the girl's arms to seep into her very pores and fuel the steadily rising aura of power around her until it grew as large as the one once circulating around the Staff of the Ancients. Looking down in horror to watch the transformed staff morph back into a simple piece of wood, Zalnaught shook his head and screamed out a bloodcurdling cry as the ultimate power at his fingers slipped away in front of him. With the last pocket of the power she had given to the staff restored to her, Kaotica furiously flexed her electrified field of darkness around her and wrenched the Staff of the Ancients out of the High Priest's grasp with one hand while her other slammed into his chest to send him flying back off his feet to land before the first ranks of the frightened Drakkaidian soldiers behind him.

With her natural energy returned and the talisman that she had taken harmless in her grasp, Kaotica let her field of ominous energy wane to a dull aura of purple light around her frame. Seeing the struggle was over, Tavin stared at the dark girl in disbelief that any of what he had just witnessed was possible. So fixated on the miracle that had just occurred before him, the Grandarian champion almost failed to notice the boy beside him push himself to his feet to slowly amble toward the girl. Rising after him, Tavin took hold of the sword at his side and nervously raised it before him not sure what to expect. Completely ignoring him, the boy made his way beside the girl already turning to face him. He stopped beside her with a faint smile of disbelief on his face that their plan had actually worked. Before he could say anything the girl extended her hand to present him with the Staff of the Ancients, making Tavin especially nervous. Noticing the Warrior of Light slowly drawing near with his blade raised, the boy turned to face him with docile blue eyes.

"You won't be needing that, Grandarian," he spoke passively. Letting the word digest, Tavin slowly let his fears

Trial of a Maven

dissipate as the girl stared at him as well and he lowered the blade to his side.

"Who are you two?" he asked in an awestruck whisper shaking his head as the bird creature that had dropped the two figures from the sky landed on his shoulder. Before any of them could respond, the sight of the shocked High Priest of the Black Church slowly rising to his feet before them with terrible fear in his trembling eyes caught their attention. Tavin instantly leapt in front of the two youths, raising his blade once more. Meeting his gaze, the mysterious boy let his smile fade and raised the staff before him in both hands. Holding it there for a long moment, the thousands of combatants around him watched as he swung it down to his rising knee to break the wooden staff in two. The moment it snapped a barely visible wave of energy quietly but forcefully spread out from the center of the staff to sweep through both armies and throw off their balance over the grassy earth. Shifting his weight to catch his balance as the energy faded, Zalnaught silently watched with his jaw dropped as the boy casually tossed the splintered halves of the destroyed Staff of the Ancients to his feet. The distraught High Priest reached down with a look of supreme pain over his visage.

"*No!*" he bellowed for all to hear. "What have you done? The power! The endless power is gone! You've wasted it all! You've—" The High Priest would never get the chance to finish as both Tavin and the three figures standing behind him saw a foot of bloody steel jut through his middle, stopping him cold with a look of contorted confusion sweeping over his face. As the life slowly drained from him, the dead body of the High Priest Zalnaught was cast to the right to reveal Verix Montrox standing behind him with an expression of cold hatred mirrored in his eyes.

"Your treason ends today, Zalnaught," the Drakkaidian prince declared just loud enough to be heard by the few standing around him. As he and Tavin stared at the fallen tyrant, their eyes shifted to the broken halves of the Staff of the Ancients as they began to slowly blacken and evaporate into the air in the form of ash. Staring in silence as the last residue of the powerful talisman drifted into the atmosphere to fade from existence, the Warrior of Light shook his head incredulously and placed his gaze on his former adversary.

"I don't believe any of this," he spoke more to himself than the prince. Verix looked up slowly, his eyes searching behind Tavin.

"Where did they go?" he asked suddenly. Spinning around in confusion, Tavin found both the mysterious boy and girl had disappeared. Wildly scanning around the field and the sky for any trace of them, the Warrior of Light shook his head incredulously.

"I have no idea," he returned throwing his arms in the air. "Who were they?"

"You don't know?" Verix pressed incredulously. "I thought the girl was your daughter."

"I've never seen either of them before in my life," he replied disbelievingly. Verix was silent at this, staring into the Grandarian's eyes hard for a long moment. At last, he opened his hand with a familiar crimson mist foaming around his broadsword to fade a moment after.

"So where does this leave us?" he asked quietly, the soldiers around them falling silent. Tavin swallowed hard, shaking his head as he wiped the sweat from his forehead.

"I'm not sure," he returned vaguely, sheathing his sword behind his back. "On a new page, though, I think. What about you?" The Dark Prince held Tavin's gaze for another long moment but at last gave a single nod and shifted in his thick armor.

"Agreed," he stated slowly. "Until we can determine what really happened to spark all this I propose a truce. If you promise us safe passage through Grandaria and agree to hold your forces at Galantia until we have withdrawn, I will move my army back to the Border Mountains. From there we will meet again. What say you?" A deep breath of relief escaping his lungs for the first time in as long as he could remember, Tavin slowly nodded in confirmation.

"You will have safe passage across Grandaria and the Border Mountains. I swear it," he promised. "If you pull out of the Valley of Galantia and wait for me while I make my report to the Supreme Granisian I'll dispatch emissaries to ride ahead of you and make sure your road is clear." Verix nodded once more, the breeze swaying his gray cape along his back.

"I'm... sorry, Tavin," he stated quickly, looking away. "Though I'm not sure what part the boy and girl played in this, I assure you that this," he said lightly kicking the dead corpse of Zalnaught, "will never be a problem again." Tavin gently bowed in response, acknowledging their agreement officially. With that, Verix did the same and slowly turned to make his way for the crimson ranks of tense soldiers behind him to order them to stand down. As the raised Drakkaidian swords and lances around Galantia began to gradually lower, the Warrior of Light deeply breathed in and out once more, turning to slowly stride back to his ranks of golden plated soldiers before the gates of his capital city, at last safe.

Chapter 47

<u>Fulfillment</u>

It was a small ridge covered in long waving grass that looked over the massive Valley of Galantia and the horde of black armored Drakkaidian soldiers gradually treading out of it for the fields to south. Though the faint breeze from the cloudy but bright Grandarian sky gently swept the green grass to and fro, a patch of the humble meadow on the ridge softly swayed heavier as a faint aura of darkness slowly descended out of the sky above it. Slowly descending, the winged form of Kaotica holding Edge by his arms gently dropped him back to his feet on the soft earth. As they landed the purple Sky Sprite hovering over them lifted back into the sky to give them their moment, sensing that both of them would want their privacy. Lowering herself beside him with her electrified field of radiating power fading once more, the pair of jagged wings on Kaotica's back dematerialized into a mist of black particles fading as Edge had seen so many times before. When the girl's power was gone and her black boots stood quietly beside Edge's she took in a long breath and turned to stare at him, wordlessly matching his satisfied gaze.

As the silence hung on, a faint layer of moisture formulated within Kaotica's eyes and she spun away to stare out at the vast army of Drakkaidians marching to the south. Lifting his head to observe what the somber girl was staring at, Edge slowly exhaled and made his way to her side. Staring at her beautiful face, he reached down to take one of her soft hands in his. She did not respond except to blink once and keep her gaze out on the fields. As they stood in silence with only the deep rumbling of troops marching away to fill the quiet Grandarian air, Edge at last felt her fingers tighten around his and she slowly turned her head to stare up into his eyes with a faint smile appearing.

Trial of a Maven

"We did it, Edgy," she managed weakly, struggling to force the words past her vast emotions. "We saved the city." Edge gave her a soft nod.

"We saved the more than the city," he returned quietly, staring off into the vast countryside before them. A faint smile of his own appearing in the corner of his mouth, he turned back to Kaotica. "I'm proud of you, Kaotica. We didn't know if what Zalnaught told you about the staff's power being harmless to you was true or not, but you still charged in with courage. I told you that you have a good heart inside you. I'm sorry I didn't see that from the beginning."

"I didn't know what I was in the beginning," the dark girl replied. "At first I didn't think about why I was here, then I decided it was for myself, but then I realized it was because I had a purpose." She looked away from him then, staring down. "Kaylan was right. We both had the same purpose. The same destiny. She made me realize I could choose for myself what I had inside." Edge let his gaze slip away from her into space once more.

"She did that for both of us," he spoke in a whisper, a tear falling from his blue eyes. Feeling the drop of liquid land on her hand, Kaotica slowly turned up to stare into his moist eyes.

"We had the same destiny because we were the same person, Edge," she said suddenly, catching him off guard. "We're still the same person. There's as much of me in the Granic Crystal with her as there is of her in me standing here with you. She's still here inside me." Edge lifted his gaze from the empty space before him and set it on the dark girl curiously, unsure what she was saying. Seeing the confusion in his eyes, Kaotica smiled and turned her entire body in front of him. "But now that it's over and our destiny is fulfilled there's no place in the world for me; there's no reason for the darkness inside me. I don't belong here—I never did. But Kaylan has a place in the world. She has a family, a home... and your heart." Edge stared at her hard, still uncertain of where she was going with this.

"You don't need a family or a home to have a place in the world, Kaotica," he told her softly. "I care about you too."

"But you *love* her," she replied shaking her head with a smile. "That's why she has to be the one to keep living in this body, not me." With that, Kaotica released Edge's hands and took a small step back. Tightening in sudden worry at what she was planning, the boy stared at her in confusion.

"What are you talking about, Kaotica?" he asked quickly. Kaotica merely smiled her ravishing smile once more as a final tear slid down her cheek to evaporate in the aura of darkness forming around her slender body.

"I already told you, Edge," she stated as small surges of electricity flashed up and down her form. "Kaylan is still alive inside me. This is her life to live. I'm giving it back to her for good." Staring at the dark girl incredulously, Edge shook his head and took a step toward her.

"Wait, Kaotica," he told her quickly. "You have as much right to live as anyone. You don't have to do this." As the aura of darkness thickened around her blurring her face from his eyes, he could see her smile one last time.

"Thank you for being there for me, Edge," she said, her voice growing distant. "However short it was, you made my life worth it." Tilting his head with overwhelming grief as he realized what was happening, the darkness around her sucked inward to transform her body into a silhouette of shadow that slowly stepped toward him to gently lean up and kiss his lips a final time. Kissing the dark girl back, Edge opened his eyes moments later to find the stale darkness over her body flaking away and rising into the air to reveal a fervent golden glow underneath that burned through the remainder of the shadow as the moments ticked by. When the last residue of the darkness surrounding her body dissipated for good, the curving body before him emanating a warm field of light limply fell to its knees. Quickly leaning down to catch it as it fell, Edge tucked the form of light in his arms and cradled it in his lap waiting for the golden aura to dim and wane into the air for the last time. Once the last shimmering wave of light sweeping over her form faded into the sunlight around them, Edge couldn't help but freely cry as the sight of Kaylan Tieloc rested peacefully in his arms again. Her long blond hair spilled around his arms and her soft blue tunic was restored to her frame the same as the time he had first met her.

Fighting back his emotions as he felt the girl stir in his arms and unhurriedly turned her head to face him, her blue eyes opened slowly to stare half awake at his figure. Letting a broad smile overtake his face as their eyes met, he watched and waited carefully for her to speak.

Trial of a Maven

"...Where... where am I?" the girl asked sleepily. Edge silently laughed in pure joy, sniffing in a wisp of air into his nostrils.

"Just take it easy, Kaylan, you're going to be alright," he told her softly. As his words registered in her mind, an estranged look of confusion passed over her delicate face.

"How do you know my name?" she asked struggling to find the strength to stay awake. "Who... are you?" As her questions digested into the boy's mind, the beaming smile on his lips slowly faded with a look of painful disbelief overtaking him instead.

"You... you don't remember?" he asked feeling his heart sink.

"We've never met, have we?" she asked calmly, trying to open her half closed eyelids to better inspect the boy's face. Her words stabbing into him, the boy stared at her incredulously for a long moment before feeling the tears welling in his eyes again and he forced himself to look away into the horizon. After all he had fought through to keep her alive and all Kaotica had sacrificed to return her to the world, fate had chosen to deal a cruel blow after all. She didn't even remember him. "Who are you?" Bringing his gaze back to the exhausted Grandarian girl in his arms, the darkly clad boy tried his best to force a smile and swallow his emotions.

"I'm..." he trailed off not knowing what to say. "...I'm... just a passing Maven." His words were flat and quiet, full of pain for having to lie. "I saw you walking from your village when you fell and hit your head. You should try to get some rest. I'll... get you home." Though obvious bewilderment lingered in her closing eyes, the girl softly nodded.

"Thank you," she said falling victim to her fatigue and drifting to sleep. Nodding in response, Edge lowered his head in sorrow and closed his eyes, unable to believe he had had her back only to lose her again. As the boy sat softly weeping over the grassy earth for the next several minutes, the faint breeze around him suddenly swept down across the long grass with a burst of vivacity that forced Edge's hair to blow up behind him. Feeling the gust fade as quickly as it had come, he was surprised to hear a deep voice speak behind him.

"Weep not for her, Revond," it spoke softly. "The Kaylan you knew will endure long after you are gone in the core of the Granic Crystal and with it her memory of you." Realizing who the voice belonged to as it finished these words, the boy did not leap up or spin around in surprise but remained motionless over the earth, staring down at Kaylan.

"Is that supposed to comfort me, sage?" Edge asked in a menacing tone. "Because if it is you'll have to do quite a bit better than that." Slowly turning his head around with his heated eyes narrowed, the boy found the gray robed spirit of the Mystic Sage Zeroan standing behind him in the breeze, his hood down to cover his bearded face as always. "You knew." Gently lowering the girl's head back into the soft grass beneath her, Edge rose with his body cramping with untold rage. "You knew all along. You knew she would have to give herself up to activate your damn crystal! You sent her—sent us—on a quest to die!"

"And yet you are both still alive," Zeroan spoke quietly. Edge threw his upper body forward to scream at the sage.

"You call being trapped for all time in that little crystal *alive*, Zeroan?" he shouted. "You played with her life like it was a game! I should have known not to trust you from the beginning!" The sprit of the sage was still for a long moment but at last shifted in his robes and opened his mouth to speak.

"For one who knows for himself that our lives are what we choose them to be, your words lack sense, young scion," he responded.

"It doesn't change the fact that you sent her to sacrifice everything without telling her," Edge shouted. "Admit it!"

"I do," Zeroan replied still calm and collected. "But what you fail to realize is that while I revealed to her this destiny it was she who had to choose it for herself. Just as you had to come to terms with your fate and choose your path, so did Kaylan. She saw the need for her sacrifice in hand with the consequence of ignoring it and she choose to save not just you but the rest of the world because she was the only one who could. Do not dishonor her sacrifice by accusing me of forcing her to do what she did for you." Though ready to explode at the sage and scream for him to be gone forever and take his trickery with him, Kaylan's final words to him before she faded into the golden crystal they had found in Godsmark echoed through his mind once more. She told him it was her responsibility. She was the only one who could save them. Though she had wished more than anything that she didn't have to leave him, after all the times he had saved her it was time for her to save him. The rage fading from his heart as sorrow flooded back inside, the boy fell to his knees on the soft earth and fought to hold back his tears once more.

"Why doesn't she remember anything?" he asked quietly. Zeroan inhaled deeply and shifted his gaze to the sleeping girl behind him before answering.

"Kaotica has completely purged herself from the body the girls shared," he stated. "Though the body was Kaotica's own after they split, the spirit of Kaylan remained a part of her no matter what physical shell she existed in. When Kaotica purged herself she purged all memory of her existence, so the Kaylan you know exists now in the Granic Crystal. This is a new Kaylan Tieloc unvarnished by any of your quest. She will not remember anything of Kaotica or your journey. She is exactly the way she was when you first met her." Blinking slowly as the sage's words sunk in, Edge shook his head in disbelief.

"How much did you know?" he pressed softly. "What else did you hold back from us?"

"You already know my sight is blurred by the presence of powerful magics in the mortal realm, Revond," Zeroan reminded him. "What little I witnessed of your quest with Kaylan and Kaotica and all of that which I did not, I could not have foreseen. All I know now is that with your help and that of Kaotica's, Kaylan was able to restore the seal to the portal of the void and save the world as her father did before her. Her heart will always be with you, but there is a new life ahead of you now, scion." Edge looked up to the sage slowly, aware of what he was saying. "You have accepted your power as the Scion of the Order of Alberic and along with it your destiny. Are you ready to become who you were born to be?" The sage's words triggering what Kaylan had told him at the portal, he remembered her telling him he had a new reason to live now. Nothing held him back. Letting her final charge to him fill his empty heart with purpose, the boy raised his head to Zeroan and nodded slowly.

"I'm ready," he answered softly. The spirit of the sage nodded behind his concealing hood.

"Then my spirit will be waiting for you within your new home, Revond," he stated. "When you are ready to meet me there I will teach you how to control your gift and commence the eighth generation of our order." Silently nodding, Edge watched as the wind swept down from the skies to slowly sway the gray robed form of the sage and pick him up, back into the winds of the world to blow him home. As the last remnant of his being faded, Edge heard his distant voice one last time. "You have done well, Revond. The trial of a scion is complete and Iairia is in your debt. For the lives of all, I thank you..." Listening as the wisps of wind faded completely, the boy named Revond slowly rose to collect the girl behind him in his arms and begin walking down the ridge for the valley below.

Chapter 48

Onward

    Jaren Garrinal sat asymmetrically folded over his favorite wooden chair in the living room of his cozy home in Eirinor Village, staring blankly out a small window toward the Tieloc house across and down the street from his. The hardy Grandarian archer had lost a particular bounce in his step in the months since he had last been inside with the full family that called it home, including the girl he loved like a daughter of his own that he had allowed to disappear almost two months ago. Jaren forced himself to look away from the empty house and set his blank green eyes on the wooden floor beneath him, deeply exhaling as he raised a hand to scratch his thick brown beard. The aging Grandarian could barely stand to look at himself in the mirror anymore after what he had done. He was the only one who knew what fate had truly befallen her. Believing it unwise to tell even his wife of the reappearance of the Mystic Sage Zeroan, he had merely informed her and the villagers that she had gone to Galantia to be with her parents.

    The lie and the truth of where she had really disappeared ate at him worse by the day. His best friend's daughter whom he swore to protect had been gone with the untrustworthy boy she set out with far longer than it should have taken them to get to even a place as hazardous as the portal to the void. The more time that passed with her missing the more solemn and restless Jaren had become. In recent days he found he could not even fall asleep with the knowledge that he might have sent Kaylan to her death. There were rumors spreading like wildfire that a third Holy War had begun and Drakkaidians were somehow marching through the Border Mountains where she was supposed to have gone. Though he had not believed it possible for Drakkaidians to find a way around the Wall of Light that had held them at bay for centuries, half of the village had evacuated to the coast or Galantia in the north when word spread that the wall had somehow fallen. Not daring to imagine what fate would befall Kaylan if she was to run into a patrol of Draks wandering the Border Mountains, Jaren brought his hands to his face to gently massage his sleepless eyes, once again silently praying to Granis that she was alright somewhere.

As the Grandarian archer sat in silence, the small tug on his long tunic sleeve caught his attention and he came back to his senses to look up and find Kaylan's brother Darien staring at him curiously.

"What's wrong Uncle Jaren?" he asked tilting his head in confusion. "You look sick." Jaren slowly dropped his hands to rest them on his knees and shook his head with a forced smile spreading across his tired face. He had been playing with his two sons and the littlest Tieloc for almost an hour though they had done most of the playing while Jaren had sat with his mind elsewhere.

"I'm fine, Darien," he replied with no witty retort that further provoked the boy's concern for him. "Just a little tired is all." Nodding as if it had been a satisfactory response, Darien set his gaze back on the wooden toy soldiers his father had carved for him years ago that they were setting up as if in a grand army. After knocking over his brigade with the brunt of his forearm while Jak and Roan continued setting theirs up by themselves, he took a seat on the floor and looked back up at his uncle.

"I'm bored, Uncle Jaren," he announced simply. "When are mommy and daddy coming home?" Jaren shook his head with an apologetic expression on his bearded face.

"They're in the middle of important business in Galantia, remember?" he told him. "They'll be back as soon as they can but things are a little hectic there right now so you have to be a big boy and be patient, all right?" Darien nodded but kept his gaze on him.

"What about Kay?" he asked suddenly. "When is she coming home? I miss her." Jaren froze at this, his heart pounding as he struggled to fight his emotions and come up with a suitable answer.

"So do I," he spoke meekly at last, deeply inhaling, turning to stare back out the window of the room. As a faint breeze blew in from outside, Darien curled up into a ball and started to shiver.

Trial of a Maven

"Can you get my blanket, Uncle Jaren?" he asked trembling. The Grandarian man quickly swept his gaze around the room and rose to pick up a small cloth beside his sons still vigorously playing in the middle of the room. Presenting it to Darien, the boy shook his head.

"That's Roan's," he informed him. "Can we go get mine in my house?" Rising with a deep breath, Jaren placed the blanket at his feet and nodded.

"I'll go get it, little man," he told him blankly. "Stay here with your Aunt. And use Roan's until I get back, okay?" Watching the small Tieloc nod his head, Jaren slowly stepped past him reaching down to rustle his short dark hair. Walking to his door and calling to his wife that he would be right back, Jaren tightened his tunic around his waist and stepped outside into his small front yard and onto the village road that led down to the Tieloc house at its far end. He swallowed hard as the thought of Darien's parents were brought up once again. Tavin and Ril were bound to be getting back soon. How would he tell them that he had let their daughter go missing for almost two months? Gritting his teeth at himself yet again, the Grandarian archer forced the thought from his mind as he stepped through the back door of the house after he had unlocked it with his key and walked into the kitchen where he had met the young Maven and the spirit of Zeroan the night before Kaylan had left. Feeling a chill creep up his spine as he walked past where the apparition of the sage had been standing that night, he made his way up the stairs to the hallway on the second level that led to the bedrooms of the house. The doors were open as usual and as he walked by he couldn't help but glance into Kaylan's room and the empty bed lying beside the single closed window. Forcing himself to look away, he continued down the hall shaking his head.

Entering Darien's room he headed to his bed to pluck a long red blanket with a passionate flame in the center that his mother had made for him after his birth. Slowly wrapping it around one hand, Jaren turned back to amble out of the room for the hallway. As he slowly tread down the corridor for the stairs, the faint sound of a breeze sweeping through the hall caught his attention. Slowing and narrowing his eyes in confusion, he wondered where the gentle wind could be coming from when he had just seen all the upstairs windows closed. Curiously turning the corner around the doorway to Kaylan's room as he peered in, the Grandarian's eyes widened and his mouth fell open as he froze in shock at what lay before him. Standing to the right of the bed beside the now open window was the darkly clad form of the Maven that had left with Kaylan so long ago. Though frozen in shock at his appearance, the second figure lying still in his arms drew the air from Jaren's lungs, a single tear forming in his eye to fall down his cheek into his beard.

The boy held Kaylan carefully in his arms, gradually setting her down to lay her slender figure on the soft bed with his gloved hands slowly withdrawing from her to fall back to his sides. Though Edge didn't see him at first, as he raised himself erect his eyes fell upon the figure of Jaren Garrinal standing before him staring with an incredulous expression on his face. The two held each other's gaze for a long moment before Jaren at last broke the silence.

"What happened?" he asked just loud enough to be heard. "Is she alright?" Edge was silent for a long moment but at last gave him a single nod.

"She's in the exact state as when she left," he replied more honestly than Jaren would ever know. "She just needs some rest and she'll be fine." Taking a slow step toward the bed sweeping his green eyes up and down the girl's form to make sure she was indeed fine, Jaren shifted his gaze back up to the motionless Maven.

"What of your journey?" he asked. "Where have you been for so long? Is the seal over the portal to the void still in place?" Edge gulped and blinked slowly before replying.

"The quest was a success," he answered vaguely. "Kaylan made sure the seal will be secure for a long time to come." Jaren raised an eyebrow at this.

"That's it?" he questioned, discontented. "That's all you're going to say?" Edge looked at Kaylan before placing his calm blue eyes back on the man before him.

"With respect, Grandarian," he stated emotionlessly, "that's all you'll ever need to know. The rest doesn't matter." Though Jaren was about to protest and insist he tell him the entire story, the sound of distant hoof beats racing into the village streets from the north side of the vale sounded through the open window of the bedroom. Looking past the boy Jaren saw the familiar sight of his best friend Tavin Tieloc riding into the village at full speed. Feeling the uncertainty around him threatening to suffocate him, the Grandarian archer

Trial of a Maven

raised his arms as if groping for what he was supposed to do next.

"What would you have me tell her parents who've been gone this entire time?" he asked desperately. Hearing this, Edge slowly turned around to observe the single rider coming into the village and find he was the same man he had saved before the gates of Galantia the previous day. Taking in a deep breath as he turned back around, he spoke once more.

"I'll leave that up to you, but just so you know, Kaylan doesn't remember anything of our journey," he informed him. "Not even who I am or Zeroan appearing that night."

"What...?" Jaren asked skeptically, unable to believe what he was hearing. As the hoof beats from the horse sounded on the dusty path of the main road of the village, Edge swept his gaze back down to the sleeping girl beneath him and swallowed hard. He slowly raised a single gloved hand to gingerly cast it down the side of her soft cheek and wipe a lock of her golden hair behind her ear as he had many times before. Aware it would most likely be the last time he would ever see her, the boy leaned down to gently kiss her on the cheek. Pulling up quick, the boy turned to the window to raise one leg to its ledge as the horse pulled into the yard in front of the house and skid to a halt, its rider leaping off to run for the house. Turning his head around to meet Jaren's gaze as he spread his arms up to the sides of the window frame, Edge stared at him with eyes that stole the suspicion from Jaren's mind.

"Just so you know, she saved us all," the Maven stated simply but with a quiet passion that softened the judgmental Grandarian archer. "Take care of her." Jaren stared at him hard, aware whatever they had been through on their journey had somehow connected the two as he had been connected to his comrades years before. Seeing the Grandarian wordlessly nod in response, Edge spun around and threw himself forward to leap out the window to land on the soft earth below and leave Jaren alone with the sleeping form of Kaylan as the sound of footsteps raced up the stairs behind him.

In the rolling Hills of Eirinor just outside the small village, the miniature form of the Sky Sprite Zephyr stood with his taloned feet perched on a small boulder sunk into the earth, waiting patiently for the form of his human companion to emerge over the hill that led to the small village just below. At last seeing a single dark body slowly ambling up the hillside toward him, his wide yellow beak faintly smiled and he unfolded his arms to spread the small feathered wings mounted on his back and lift up off the rock and hover there waiting for him. As Edge closed the gap between them staring into space the entire way, he at last stopped beside his partner to turn and gaze back into the small village of Eirinor. Hovering in the silence for several long minutes, Zephyr at last landed on the boy's left shoulder.

"Did you see the rider coming in before you left?" he asked, to which Edge replied yes. "Did you know he was Kaylan's father when you saved him yesterday?"

"No," Edge spoke simply, "but I could have guessed. He had her eyes—courageous." Zephyr nodded, smiling as he remembered the warm determination he always found there when staring into her beautiful eyes.

"Do you think he'll be able to piece together what really happened?" he asked. Edge merely shrugged.

"I don't know," he returned blankly. "He is the Warrior of Light. Maybe he already knows. But I think you and I are the only ones who will ever know the whole truth." Watching his partner's eyes soften as they stared hard at the rooftop under which he had left the blond haired girl, Zephyr relaxed and let his thoughts come out freely.

"She's going to be alright then?" he spoke softly, turning to stare at his partner. Edge remained still for a long moment but at last nodded.

"As if nothing had ever happened at all," he answered. Noting the lingering sorrow in his voice, Zephyr took a deep breath.

"Which doesn't mean it didn't," he chimed in. "What you went through was real—what you felt together was real. Nothing can ever take that away from you, partner." Letting the words sink in, Edge gulped down his final regrets and turned to his friend with a grateful look in his eyes.

"Thanks, Zeph," he told him sincerely. "For everything. After all I put you through and all the times you saved us along the way, I'm in your debt now. You're the best friend this lost boy could have ever hoped for. A better partner—

there is none." The purple sprite merely smiled placing a finely feathered hand on the boy's neck.

"That's what friends are for, Edge," he stated graciously. His eyes widening at the sprite's last word, the boy suddenly broke his gaze from him.

"Can you do me another favor, Zephyr?" he asked, catching the sprite off guard. When Zephyr replied anything he needed, the boy brought his eyes back to him. "My name is Revond." Though remaining still for a long moment, Zephyr's beak slowly widened to a grin as he wordlessly nodded in response and lifted off the boy's shoulder in a sphere of Lift Power. Matching his partner's modest smile, the boy nodded to himself that everything was finally right and he indeed had a new purpose as Kaylan had told him. Pulling his worn black gloves tight against his hands and turning from the small village of Eirinor, he began walking south as a familiar breeze rustled down from the cloudy sky, blowing at his back as if to push him on and guide his way.

Tales of Iairia
Trial of a Maven
The End

About the Author

Tyler Tullis is a young man from Washington State with a passion for writing and stories centered around the clash between good and evil. He began writing his *Tales of Iairia* trilogy in high school and independently published the first installment, *Shards of Destiny*, before graduating. He has since begun college at Gonzaga University in Spokane, Washington. During his freshmen year he completed *Trial of a Maven* and plans to write the final installment of the trilogy as well as a prequel before graduating. Though his aspirations for his writing career extend beyond the *Tales of Iairia* series, he is currently content honing his craft at college. Upon finishing his second novel Tyler was 19 years old.